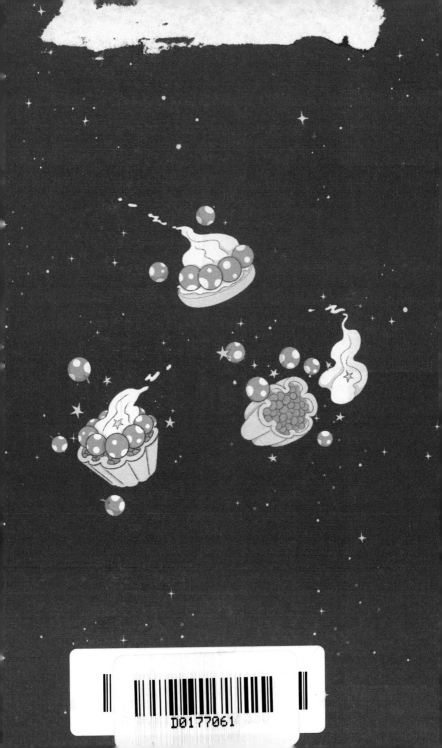

EXTRA WEIRD CREATURES

Books by Mark Powers

The  series

Illustrated by Dapo Adeola

Space Detectives

Space Detectives: Extra Weird Creatures

The  series

Illustrated by Tim Wesson

Spy Toys

Spy Toys: Out of Control!

Spy Toys: Undercover

SPACE DETECTIVES

EXTRA WEIRD CREATURES

MARK POWERS

Illustrated by
DAPO ADEOLA

BLOOMSBURY
CHILDREN'S BOOKS

LONDON OXFORD NEW YORK NEW DELHI SYDNEY

BLOOMSBURY CHILDREN'S BOOKS
Bloomsbury Publishing Plc
50 Bedford Square, London WC1B 3DP, UK
29 Earlsfort Terrace, Dublin 2, Ireland

BLOOMSBURY, BLOOMSBURY CHILDREN'S BOOKS and the Diana logo
are trademarks of Bloomsbury Publishing Plc

First published in Great Britain in 2021 by Bloomsbury Publishing Plc

A catalogue record for this book is available from the British Library

ISBN: PB: 978-1-5266-0320-3; eBook: 978-1-5266-0329-6

2 4 6 8 10 9 7 5 3 1

Printed and bound in Great Britain by CPI Group (UK) Ltd, Croydon CR0 4YY

MIX
Paper from
responsible sources
FSC® C020471

To find out more about our authors and books visit www.bloomsbury.com
and sign up for our newsletters

To Sylvia Thompson & Nick Devereux

With thanks to Jo, Kate, Zöe and
all at Bloomsbury
— Mark

For Matt, Meg and Jet. Thank you for your
help bringing this book home :)
— Dapo

PROLOGUE

PING!

Somewhere in Starville, a text message arrived on someone's mobile communicator. It was late – past midnight – and the owner of the mobile communicator had been in bed, asleep. Blearily, they reached for the device and read the message.

IS IT DONE???

Yawning, and with tired, fumbling fingers, the owner of the device typed a reply.

YES. WE SHOULD SEE
RESULTS IN THE MORNING.

A pause. Then another message **PINGED** in.

EXCELLENT!!! OUR FIENDISH PLAN NEARS COMPLETION! TOGETHER WE SHALL BRING CHAOS, CONFUSION AND MISERY TO THE INHABITANTS OF STARVILLE – AND GROW STAGGERINGLY RICH IN THE PROCESS! HAHAHAHAHA-HAHAHAHAHAHA!

After a few seconds, it added:

NIGHTY-NIGHT, THEN.

The owner of the communicator put down the device and slumped back on to their pillow. Soon, they were deeply and comfortably asleep.

Chapter 1

Felix Plum
is unwell

Mrs Plum rapped her knuckles three times on Felix's bedroom door.

'Your breakfast will be in the kitchen in five minutes, darling, or in the cat in ten. Up to you.'

Through the door there came a low, muffled groan.

Mrs Plum heaved a sigh. She'd seen hundred-year-old giant tortoises with more get-up-and-go than her son. She knocked again.

'Come on. The rocket bus will be here at eight thirty.'

'I don't wanna go to school,' came Felix's voice.

'It's the last week of term. You want to see all your friends, don't you?'

'I don't want to do anything. I feel funny and I've got a headache.'

'Oh, not that old fib,' sighed Mrs Plum. 'You realise kids have been trotting out that excuse since the dawn of history? I bet kids in caves used it to pull sickies from hunting mammoths. Come on, Felix. Stop wasting time.'

'I really have, Mum. I don't feel well. *At all.*'

Mrs Plum frowned. Normally Felix would snap out of his laziness, but today something felt different. A sudden thought occurred. Her son couldn't actually be ill? Could he?

She pushed open the door. Felix lay sprawled on the bed under an untidy heap of cushions and pillows, the duvet pulled over his head. Gently, she sat on the edge of the bed and cleared her throat.

'Felix, darling? Come out from under there, please.'

A small pair of hands appeared over the top edge of the duvet and pulled it down a few inches, revealing a scruffy mop of brown hair and a pair of watery blue eyes.

'Good heavens!' cried Mrs Plum. 'You look terrible, darling!' She laid a hand on Felix's forehead. 'And you have a temperature, too! You really are poorly! Is your head terribly painful?'

The boy nodded. 'Yeah. And there's this really weird feeling in my shoulder. I don't know what it is.'

'Oh dear. Let me see.'

Felix sat up and pulled down the duvet.

Mrs Plum gave a startled gasp and backed away from the bed. 'Oh my goodness!'

Felix yawned. 'Hmm? What's up?' He noticed his mum was staring, horrified, at his right shoulder. He swivelled his head to see what she was looking at – and let out a blood-curdling scream.

Chapter 2
Head boy

High above the planet Earth floated the gigantic space station known as Starville. It was a single, vast city enclosed under a great glass dome, a breathtakingly beautiful place of long, elegant streets and lush green parks, home to over a million humans and aliens. The most astounding place in the whole solar system.

Located halfway up a glittering skyscraper in one of Starville's fancier districts was the office of the *Space Detectives*.

Connor Crake and Ethan Kennedy were two ten-year-old boys from Earth who were staying on Starville with Ethan's uncle Nick for the summer holidays. The pair had always been keen mystery solvers and, after recently saving Starville from an evil plot to send it crashing into the Moon, they had been given this marvellous office filled with the very latest detecting technology by Starville's grateful Supreme Governor.

Ethan was on his swivel chair, spinning rapidly, giggling as the world flashed by in a blur. His shirt front was streaked with filling from the pastry he'd eaten for breakfast. He was a short, squat boy with the nervous energy of a puppy.

'Will you stop doing that?' asked Connor irritably, adjusting his thick-lensed glasses. He was taller and thinner than Ethan and was sitting nearby at his desk,

studying the local news on his computer screen. 'It's incredibly distracting. One of these days you'll spin so fast you'll take off like a rocket-copter and fly out of the window.'

Ethan grabbed hold of the edge of his desk and the rapidly rotating chair came to an abrupt halt. He shook his head, which was woozy after all the spinning, and gave an apologetic shrug. 'Sorry, mate. I'm just so completely and utterly bored out of my skull. We've had nothing decent to investigate all week, have we?'

This was true, Connor knew. In the past few days, the Space Detectives had solved a grand total of three mysteries, none of which had offered much of a challenge to their powers of investigation. He brought up the case notes on his computer screen to remind himself:

MYSTERY	SOLUTION
Stolen antique ring	Found inside slipper under bed

MYSTERY	SOLUTION
Ghost of Winston Churchill spotted in hallway	Reflection in hallway window from TV in building opposite showing Earth History Channel

MYSTERY	SOLUTION
Horrid smell in kitchen	Horrid, out-of-date cheese in fridge

Nothing to tax the minds of two bright young detectives there. In addition to being ridiculously easy to crack, these three cases shared something else in common. They had all been brought to Connor and Ethan's attention by the same person – a rather scatty old woman called Florence Quail, who lived by herself in the apartment next to their office. She was a kindly soul, often stopping by to bring the boys home-baked cookies, but Connor and Ethan had begun to wonder whether she was inventing these so-called mysteries to inject a bit of excitement into her otherwise uneventful life.

The office doorbell rang.

'That better not be Florence Quail again,' said Connor.

'If it is her, let's hope she's brought some of those Venusian cupcakes she made on Monday,' said Ethan, getting up to answer the door. 'They were the business.'

He swung open the door to find not Florence Quail but a middle-aged woman and a glum-looking boy aged about ten standing in the hallway. The boy was carrying a large cardboard box labelled **Nutty Choc Blobs** on his shoulder. Ethan's eyes lit up. He liked Nutty Choc Blobs even more than Florence's Venusian cupcakes.

'Are you the Space Detectives?' asked the woman. She had a grey, haunted look on her face. 'I need help. Urgently.'

'Come in,' said Ethan. 'I think we can spare you a few minutes.'

The woman introduced herself as Mrs Marjorie Plum and the boy as her son Felix. Ethan showed them into the office and asked them to sit on the long, comfortable sofa facing the two detectives' desks. He expected Felix to put down the cardboard box – hoping he would open it and offer its contents around – but to his surprise the boy kept the box held firmly on his shoulder. It looked very uncomfortable.

'I'm Connor,' said Connor, 'and that's Ethan. We solve problems. What can we do for you?'

Mrs Plum took a deep, shuddering breath. She seemed to be gathering herself to deliver some shocking revelation. 'It's probably easier if we show you,' she said, and nodded at Felix, giving his arm a gentle nudge.

'I'll show you, guys,' said Felix morosely, 'but you've got to promise to be cool about this and not freak out.'

Connor and Ethan exchanged a curious glance.

'We promise,' said Connor.

'We'll be cool,' said Ethan.

'OK,' said Felix, 'but remember. You promised.'

He lifted the Nutty Choc Blobs box from his shoulder and placed it on the floor.

Connor and Ethan blinked. Then blinked again. Then rubbed their eyes and blinked some more.

It must be extremely difficult to be cool and not freak out when a boy reveals an **extra head** sprouting from his shirt collar, but a promise is a promise and somehow Connor and Ethan managed it. They stared as politely as possible and tried their hardest not to say things like **wow** and **oh my gosh** and **blinking heck, mate, you've got two heads!**

Felix's second head was a perfect copy of the first, right down to the scruffy mop of brown hair and the small mole on his right cheek.

'Thanks for not freaking out,' said Felix's first head. To both Connor and Ethan's astonishment – not that they weren't already thoroughly astonished – they noticed that when Felix's first head spoke, the second head spoke exactly the same words at exactly the same time. The effect was a bit creepy.

'It was just *there* when he woke up this morning,' explained Mrs Plum. 'I swear he only had the one when he went to bed last night. Our family doctor doesn't have a clue how this could have happened. She said there's no known disease in the universe that can suddenly cause a person to grow an extra head. A total mystery. So that's when I thought of you. I'd seen one of your adverts online. You solve mysteries, don't you? Well, here's one for you. How did my son grow an extra head and is there anything we can do about it?'

The office doorbell rang again.

'Get that, would you?' said Connor to Ethan. 'And if it's Florence Quail, tell her we're busy.' He turned to the visitors on the sofa. 'We'd be delighted to take your case, Mrs Plum. Things have been quiet here lately, so I can promise you our full attention. Ethan and I will put our heads together and see what we can do.' He winced. 'Sorry. Poor choice of words.'

Wearing a dazed expression, Ethan returned from the door and whispered in Connor's ear. 'Mate. There's about twenty people out there. And all of them have got

extra heads!
Or extra arms. Or legs.

Something **extremely odd** is happening on Starville today!'

Chapter 3
Nosing around

An hour or so later the two young detectives were sitting on a bench in the small, neat park opposite their building. Connor and Ethan often found a bit of fresh air helped when trying to figure out a mystery. Ethan had taken the details of everyone who had shown up at their office that morning with unexplained extra body parts and was reading them aloud to Connor from his electronic notepad. Connor was using his own device to plot where everyone affected lived on a map of Starville.

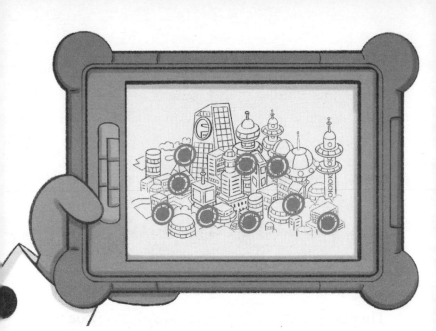

'... then there's Clive Osprey, the maths teacher from Starville Central High. He's got five extra arms. Should be useful when marking homework. Next was Ibrahim Khan, rocket-bus driver. He's another member of the two-heads club. Then we saw Lizzie Newtbiscuit, the three-legged architect. And finally there were the Armitage twins, Pip and James, who between them have a total of twelve extra limbs. That's everyone.'

Connor adjusted his glasses, pushing them further up his nose, which he always did when he was thinking. 'What do all these people have in common? There must be something they all did recently or something that happened to them that's the cause of all these extra body parts.'

'I haven't noticed anything,' said Ethan. 'They're a real mix. Young, old, rich, poor. Some people were at home yesterday, some at school – the school terms are long here compared to Earth ones – some at work …'

'All human? Or were any of Starville's alien inhabitants affected?'

'Mostly human,' said Ethan. 'Except for a couple of Martians and one Plutonian Cow Person.'

'Any ideas?'

'Not a sniff.'

'Hmmmm,' Connor said, and stared

thoughtfully into the distance. Was some strange alien virus the cause of people randomly sprouting arms and heads? His eyes flitted idly across the shimmering trees and grass of the park in a slow semicircle until he was looking at his friend again – then he gave a squeak of alarm and nearly fell off the bench.

'What's up with you?' asked Ethan. 'You look like you've just remembered you left a bath running somewhere.'

Connor was staring at Ethan in open-mouthed amazement, his jaw flapping like the tail of a recently landed trout. He pointed to his nose with a trembling hand.

'Something up with your nose?' asked Ethan.

Connor shook his head dumbly. He seemed to be summoning the strength to speak. 'Not mine,' he managed to say eventually.

'Look.' He took Ethan's electronic notepad and switched on the selfie camera, holding it up so Ethan could see himself.

Ethan goggled.

'Whaaaaaaaaaaaaaaaat?'

He touched his face gingerly. Once, twice, a third time. The image on the screen was no lie. It had really happened.

He had five noses!

Somehow, in the past few seconds, a pair of new noses had sprouted on each cheek. They were exactly the same shape as his usual nose and even had the same light sprinkling of brown freckles.

'This is ... unusual,' said Ethan in a small voice. He pinched a couple of his extra noses, as if hoping he was dreaming and might wake himself up.

'I know! How the heck did this happen?' asked Connor. 'You looked fine a moment ago.'

'This is potty!' groaned Ethan. 'I can't go through life with five noses! My hay fever's bad enough with just one!'

He gave a sniff through each of his noses. The combined sound was as loud as a small spaceship taking off.

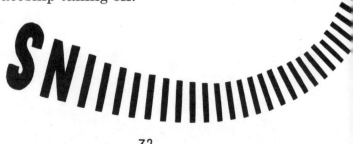

FFFFF!!

Connor gave a sympathetic shrug. 'All we can do is try to solve the mystery. Find out how this happened and how we can fix it.'

'It's all right for you to say that,' said Ethan. 'You're not the one who's going to need four more sleeves sewn into his jumpers to wipe all the extra snot on.'

'Can you think of anything unusual that's happened to you lately that might be behind this?' asked Connor. 'Anything at all?'

Ethan gave a bitter little laugh. 'Mate, since we moved to Starville it's been nothing *but* unusual twenty-four hours a day. It could be *anything*.'

A friendly bark interrupted their conversation.

'Look,' said Ethan, 'it's Winston.'

Winston was a stray collie that the two young detectives saw most mornings when they were arriving at their office. He was a friendly dog with long white-and-brown fur who seemed content to survive on the streets, stealing odd morsels of food out of bins and even occasionally from market stalls. He was such a cheerful, good-natured animal that no one ever minded.

Today Winston was trotting contentedly down the path that ran along the edge of the park, pausing to sniff everything that came his way.

'Notice anything different about Winston today?' asked Connor.

Ethan stared at Winston, momentarily forgetting his own woes. 'He's got three tails!'

And so he had. Sprouting from Winston's rear end as he padded along the path were three lively, wagging tails that whipped and thrashed chaotically like a trio of excited snakes.

Connor suddenly gripped Ethan's arm.

'Ow! What is it?'

'I've had an idea!' said Connor.

'I hope it's a good one,' said Ethan, rubbing his arm.

Connor adjusted his glasses. 'Dogs are territorial, right? That means they keep to the same area all the time – their territory.'

'OK.'

'That means the chances are, whatever happened to Winston happened when he was patrolling his territory, probably yesterday.'

'So?'

'So. If we follow Winston now as he patrols his territory, he might take us to wherever he picked up those extra tails from!'

Chapter 4
Tailing Winston

Winston sniffed at a lamp post near the park entrance and then trotted across the road, heading for a long parade of shops.

Connor and Ethan followed at what they hoped was a safe distance, trying their best not to attract Winston's attention in case it made him stray from his usual route.

His three tails flicking and flailing, Winston pawed at the half-chewed remnant of a hamburger outside a takeaway before wolfing it down in a single gulp.

'Make a note of that takeaway,' whispered

Connor to Ethan. 'It's FluffyCorp Smileburgers.'

'I'm sure that place was called Zap and Pongo's Tremendous Space Burgers last week,' said Ethan. 'It must have been taken over.'

Next Winston rummaged in a litter bin outside the Royal Bank of Saturn, pulling out what looked like an old orange peel, which he sniffed a few times and then ignored.

From there he scampered past a branch of the Jetpack Phone Warehouse and towards the department store Mars & Spencer.

Ethan kept careful note of everywhere Winston went and every scrap of food he scavenged or even just sniffed. 'Any ideas yet?' he asked Connor.

His friend shook his head. 'It could be any of these places. Or none of them. Let's keep going. Hey, look where he is now!'

The collie was sitting obediently outside a chemist's called Hootenbiffle's All Night Pharmacy. It was a rather scruffy, run-down sort of place compared to the flashier shops around it, with a faded sign and a rectangle of damp cardboard in its door where the window had been broken.

'This is where I get my hay fever tablets!' said Ethan.

'Is that so?' said Connor.

They hid behind a parked hover-van and peeped around. After a moment, the door of the chemist's opened and an old man with a droopy grey moustache emerged carrying a small metal bowl, which he placed on the ground in front of Winston. Immediately, the collie began to lap thirstily at its contents.

'Interesting,' whispered Connor. 'From the way he was waiting outside the shop, it looks like Winston probably comes here for a drink every day.'

'Maybe the chemist's been handing out dodgy medicines to people and that's what's made them sprout extra heads and stuff?' wondered Ethan. 'Perhaps his entire shop is contaminated with some weird chemical and it's even affecting the water he gives to Winston, which is why he's grown those extra tails?'

Connor nodded approvingly. 'What an excellent theory.'

Ethan glowed with pride. Compliments from his brainy friend were rare.

'Although,' continued Connor, 'if the whole shop was contaminated, you might expect the owner himself to be affected. And he looks fine.'

Ethan groaned. 'I knew it was too good to be true.'

Soon, Winston lifted his head from the bowl and shook the last few drops of water from the fur of his muzzle. The old man reached down and picked up the bowl, a happy smile on his face. Winston barked once, as if in thanks, turned his tails and trotted away towards the entrance to a narrow alley.

'I'll speak to the chemist,' said Connor. 'You follow Winston.'

Ethan sniffed the ground, his five noses twitching. 'I've got his scent. My sense of smell is five times stronger now. He won't get away.' He tiptoed hurriedly after the dog.

'Excuse me,' said Connor as he approached the old man. 'Would you be Mr Hootenbiffle?'

'That's me,' said the old man in a voice as thick and scratchy as a sandpaper milkshake. 'Whaddya want, kid?'

'Do you give that dog water every day?'

'The dog? Yeah. He's a good mutt. Chased away the rats in my backyard, so now I give him a daily drink. What's it to you, kid?'

'He's grown extra tails. Have any of your customers complained about growing extra limbs after using your medicines?'

Mr Hootenbiffle's moustache quivered with outrage. 'No! No one has complained! What are ya tryin' to say, kid? My business'd get closed down in a week if my products gave people crazy side effects like that.'

Connor cupped his chin thoughtfully. 'What kind of substance would it take to make a person grow extra heads or noses?'

The old man gave a snort. 'Nothing I sell. You'd need a fancy lab full of scientists to come up with something capable of genetically altering a person that much.'

Connor nodded. 'Thanks for your help, Mr Hootenbiffle.'

'No problem.'

Connor's electronic notepad made a chirruping sound to indicate an incoming message. He read it.

FROM: ETHAN

HEY, MATE.

THINK I FOUND SOMETHING.

JOIN ME IN THE ALLEY.

BUT BE *REALLY REALLY* QUIET.

Connor tiptoed into the alley. He found Ethan crouching behind a large and stinky dustbin, his five noses wrinkled in disgust. He gestured for Connor to join him.

'What have you found?' whispered Connor.

Ethan pointed down the alley.

Connor saw Winston and two other dogs he'd never seen before snuffling inside an overturned bin. He noticed that one dog, a brown-and-white dachshund, had six legs and the other, a small yappy terrier, had three heads.

'Look what's written on the side of the bin,' whispered Ethan.

Connor squinted into the distance. 'It says property of Pokeweed's Perfect Pastries. So what?'

'Pokeweed's bakery backs on to this alley. I bought a pastry from there this morning!'

'Interesting,' said Connor. 'Give me a moment.'

He whipped out his electronic notepad and examined the map he'd marked earlier with the addresses of all those afflicted with extra limbs. 'Aha!' he announced, turning the device towards Ethan. There was a ring of red dots on the map. 'Check this out! The addresses of everyone who came to see us this morning form a rough circle. And look what's exactly at its centre!' He tapped a label on the map.

Ethan peered at it. The label read:

Pokeweed's Perfect Pastries

'Hello, Mrs Plum. It's Connor Crake calling from the ***Space Detectives***. How is Felix doing? Oh dear. Yes, it must be awful having dinner with a boy who talks with *both* mouths full. Speaking of food, I have a question about what Felix may have been eating yesterday ...'

'Mr Waterbuck? Ethan Kennedy from Space Detectives. Hi. Hope I'm not disturbing you? Having twelve extra legs must be disturbing enough. Help me out with something. Are you a fan of pastries ... ?'

It didn't take long. Within a few minutes they had called every one of their new extra-limbed clients and every single one of them had given exactly the same answer to their question.

'Snorgleberry tart!' said Ethan. 'Everyone who's grown extra bits has eaten a snorgleberry tart from Pokeweed's Perfect Pastries in the last twenty-four hours. Including me.'

Chapter 5
Baking bad

Pokeweed's Perfect Pastries was a small shop with a brightly painted sign and a large window at the front displaying rows of mouth-watering golden-brown pies, cakes and pastries.

Ethan pressed his noses eagerly against the glass.

'Don't even think about eating anything from this place,' said Connor sternly. 'You have enough extra bits as it is.'

'I wasn't thinking about eating anything,' protested Ethan.

Connor snorted. 'The only time you're not thinking about eating is when you're asleep, and even then you're probably dreaming about eating. Are you clear on our plan?'

'Of course. It's gonna be a piece of cake.'

'See? You're still thinking about food.'

'I'm not. Stop making a meal of this.'

'You did that on purpose! And don't forget to cover your noses before you go in or they'll realise something's up.'

Ethan had bought a long green scarf from a nearby boutique, which he now tied around his face, hiding his noses. He pushed open the shop door. 'Come on.'

Inside, their nostrils (all twelve of them) were greeted by a gorgeous smell. Behind a long glass counter stuffed with delicious-looking baked goods stood a plumpish elderly woman wearing an apron. Her cheeks were rosy red and her eyes twinkled with good cheer.

'Good afternoon, gentlemen!' she said warmly, a broad smile spreading across her dimpled face. 'I hope you're both well on this fine afternoon. What can I help you with today? May I recommend our ginger and spoffleblob muffins, freshly baked this morning? They go extremely well with a helping of East Starville gruntcumber cream and a pot of tea. We have a two-for-one offer on them today.'

'No thank you, ma'am,' said Connor. 'We're here on business.' He quickly flashed the screen of his electronic notepad at her. 'This is our authorisation to prove that my colleague and I work for the **Starville Daily News** website. We understand Pokeweed's Perfect Pastries is one of the best-loved shops in the whole of Starville and we'd like to do a feature on your fabulous food.'

The old woman's eyes lit up with excitement and pleasure. 'Oh my! The **Starville Daily News**! How terrifically exciting! Of course! Be my guest!'

'Thank you, ma'am,' said Connor. 'Oh, by the way. Excuse my friend wearing that scarf over his face. He has a touch of Martian Sniffling Sickness and doesn't want to spread his germs.'

'Of course, I understand,' said the old woman. She looked suddenly perplexed.

'So how can I help you?'

'Am I right in thinking that you're Daphne Pokeweed, the owner of this bakery?' asked Connor.

The old woman gave a tinkling chuckle. 'Oh no! You're thinking of my granddaughter. She's Daphne. I'm her grandma, Isabella Pokeweed. Looked after her since she was orphaned as a baby, I have. She always loved baking, so when she turned eighteen I bought her this shop so she could follow her dream. Not that you'd ever hear her thank me for it! Oh no! More important things to do, apparently. Still, enough of my prattling. I suppose you want to see Daphne, do you?'

'Please,' said Connor.

'She's in the back,' said Isabella Pokeweed. 'Preparing tomorrow's batch of hazelnut asteroid bites. Would you like to come and meet her? It might be nice for you boys to see what goes on behind the scenes here.'

Connor nodded keenly. 'Yes. We'd like that very much. Wouldn't we, Ethan?'

'Sounds like a brill idea,' said Ethan.

Isabella led them through a door behind the counter and into a small kitchen area. The cramped space was dominated by a huge oven that took up an entire wall and by a large wooden table covered with metal cake trays. In each compartment of the trays sat a whitish blob of uncooked cake mixture. A young woman stood hunched over the table, an icing bag in her hand. She had very big dark eyes and long dark hair piled up in a heap on top of her head.

'Daphne,' said Isabella. 'So sorry to interrupt you, my angel. These two young gentlemen are here from the **Starville Daily News**. They've heard wonderful things about our products and have come to see what we do for themselves. Isn't that exciting, dear?'

'What?' exclaimed Daphne, suddenly glaring up from her work. 'Has your brain turned to mush, Grandma? Why would I want a pair of horrid journalists nosing around my beautiful kitchen and stealing my recipes? Get them out of here!'

She put down her icing bag and shooed Ethan and Connor from the kitchen like a pair of disobedient dogs. Then she returned to her work, slamming the door furiously behind her.

Ethan and Connor exchanged a knowing look.

'Oh, so sorry about that, gentlemen,' said Isabella. 'She's a highly strung one, my granddaughter. Takes her baking ever so seriously. More seriously than good manners, anyway, it seems.' She tiptoed to the opposite end of the shop and beckoned for Connor and Ethan to follow. 'Between you and me,' she whispered, one eye on the door of the kitchen, 'I'm worried about my Daphne. She's been acting *very* strangely lately.'

'How so?' asked Connor.

'She's been cutting a lot of corners. She reckons she's such a brilliant baker she can work miracles with the cheapest, nastiest ingredients. Only last Thursday she ditched our normal snorgleberry supplier for some dodgy outfit down by the space docks. She's letting our standards slip, if you ask me, and if we end up making a customer ill we could be shut down. Please don't mention this in your article, gentlemen, but I had to tell someone.'

The two Space Detectives shared another knowing look.

'Do you have the address of this new snorgleberry supplier?' asked Connor. 'We'd like to check them out.'

The address Isabella Pokeweed gave them turned out to be a large dingy warehouse with cracked, dusty windows in a deserted street near Starville's space docks. Its huge double doors were locked with a thick chain and a large, chunky padlock. A faded sign above read:

TOBY HAWKMOTH WAREHOUSE

Ethan glanced about. 'No security guards around. How long would it take that big brain of yours to pick this lock, Connor?'

'I don't know,' replied Connor, 'but it would save a lot of time if we just snuck in through this hole in the wall.' He pointed to a triangular gap he'd just found in the corrugated metal wall of the warehouse.

The two boys squeezed through the narrow opening and emerged into the gloomy interior of the warehouse. Connor activated the torch feature of his electronic notepad. Its thin yellow beam illuminated rows of huge boxes and crates stacked up to the ceiling. The air was stale and musty.

'Yuck,' said Ethan, tying the scarf around his noses once more. 'This doesn't seem like the best place to store fresh fruit for Starville's most popular bakery, does it? It looks like no one's been here in ages.'

'The hole in the wall and the lack of security guards would suggest that,' said Connor, adjusting his glasses. 'Hello. What's this?'

His torch beam lit up a stack of wooden crates. Stencilled on the side were the words:

TOBY HAWKMOTH'S
CUT-PRICE SNORGLEBERRIES
WHY USE THE BEST WHEN YOU CAN USE OURS?

'Cut-price snorgleberries?' said Ethan. 'That doesn't sound very—'

His words were cut off by a rasping, roaring noise that echoed off the warehouse's metal walls. A huge menacing shape emerged from behind the stack of crates and began to advance on them …

Chapter 6
The pigeon
and the cat

In the veering light of Connor's torch, they could make out a muscular grey body and two enormous clawed feet. The roaring grew louder and fiercer.

The two boys blundered backwards, tripping over a stray wooden crate and sprawling to the dusty floor. Connor swung the beam of his electronic notepad towards the approaching form.

It was huge and two-headed. It was a pigeon.

Ethan blinked. That didn't seem quite so scary after all.

The enormous two-headed pigeon roared again, and this time the sound quickly transformed itself into a throaty cough. The pigeon halted and slapped itself hard on the chest a few times with one of its wings. After a moment, the awful noise subsided.

'Sorry, lads,' it said. 'All the dust in here, see? Gets right in the back of your throat. What can I do for you?'

Connor and Ethan stared, dumbstruck, at the enormous pigeon. Its two heads bobbed gently back and forth. Perched on the top of one of those heads, they noticed, was a very small bowler hat.

Connor was the first to recover his wits. 'Oh, erm, hi. We're investigating some odd goings-on. Do you mind if we ask you a few questions?'

The pigeon blinked its four eyes. 'What

sort of questions?'

'Well,' continued Connor, 'can I ask how long you've had two heads, if that's not too impolite?'

'Oh,' said the pigeon, a note of disappointment in its voice. 'You noticed, did you? Is it very obvious, then? The extra head? I thought I might be able to draw attention away from it by wearing the hat on my other one.'

'I'm afraid it is a bit noticeable, yes,' said Connor.

'But it looks very nice,' added Ethan, quickly.

'Kind of you to say,' said the pigeon. 'I must admit it was a bit of a surprise when I found it there this morning. Yesterday I was a normal pigeon of the one-headed, non-talking variety. Now look at me. But I have to say, these odd transformations have made me realise that most pigeons are pretty stupid creatures. Spending all day flapping about in dirt. I've got ambitions now. I'd like to open my own antique shop. I reckon I can make it work.'

'Sounds brill,' said Ethan politely. 'Lots of people on Starville have recently grown extra heads and arms and stuff. We think it might be connected to a dodgy batch of snorgleberries stored in this warehouse. Have you eaten any snorgleberries in the past twenty-four hours?'

The pigeon scratched its beaks. 'Maybe. I'm a pigeon. I eat a lot of random stuff. I ate a pair of mittens once.'

'Snorgleberries are those little round purplish things,' said Ethan. 'There's a couple of big crates of them back there.'

'I think maybe I did, now you mention it,' said the pigeon. 'Sometime yesterday evening. I'd only eaten a couple of discarded chips all day so I was still a bit peckish. As I recall, those crates were delivered here yesterday by a hover-lorry with the name FluffyCorp on the side.'

'FluffyCorp?' repeated Connor. He looked at Ethan. 'They took over that burger place we saw earlier, didn't they?' He cupped his chin thoughtfully and searched online for the name with his electronic notepad. 'Hmmm. They're a massive corporation. They make all sorts of things and sell them really cheaply. They've put loads of smaller companies and shops out of business.'

'Why would this FluffyCorp company want to deliver a bunch of snorgleberries that make you grow extra limbs to this abandoned warehouse?' asked Ethan.

'That,' said Connor, 'is what we're going to find out right now. At least, *I'm* going to find that out. *You're* going to go back to Pokeweed's bakery. Get as much info on Daphne as you can from her grandmother. And be careful. There's no knowing what this Daphne might do.'

Ethan nodded. 'Right.'

'Oh, you can't go,' said the pigeon, 'because I'm going to eat you both now.'

Ethan and Connor's blood froze.

'Whaaaaaat?'

they chorused.

'Only joking!' laughed the pigeon. 'Ha! You should see the looks on your faces!'

In contrast to the dingy warehouse of Toby Hawkmoth, the headquarters of FluffyCorp were in a huge, gleaming new skyscraper in the centre of Starville's business district.

A set of glass doors swished open automatically as Connor stepped into the wide, comfortable reception area. Inside, small messenger robots like shoeboxes on wheels raced in all directions on various errands, some carrying letters and documents, some cups of steaming coffee. There were huge TV screens everywhere showing commercials for FluffyCorp products.

'Can I help you, sir?' asked the android receptionist.

Connor could tell she was an android because no human could possibly have a grin that wide.

'Yes,' he replied. 'I was wondering if you could give me a security pass that will let me go anywhere in this building? I'd like to have a general snoop about and see if you're up to no good. Would that be OK?'

There was a pause. Circuits beeped in the receptionist's head. 'Certainly, sir,' she said, grinning her ultra-wide grin, and handed him an **ACCESS ALL AREAS** pass.

'Most kind,' said Connor, attaching the pass to the front of his shirt. He smiled smugly. Before arriving, he had hacked into FluffyCorp's computer system and reprogrammed the receptionist to obey his commands.

There was a sudden hubbub. A door opened and an extraordinary figure emerged, surrounded by several of the shoebox-like messenger robots. The figure was an immensely fat tiger wearing a smart business suit and tie. It waddled along self-importantly on its hind legs, stroking its long whiskers from time to time and growling commands at the robots.

'Move my golf game with the Supreme Governor to after lunch tomorrow,' it rumbled. 'Fire all the workers at the FluffyCorp Cola bottling plant and replace them with trained chinchillas. It'll save a fortune. Look into property prices on Jupiter's moon Ganymede. I fancy owning a holiday home with a view of the asteroid belt. Open up a new—'

It suddenly stopped in its tracks and stared at a small cardboard box perched on the reception desk, its great fanged mouth hanging open.

'What is *this*?' it rumbled.

'A box of Pokeweed's Perfect Pastries, Mr MacGillicuddy,' answered the receptionist. 'We thought it would be nice if visitors could have a pastry while they're waiting for their meetings.'

With a huge claw, the tiger swept the box from the desk, scattering its contents all over the floor. Immediately, a fleet of tiny cleaner robots appeared and began to vacuum up the mess.

'Pokeweed's Perfect Pastries?' roared the tiger. 'What's wrong with FluffyCorp Tasty-Pastries? Can't we at least offer people one of our own products?'

'We tried that,' said the receptionist, 'but people prefer Pokeweed's. They say they taste much nicer.'

'What?' roared the tiger. 'Ridiculous!' It leaned in close to the receptionist so that its massive fang-filled mouth was mere centimetres from the receptionist's face. 'FluffyCorp products are always best!' it growled menacingly. 'The next time I see a box of Pokeweed's so-called perfect pastries in here, I shall be a very, very angry tiger indeed. Understood?'

The receptionist nodded dumbly.

Brushing flour from her apron, Isabella Pokeweed led Ethan through the kitchen and into a poky living room filled with old, worn-looking furniture.

'Is Daphne about?' asked Ethan, glancing around. 'Are we OK to talk privately?'

'She's just popped out to the hypermarket to buy some currants, so we should be fine for a little while,' said Isabella.

'I need to ask you some more questions.'

'Of course,' said the old woman with a dimpled smile. 'Anything to help. Have a seat. I'll make us a nice pot of tea.'

She shuffled out again.

Ethan sat down heavily on to the saggy sofa. He noticed a large framed photo on the mantelpiece. He stood up to examine it and found it showed Isabella and Daphne in their kitchen wearing chef's hats. Daphne was smiling sweetly and looked nothing like the sort of person who would want to inflict unwanted extra limbs on strangers.

But then Ethan guessed that was why you could never tell who the bad guy was going to be. That was also what made detective work so difficult.

The photo frame was resting on a slip of shiny paper. With a quick check to make sure Isabella was still in the other room, Ethan slid out the slip of paper and held it up to the light.

It was a ticket for an interplanetary cruise leaving that evening, and at a cost of fifteen million Starville dollars, a staggeringly expensive one. How could the old woman afford it? The bakery was successful but it hardly sold enough cakes and pastries to allow its staff to take luxurious space cruises. And if the family was that rich, why did they live in these cramped rooms behind the shop filled with tatty old furniture?

There was a business card attached to the ticket with a paper clip. He slid it out and read it.

MORTIMER J. MACGILLICUDDY
MANAGING DIRECTOR, FLUFFYCORP

And written below that in ballpoint pen were the words:

Thanks for all your help, Isabella! FluffyCorp appreciates it! MJM

'Oh dear,' said a voice.

Ethan spun round, the business card still in his hand.

Isabella Pokeweed was standing in the doorway holding a tray laden with teapot, cups and little cakes.

'I'm sorry you had to go snooping into things that are none of your business,' said the old woman flatly. 'Now I'm going to have to shoot you with my stun-ray.'

Ethan snorted. 'How can you shoot me if you're holding that tray?'

A third arm emerged from inside Isabella Pokeweed's apron. Clutched in its hand was a bulbous stun-ray pistol. She aimed it at Ethan and fired. The boy slumped to the floor.

'Quite easily, as it happens, dearie.'

Chapter 7
Spirit in the sty

In a gleaming laboratory somewhere in the headquarters of FluffyCorp, a pig was playing the piano. As it played, it sang in a low, mournful voice:

'Woke up this mornin', I was in a muddy sty

Yeah, I woke up this mornin',

I was in a muddy sty

I'd rather live in a bungalow,

'least then my feet'd be dry ...'

A young scientist in a white coat was watching the pig and making notes as it performed its sorrowful little song. She sighed irritably. 'Oh, come on, Kieran. Why do you keep playing all this sad stuff? You've got a heap of happy songs to learn before Friday. "The Sun Has Got His Hat On", "Yellow Submarine", "If You're Happy and You Know It" ...'

'But I ain't in no happy mood,' protested the pig. 'I gotta sing what's in my heart.'

'But our market research shows people like happy songs best,' said the scientist. She handed the pig some sheet music. 'Try this one. It might be more up your street.'

'"Old MacDonald Had a Farm"?' snorted the pig. 'I'll practise it, but I won't *feel* it.' Moodily, it started to play the song.

There was a knock at the door. The scientist answered it and found a young boy standing in the corridor.

'Hello,' said Connor. 'I'm doing a school project on FluffyCorp. Can I ask you some questions, please?'

The scientist noticed he was wearing an **ACCESS ALL AREAS** pass. She'd better be helpful, then. 'Hi. I'm Angela Puffin,' she said brightly. 'What would you like to know?'

'I just have a few questions about—' He stopped abruptly. 'Why is that pig playing the piano?'

'Young Kieran here is our latest product,' said Angela. 'Here at FluffyCorp we've had great success genetically engineering animal workers whose skills vastly exceed those of human beings. Dogs that drive hover-taxis, snakes that design clothes, ducks that act in TV soap operas. So we thought a piano-playing pig might prove popular. Kieran has all the musical talent required, but for some reason he never wants to play the songs we give him and keeps making up his own blues numbers. It's very irritating.'

'You think that's irritatin', you wanna try playing some of this garbage,' called over Kieran the pig.

'How fascinating,' said Connor politely to Angela, even though it sounded like one of the silliest things he had ever heard. 'And how do you do that?'

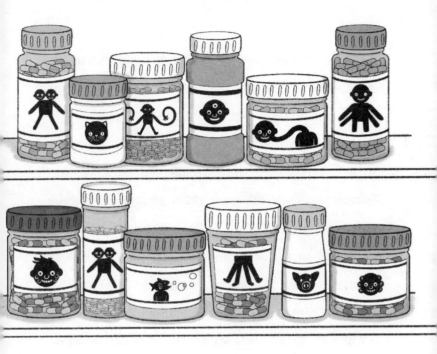

She pointed to a shelf of jars filled with pills, tablets and capsules of every shape and size. 'The medicines in each of these jars contain a special chemical formula that affects a different part of a living thing's DNA. You do know what DNA is? It's the stuff in all the cells of your body that tells each bit of you how to grow.'

'Yes, I think so.' Connor was actually rather a whizz at biology but he saw no sense in letting her know that.

'By adding a combination of different pills into a creature's diet we can make it larger, smaller, cleverer, give it more heads, legs – whatever we want.'

'These pills would be pretty dangerous if they fell into the wrong hands.'

'Fortunately, none of them have,' said Angela. 'We're very strict about these things.'

'Speaking of being strict,' said Connor, 'who's the tiger with the short temper I just saw in reception? Mr MacGillicuddy?'

Angela raised her eyebrows. 'Mortimer J. MacGillicuddy. He's the managing director – the big boss, basically – of the whole of FluffyCorp.'

'Seems a pretty scary guy to work for.'

'Funny story, actually,' said Angela. 'Well,

half funny, half a bit terrifying. Last year we were asked to genetically engineer a tiger who'd be ruthless and successful in business. We thought they'd sell well to small companies who can't afford to hire a lot of people. Mortimer J. MacGillicuddy was our first attempt. But he was so clever and so ruthless that he ended up taking control of FluffyCorp and now he's *our* boss! And, boy, is he a tough cookie. Wants us to be the best in every way and gets mighty angry if any of us fall short.'

'Hmmm.' Connor rubbed his chin thoughtfully. In his mind, the pieces of a strange and complicated jigsaw were falling into place.

His electronic notepad **PINGED** to indicate an incoming text message. He reached into his pocket for the device but it slipped from his fingers and clattered to the floor underneath Angela's desk.

'Butterfingers!' laughed Angela, and scrabbled under the desk to retrieve it for him. A moment later she emerged and handed him the device. Connor thanked Angela for her time and slipped out into the corridor to read his message.

'The farmer woke me up this morning,' sang Kieran, 'as I was enjoying a snooze. He won't let me lie around in mud all day, I got those lazy pig blues.'

'I quite like that, actually!' said Angela. 'It's catchy!'

'You'd better believe it, baby,' said Kieran.

Out in the corridor, Connor read his message.
It was from Ethan.

HEY, MATE.

ANY CHANCE YOU COULD

SPARE FIVE MINUTES

TO SAVE MY LIFE … ?

Chapter 8
Hot stuff

With a clatter, Ethan's electronic notepad slipped from his knee and on to the floor. He groaned and struggled against his bonds but was unable to move.

A few moments earlier, he had woken up to find himself tied to a chair in a mysterious dark room. It was a tiny place, a bare chamber with featureless grey walls. With a little effort, he had managed to prise his electronic notepad from his pocket and send Connor a quick text outlining his predicament. And then he'd dropped it.

'What's going on?' cried a high female voice. It seemed to come from behind him. Ethan thought he recognised it.

'Is that you, Daphne?'

'Yes. I'm tied to the chair behind yours,' said the voice. 'And who are you exactly?'

'Ethan Kennedy,' said Ethan. 'One of the Space Detectives.'

'One of the *what*?' snorted Daphne.

'The Space Detectives,' said Ethan. 'We solve mysteries, help people with problems. We came to your bakery earlier pretending to be from the *Starville Daily News*.'

'But why?'

'It seems everyone who's eaten a snorgleberry tart bought from your bakery in the last twenty-four hours has grown extra body parts. Including me. I've got five noses now.'

'Good heavens! I had no idea. You should

know it's my gran Isabella who's behind all this tomfoolery. Don't fall for the kindly old granny act. She's the wickedest old trout you could ever have the misfortune to meet.'

'Yeah,' said Ethan patiently. 'I'd sort of gathered that from the way she shot me with a stun-ray pistol and locked me in here. She seems to have at least one extra arm herself now, too. Where are we, anyway?'

'In the oven,' said Daphne. 'Let's hope the old bat doesn't turn it on or we'll be baked like a pair of muffins.'

Ethan felt a cold hand of fear clasp his heart. 'Oh, great.' He tried to stretch out his foot to reach his electronic notepad but it was useless. He heaved a sigh. 'The reason why your gran is putting strange limb-growing chemicals in the baked goods is something to do with the company called FluffyCorp. It was them who provided the tainted snorgleberries, and I found a ticket on your mantelpiece for a mega-expensive space cruise for your gran and attached to it was the business card of FluffyCorp's boss.'

'Of course!' groaned Daphne. 'Now I understand what's been going on.'

'What is it?' asked Ethan, straining to turn towards Daphne. 'Please explain!'

There was an ominous rumbling noise, and a powerful lamp on the ceiling of the oven lit up with a bright orange glow.

'Is it me,' said Ethan, 'or is it getting warmer in here?'

Daphne gave a bitter laugh. 'I think someone just ordered two well-baked muffins to go.'

The hover-scooter streaked like a comet over the busy pavements of Starville, weaving in and out of towering office blocks and narrowly avoiding a flock of cyber-starlings that was circling lazily in the air over the park. Connor gritted his teeth into the howling wind and pushed down hard on the scooter's accelerator pedal ...

Drip drip drip ...

The sweat pouring from Ethan's and Daphne's foreheads was beginning to form little puddles on the floor of the oven.

'My gran's being really silly just sticking us in the oven like this,' panted Daphne.

'Oh, really?' replied Ethan. The air was so hot that it hurt to breathe it. He wondered if this was because of his extra noses and tried breathing through his mouth instead. That seemed to help.

'Yes,' continued Daphne. 'If I was cooking humans I'd make sure to baste them in a nice barbecue sauce with minced garlic and onion first. You get a much fuller flavour that way ...'

Poor woman, thought Ethan. *This awful heat is driving her out of her mind*. He tried once more to wriggle from the rope that bound him tightly to his chair, hoping his sweat might have loosened its hold, but it was hopeless. The very air itself now seemed to be singeing, as if the oven and its contents had been caught in a dragon's fiery breath. Ethan swore he could feel his eyelashes starting to crisp …

CLANNNNNG-SCOOOOOOOOOOOCH!

The oven door suddenly flew open, letting in a gorgeous blast of cool air. A long wooden paddle was thrust inside and scooped out Ethan and Daphne like a pair of steaming pizzas.

'Connor!' gasped Ethan happily as his friend untied his and Daphne's bonds. 'I thought I was toast! We need to catch Isabella fast. Mortimer J. MacGillicuddy of FluffyCorp has paid her to put limb-growing chemicals in the snorgleberry tarts.'

'I know,' said Connor. 'FluffyCorp wants to put Pokeweed's out of business because everyone prefers Pokeweed's pastries to their own.'

'Sneaky,' said Ethan. 'That is *well* sneaky.'

'We have to hurry,' said Connor. 'We need to track down Isabella before she escapes.'

'She's on her way to the East Spaceport,' said Ethan. 'She's planning to leave for an interplanetary cruise tonight on the Starship *Solar Queen*. I saw her ticket. But how are we going to stop her?'

Connor showed Ethan a handful of differently sized pills. 'I swiped a bunch of stuff from the lab at FluffyCorp when their scientist wasn't looking. I'm sure there's something here we can use. Let's get going.'

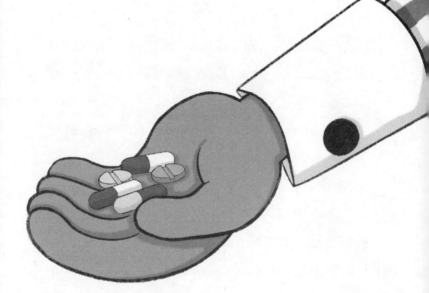

'I apologise for my gran,' said Daphne. 'She's not normally *quite* this evil.'

Chapter 9
Spider-Nan

Among the hundreds of vessels buzzing around Starville's East Spaceport lay the elegant form of the Starship *Solar Queen*. In shape, the enormous space liner resembled a dolphin – sleek and grey with long powerful fins. A line of passengers carrying suitcases was travelling up the narrow escalator from the Space Passport Control building towards the entrance portal, where a robot cabin crew was greeting them with cocktails to the happy sound of a steel band.

Isabella Pokeweed was among the excited

holidaymakers ascending towards the huge starship. How beautiful it looked, she thought, and what a trip she was going to have! She'd spent far too long helping out her wet niece in that crummy bakery. Well, now, she thought, it was time to have a little fun herself.

A low buzzing drone filled the air. She glanced around and saw a small hover-scooter hurtling through the sky towards her. Aboard it were – she squinted into the distance – those two interfering brats who had called at the bakery earlier! That five-nosed squirt must have escaped somehow!

Isabella shouldered aside the young couple in front of her on the escalator and hurried up it, bulldozing aside everyone in her path and drawing annoyed cries of 'Hey!', 'Watch out!' and 'Well, *really*!'

'Right there!' yelled Connor above the hover-scooter's whining motors. 'Fighting her way through the crowd on the escalator. You see her?'

'Yep,' said Ethan. 'I'll take us as close as possible. You get ready with the straw.'

'Will do.'

The hover-scooter streaked through the air towards Isabella Pokeweed. Hearing its approaching engines, the old woman quickened her pace.

Connor reached into his jacket and drew out a small green liquid-filled capsule and a fat plastic drinking straw. While Angela Puffin had been trying to retrieve his electronic notepad from under her desk, Connor had been helping himself to the jars in the lab. One had been labelled:

SLEEPING TABLETS – XXXXXTRA POWERFUL

Desperately trying to keep his balance,

Connor raised the straw to his lips and inserted the glossy green sleeping tablet into the end. The escalator loomed up ahead, Isabella still jostling her way through the crowd of passengers.

SSSCCCZZZHHHHUUUUUUUUUUMMMMMMM!

The hover-scooter seemed to skid through the air, coming to rest hovering just a few feet over the escalator ...

Connor blew sharply and the tranquilliser capsule shot out of the drinking straw like a cork from a bottle ...

FFFPPHHHHLIIIIIIIIIIIIPFF!

Isabella looked up and emitted a startled grunt. In an instant, an extra set of arms sprang out from her dress. Using all six limbs, she sprang on to the handrail of the escalator and began to scurry up it like an enormous insect.

The tranquilliser capsule sailed past her

and exploded against the top hat of an expensively attired man who was standing on the escalator next to his equally expensively dressed wife. Immediately, the two of them collapsed in a deep sleep, causing the people standing behind them on the escalator to trip over, who in turn caused

the people standing behind *them* to trip over ... Soon everyone on the escalator was tumbling down it like helpless human skittles.

Seeing a strange six-limbed woman scampering towards them, the cabin crew at the entrance to the *Solar Queen* quickly shut the portal's hatch with a loud clang. The old woman cursed her luck and leaped on to the outer hull of the ship, clinging to it like a fly to a wall. There she raised her head and scanned the sky for the hover-scooter. She'd fix those two meddlesome little maggots ...

Ethan gave a groan. 'Great shooting, mate. Looks like Spider-Nan's getting away.'

Connor winced. 'Sorry.'

'How many of those tranquilliser capsules have we got left?'

'In total?' said Connor. 'Er, none, I'm

afraid. It seems I dropped them as we were doing that last manoeuvre. There are a few more pills here, but they got jumbled up in my pocket and I can't remember what each one does.'

'For the cleverest person I know, you can be extremely thick sometimes,' said Ethan.

But before Connor could reply, a pair of strong hands took hold of the hover-scooter and plucked it from the sky. He and Ethan found themselves staring into the grinning, wrinkly face of Isabella Pokeweed. She was using her other arms to cling to the hull of the *Solar Queen*.

'You pathetic pair of drips,' she growled. 'Nothing's going to stop me escaping. You two boys think you're so high and mighty with your little investigation. Well, I reckon it's time someone brought you *down to Earth* ...'

With a gargantuan grunt of effort, she lifted the hover-scooter high above her head and hurled it at the ground. Ethan struggled to regain control of the vehicle but none of its throttles or pedals would respond. The two boys scrabbled to free themselves from their safety belts but before they could find the release switches, the hover-scooter slammed into the ground with a shattering

SMASSSHHHH!

The two Space Detectives lay sprawled on the concrete floor of the spaceport among the wreckage of their faithful hover-scooter. Connor shook his head slowly. He felt dazed and bleary but otherwise unhurt. Gently, he nudged Ethan.

'How are you doing? Anything broken?'

'Loads of things broken,' moaned Ethan. 'The fuel tank's got a big hole in it, both primary and secondary motors are trashed, the handlebars are twisted completely out of all shape ...'

'Not the scooter, you dummy! You!'

'Me?' said Ethan. 'Oh, I'm fine, mate.'

A huge shadow suddenly fell across them and there was a tremendous **WHOOSHING** noise from above.

Ethan peered upwards. 'Is that what I think it is?'

Connor shot a quick glance upwards. 'I don't know. Tell me what you think it is.'

'It looks like a spaceship about to land on top of us.'

'Yes. That's precisely what it is.'

Above them, a huge space freighter was gently lowering itself towards the ground, one of its four gigantic landing gears directly overhead. In a few short seconds, it would squash them flat like grapes under a steamroller.

With frantic grunts they struggled to free themselves from the safety belts that pinned them to their ruined hover-scooter, but the release switches refused to open.

'I'm starting to think these safety belts aren't that safe after all,' muttered Ethan glumly.

Connor could do nothing but stare upwards in horror as the space freighter's enormous landing gear descended unstoppably towards them ...

On the ground nearby he noticed a greyish feather, probably belonging to a pigeon. A sudden brainwave struck him. He snatched up the feather and began to tickle Ethan's five noses with it.

'What are you doing? Can't you see we're about to be –

ATTTTTTCCCCHH

Ethan suddenly gave an explosive five-nosed sneeze, the loudest, most powerful sneeze Connor had ever witnessed. Its force propelled the two boys and their wrecked hover-scooter from under the space

HHHHHOOOOOOO!'

freighter's landing gear and sent them
hurtling along the ground until they crashed
into a lamp post with a crunching impact of
shattering plastic and glass.

The huge space freighter touched down several metres away, the deafening roar of its engines slowly fading to silence.

With aching limbs, the two boys finally managed to wriggle out of the straps that held them to the now hopelessly ruined remains of their hover-scooter.

Ethan took out a handkerchief and wiped all five of his noses, which took some considerable time. 'I thought we were a pair of pancakes for sure. Any sign of Isabella anywhere?'

'There you go again,' said Connor. 'Thinking about food.'

A sleek, compact spacecraft whistled over their heads and sped off into the distance, heading for the enormous airlock through which all space traffic entered and exited from Starville. Connor could just make out Isabella in the cockpit.

'There she goes!' cried Connor. 'In that stolen hover-roadster! Once she gets out into open space there'll be no stopping her!'

'And how can we do that without transport?' groaned Ethan. 'Contact the staff who operate the airlock?'

'No time,' said Connor. 'There's only one thing to do.' He delved into his pocket and produced a tiny cylindrical pill.

'But I thought you couldn't remember which pill did what!'

Connor shrugged and popped the capsule in his mouth. He swallowed and gave a grimace. 'We'll just have to take our ...'

There was a sudden loud popping sound. Connor gritted his teeth, waiting for an extra head or leg to burst forth from his body. Looking down at himself, he counted the usual number of limbs, and a swift glance at each shoulder confirmed he had not grown any extra heads. Maybe the capsule hadn't worked? Then he noticed ...

'Your arms!' gasped Ethan.

Connor gaped in bewilderment and watched as his arms rapidly began to grow longer and longer and longer, telescoping out from the sleeves of his jacket and stretching away across the ground. Within a couple of seconds, they were ten metres long, then fifty, then a hundred.

'This is incredible,' breathed Ethan.

'This is amazing,' murmured Connor.

'Well, don't just stand there,' said Ethan. '*Do* something with them.'

Connor tried to lift his arms, which were now almost a hundred metres long and snaking off into the distance. He expected them to be heavy, but to his surprise he found he could use them as easily as ever. Soon his hands were almost level with the speeding hover-roadster. He took a deep breath. Then he seized the vehicle firmly by one of its fins. Instantly, it stopped, engines puttering. These super-long arms of his were also super-strong, it seemed.

With his other hand he smashed the vehicle's windscreen, reached inside and pulled out Isabella Pokeweed like a stone from a peach.

'I suppose that's what you call the long arm of the law, eh?' sniggered Ethan.

'That joke would work better if we were policemen rather than private detectives, wouldn't it?' said Connor.

'Don't spoil the moment, smart alec,' said Ethan. 'We've just saved the flipping day.'

Chapter 10
Life and limb

The office was crammed with partygoers and the air was full of happy piano music and even happier chatter.

It had seemed the right thing to do, thought Ethan and Connor – to invite everyone involved in the Pokeweed case to celebrate the solution to one of the Space Detectives' most puzzling cases. There were two notable absences – Isabella herself, of course, who was beginning a long jail sentence in a high-security detention bubble. And Mortimer J. MacGillicuddy, who had been fired from his position as Managing Director of FluffyCorp for adding dangerous chemicals to foodstuffs, and who was now employed making licence plates for hover-cars. Also in a high-security detention bubble.

'Great party, guys!' said Felix Plum to Ethan and Connor as he and his mum piled their plates high with Pokeweed's pastries from the buffet that Daphne had specially prepared. The young boy looked much happier now that a course of pills from FluffyCorp had removed his extra head, and his mum, Mrs Plum, also looked considerably less stressed.

'Nice to see you, mate,' said Ethan. 'What's that you're eating?'

'Snorgleberry tart, of course,' said Felix.

'And most delicious it is, too,' said Mrs Plum.

'The whippleplofter fancies are terrific, too!' said Angela Puffin, her mouth full as she piled five of the small orange cakes on to her plate.

Further up the buffet table, the Space Detectives' neighbour Florence Quail was helping herself to one of a tray of Venusian cupcakes she had baked for the occasion. Daphne had already asked for the recipe.

'These really are very tasty,' said a voice. Florence looked around – and was astonished to find a giant two-headed pigeon standing behind her.

A brown-and-white collie dog brushed past the scientist's legs and began to lap water happily from a bowl placed on the floor, its long tail wagging with excitement.

Connor and Ethan went to the small kitchen area at the back of their office to fetch more cups. Connor opened a cupboard and struggled to reach a pile of saucers from a high shelf.

'Still wish you had those long arms?' asked Ethan.

Connor gave a chuckle. 'No. Perfectly happy for you to go and fetch me a stepladder. What's it like having only one nose again?'

'Fantastic, mate. Sometimes I wish I still had them when I smell the amazing stuff Daphne's baked for us today. But imagine how long it would take to pick five noses! There just aren't enough hours in the day!'

Sitting at a piano in the middle of the office, Kieran the pig began to sing:

'It wasn't no fun for folk
Sprouting them extra arms and heads
Clothes didn't fit no more
And not enough room in their beds
That's the kind of dilemma
That every person dreads

Connor and Ethan
These two boys saved the day
They cracked the Pokeweed case
Proved crime doesn't pay
And now everyone's rejoicing
Cos Isabella's locked away

Yes, Connor and Ethan
Their investigations proved effective
They solved the big mystery
Even though their hover-scooter's defective
They're just what Starville needs
Two groovy *Space Detectives*.'

Kieran's song finished and everyone applauded wildly.

'Thank you, thank you, guys,' said Kieran. 'Glad you enjoyed it. Any requests?'

COULD YOU BE A SPACE DETECTIVE?

WERE YOU PAYING ATTENTION?

TAKE THE QUIZ AND FIND OUT!

1. Which body part did Felix Plum grow an extra one of?

    a) Head
    b) Arm
    c) Leg

2. How many extra noses did Ethan sprout?

    a) 3
    b) 4
    c) 5

3. What sweet treat did everyone with extra limbs eat?

    a) Snorgleberry tart
    b) Ginger and spoffleblob muffin
    c) Whippleplofter fancy

4. What creature did the Space Detectives encounter in the warehouse?

    a) A sparrow
    b) A magpie
    c) A pigeon

5. Who bought a very expensive interplanetary cruise ticket for Isabella Pokeweed?

    a) Daphne Pokeweed

    b) Mortimer J. MacGillicuddy

    c) Mr Hootenbiffle

6. What animal was playing the piano at FluffyCorp headquarters?

    a) Cow

    b) Pig

    c) Duck

7. How many extra limbs did Isabella have (she has two arms and legs already)?

    a) 2

    b) 3

    c) 4

8. How did Ethan stop Isabella escaping?

    a) With a giant sneeze

    b) With a giant burp

    c) With a giant fart

9. When Connor took the last FluffyCorp pill, he grew ... ?

    a) Super-long legs

    b) Super-long ears

    c) Super-long arms

Answers: 1. a, 2. b, 3. a, 4. c, 5. b, 6. b, 7. a, 8. a, 9. c.

HAVE YOU READ THE FIRST INTERGALACTIC MYSTERY STARRING THE *SPACE DETECTIVES*?

Turn over to read an extract ...

PROLOGUE

The lone figure stared at the laptop screen and gave a chuckle.

In the darkened room, it was impossible to tell whether the figure was young or old, male or female, human or alien. But there was no mistaking the pure evil in its laugh.

The task that lay ahead was difficult. A few details remained to be checked. But if the plan succeeded, the result would be unimaginable terror ...

A muffled voice called, interrupting the figure's thoughts. The figure closed the laptop and went downstairs for dinner. It was fish fingers.

Chapter 1

Welcome to Starville

It was another perfect day on Starville – the most astonishing place in the galaxy. A gigantic space station, Starville sailed silently overhead in orbit around the Earth and was home to over a million humans and aliens. It was a single, vast city brimming with skyscrapers, lush green parks and even a sparkling artificial sea, all enclosed by a huge and incredibly strong glass dome. Seen through a telescope from the world below, it looked like a gleaming snow globe gliding majestically through the night sky.

At the edge of a wide, tree-lined square near the centre of Starville's fanciest shopping district, two ten-year-old human boys stood behind an ice cream stall. One was tall, gawky and looked a bit like an ostrich wearing glasses. His name was Connor. The other was short, squat and constantly bristling with energy like a terrier. This was Ethan.

The square was full of humans and aliens enjoying the sunshine. Business at the ice cream stall was brisk.

'Wow,' said Ethan as he watched their latest customers, a family of tall, two-legged, blue-skinned, cow-like creatures, walk away licking their lips. 'Those Neptunian Cow People really love our Extra Minty Grapefruit and Smoky Bacon flavour! That's the fifth lot we've sold to them today.'

Connor adjusted his glasses, a sure sign there was something on his mind. 'Actually, Ethan, the Cow People are from *Pluto*, not Neptune. You should try to remember that. We wouldn't want to offend any of our customers.'

Ethan had to laugh. 'Give me a chance, mate! We've only been on Starville a week. I haven't learned all the alien races who live here yet.'

'Well, you could have memorised them all
on the rocket trip up here, like I did,' said
Connor. 'What were you doing?'

Ethan shrugged. 'Looking out of the

window and going, **"Blimey, I'm on a flipping rocket!"**

That and eating the cakes my mum baked for the trip. You can't learn everything in books, you know. Sometimes you need to just look around you. Or taste around you.' He scooped a stray blob of ice cream from the machine's dispenser nozzle with the end of his finger and popped it in his mouth.

Connor glared at him. 'For the last time, stop doing that. It's unhygienic. You'll get us closed down.'

'Oh yeah,' said Ethan. 'Sorry.'

'Anyway, I'd recommend getting to know all the different alien races now we're here,' said Connor. 'It might be handy for a case.'

'A case!' said Ethan, staring off into the distance. 'That's what we need!'

'Tell me about it,' grumbled Connor, folding his arms. 'I hardly think standing around all day selling ice cream is a good use of our skills.'

These boys were more than just ice cream sellers. They were **detectives**! Back home on Earth, Connor and Ethan had solved many mysteries together in their spare time, such as finding their head teacher's missing antique letter opener (long story short: magpie). As a result, the two boys had got rather good at finding the solutions to people's thorny problems. So when Ethan's Uncle Nick had invited them to spend the long summer holidays working on his ice cream stall on Starville, the pair had accepted instantly. This was their chance to be *Space Detectives*!

**LOOK OUT FOR ANOTHER
INTERGALACTIC MYSTERY**

IN

**COSMIC PET
PUZZLE**

COMING SOON!

Mark Powers has been making up ridiculous stories since primary school. He grew up in North Wales and now lives in Manchester. If he could go anywhere in space he'd like to go to the Planet of the Doughnuts (that is a thing, isn't it?).

Dapo Adeola is a total sci-fi enthusiast who loves creating characters for books and animation. He grew up in South London and now resides in East London, which according to him is about as close to another world as you're gonna get here on Earth.

Dan is a teddy bear.
He's made for hugging.
Aw, so cute, right?
WRONG!

Dan's so strong he can CRUSH CARS.
But what makes him a FAULTY TOY
could make him the PERFECT SPY.

With a robot police rabbit
and one seriously angry doll, Dan is in
a **TOP SECRET TEAM** designed to
STOP CRIMINALS in their tracks.

It's all up to the

SPY TOYS!

William Shaw was born in Newton Abbot, Devon, raised in Nigeria and lived for sixteen years in Hackney. For over twenty years he has written about popular culture and sub-culture for various publications including the *Observer* and the *New York Times*. He lives in Brighton.

THE BREEN & TOZER SERIES

A Song from Dead Lips
A House of Knives
A Book of Scars

The Birdwatcher

A
BOOK
OF
SCARS

WILLIAM SHAW

Quercus

First published in Great Britain in 2015 by Quercus
This paperback edition published in 2016 by

Quercus Editions Limited
Carmelite House
50 Victoria Embankment
London EC4Y 0DZ

An Hachette UK company

A CIP catalogue record for this book is available
from the British Library

PB ISBN 978 1 78206 427 5
EBOOK ISBN 978 1 78429 088 7

10 9 8 7 6 5 4 3 2 1

Typeset by Hewer Text UK Ltd, Edinburgh

Printed and bound in Great Britain by Clays Ltd, St Ives plc

To the very patient members of what Chris once called
the Crucible: Roz Brody, Mike Holmes, Janet King
and C. J. Sansom.

'If we are going to sin, we must sin quietly.'

Eric Griffith-Jones, Attorney General, Kenya, June 1957

She lies in soft tufts of grass, July sun warming her skin. Above her, ash branches droop, heavy with pale seeds. They sway, gently pushed by a southerly breeze. The thick smell of cut hay obliterates every other scent.

This spinney used to be her special place. Her secret. As a small child she used to scramble through the blackthorn to escape here when her mother needed help mucking out the chickens, or when her annoying older sister got on her nerves. They never found her. A hidden dip between old hedgerows thick with dogwood. A perfect hideaway.

Around her, roots swell, nuts thicken. The berries of a cuckoo-pint redden. A fat bee stuffs itself into the bell of a foxglove flower, fizzing angrily as it tries to back out. She lies so still a gatekeeper butterfly rests on her hand, opens its wings, the dark russet colour making her skin look paler than it is. Over the last two weeks it has been dry and warm.

Yesterday, while her sister had worked harvesting hay in the top field, she had sprawled face down on a towel by the estuary, bikini top unbuckled, soaking up ultraviolet. From above, on the footpath that ran across the railway bridge, a trainspotter had spied on her, licking his lips and focusing his binoculars on the pale bulge of flesh that pressed against the ground.

'Alex,' a voice calls now. That's her big sister. A flat-chested young woman, jealous of her younger sister's beauty and idleness. Of the way the men flock around her. 'Alex?'

Her sister has been calling her name for an hour, at least.

'It's your bloody turn to do the milking. I done it this morning.' A thick West Country accent.

It has been a summer of discotheques and cigarettes. Excitement. Glamour. Periods. A Bri-Nylon bra that she had to buy with her own pocket money. Real French perfume. Rich men with cars, eager to take her out. Dad shouting at her for coming in so late. Mum complaining that she should have phoned. The magnificent power of beauty in an age in which the young rule the world.

There are more important things too that touch somewhere much deeper. Watching *A Hard Day's Night* at the Riviera. Crying silently to John, Paul and George singing 'If I Fell'. And that new one, 'It's All Over Now'. The way Jeanne Moreau crosses her legs in *Jules et Jim*.

Everything new that is blowing away everything old. A life beyond this stupid, drudging farm.

Alexandra has a list she keeps in her other Secret Place. Not this one. The loose skirting board behind her bedside table in her stupidly small room. She made it on New Year's Day (after skinny-dipping in the estuary at night, drunk on cider).

1964

I WILL BE 17 AND THIS WILL BE MY BEST YEAR
EVER. I PROMISE I WILL –
  Go in a plane
  Meet J. Lennon
  Do the beast with two backs!!
  Learn 2 drive moped
  SMOKE FRENCH FAGS
  Go to Liverpool
  Go to London

LEAVE HOME 4 EVER

'It's not bloody fair,' the sister is shouting.

Far away, the beetle stops. Wiggles its antennae in the warm air. Sensilla activate. Process what they've gathered.

On the grey tree trunk it clings to, the beetle pauses a moment. Then waves the antennae again. With an almost inaudible click, the wing cases pop open. Two veiny wings, larger than it seemed possible for it to store in that slender abdomen, emerge and spread.

It has found its purpose.

Buzzing faintly, it flies, following the signal of airborne molecules. They pour towards it over woodlands green with summer leaves, over cow pastures and fields full of wheat, over warming water. And as it travels, their scent grows stronger.

Long, black and grey, almost ant-like, it is not a beautiful beetle, but it is a fortunate one. It has been an exceptionally warm July.

After an hour it lands on red mud. Close. Very close.

A scrabble through twigs and seedlings and then it is there.

Home.

Without pause, it starts to cut through soft skin with its mandibles. The flies are already here, buzzing. They will make maggots for the beetle's progeny to feed on.

The sun moves slowly across the sky. The dappled light travels in the opposite direction across her nakedness. The chiffchaffs start their banal song again.

Her dad is shouting. 'Alexandra!' Anxious now. A quiet man who rarely shouts. But he is bellowing, 'Alexandra?'

Always Alexandra, never Alex.

At dusk a badger, cautious of her human scent, ducks back down into the sett and waits, snout sniffing the air.

The bluebottles are crowding where her nipples had once been; where the knife had removed them. Dark black blood-crusted rings on her teenage breasts. They are laying eggs on her skin, so the maggots can burrow beneath it. Flies crowd into her open mouth, skitter across her dry eyeballs.

A puffball breaks the ground by her thigh. At night a vixen approaches, cautious at first. She trots round her, sniffing before tentatively starting to feed where the skin is already broken on the belly. But a dog fox barks somewhere and she leaves the feast.

The list lies undiscovered behind the skirting.

She has smoked Gauloises and had sex. The other items are still unticked and will remain that way. The local police who will search her room, turning out her drawers, peering under the mattress, will never find it. Nor who mutilated her, tortured her and left her dead like this on the farm where she had been born sixteen years earlier.

ONE

1969

'Paddy. Wake up. You were screaming.'

A woman's voice, close to his ear.

Cathal Breen opened his eyes but saw nothing in the dark. What was a woman doing in his flat? How did she get in? Had he brought someone home with him? Had he been drunk? His head felt heavy enough. But no. Not drunk.

'Was he having another nightmare?' Another woman's voice in the darkness. Two women?

Breen leaned over to switch on the bedside lamp and hit a wall hard with his fingertips. A wall next to his bed? What was that doing there?

Fingers smarting, he realised, fuzzily at first, that this was not his bed at all. He was not at home in London.

It was starting to come back to him as he surfaced from the dark. He had been dreaming about the shooting again. He was here to convalesce from his injuries. That pain in his shoulder; the bullet wound. Where was here?

He turned to the other side of the bed, almost knocking the bedside lamp to the floor as he fumbled for the switch.

Light. He blinked.

They were standing around his bed as he struggled to wake:

Helen Tozer and the strange one who called herself Hibou. Signed off sick, he was at the Tozers' farm in Devon.

'Are you OK?'

'Did we wake you?'

'You were having a bad dream.'

He was still panting. Helen sat on the bed next to him and put her cold hand on his forehead. Breen started to relax.

Hibou hovered at the end of the bed. 'What were you dreaming about?' she asked.

'I don't remember,' said Breen.

'Shh,' Helen scolded Hibou. 'Not now.'

He knew where he was finally. The dead girl's room.

'You're the one who's always telling me that if I don't talk about stuff like that, I'll explode,' said Hibou. 'He should talk, too, after what happened to him.'

In his dream he had been shot again; only this time it was him who had fallen from the tower block, not Cox. He focused on his watch. Ten minutes to five. The girls would be getting up for work soon anyway.

He could already hear Helen's mother downstairs, stoking up the stove. She would appear soon with the first of her mugs of tea.

He sat up properly now, fully awake. Behind the curtain, it was black outside. Winter was hanging on.

Helen stroked his forehead. 'Poor Paddy. You need a bit of time to get better, don't you? Not just from the wound, is it?'

It was soothing, her hand against his skin. Like a mother's, almost.

'It would be better if he talked about it, though, wouldn't it?' said Hibou. 'I mean, he almost died. That has to mess with your head, doesn't it?'

Hibou would be seventeen this week, but looked older. It wasn't just the borrowed winceyette nightdress. It was the visible curve of

6

her body beneath it. He closed his eyes again. Two women in a bedroom with him; a man, he should be happy, but he wasn't. He was losing all sense of himself. He woke up scared. He didn't feel like a policeman any more. Something had been taken.

And he shouldn't be here, anyway. He didn't belong. The bedroom was not his own. It was the dead girl's. Tozer's sister.

It would be better if he talked about it, he thought.

No one talked about the dead girl in whose room he slept any more. Cathal Breen understood that. Some things you hide.

He had been on the Tozers' farm a week now. But though they didn't talk about her, not a day went past when she wasn't present in some way. The pauses in the conversation. The flicker in her mother's eyes and the long silences at the dinner table. The photograph on the dresser downstairs of them all standing next to the family car: a Morris Oxford. Mrs Tozer in the middle, Mr Tozer next to her with his arm around Alexandra, who smiled brightly at the camera. Helen standing a little apart from the rest, frowning. Alexandra: the beautiful one, feminine and womanly even as a teenager. Helen: the difficult one, long-limbed and awkward. The space between them, even when Alex had been alive.

Time passed so slowly here. Every hour was like lead. It was driving him mad. Around eight he got up, dressed slowly, then mooned around the house.

'Are you up, dear? That's nice?'

Read the paper. Tried a Len Deighton book. Tried the crossword. Gave up.

'Where you going, m'dear?' called Mrs Tozer from the kitchen.

He was a Londoner. A police sergeant. There was nothing for him to do in a place like this except eat and sleep and grow sluggish on Mrs Tozer's food. But sleep brought the nightmares.

7

'Just out for a walk,' he called back, irritated that she had noticed him leaving. He had hoped to make it out of the front door without attracting any attention.

'You wrap up and be careful. There's a wind.'

He had spent the first days in bed, feeling the farmhouse wrapping itself around him. Its thick walls and ticking clocks were deadening. Mrs Tozer's food made him pasty. He needed to get out.

He walked through the passageway down to the front door, conscious of being observed by a second pair of eyes, pale in the darkness. Mr Tozer, Helen's father, lurked in the living room, smoking cigarette after cigarette behind drawn curtains. He's not been himself, they said. Breen had tried to make small talk with him but failed. His only topic of conversation seemed to be cows, and recently he had even lost interest in them. Would it be better if old man Tozer talked about it?

It was a lightless morning. Outside the front door, Breen looked right, down to the black estuary, then left, up towards the hills. Instead he walked straight ahead, crossing the rutted driveway and into the front field. The grass was brown, dead and thistly. He kept away from the middle, edging around towards the clump of trees, assuming he was less likely to be spotted if he kept close to the hedgerows.

The ground was slippery and uneven. He had to be careful. He had only been out of bed a day and the wound in his shoulder was still sore, his arm wrapped up in a sling within his coat.

He looked down at his brogues. He should have worn better shoes. The leather soles slid on the wet grass and he fretted about getting cow shit on them.

The spinney was less choked in winter but after more than four years, the thorns that the police had cut their way through to reach the site had grown back.

Breen peered into the dark depression, but could make out

nothing. The undergrowth was too thick, the light too low. Between the finger and thumb of his good arm, he clutched one of the bramble stalks and started to tug it out of the way. Instead the stem flailed in the air, snagging on his duffel coat. Picking it off, a single thorn wedged into the round of his thumb. Breen pulled his hand away and stared at the round glob of blood that emerged from his skin, then put it in his mouth and sucked it clean.

Now he peered a little further into the darkness, trying to guess where the body had been left. He could smell rotten mud and standing water. He felt stupid, ill-equipped for this, one bad arm tucked inside the coat, and almost turned back. The farmhouse would be warm. Mrs Tozer was making scones.

A cry came from one of the upper fields. Breen ducked low. He didn't want to be seen, not here at least.

'Steady. Steady.' A woman's voice, still far away. 'Back her up.'

Breen relaxed. The shout had not been intended for him. He had not been spotted. He straightened again. It was Helen shouting orders to Hibou somewhere over the ridge of the hillock. Winter days were short on the farm. There was a lot to get done in a few hours. Helen Tozer worked hard. Hibou didn't seem to mind the life either. There was a new pinkness in her cheeks. She seemed to love it here.

Breen leaned forward once more, peering into the black, past the thickets and an ancient rusting bed frame. The local police would have searched it thoroughly of course. There would be nothing to find. It was pointless coming here. All the same, he kicked the debris aside to push his way further into the copse.

Go careful now. You are supposed to be recuperating.

There was a hint of old pathway, leading down. Encouraged, he grabbed a dead elder branch for support. He was only going to have a quick look, wasn't he? He leaned forward again.

9

Then his left foot slipped on the slick red mud.

A loud snap. The dead branch gave. Body twisted as feet skidded from under him, thumping down sideways onto the cold ground. Rooks exploding into the air above him.

Pain, pain, pain; his left shoulder screamed. Blinding, all-enveloping pain.

He curled up on the cold wet ground, eyes firmly clamped shut, trying not to shout out loud.

Shit, shit, shit.

The smell of musky rot. And the mud and rabbit shit all over him.

Now Cathal Breen lay back in the same bed again, in the room that had been hers.

'So you're a policeman,' said the doctor. A man with yellow ridged fingernails and huge eyebrows.

'Yes,' said Breen. The pain had dulled now.

'Well, well.'

The doctor cut another piece of pink plaster and stuck it to the bandage on Breen's shoulder. Breen tried not to wince as the doctor pressed down.

'From London?'

'Yes,' said Breen again.

'The big smoke, eh?'

'That's right.'

'Friend of young Helen's, I hear?' The doctor's nicotine fingers shook as he laboured.

'I worked with her when she was in the Met.'

In half-moon glasses, the man tilted his head back a little to examine his work, looking down his nose at Breen. 'Down here to get better, I hear?'

'That was the idea.'

'I knew that wouldn't last with young Helen. No job for a lady, the police,' said the doctor. 'I know her mother's happy to have her back where she belongs, isn't she?'

'I am so glad,' said Mrs Tozer from the doorway. Helen's mother. Rounder, shorter than her angular daughter.

'I expect she's helping her father with the farm now?'

'Hel's doing most of it these days. Mr Tozer's not been himself.'

'No. I heard that.'

'We got the new girl helping too. From London. Another waif and stray.'

'All mouths to feed, Mrs T.'

'I don't mind. I like a bit of company. It was too quiet when Helen was away.'

The doctor tutted. Licked his lips. Cut the last section of sticking plaster. The scab had cracked and bled again because of the fall.

'A bullet wound, I gather,' said the doctor finally. He'd clearly been dying to say something about it throughout the whole time he'd been there.

Breen looked at Helen's mother, still hovering by the bedroom door. 'Yes,' said Breen.

The doctor whistled. 'Only, you don't get a lot of those around here.' A giggle.

'I washed the shirt,' said Mrs Tozer. 'Left it to soak in cold water. A bit of vinegar will have the blood out.'

'Very good, Mrs T.'

'He going to be OK, Doctor?'

Breen lay back and looked at the cracks on the ceiling. He knew what the doctor was dying to ask him. But people round here were not like Londoners. They didn't come out with it. How did you get shot? They were just as nosy, probably, only didn't show it.

The doctor frowned as he worked. 'The projectile must have grazed the clavicle a little, I should say. You were lucky.'

'That's what they told me in London.'

The doctor replaced his scissors in his black leather case.

'You shouldn't have been up and about, anyway. You're a naughty boy. You have to stay still. Mrs Tozer? See this young man stays inside.'

Helen's mother, still at the bedroom doorway, nodded.

'Have I messed it up?' said Breen, feeling for a cigarette on the bedside table with his good hand. 'Will it still heal OK?'

'I'm confining you to quarters. No getting up and wandering around. Don't want a wonky arm, do you?'

Breen lit the cigarette, not offering one to the doctor. He was going to go mad, just lying here, he thought. In this small room. This room particularly.

They had put the family radio in his bedroom. When the doctor had gone, Breen listened to the news. The government was calling up reservists to put down some rioting in Ulster. Someone reckoned Soviets were planning to send bacteria to Venus to generate oxygen in the atmosphere there. In London, they were selecting jurors for the Kray brothers' trial at the Old Bailey.

Just the thought of London made him homesick.

He switched from FM to VHF and twisted the tuner until he came across a police frequency. On it, you could only ever hear half of the conversation.

A lorry broken down on a hill somewhere. A pensioner complaining about a tramp stealing vegetables from an allotment. Ridiculous country crimes.

Breen switched off the radio and looked at the cracks in the ceiling again.

Nothing happened around here. He should not have agreed to come.

Around five, Mrs Tozer returned with shepherd's pie and cabbage and white bread. She refused to believe that Breen did not like tea, so there was a cup and saucer there too. He ate out of boredom.

Helen Tozer came up at around eight, smelling of the milking shed.

'You've got gravy on your face,' she said, and sat on the bed next to him.

'Where?' he asked.

She pulled a checked cotton hanky out of her jeans pocket and dabbed his chin.

'You look tired,' he said.

'Another cow's gone dry. And we're going to have to buy hay in.'

She put her handkerchief back into her pocket. They could hear her mother in the kitchen, her father in the front room, telly on loud. *The Dick Emery Show*.

'My bloody dad didn't grow enough fodder for the winter. I don't know what got into him. He never used to be like this.'

'And you? Are you OK?' he asked.

Helen Tozer looked different down here on the farm. In London she'd worn miniskirts and mascara. Here she wore loose jeans and jumpers that unravelled at the elbows. It wasn't just the way she looked, though. She was as lost here as he was.

She shrugged. 'Not really.'

He enjoyed her closeness now, her body warm against his. It didn't happen often.

They had met in London when she was a policewoman, before she had come back down here to look after the farm. They were never lovers. Not properly. They had had sex just once in his under-heated flat in Stoke Newington. Both of them drunk. He had hoped for another chance, but it had never come. When he came down to Devon to recuperate from the gunshot wound, he had imagined she would be looking after him. Instead she was out all day, working. Someone had to run the farm, didn't they? Her parents only had the one child now.

'Stay for a while,' Breen said, reaching out to take her hand. The skin was rougher. She pulled the hand away and rolled off the small bed onto her feet.

'I'm going to have a bath, then I'm going to bed,' she said. 'I'm up at five.'

She picked up his tray, but instead of leaving she stood by the door, watching him.

'What?' he said, irritated at the way she was keeping her distance from him.

'Dad saw you,' she said, 'by the spinney.'

The spinney where Alexandra's body had been found. Down the hill a little way from the farmhouse, the piece of land that was too steep, too awkward to plough. He tried to read the flat expression on Helen's face.

'Was he upset?'

'He doesn't like people going there.'

'I was curious, that's all,' said Breen. 'I wanted to see . . . . I get bloody bored, just lying here.'

'Well, you're going to bloody well have to lie there now, aren't you?' she said, and pulled the door behind her.

Murdered people never really go away. They stay with you. If you never discover why they were killed, or who the killer was, it's worse. As a policeman he knew this from the families and friends of victims that he'd met over the years. Now, living here, the dead girl was all around him in this house.

From downstairs came the noise of washing-up. Clattering plates.

He turned the radio back on. 'Gamma One. Can't hear you, over.'

Something about someone pilfering eggs from a kitchen window ledge now.

The hills here made communication hard. He decided he didn't like hills. He longed for the grey flatness of London. The possibility that something was going to happen.

When he had worked with her back in London, Helen Tozer had never wanted to tell Breen about her sister. Breen had insisted. Women were more emotional than men, weren't they? Less rational. It would affect her work. Wanting to understand why she had joined the police in the first place, he had insisted she talk about it. She had resented having to tell him about Alexandra, but in a way, that had been the start of their friendship.

He lay awake with it all going around in his head still.

Had the dead girl been left there? He assumed so. She had been subjected to a violent assault, he knew that. No one would have been able to murder a schoolgirl in the middle of a farm without someone noticing, would they? So why would you go to the trouble of dumping the body back here? There had to be a reason for that. Somebody wanted the body found. Yes. Did it mean that the killer was someone who knew the farm well? The local police would have been through everything, of course. There would be reports.

He tried rolling over onto his left side but the pain was too bad, so he sat up straight instead. This was stupid, lying awake like this. There was nothing he could do, anyway. He should try and sleep. Or think of something else at least.

She'd told him then that her sister had been raped, beaten and knifed. A brutal murder. Sometimes killers got away with it, he knew that. But how good had the investigation been?

It was only when the noise of Helen going out to do the morning milking in the winter darkness woke him, at around five in the morning, that he realised he had slept at all.

A little after eight the sun rose behind the curtains and Mrs Tozer came in with a tray of bacon and sausages and took away his ashtray.

He tried reading his paperback, but did not enjoy it any more than he had yesterday. Got to his feet and pulled a chair to the window. Helen had brought him a pad and some pencils; she knew he liked drawing. But whenever he tried to draw the scene he saw through the small, square window, his efforts looked childlike. It was hardly his fault. The cosy round hills and the fat hedgerows looked like a child's drawing to start with. He preferred drawing faces. People. Things.

He got back into bed. Yawned. Dozed.

Later, in the morning, Hibou came and sat with him for a while. Her break from the fields.

'Did Helen tell you to come?' Breen asked.

'Yes,' she said, blushing. There were an awkward few seconds, then she said, 'I don't mind.'

In London Hibou had looked fragile and feminine. A runaway, she had been taken in by squatters who had fed her drugs and used her for sex. She had been timorous and shy. Here in the countryside she was still strikingly pretty in a pink-skinned, English way, even in her dungarees and Land Girl headscarf. She was more confident, more muscular. The farm seemed to suit her. She was coming alive.

'We got a hundred and two gallons of milk this morning, Hel said.'

Breen tried to sound interested. 'Is that good?'

'Better. Was only getting seventy last week. We should be getting twice that, though. They say cows like music.'

'Are you going to sing for them?'

She snorted. 'That'd curdle it. I asked Mrs T if I could try to make some butter from it. Eggs are down, though. Don't know why.'

'Could somebody be stealing them?'

She curled her lip. 'Round here? Doubt it. Why?'

'Just something I heard on the radio. You like it here, don't you?'

Hibou nodded. 'I think I'm good at it,' she said. 'It's looking after things.'

Hibou was Helen's project. Helen had brought her here from London so she could have a place to quit heroin. She was the same age Alexandra would have been when she died. Breen had always assumed that was why Helen had wanted to save her.

'I think everyone should grow food,' said Hibou. 'It's about being connected.'

'Connected to what?' said Breen.

'The land. Nature. Everything. The Earth.'

Breen turned away.

'You're laughing at me,' she said.

'Sorry.'

'Don't you feel it? Back when we all lived on the land, we would all have been connected to the Earth energy and to the moon and stars.'

'The Earth energy?'

'You don't feel it because you don't want to be connected to nothing but yourself.'

'I thought Helen had sent you in here to cheer me up?'

'You think of something to talk about then,' she said.

'Do you think Helen is happy here?'

'Why wouldn't she be? I was asking her if maybe I could plant a biodynamic vegetable plot in the spring. And try and sell them at the market.'

'Biodynamic vegetables?' asked Breen.

'You know. Health foods. Grown without chemicals. Planted according to the moon's cycles. More natural.'

Breen looked at her. 'They've been farming on this land for generations,' he said. 'They don't want someone coming along and telling them how to do it, especially not someone with a head filled with hippie . . . stuff.'

She reached up and undid her headscarf, letting her long blonde hair down. 'Actually, Mr Tozer says it's fine,' she said, shaking her head. 'He's going to dig over a quarter-acre behind the house for me to use. For your information.'

'He is?'

Mr Tozer had rarely shifted from the living room for weeks. 'Old man Tozer is digging over a place for you to grow funny vegetables?'

She had a so-there smile on her face. 'Biodynamic,' she said. 'Not funny.'

Breen was silent.

'Anyway, the other thing is, Helen says to say we should all go out on Friday night as a treat,' she said. 'If you're well enough.'

'Go out? Around here?' A small market town a couple of miles away with a few rough pubs and a cider bar, and that was it.

'It'd be fun. Get your mind off it.'

'Off what?'

'Whatever it is that's making you so grumpy.'

'Will you be OK? Going to the pub?'

'I'm not a nun,' she said. 'It's my birthday Saturday, actually. So it's kind of a celebration. You think Helen would lend me something to wear?'

'Do you still want it? You know . . . the drugs?'

She shook her head. 'Not really. Only if there's nothing to do,' she said, looking away. 'It's why I like working.'

'Your parents will be thinking of you,' he said. 'I would imagine birthdays are hard for them, not knowing where you are.'

'Hel keeps telling me I should write a letter to them.'

'You should. Are you going to tell them where you were?'

She shook her head. 'I don't think so.'

'Do you miss them?'

She blushed. 'No,' she said, but looked down at her hands as she spoke.

'Everyone misses their parents,' Breen said. His father had died last year.

'Not me.' She looked young again; less of a woman and more of a teenage girl.

He rolled over. 'I'm tired,' he said. 'I want to sleep now.'

'Suit yourself.' She stood. 'I only came here to talk to you because I was asked.'

'You're going to be seventeen?'

She nodded. 'I know. So old,' she said, and closed the door behind her.

That night, he left the window open, even though it made the room cold. He lay awake, listening to hooting owls and the night trains. At one point he thought he heard someone moving outside, and got up and stood by the window, shivering in the chilly air as he peered into the blackness, but could see no one out there.

He dressed himself carefully, put on a vest and a woollen shirt of Mr Tozer's and went downstairs.

'Where are you going?' said Mrs T.

'Just stretching my legs.'

'You stay out of trouble this time,' she said, but she smiled at him.

There was a long wooden henhouse roughly in the middle of the hen enclosure. As he approached, the birds came towards him, expecting food.

He squatted down and looked at them. Strange creatures, with their lizard eyes and mechanical movements. There was a gate, but it wasn't kept locked. It would be easy to sneak in after dark to steal eggs, he reckoned.

He pulled back the latch and moved gingerly into the pen. The chickens clucked and cackled around him, pecking the dirt where the grass had been worn away. He walked towards the henhouse. There was a ramp leading up to a small door. He squatted down and peered in, and was hit by an acrid smell. He retreated, blinking, and bent to examine the patches of bare soil. Was that a footprint? He lowered his face towards the ground to look as closely as he could. It was too large to be Hibou's. It could be one of Mr Tozer's, though.

On the way out he opened and closed the latch a few times, listening for the noise it made.

What was he doing? This was stupid. He was losing his mind, out here.

The chickens watched him, unconcerned.

TWO

On Friday, Hibou opened the door at the bottom of the stairs and silence fell in the kitchen.

'What? Do I look daft?' She looked down at what she was wearing.

Nobody had seen her out of overalls or jeans since she'd been at the farm. Now she was wearing a short blue corduroy skirt and a suede jacket, open over a pale turtleneck jumper.

Mrs Tozer had been mixing a batter. She paused, bowl under one arm.

'They fit really well, don't they?'

Old man Tozer made a strange noise: half splutter, half groan.

'Why is nobody saying nothing? Hel? You said I could borrow your clothes.'

A dollop of batter splodged onto the floor. Still nobody moved.

'Those aren't my clothes,' said Helen quietly.

'Oh. But I thought you said . . .'

Breen looked at Helen's parents, both open-mouthed.

'They were in Paddy's room,' Hibou explained. 'And I thought they were yours . . . I'm sorry.' She turned to head back up the stairs. 'I'll go and change them.'

'I never threw them away,' said Mrs Tozer.

'No,' said old man Tozer, finding his voice. 'It's OK.'

Everybody turned to look at him now. His eyes seemed redder than usual.

'I thought they were a bit, you know, bigger . . .' said Hibou.

The clothes fitted Hibou well. They made her look much older than her seventeen years; much more sophisticated. Helen was skinny. Breen looked at the swell beneath the suede jacket. Her sister, Alexandra, must have been larger than her, too.

'You look lovely, my dear,' said Mrs Tozer, wooden spoon starting to move again.

And Hibou beamed and shook out her blonde hair. Briefly, Breen caught Helen's eye. She looked away, unnerved.

The spoon clacked against the side of the pudding basin.

'Don't look,' said Helen. 'It's my ex.'

'Where?' said Hibou.

'In the lounge bar. By the window. Oh, God, no.'

The public bar was standing room only, air damp from wet clothes and thick with smoke. There was a jukebox playing Elvis Presley.

'The one with the little moustache? He looks OK,' said Hibou, peering past the bar into the room beyond.

'You are blind.'

Breen was having trouble protecting his arm from the jostling around him in the Union Inn. Neither he nor Hibou was drinking. In a pub like this it wouldn't have mattered she was underage, but she didn't like alcohol, she said. He was still on antibiotics.

'You really went out with him?' Hibou said. 'When was that?'

'Yonks ago. We were engaged for a bit. Almost married.'

'Never? You? I can't imagine that.'

'That was the problem. Neither could I.'

Breen was drinking Coca-Cola. Helen was on rum-and-black.

'See? This is why I hate being back here. This place is too small.'

'In London I felt lost,' Hibou said. 'People are friendly here, I think.'

''Cause you're in a miniskirt,' said Helen. 'That's why they're friendly.'

'Don't,' said Hibou, but she smiled all the same.

It was true, though. Hibou exuded a kind of obvious sexiness that Helen didn't have. People turned their heads. Men stared at the bare legs, then upwards to the rest of her. Breen wondered if it had been like that with Alexandra, too. He also wondered how aware Hibou was of the effect she had. A little too aware, perhaps.

'I'd have hundreds of children if I was married. Would you have kids, Hel?'

Helen shuddered. 'I don't ruddy think so.'

'Why not?'

A young man with sideburns approached. Through a straggle of long hair, Breen noticed a tattoo of a swallow on his neck. He leaned forward, towards Hibou, putting his hand on the wall behind her. 'You new around here?'

'She's helping us out on the farm,' said Helen. 'Leave her alone, Spud.'

'I like shy, me. You want to be a farmer, do you, darling? I'm a farmer.'

Helen said to Breen quietly, 'You OK?'

'Not my thing, really,' he said.

Spud and Hibou were talking. She didn't seem to mind. She was laughing at something the young man was saying.

Helen said, 'What were you looking for, up at the spinney, when you fell?'

'I'm sorry. I shouldn't have gone there. Did I upset your father?'

She looked past him, towards the lounge bar. 'Did you find anything?'

He shook his head. 'I just fell. I don't know what I was expecting to find. I just thought if I looked I might see something. I'm supposed to be a policeman.'

'Supposed to be,' said Helen.

'Did you ever see any reports? Any paperwork about what they'd done?'

She shook her head. 'I always got the idea they never told us everything. Didn't want to upset us.'

He nodded. 'You look tired,' he said.

Helen glanced over towards Hibou. 'Oi, Spud! She's only sixteen.'

'I don't mind if she don't.'

'Seventeen, actually. Almost.'

'The farm's losing money,' Helen said. 'Our herd's yield is way down and we had too many new stillborns. Milk prices are down since they scrapped free milk for secondary schools. I don't know where the money's coming from, be honest. We need to get through this winter first, then sort it out.'

'You're a different woman down here,' said Breen.

'Boring, you mean.' She swilled down the rest of her glass and licked the rim.

'When I'm back in London,' said Breen, 'will you come and visit me?'

'I miss London so much already,' she said.

'Heard of Tyrannosaurus Rex?' Spud was saying to Hibou.

She nodded. 'They're OK.'

'I'm getting tickets. Next month. Want to come, Hel?'

Helen sniffed. 'They do all that Hobbity stuff.'

'It's, like, psychedelic.' He mimed smoking a joint.

Hibou giggled. Spud, reaching to put his arm around her, said, 'I'm going to Marrakech in the summer. Hitchhiking.'

'You? You've never been further than Bristol,' said Helen.

'Bollocks,' said Spud. 'I went to London when I was eighteen. Tower of London. Everything.'

'People who go to Morocco don't come back,' said Hibou. 'Boy from the squat I used to live in said he knew someone who went there. Disappeared.'

'Too much wacky baccy I expect,' said Helen.

'No. Seriously. Just vanished. Him and the other guy he was on the road with.'

'You used to live in a squat?' said Spud, impressed.

'Oi, Spud. Leave that poor girl alone and get us another.' Helen held out her glass to him.

'Bloody hell,' said Spud.

'I suppose you want one, mister?' Spud asked Breen.

Breen shook his head.

'You OK?' Helen said to Hibou when he was at the bar. 'I'll tell him to bog off, if you like.'

'He's a bit of a laugh, that's all.'

'You written that letter?'

Hibou shook her head.

'You promised me. God. He's spotted us,' said Helen.

'Who?'

Breen looked. Her ex was waving across the bar to them.

The fact that, apart from Hibou and himself, everyone was drunk made Breen feel even more sober. Sergeant Sharman was pushing his way through the crowd towards Breen, hand out, bouncing off other drinkers as he made his way across the room. They had met before; he was younger than Breen by a couple of years, but jowlier and rounder at the waist.

'Breen, isn't it?'

Breen held out his good hand to shake.

'Hadn't expected to see you back down here, city boy,' Sharman said, looking Breen up and down. 'Don't tell me. You and Helen must be courting, then?'

'No,' said Breen. 'It's not that.'

'Word to the wise, chum. She's a tricky one.' He laughed. 'I know that from personal experience. But good luck to you.'

'We're not going out,' said Breen. 'I'm just down here on sick leave.'

'Hel. She's a bit of a handful, ain't that right, Spud?'

Spud, returning from the bar with a rum-and-black, scowled.

'Mind you, you're a bit of a handful yourself, so I hear,' he said to Spud. 'We're keeping an eye on you, lad.'

'I'm not going out with Helen,' Breen shouted above the noise.

'Sick leave? Bit of skiving?'

'He was shot,' said Hibou.

'What?'

'He was shot,' shouted Hibou louder, and the pub suddenly went quiet.

Everybody seemed to turn and look at Breen.

'What?'

'Almost killed,' said Hibou more quietly.

'Ruddy hell. Where was he shot?'

Hibou pointed at Breen's shoulder.

'Did you get him?' asked Sharman.

'Sort of,' said Breen. He remembered the nightmare he'd been having. The man who shot him eventually fell nineteen floors from the top of a London tower block.

'Bloody hell.'

A man in a worn overcoat said, 'What's that like, then, being shot?'

Everyone was clamouring around Breen now.

'Bet it bloody hurt.'

'Drink, boy?'

'Proper hero, you are.'

'That right?' said Sharman. 'You were shot?'

Breen nodded.

'Bloody Nora. London. Mad, in't it?'

'Let him sit down. He's injured.'

Somebody got a chair and pushed it at Breen. Sharman pulled one up next to him.

'We don't get that many shootings round here,' said someone, thrusting a pint of beer at him.

Sharman asked, 'Where did Helen go?'

'Lav,' said Hibou.

Drunk, Sharman looked her up and down, licked his moustache, then turned his attention to Breen again.

'Hurt still?'

Breen nodded.

He pulled his chair closer to Breen. 'How is Hel? Police weren't to her taste, then?'

'No, no. She had to come back because of her father.'

Sharman stopped smiling. Everyone knew why Mr Tozer had fallen apart. He hadn't been the same since his daughter was murdered. No policeman liked to be reminded of cases they have failed to solve.

'Helen says he turned in on himself after her sister was killed. But it got really bad this winter. He'd pretty much given up on the farm.'

The chatter of the pub drifted back.

'Terrible thing,' said Sharman. He looked around uncomfortably. 'Expect you're bored silly. Play darts? We got a team at the station in Torquay. You could come down. Got a board in the canteen.'

'Bad shoulder,' he said. He was grateful for the excuse. He didn't want to spend his time here in a country police station.

'Something else then. Maybe you should come out with us boys one evening. You probably need a bit of a laugh.'

'Maybe,' said Breen.

'Course you do.'

Helen was weaving her way back from the Ladies, scowling.

'Hello.' Sharman stood, smiling, leaning forward towards her.

'Thought you were a married man,' said Helen.

'Don't mean I can't go out for a drink on a Friday night. We've missed you.'

He leaned towards her to give her a hug.

'Get off.' Helen scowled, lit a cigarette without offering him one. 'How's the kiddies?'

'Just the one,' he said. 'Come on. We used to be mates.'

'Get us a drink then,' she said. 'Double rum-and-black. You want anything?' she called to Hibou, who shook her head.

Hibou was on her own again; the lad she'd been flirting with had made himself scarce now Sharman was around. 'You all right? Want to head home soon?'

'I'm OK,' she said.

A man was selling raffle tickets for a leg of lamb. Breen shook his head.

Helen and Freddie Sharman were in conversation now. Sharman had his arm around her and Breen noticed her leaning into him, her lips close to his ear. As she talked, Sharman glanced over and looked straight at Breen. Were they talking about him? They must be.

Breen felt irritated. She would be telling him about how he was hating it down here, probably. Breen didn't mind Sharman. He was a good enough copper. But she shouldn't be fooling around with him like this.

Now Sharman was shaking his head. Helen was smiling at him still.

He realised that Hibou was looking at him, too. She must have noticed the look on his face as he watched Helen and Sharman.

'Helen said you had a thing with her in London,' said Hibou.

'Yes,' he said. 'Nothing serious.'

'Why not?'

'She's not my type. Or I'm not hers.'

'Your type?' she said. 'What's all that? You're just building walls around you.'

'What do you know? You're just sixteen.'

'Seventeen tomorrow.'

He looked around the pub full of drunkards and farm boys. The window was dripping with condensation. Outside, it was dead and black. The London streets would be bright, full of artificial light. They would be busy with buses and taxis. People you didn't know doing so many different things, talking in different accents, dressing in different clothes. There would be films to see and concerts to go to.

It was that feeling of wanting to hear a well-loved song again. He would kill for a decent cup of coffee, too.

Breen and Hibou walked back from the pub together, Hibou quiet, self-absorbed, Breen silently angry at Helen. There was a lock-in back at the pub. 'You go home, Paddy. Not your scene,' Helen had said.

When they got to the farm Breen opened the small cupboard under the stairs and pulled out the big silver torch. Hibou watched him, puzzled, but didn't ask what he wanted it for.

That night, again, he lay in bed wide awake. At around one by the luminous hands on his watch he heard Helen returning from the pub, tripping up the stairs. However drunk she was, he would have liked it if she had come to knock on his door on her way to bed, but she didn't. Soon he could hear her snoring softly at the other end of the corridor.

At around two he sat up straight, yanked himself from the bed. At the window he switched on the torch. The light barely made it across the farmyard to the henhouse. He waved the torch backwards and forwards, but there was no one there. The gate was still closed. He had thought he heard someone moving around out there, perhaps opening the gate to the enclosure, but it must have just been his imagination.

He switched off the torch again and the world became completely black.

THREE

Early on Saturday morning, the windows of the farmhouse began rattling.

'Miracles,' Mrs Tozer said, looking out from the kitchen. A puff of two-stroke smoke drifted past. 'The girl's done that, you know.'

'Hibou?' said Breen.

'That's right.'

Bony hands on the rotavator's handles, old man Tozer was noisily churning up a patch of soil at the back of the house, moving slowly backwards and forwards behind the battered old machine as it spat out clods of wet earth. The engine's splutter sped and slowed, threatening to stall at any moment from the strain of it. Mr Tozer chewed his cheek steadily as he worked.

It was Hibou's birthday. Mrs Tozer had baked a cake with a big iced owl on it. 'That's what Hibou means, you know. She told me. Funny name, though, isn't it? "Owl". I asked her what her real name was, only she wouldn't tell me.'

'She won't tell anyone,' said Breen. 'In the squat where she lived, they all had made-up names.'

Mrs Tozer had made the birthday cake and Mr Tozer was giving her a vegetable garden.

Hibou was there, in blue overalls and wellingtons, watching him break up the soil.

Old man Tozer turned a switch and the engine died. Hibou put down the basket she was holding and kissed Helen's father on the cheek.

Breen and Mrs Tozer watched them. Mr Tozer had picked up a handful of soil and was discussing it with Hibou. She took the earth from him and smiled. Sniffed it. For a second Breen thought she was even going to taste it. Then Mr Tozer turned and started tugging on the starter cord until the engine blurted back into life.

Helen came down the stairs in an old quilted dressing gown of her mother's. 'What the crapping hell's he doing at this hour?'

'Language,' said her mother.

Helen joined them at the window. 'Today's supposed to be my bloody lie-in. One morning when I don't have to get up for the cows.'

Helen's mother tutted, went to the range and started making tea for her.

'It's Hibou's birthday.'

'Besides, I'm coming down with a cold,' said Helen.

'Drank too much last night, more like,' said her mother. 'I could hear you snoring.'

'Thanks for the sympathy, Mum. Fab.' She smiled and gave her mother a little hug.

Hibou came in now, sitting on the edge of the bench to tug her wellingtons off.

'That outside, that's for your vegetable thing?' said Mrs Tozer.

'Biodynamic,' said Hibou. 'It's what we did at the squat in London. You have to plant the seeds when the moon and the signs of the zodiac are right. It's amazing.'

'Amazing,' said Helen, rolling her eyes.

'No harm trying,' said her mother.

'Nobody round here is going to want stuff like that anyway. Waste of effort.'

'I'll do it in my own time,' said Hibou. She put down the basket. It was half full of eggs.

Mrs Tozer fetched a pile of egg boxes and started counting them, placing them in the boxes. When she'd finished she made a note in a small, well-thumbed notebook. 'Eggs are still down, too,' she said.

'Really?' said Hibou.

'Only twenty-five today,' Mrs Tozer said.

'Maybe you should sell them as free range. Get a better price than the Egg Marketing Board,' Hibou said.

'Free range,' muttered Helen. 'They're just eggs. Have you written that letter, Hibou? Like you promised?'

'It's her birthday,' said Mrs Tozer. 'Leave her be.'

'It's her birthday and her parents will be thinking about her. They won't know where she is. Of all people, you should know what that's like.'

Her mother tutted. 'Don't, Helen.'

'Yes, actually I have. As it happens,' said Hibou, holding her head up and looking Helen in the eye.

'And have you posted it?'

Hibou shrugged. 'Don't have a stamp.'

'Fetch my purse, dear,' said Mrs Tozer. 'There are some in there.'

'I wish he'd stop that noise,' said Helen. 'It's giving me a headache.' She disappeared up the small staircase at the back of the kitchen.

'Maybe it's foxes scaring the hens,' said Hibou. 'That's why they're not laying so many.'

'Just our luck,' said Mrs Tozer, digging her purse. 'I suppose.' She pulled out a fourpenny stamp.

'But it's a Christmas stamp,' said Hibou. Two children playing on a rocking chair.

'That don't matter,' said Mrs Tozer.

Helen returned, clutching her present. 'Sorry 'bout the wrapping. I'm no good at that sort of thing.'

It was a record; you could tell from the shape. The young girl threw her arms round Helen.

'Get off,' Helen said. 'Any chance of a fry-up, Mum? I'm starving.'

Hibou unwrapped the package. It was a copy of The Beatles' new album, *Yellow Submarine*, cover brash, bright and childish. 'For me?' she said. 'Really? That's super.'

Helen grunted, last night's make-up still on her face.

Mrs Tozer took a couple of thick rashers out of the fridge and laid them into an old black pan. The rotavator stopped, finally.

'Alleluia,' said Helen.

Quietness.

Breen wasn't used to the kind of silence there was here. All you could hear was the occasional motorbike on the road above the farm; seagulls squawking above the estuary below. A yawning day inside this small, dark farmhouse, with nothing to do.

Old man Tozer came in and said, 'You doing some rashers for me?'

'You already had yours.'

'Want more,' he said.

'Want more, *please*,' scolded Mrs Tozer, but she was smiling.

'This is a fab birthday,' Hibou said, kissing Helen's father on the cheek as he washed his hands in the sink. He smiled and blushed.

'I don't know what you want to grow vegetables for anyway,' said Helen. 'We got our work cut out doing the cows.'

'I'll make time,' said Hibou.

'Leave her alone,' said Mr Tozer.

'God's sake. There. You got the stamp. Give it me and I'll post it,' said Helen.

'I can manage that myself, actually,' said Hibou.

'Do it today.'

'OK, OK.'

'Who took the torch?' Mr Tozer said. 'Hibou went out to do the milking this morning. No torch.'

'Sorry,' said Breen. 'I did.'

'What for?' said Helen.

'Sounds stupid now. I thought there might have been someone nosing around the farm at night. So I wanted to take a look.'

'And?'

'I didn't see anyone.'

Helen snorted. 'The great detective. There's no one sneaking around this farm.'

'You got out of the wrong side of the bed this morning, didn't you, madam,' said Mrs Tozer.

Breen went back to bed to lie down and smoke a cigarette. On the way out to help on the farm, Helen put her head around the door as he lay there, doing nothing.

'I'm going mad here,' he said.

'Imagine what it's like for me, then,' she said. 'You'd have thought the sun shone out of her bum.'

'You're the one who brought her here.'

'I know.'

'Are you sure about her?'

Helen said, 'Why shouldn't I be?'

'We don't know anything about her. All we know is that when she was in London, when we found her, she was a drug addict. She won't tell us why she ran away from home. She won't even tell us what her real name is.'

'She's just young. And pretty. And full of hope.' She wrinkled her nose. 'Do I sound fed up?'

'What if she gets back into drugs? People do, you know. Your parents trust her. They're taking her in as if, I don't know, she's their daughter . . .'

She took a cigarette from his packet without asking him. 'You think we should chuck her back out?'

'That's not what I'm saying. I just don't know anything about her.'

'I have to go.'

'Stay and talk.'

'Can't,' she said.

'Are you happy your dad is getting on so well with her?'

'You noticed then?'

'Hard to miss.'

'Why wouldn't I be?' she said, and closed the door behind her.

He was woken the next morning by someone shaking him gently. It was Sunday, he remembered. He was deep in sleep. He never slept like this, but the sheets always seemed clean in this house and smelt of the air they were dried in and the lavender Mrs Tozer sewed into little packets and left in the cupboards. Like some weird storybook spell was being cast.

It was Helen doing the shaking. 'Morning,' she said. She was on the edge of the bed next to him.

He was blinking, struggling to wake. She looked different. 'What time is it?'

'Half eight.'

She was in a dress. Breen sat up. Something was going on. She never wore dresses, even in London. Miniskirts and tops, but never dresses. Before he could ask, she said, 'I'm taking Mum and Dad to church.'

'I didn't think they went any more.'

'I thought they should. I said I'd give them a lift.'

He looked at her, suspicious. 'You told them to go to church? I didn't think you believed in anything.'

'It's nothing to do with God. It's just trying to get things back to normal again. Like it used to be.' She reached out and brushed hair out of his eyes. 'You need a haircut,' she said.

Breen nodded.

She stood. 'And besides, I've arranged for you to have a visitor.'

'A visitor?'

'You're bored. It's not good for you; I can see that. But it's someone I'd rather Mum and Dad didn't meet. So I thought I'd get them out of the way.'

A voice from the kitchen: 'Hel, we're ready. Are you coming?'

She stood and blew him a kiss.

'Who?'

She raised her fingers to her lips. He rolled over and lay there, awake now.

Eventually he dressed and went downstairs. The Tozers had already gone. Hibou was finishing the washing-up. He stood in the warm kitchen and stretched. His shoulder was feeling a little looser this morning. The ache from his fall seemed to be subsiding.

Hibou dried her hands on one of the cloths on the stove and reached down one of Mr Tozer's coats from the back of the kitchen door.

'I thought I'd go for a walk,' said Hibou.

'Not going to church like the rest of them?'

'I don't believe in the Abrahamic god,' said Hibou. 'I'm a pantheist.'

'You're sixteen,' said Breen.

'Seventeen.'

'Bully for you,' said Breen. 'Did Helen tell you to go out?'

'No. I just fancy it,' she said. 'Helen says there's avocets on the river.'

'What?' said Breen.

'Birds,' said Hibou, thumb already on the latch of the back door. 'I made you sandwiches,' she said. 'Cheese and onion. Don't forget them.'

'For me?'

'Helen said I should do it.'

'Why?'

'Don't ask me.'

When she'd gone he watched her walking away, down the slope towards the estuary. She was walking with a sense of purpose, as if she knew exactly where she was headed. He stepped outside into the yard and watched her as she crossed past the pond. At the edge of the estuary she took a path to the right, towards the town, before disappearing from view behind the scrubby oaks that lined the waterside.

It was cold. He shivered. He was about to go back inside when he heard a car crackling down the gravel track towards him.

He turned and saw the pale blue of a police car. It pulled up at the front of the house.

Sergeant Freddie Sharman didn't get out. He leaned over and opened the passenger door.

'Get in,' he called, unsmiling.

'Morning to you too,' said Breen.

'This is not my idea.'

Breen leaned down and peered into the car. 'Where are you taking me?'

'Didn't Hel say?'

Breen shook his head.

'She didn't say anything? What she wanted me to show you?'

'No.'

'Bloody hell,' he said. 'I feel like her lackey.'

'I know exactly what you mean,' said Breen, getting in. And the car drove up the rutted track out of the farm.

Torquay Police Station was a dirty Victorian building at the corner of a steep street, Gothic grey stone and dark wood-panelled rooms. Like the station he had worked in at Stoke Newington, it was reassuringly solid and old-fashioned. This felt more like home.

'In on a Sunday, Fred?' said the desk officer, chewing on a pencil.

'No,' said Sharman. 'I'm not here at all, matter of fact. And neither is this gentleman.'

'Who said that?' said the copper, pretending to look around. 'Could have sworn I heard someone speak.' And went back to chewing.

The station was quiet. Sharman and Breen walked down a short corridor, past a room where a couple of coppers sat drinking tea and listening to the radio. Sharman led him up a thin staircase to a room on the second floor, under the eaves. It was filled with filing cabinets of all shapes and sizes, crammed in around the walls and arranged in a small square in the middle of the room. There was just enough space to walk around them. Sharman went straight to one in the far corner and opened up a drawer.

'It's all in here,' he said.

Alexandra Tozer had her own cabinet: three drawers, filled with hanging-file folders. Without even looking, Breen could see the coloured paper of different forms, the yellowing photographs, the bulging roneo'd reports.

'Nothing leaves this room without my say-so,' Sharman said.

Breen looked around. There was a small old-fashioned desk by the radiator, an empty inkwell at the corner.

'Did you work on the case?'

'Everybody did. This isn't the Met. When something like that happens everyone's involved. I was new to CID then, I'd just made sergeant. But, yes, we spent weeks going over the land on the farm. And tramping around up on the moor above it. There were all sorts of theories about where she'd been killed before she'd been dumped on the farm, but nobody ever found anything.'

'Why not?'

'I know what you're thinking,' said Sharman. 'Local boys. Funny accents. What do they know? But round here a murder like that meant something. Everyone was close to it. Not like the Met. I expect you get a new murder most days up there. As far as I'm concerned, a fresh pair of eyes, that's great. But tread careful.'

'Right.'

'This is just a favour, to Helen. Because you're here. In the vicinity. And you're going to see all sorts of things in those files. None of it gets back to the family.'

'Why?'

'You'll understand when you see it.'

'Helen arranged this. I won't be able to keep it from her.'

Sharman rubbed his lower lip against his moustache. 'We told them it was brutal. We never told them how bad, though.'

Breen stared at the cabinet.

Sharman said, 'There's stuff in there they never told the papers or the family. Not even Helen. It was . . . pretty weird, ask me. Awful.'

'What if she wants to know?'

'That's for you to deal with. But I care about her. I know you do too. I don't want her getting upset.'

Breen leaned over the top drawer and looked down at the thick wad of documents.

'I'm going home,' said Sharman. 'Sunday dinner. I'll come and drop you back.'

'OK.'

'You got sandwiches or something?'

He thought of the packed lunch Hibou had made him. It was still sitting on the kitchen table in a brown paper bag. 'I'll be fine,' he said.

Sharman hesitated by the door.

'Just 'cause you're down from London, don't go thinking we didn't do our best. We busted a gut to find out who killed that girl.'

'I'm sure you did,' said Breen.

'So don't go digging around to say we didn't do it proper, is all I'm bloody saying.'

And Sharman closed the door behind him.

Breen looked around the room. An empty tea mug on top of one of the cabinets and an ashtray full of old butts.

He wondered how Helen had persuaded Sharman to do this.

In the three drawers, the files weren't in any particular order. Papers had been crammed in, buckling edges, spilling pages from their clips. It was as if they'd been taken out, rifled through many times and put back in. The disorder seemed to show the sense of frustration there must have been with this case.

Breen didn't mind. The order that tidy people put things in often concealed delicate connections. This last few months had taught him that chaos could be useful. He squatted in front of the cabinet and started leafing through a drawer.

The crime-scene photos were right at the front. Black-and-whites, eight by ten inches. They had pinholes at the corners. Breen took them out and looked at a few of them.

The first was of her face, taken in the bright light of a pathology laboratory, he guessed. Pale and overexposed. Eyes vacant. But even with the dark bruising around the mouth he could see the resemblance to Helen. The curve of the eyebrow. The twist of a lip. But Helen's angular face came from her father. Alexandra had had her mother's softness. There were cuts to the side of her head, as if from a struggle. Even like this you could tell she had been beautiful.

He put the photograph on the desk and dug back into the folder for more. The second photograph made his stomach lurch.

It was of the mutilations on the dead girl's breasts. Her nipples had been cut off. A knife dug into the skin; an irregular, circular wound.

He stared at the photograph for a while, trying to distinguish between pre- and post-mortem injuries. How much of this had been done while she was still alive? That would be in the pathologist's report. Then he pulled out a third one. The body as it was found, on the Tozer's farm, lying in the spinney which he had tumbled into a few days earlier.

It was a good-quality photo. She was lying on her back, legs straight, arms by her side. You could see the texture of the grass and fallen leaves around her; the dappling of the light. Though animals had gnawed the dead flesh, they didn't seem to have moved her.

There was something unsettlingly poetic about the way the photographer had composed the picture: the tree roots poking through soil, the shine on a policeman's boot a couple of feet away from her head. It was almost as if whoever had taken it had wanted to show that they were more than just a functionary.

But it wasn't only the photographer who had composed the scene, Breen realised. The body had been laid there carefully. Respectfully almost. Though that seemed an absurd thing to say after what the killer had done to the victim; but the position seemed to be very deliberate. A body wouldn't have fallen into this position.

It had been arranged, limbs straight, hands against the soil. What did that say? Was there some ritualistic element to the killing?

If he had been investigating, what would he have done first? He would have looked at where the body was found. Breen returned the photograph and started looking for any notes, made at the time, that would describe the scene. Eventually he found a typewritten crime-scene report written in stodgy English ('the deceased's body was found lying with its head to East-North-East'). It was sixteen pages long.

He looked around for something to make notes on.

A sign on the wall read: 'No HOT drinks alowd!!!' Breen unpinned it and used the back to copy sections from the report. He wrote his notes as small as he could to save space.

The scene-of-crime report alone took him a couple of hours to go through, by which time his first sheet of paper was full. There were two more copies of the scene-of-crime photo in a brown envelope. Breen took them out, tore the envelope into two sheets and started filling them, too.

It felt good to do this. As if he were emerging from a long, heavy sleep. Something to think about. Something to do. He could feel the blood start to move around his body again.

There was a folder with a photo of a man clipped to it. A transcript of an interview inside, plus some handwritten notes. A suspect? Breen started scanning through the drawer for similar ones.

Flicking from front to back in three drawers, he found fourteen similar folders. He took them out and laid them on the floor in a large rectangle. Each appeared to represent someone the police had interrogated in the days after the killing. Some were thick, bulging with paper that spilled out, and well-thumbed. Others contained just a sheet or two.

It would take days to go through them all properly. He began by noting down all of the names, then started to delve through them where they lay on the floor.

At the Met they loved to assume that forces outside of London were all yokels, soft-headed men who had it easy. But there was no sign that the Devon police hadn't thrown all they had at it.

One folder was titled 'Edward Tozer'. Breen hesitated over it. Helen's father had been interviewed. He would have to have been considered a suspect too. It was only reasonable.

It contained a signed statement and the transcripts of two interviews, one conducted two days after the discovery of Alexandra's body, the second around two weeks later.

Breen read through the first interview:

SGT BACON: Did you and your daughter ever argue?
MR TOZER: Yes.
SGT BACON: What did you and yr daughter argue
    about?
MR TOZER: (Says cannot remember.)
SGT BACON: (rpt q.)
MR TOZER: Not coming back from school on time.
    Playing music late. Not dressing decently.
    Not eating food properly. Talking back to
    her mother.
SGT BACON: (Asks about last time saw AT.)
MR TOZER: Wed a.m. She was going to school.
SGT BACON: Was there an argument on way to
    school?
MR TOZER: No. I don't remember.
SGT BACON: What about boyfriends?
MR TOZER: Never saw any.
SGT BACON: AT was good-looking girl.

MR TOZER: I know she had boyfriends. She never
    dared bring them to the farm. I didn't
    approve.

The transcript was stilted; he couldn't imagine Mr Tozer talking
like that, but it was surprisingly detailed nonetheless. The officer
taking notes had been thorough. They were probably better records
than most of the ones they kept at Marylebone.

SGT BACON: Go through everything you did on that
    day.
MR TOZER: (Asks for clarification.)
SGT BACON: 15th July. (Day of murder.)
    (Mr Tozer became angry and refused to
    continue with interview.)

The statement was a carbon copy. It would have been written by
the investigating officer from the interviews for Mr Tozer to sign.
There was the name of a solicitor who had also been present. Breen
would have asked the same questions as the policeman. They would
have needed to find out what old man Tozer had been doing on
the day his daughter was murdered.

He read the statement.

On Thursday, 16 July at approximately 11 a.m.
I noticed one of the dogs going into the
spinney. Though I shouted he would not return.
I was made curious by this. I followed the
dog there and discovered the body of my
daughter. I did not call the police for
approximately fifteen minutes because Mrs Tozer

45

was distressed. When police asked why the dog had not discovered the body earlier I explained that the dog had been tied up the previous day for biting a calf.

He closed Mr Tozer's file and picked up another at random. Outside, it had clouded over. The room was getting dark. He stood and switched on the light, a single bulb dangling from a cord in the middle of the room.

'Bloody hell. You made a mess.'

Sergeant Sharman was at the door. Kneeling, Breen looked around him. There were piles of paper everywhere, covering the floor, on top of cabinets, on top of the small desk.

'There's a lot of material.'

'Told you, didn't I?'

Breen rubbed his eyes. 'Can I have a bit more time? I feel I've only just started.'

'It's my day off. I'm only doing this as a favour,' said Sharman. 'I said I'd drop you back at three. It's ten to now.'

Breen looked at his watch. Had he really been here four hours? He frowned, stood, went to the desk and picked up the sheets of paper he'd been writing on. Six pieces of paper, covered in tiny script. 'What about another day?' he asked.

'Not sure. We'll see.'

'Give me ten minutes. I'll tidy up.'

Sharman sighed. 'Five,' he said. 'I'll see you downstairs.'

Breen began piling up the folders on the floor, making a few last rapid notes. They were disorganised when he got here, but he wanted to make sure he kept the papers he had read separate from the ones he had not yet had a chance to look at, so he was trying to be as methodical as he could. While putting them back in the drawer, he came across three copies of the pathologist's report.

One was clearly a top copy; the others were carbons. The top copy had the instruction 'Confidential. Do NOT share' written in red biro. He hesitated, then folded one and tucked it into his jacket, along with his notes.

FOUR

'See? We done it proper. Told you.'

The police car was parked on the road above the farm; they didn't want the rest of the family to know where Breen had been. It was already getting dark now. Breen opened the door.

'And you eliminated every single one of the suspects?'

'Yes. All had alibis that put them in the clear. Every single one. Apart from Mr Tozer, but they didn't figure that one at all. I mean, you've got to be careful. But it wasn't Mr Tozer.'

Breen shook his head. 'So you think it must have been someone else. Someone you haven't even considered yet.'

'That's the only option.'

Breen nodded.

Light glowed from the farmhouse windows. Breen walked down the track, stumbling over loose stones as he made his way towards it.

Breen woke with a start in darkness. He cried out something form-less, syllables without shape.

'Shh.' A hand on his face. 'Just me,' said Helen.

Heart galloping, Breen leaned over and switched on the bedside lamp.

She said, 'I wanted to talk. About yesterday. I didn't get the chance at dinner.'

He had taken a long time to go to sleep. Lying in bed, alone in his room, he'd started to read the pathologist's report. It had been thorough, detailed and ugly. And the facts of Helen's sister's death were horrible. As a younger man the details would not have upset him this way. He had seen bad things with his own eyes. Not as bad as this, maybe. Was it that he knew the victim's sister? He had become thinner-skinned.

Helen was dressed in an old brown jumper of her father's that was fraying at the cuffs.

'I didn't mean to scare you.'

God. Had he put the pathology report away before turning the light out? He checked the bedside table and was relieved to see it was not there, so he must have put it in the drawer.

'What's wrong?'

'Nothing.'

'So? Did you go to the police station?'

'Yes.'

'Did Freddie show you what was in the files on Alex?'

Breen nodded.

'What do you reckon?'

Breen was still blinking in the light, trying to wake up. 'I don't know . . . What time is it?'

'Just gone five. It's my turn for the milking. Did you find out anything?'

It felt like the middle of the night. He could only just have fallen asleep. Breen sat up slowly, guarding his shoulder. 'Why did you ask him to take me there?'

'Don't think I haven't noticed how bored you've been this last couple of days.'

'So you were doing this as a kindness to me?'

'Sarky doesn't suit you, Paddy.'

'Seriously,' said Breen. 'What are you doing opening up all this stuff, Helen?'

'It's true, though, isn't it? You're going mental down here. That's why you were digging around in the spinney the other day.' She leaned over and touched his hand. 'And I just wanted you to take a look. Let me know what you thought.'

'Things are getting better with Hibou here, aren't they? It's like there's a corner being turned. You sure you want this stirred up?'

'Stirred up? Like it's some unfortunate family bust-up that's best forgotten? Alex was killed and whoever killed her got away with it. You can't ever let that go.'

Breen reached out his hand and pulled at one of the loose threads in her jumper.

'So?' she said.

The wool unravelled in a series of tiny jerks. 'They put in a lot of time,' said Breen. 'You could tell from how much stuff there was. But whether they did it well or not, I don't really know . . . It would take weeks to go through it.'

She was thinner than she had been in London, if that was possible. There were bags under her eyes.

'I know they put in a lot of time. I was here. Remember?'

'You can't just review a case in an afternoon.'

'Still. If I could persuade Freddie to let you in there again?'

'You sure you know what you're doing, Helen?'

'I'm doing the milking. That's what I'm bloody doing,' she said, and stood.

Breen lay down in the darkness and tried to avoid falling back to sleep.

Grey drizzle fell outside. Hibou said, 'What is it with you and Helen? I don't get it.'

They were in the fug of the kitchen, condensation dripping down the windows.

She had just come in to make a Thermos of tea.

'What do you mean?'

'You row like you're girlfriend and boyfriend. Why not admit it and just go out together?'

'We're not in love.'

'Looks like it to me.'

'And we don't row.'

'So how come she's in such a foul mood this morning? I saw her coming out of your room all mardy.'

'It wasn't a row,' said Breen.

'You two spend your time mooning around each other like you're lovers, but neither of you actually do anything. It's pitiful.'

Breen put down the spoon he was eating porridge with. 'Because we're not lovers.'

Hibou poured hot water into the chipped enamel teapot and shrugged.

Mrs Tozer came in with a basket full of washing. There was a rack that hung on pulleys from the ceiling that squeaked as she lowered it.

'What do you say, Mrs T?' said Hibou. 'I said Cathal and Helen should be going out.'

'None of my business,' said Mrs Tozer, loading clothes on the rack. 'None of your business neither.'

'Just larking,' said Hibou.

Breen grunted and went to put his bowl in the sink. 'Leave it, dear,' said Mrs Tozer. 'I'll do that.'

'I don't mind.'

'I wouldn't dream of it.'

It irritated him that he couldn't do anything around this house.

He wasn't allowed to. He had lived alone, or looked after his late father, for years. He enjoyed cooking, and didn't mind washing up. But Mrs Tozer wouldn't let him anywhere near her pots and pans. The most Breen had been allowed to do was help dry dishes on Sundays, the one day of the week that old man Tozer washed up.

He went to the bedroom and bolted the door, and started going through the notes he had made yesterday. He was in a bad mood. He turned back to the pathology report. He read four more pages, then put it down.

After lunch he announced he wanted to go out for a walk. He felt the house closing in on him again.

Mrs Tozer frowned. 'Are you well enough?'

'Of course I am,' he snapped at her.

She didn't answer. Went back to mending a pair of Mr Tozer's spectacles with sticking plaster.

The drizzle had finally stopped. He walked up the steep lane out of the farm and onto the main road, twisty, high-hedged and dotted with puddles. When he heard cars coming he pressed himself into the bank to stay safe. People around here all drove like lunatics.

The nearest village was around a mile to the east. Breen found what he was looking for on the outskirts. A red phone box under a huge bare oak tree at a road junction; one of the old-fashioned boxes that you had to feed money into before you could dial.

He could have used the phone in the house, but there was no privacy there.

'Sergeant Sharman,' he said to the woman who answered.

Sharman was at his desk, fortunately. 'Well?' he said cautiously.

'I wanted to ask,' Breen said. 'There has never been another murder like it . . . that same way?'

'You don't think we asked? Every time I read about another girl getting murdered I always check. Nothing like that,' he said. 'I mean, a murder that disgusting. You'd hear, wouldn't you?'

There was a pause. A motorbike came roaring up the lane so loud, neither of them could speak anyway.

'Is that all?' said Sharman.

'How many people did you interview, altogether?'

'I don't know. Hundreds, it would have been.'

'But you created a suspect list?'

'That's right.'

The pips went. Breen added more pennies. 'I know. But there were fifteen altogether on the list, by the look of it.'

'I can't remember.'

'But there were only fourteen folders.'

'What are you saying?'

'At some point someone numbered all the suspect folders, one to fifteen. There's a number written in the same pen on the top left-hand corner of all the folders. Edward Tozer is number one and the numbers go up to fifteen. But there are only fourteen folders. Number six is missing.'

There was a pause.

'All I know is we ruled all of them out. Everyone had an alibi apart from Mr Tozer, but nobody really ever thought it was him. None of the people we interviewed could have done it.'

'So who was number six?'

Sharman sighed. 'Are you quite sure there was one missing?'

'I checked.'

Sharman said, 'Call me tomorrow. I'll ask around.' And he put the phone down.

Breen looked through the steamy windows of the phone box.

Maybe he should walk more. It felt good to be out of the house. He needed to think.

He walked through the small hamlet, lingered in a poorly tended graveyard, looking at the writing on the stones until his feet started to feel cold, then headed back. He was a quarter of a mile down the lane when he spotted something pale stuck into the leafless hedge. A piece of paper. He was about to walk on when he noticed the stamp. A fourpenny Christmas one. As rain started to fall, he reached into the hedge and pulled out a crumpled envelope.

It was addressed to a Mr and Mrs Curtis; an address in Buckinghamshire, written in a round, girlish hand.

He wondered, for a second, whether Hibou had dropped it. The rain was coming thicker now. He wouldn't have opened it, only it was unstuck anyway in the damp. In it, a single, blank sheet of paper.

'What happened to you?' said Mrs Tozer.

He was soaked, wet from head to toe, and shivering.

'I was walking along the road. A bread van hit a puddle and splashed me.'

'What were you doing walking along the road anyway?' she tutted. 'Get them clothes off. I'll dry them.'

Breen went upstairs to his bedroom and pushed the door. At first he thought it was stuck. He pushed harder.

'Who is it?'

'It's me. Can I come in? I need to change.'

His bedroom door had been bolted from the inside. 'A minute,' said Helen.

'Are you OK?' he said. He thought he heard crying.

No answer.

*

The pathology report was laid out on the bed, the sheets crumpled now.

'I shouldn't have brought it home,' Breen said. 'I'm sorry. You weren't supposed to see it.'

Helen had dried her eyes, but they were still red-rimmed. She glared at him.

'They never said it was like that,' she said. 'They told us she was killed quickly. Why did they lie?'

'Because they didn't want to upset you. It was bad enough for you anyway.'

She snorted. Breen closed the door behind him and locked it again. He went to the bed and picked up the papers.

'She must have been so bloody scared,' she said.

'Yes. She must.'

Alexandra Tozer had not been killed quickly. The pathologist estimated that the sixteen-year-old had been tortured for around twelve to twenty-four hours before she died.

'A boiled egg,' said Helen. 'I mean. That's so . . . so . . .'

Often pathologists' reports were handwritten and barely decipherable. This one had been typed, at least, but Breen had had to read the covering letter several times before he had understood what the pathologist was trying to say. The torturer had mutilated her body in several ways while she was alive. He had cut off Alexandra Tozer's nipples, cut diagonal marks onto her belly and had burned cigarettes on her skin. But that was not the part that Breen had found most disturbing. Breen had re-read the sentence over and over to make sure he was not misunderstanding it. The killer had placed an egg in her vagina.

The pathologist had written: 'Upon opening the egg, we found its contents to be hard-boiled.' Breen had had to put the report down at that point, the horror mixed with the absurd image of a man in a laboratory tapping an egg with a teaspoon.

The hot egg had seared her skin as it entered. 'Traces of burnt tissue,' said the report.

Traces of burnt tissue.

And it had still been inside her when the body was found.

Helen was shaking slightly. 'I mean. It's fucking horrible. Christ.'

Breen would have had to admit, if asked, that he didn't really understand some of the anatomical terms being used. He wished his generation understood more about female biology.

Helen said, 'What is that? Something symbolic? Placing an egg there. What does it mean? Oh, God. I hadn't expected that.'

Breen sat on the bed beside her and put his arm around her, tentatively at first. Her shoulders jerked in small shivers as she leaned into him. He was not used to seeing her like this. She had always been so tough.

'I'm really stupid,' said Breen. 'I should have hidden it.'

She yanked away from him. 'Why? If you believe that, you're as bad as them. Thinking we shouldn't know this stuff. She was my sister. I should know this.'

'I know. But.'

'I know what the police are like. Keep everything to ourselves. Don't trust anyone.'

'They just didn't want to hurt you.'

She glared again. 'Well, that worked well, then, didn't it?'

Breen knew better than to argue.

She shrugged away from him, stood up and looked out of the window. 'I mean, I knew it must have been a loony. But bloody hell.'

And she shivered again.

A voice from downstairs. 'Supper.' Her mother, summoning them down. More food.

'In a minute,' called Helen.

'Are you going to be OK?' he asked.

'I heard that she'd been mutilated. Her breasts and stuff. But they told me that was after she died. Poor Alex.'

'Yes.'

'God. How do I look? Will they see I've been crying?'

Her eyes were still red.

'You might get away with it,' he said.

All last night he too had been thinking, why an egg? Did it mean something? The other mutilations were perverse enough.

'You think?' she said, peering at the small mirror.

But an egg. An egg in a place where eggs come from? Was it supposed to symbolise something?

She was blinking, rubbing her eyes with the backs of her hands, trying to get her eyes to look normal. Helen Tozer didn't cry. She wasn't that type of girl.

The mirror Helen was looking into would have been Alexandra's once. She would have looked into it too; the pretty one of the two sisters. The one who was into make-up and boys. Maybe even the day she was killed, standing here with her mascara, putting it on for someone. Now her sister was drying her eyes in it.

They ate supper talking little. It was steak and kidney pie. A dark, rich sauce. Breen felt the flab poking out over his waistband.

Helen took a little pastry, but barely touched the meat. She sat there, head down, looking at the table.

'You all right, Hel?' her father said. She was uncharacteristically quiet. He, on the other hand, was becoming more talkative by the day.

Helen didn't answer.

Hibou said, 'They say if you stuff the skull of a cat with oak bark and bury it in the ground, it makes your soil more fertile.'

'That right?' said Mrs Tozer. 'Who says that, then?'

'God's sake,' said Helen, putting down her fork. 'Don't be ridiculous.'

'Only saying,' said Hibou. 'Making conversation.'

'Something wrong with the pie, lovely?' asked her mother.

'I've got a headache, that's all,' Helen said, and pushed the plate away.

They ate the rest of the meal in silence until Helen stood suddenly and left the room, leaving the door at the bottom of the stairs wide open.

'I'll do the cows tonight if you like,' said Hibou, calling up the stairs after her as she stood to close the door to keep the warmth in the kitchen.

'What's wrong with her?' said her father when she'd gone.

'Another lover's tiff, most like,' said Hibou, looking at Breen.

Breen didn't want to eat any more either, but he felt he had to now, chewing his way slowly through a piece of beef. As he swallowed he could feel the meat sliding slowly down his gullet.

'Is she all right?' said her father.

Sounds of Helen retching were coming from the bathroom upstairs.

'I'll go and see what's the matter.'

Her mother stood and followed Helen upstairs, leaving the three of them with their half-finished plates of food.

FIVE

Helen Tozer was sharing her bedroom with Hibou. Hibou slept on a folding bed under the window. Hibou's bed was neatly made, eiderdown tucked in over the blankets.

Helen's clothes were all over the floor, a pair of white knickers poking out of the top of a muddy pair of jeans, bra on top of them.

She lay on the bed looking pale. 'I feel manky.'

The wall above her bed was covered in photographs. Bob Dylan. Jean Seberg in *A Bout de Souffle*. Several of George Harrison. Brian Jones in a fur coat. A still from the movie *Yellow Submarine*. A yellowing cover of *Nova*.

'It was a shock,' said Breen.

'Can say that again.'

The morning after she'd read the pathologist's report, Helen had stayed in bed, leaving the farm work to Hibou. Jimmy Young chattered on the transistor on her pillow. 'I couldn't sleep, neither,' she said. 'It was all going round in my head.'

'Tell me about your sister,' said Breen. 'What was she like?'

Helen sighed. 'Prettier than me. All the boys fancied her. She was sixteen and she had proper bosoms. Not like mine.' She looked down at her chest. 'She loved it that all the boys I knew fancied her more. She was so competitive.'

'And you're not?'

Helen ignored him. 'Got a fag? Settle the stomach.'

'Did you remember any boyfriends?' He took a packet of Regals from his dressing-gown pocket.

'Why you asking?'

'Why do you think?'

Her mother didn't like her smoking in bed. 'The boys fancied her, but she didn't hardly ever go out with them. You know. Proper ones who brought her flowers and wanted to take her out in their cars. I think she enjoyed turning them down. Dad would have never let them take her out anyway.'

'Anyone in particular chasing after her?'

She shook her head. 'The police asked me all this. There were a few prats from school. Sixth-formers. But she didn't really have much to do with them over that last year. I mean, I always thought she must have had boyfriends, but she didn't let on who.'

'She never said who these boys were?'

Helen shook her head. 'Didn't tell me, case I told Dad.'

'Would you have?'

Helen shrugged. 'For her own good.'

Breen laughed. 'You sneaked on her?'

Helen took a pull of the cigarette and a piece of ash fell onto the blanket. 'There was this bloke who worked in the garage. I'd really fancied him.' She brushed at the ash. 'Thought he fancied me too. And then Alex told me she was going out with him. Just out of spite, really.'

Breen remembered one of the men in the suspect list had worked in a garage.

'She was so annoying,' Helen said, and wriggled down into the blankets. 'She used to think it was funny that I never had boyfriends and she had loads.'

'You must have had some boyfriends.'

'I was the shy one, those days. Not really shy, I suppose. But less sure of myself with blokes. Back then, Alex was really . . . smug. It's hard. When someone that close dies. You love them. Course you do. But it's complicated, isn't it? Half the reason you feel so bad is that you feel guilty for not loving them enough. There were times when I really hated her. I mean, really hated. I was the oldest, only she was the one who got to do everything first.'

'Like what?'

'You know. Drinking. Sex. She lost her virginity when she was fifteen and boasted to me about it. My friends all called her a slag, but you could tell they were a bit jealous too.'

'And you weren't?' said Breen.

'Bog off.'

'I was only trying to find out what things were like between you.'

She glared. 'You don't know what it's like. You never even had brothers or sisters.' She stubbed the half-smoked cigarette out and put the dog-end into an old packet, closed it, then she rolled over, her back towards him.

It was true. His father had been the only relative he had known. He had grown up wishing he'd had a proper family, a brother to play with.

'Go away now. I've got a headache,' she said.

He stood.

'No,' she said. 'Sorry. Don't go.' He sat back down again. 'Oh, God. I think I'm going to be sick again.'

She pushed him out of the way and stood by the bed for a moment, blinking, holding one hand over her mouth, unsure whether she would vomit or not. She was dressed only in a long cotton vest that came down to the top of thighs, her legs long, pale and muscular from working on the farm. Breen looked away.

★

The wellingtons were too big, plopping against his calves as he strode across the uneven soil.

Breen looked around. The fields sloped down to the muddy estuary. There was a footpath that led up from the water's edge, about a quarter of a mile away. Very occasionally a rambler, binoculars in hand, would come nervously ambling up it.

Helen had said she didn't feel like lunch. Hibou had announced she was making some sandwiches and going out for a walk.

'But you've only just come in,' Mrs Tozer had said.

After she'd been gone a few minutes, Breen had followed. He had watched her walk down to the water's edge again, turning right along the footpath, just as she had the last time.

By the time he'd made it to the water's edge his socks had slid to the bottom of his boots. Hibou was out of sight, having disappeared down the pathway, behind the tall brown reeds on either side. Breen sat on a rock and pulled off the boots, rubbing the side of his calves where the rubber had chafed them. A train rumbled slowly along the side of the water.

He considered following her but his legs hurt, so he waited on the rock. The wind was starting to come up. A curtain of rain crossed the water. He replaced the boots and lit a cigarette.

She came back along the path after a little while.

'Where did you go?' he asked her.

'Just for a walk,' she said. 'Like I said. Why?'

'No reason.'

He paused, then said, 'Did you post that letter to your parents?'

'Yes. Course I did.'

Breen looked at her. She was a good liar, he thought. They walked back up the hill together, saying nothing.

★

'There was a phone call for you, Cathal,' said Mrs Tozer. 'Freddie Sharman. What's he want?'

Helen was sitting at the dining table, reading the local paper. 'Freddie?'

'Poor poppet,' said Mrs Tozer. 'You should go to the doctor. Shall I give him a call?'

'I'll be fine, Mum,' she said. 'Just leave me alone.'

Val Doonican came on the radio; Mrs Tozer started singing along. '"If I knew then what I know now . . ."'

'God. Please, Mum. Switch it off.'

'Thought you liked the radio.'

'Where's Dad?'

'Out with Hibou mending a gate up at Low Barton. He's helping her put it back on the hinges. Why's Freddie calling?'

'May I use the phone?' asked Breen. He felt in his pocket for change to put in the tin.

When he returned he asked Helen, 'Can you give me a lift?'

Mrs Tozer said, 'You're not thinking of going out now, are you, Hel? You're not well.'

'I'm much better now. Hibou's out with Dad, you said?'

Mrs Tozer smiled. 'I know.' She paused, potato peeler in one hand.

'How come he never goes out with me?' Helen said.

'Last few days, I think he's getting back to his old self, isn't he? And he did the milking this morning too on account of you were sick. First time in weeks.'

'That's good, I suppose.'

'It's the girl, I think. She brings good luck. Best thing you did, bringing her down here.'

Helen scowled.

'How come you're meeting up with Freddie?'

63

'He was thinking of joining the Met,' lied Helen. 'Wasn't he? Wanted to have a chat to Paddy about it.'

'Freddie go to London? I don't think he'd like it there,' Mrs Tozer said.

'That's what Paddy's going to say, isn't it?' said Helen.

Breen didn't answer.

Helen stopped the old Morris up by the gate. Her father was levering it up onto its hinges while Hibou stood over the post, guiding it onto the pins.

'I don't mind,' shouted Hibou. 'Me and your dad will manage.'

'I can see that,' said Helen.

Her dad was grinning, unable to wave, both arms pressing down on the length of wood he was using for a lever, gradually releasing the pressure so the gate lowered onto the post.

'Did you see that?' she said as she drove away. 'He never smiles like that for me.'

'It's like she's taking the place of your sister, isn't it? You're competing with her just like you did with Alexandra.'

'That's the stupidest bloody thing I ever heard you say.' She ground the gears and said, 'Is there any chewing gum in the glove compartment? I still got the taste of sick in my mouth.'

She accelerated into the lane. 'Slow down,' said Breen.

'You always want me to slow down.'

'I thought I saw someone there. In the hedge by the gate.' A man dressed in a long dark coat.

'So?'

'Nothing.'

They were on the main road now, winding towards Torquay. A blast of rain hit them just as they were coming over a rise in the road. The rubber on the left-hand wiper had perished, leaving Breen's side of the windscreen blurry.

'She's just like your sister, though, isn't she?' said Breen. 'Right down to the fact that you're jealous of her.'

'Bog off,' said Helen. 'You've got it all wrong. As per usual.'

A car came at them, flashing its lights in the rain. Helen blared her horn in return.

'Get over to your bloody side of the road,' she shouted.

'It's you who were on the wrong side,' said Breen.

'Shut up, Paddy,' she said, gripping the wheel, pushing her foot down onto the accelerator and racing down the narrow roads.

A storm lashed up waves in the bay; in the far distance white yachts bobbed on their moorings. The sea was grey, waves topped with froth. The view was smeared by rain on the glass of the front of the Palm Court Hotel. Tourist season was still a long way off. The pavements were empty. Cars crawled past along the coast road, drivers peering close to windscreens.

At a small table, covered in a starched cloth, Helen Tozer was scarfing fondant fancies.

'Feeling better now?' said Breen.

'Starving. I couldn't touch breakfast.'

'Don't you have real coffee?' said Breen, looking down at his cup.

'He's from London,' explained Sergeant Sharman to the waitress, who stood nervously in her black dress and white pinny.

'Oh,' she said.

Helen shifted her saucer to cover a blot of spilt tea.

'So?' said Breen.

'I looked,' said Sharman. 'You're right. They must have removed one file.'

'Whose was it?'

'Confidential, OK?'

'Why?'

'It's just a bit sensitive, is all.'

'Who, then?' said Helen, leaning forward.

'James Fletchet.'

'Jimmy Fletchet?' said Helen, crumb-mouthed.

Sharman nodded.

'Why are you going on about Jimmy Fletchet? Who is he?' asked Breen, but Sharman had his eyes fixed on Helen now.

'You didn't know?' Sharman asked.

Helen wiped her mouth. 'Know what?'

'James Fletchet was going out with your sister. They had a fling about a month or so before she died.'

Helen spurted crumbs. 'You're joking. He's bloody your age.'

'Who is he?' asked Breen again.

'That's disgusting.'

'Who?'

'A local toff. A swank. An MG man,' said Helen. 'She never said nothing about him. James Fletchet was . . . with my sister? Oh, Christ. You think it was him?'

'Shh,' said Sharman. 'Keep it down, Pete's sake. All this is confidential.'

'Oh, my God. What a slimy . . .'

'Please, Hel. I'm not happy telling you any of this.'

'You're not happy?' Helen shook her head. 'Was it him?'

'No. It was definitely not James Fletchet who killed your sister. That was ruled out. It couldn't have been.'

'But how do you know?'

'If you'd let me explain, Hel. I just spoke to a couple of fellows down the station. They were the ones who interviewed him.

Apparently him and your sister met at the races. They went on a few dates. He thought she was older. Was shocked to find she was only sixteen and ended it. That was before the murder.'

'But that doesn't stop him from having done it.'

'Give us a chance, Hel.'

'How come you found out and I didn't know anything about it?'

Sharman said, 'We found a couple of letters in her room.'

'From him?'

'Yes. They contained details of their . . . affair. And him ending it.'

Condensation dripped down the inside of the glass.

'What do you mean, details?'

Sharman looked past her, out of the window. 'You know. What they did in private.'

'About him fucking her?' said Helen.

The rattle of teacups from an elderly man at next table.

'Quite detailed, yes,' said Sharman uncomfortably.

Outside, herring gulls swirled in the air.

'Christ.'

Helen dug out a cigarette and lit it, not offering her packet around. A trawler was chugging its way across the bay, pitching in the waves.

'At least she had some bloody fun, I suppose,' Helen said. She blew out smoke.

A disapproving cough from the next table. Helen ignored it.

'I didn't see any of his letters in the files you showed me,' said Breen.

Sharman said, 'Apparently we gave the letters back to him. At his request. He had cooperated fully with the investigation. The letters were personal. As I matter of fact, I think he cared for her a great deal.'

'Cared for her,' sneered Helen.

'They told me he seemed very upset about the whole thing.'

'I should ruddy think he was,' said Helen.

'And we were able to rule him out definitively,' said Sharman.

'I mean, he's married. What an old bugger. She was a child.'

'Technically she was above the age of consent.'

Helen closed her eyes.

A gust of wind whacked at the large glass window with a bang, sending condensation running down in jerky lines. The large hotel lounge was almost empty. The small potted palms looked as if they were struggling to survive in the climate.

'So why wasn't his name included on the list of suspects? The CID just removed his information from the file?' said Breen.

'He's a man of some importance around here, I suppose,' said Sharman. 'It was an affair with a teenage girl. I'm guessing he was scared that it would get back to his wife and that's why he asked us to remove the file. As we had absolutely ruled him out I suppose it must have seemed reasonable to do it.'

'How?' said Breen. 'How did you rule him out?'

'He had a pretty watertight alibi,' said Sharman. 'And he co-operated fully with the investigation.'

Helen shivered. Stubbed out her cigarette on the saucer. 'I can't believe you didn't say any of this to me, Freddie. I mean, we were pretty bloody close.'

'Don't be angry, Hel. I didn't know all this. I wasn't leading on it at the time.'

Breen said, 'What was the alibi?'

'Good old boys,' Helen muttered.

'He was with a copper all that day,' said Sharman.

Helen said, 'Let me guess. Milkwood?'

Sharman nodded.

'Who is Milkwood?' asked Breen.

Helen said, 'Sergeant Milkwood. They were pals. I remember. Milkwood was always dropping his name. What if he was in on it too? I mean, he could have been.'

'No chance,' Sharman said. 'Plenty of witnesses. Otter hunting. Nutty about it, both of them. Fletchet was master of the hunt. The kennels are up on his estate. Milky and him used to run the dogs over the moors once a week to keep them fit. Make a day of it. They were both there when your sister was killed. Several of them from the hunt confirmed they were both there all day. No question.'

'Otter hunting?'

'They'll kill pretty much anything round here,' said Helen. 'Badgers. Foxes . . .'

'What about his statement? He might have had things to say about Alexandra,' said Breen.

Sharman said, 'It wasn't me who made the decision to remove that file. Between you and me, I would rather it hadn't been done. I'm guessing it was Sergeant Milkwood. As you say, they were friends.'

'And Fletchet is posh.'

Sharman said, 'Probably true.'

'Could I talk to him?' said Breen. 'James Fletchet?'

Sharman looked uneasy.

'She had secret lovers. We know that. What if the killer was one of them that you hadn't identified?' said Breen.

'But we ruled every one of them out.'

'God,' said Helen, putting her head in her hands. 'You make it sound like there were loads.'

'Can you be sure?' Breen asked.

'You've seen the files, Paddy.'

'I only had one afternoon. And besides, I didn't see Fletchet's file.'

Helen looked up. 'Maybe there was something important in the interview.'

'I can't help you there,' Sharman said. 'It's not my department any more.' He looked at his watch. 'You do what you need to. Just don't let it come back on me, right?'

'What about Milkwood?'

'He transferred three years ago. With your lot now.'

'The Met?'

'That's right.' He stood and pulled out a pound note for the tea and put it on the table. 'Look after yourself, Helen,' he said.

Helen scooped up crumbs from her plate with her finger and sucked thoughtfully.

A woman in a sequinned dress sat down at a grand piano behind the arches and began playing 'Some Enchanted Evening'.

'What if Fletchet did it?' said Helen when he'd gone. 'I mean. I bet it's him. Maybe got someone else to do it. What if he got her pregnant or something?'

'She wasn't pregnant. It would have been in the report.'

'I mean, a bit convenient, isn't it, that he's there with trillions of other people when she's getting killed?'

'You're angry. You've just found out he was having . . . relations with your sister.'

'Fucking her, you mean. She was sixteen.'

'And when did having a good alibi become a proof of guilt?'

'Yeah, but.'

Breen said, 'What if digging into this stirs other stuff up? You're upset already.'

'You think it's nice to hear that your sister was sleeping with older

70

men? Not just a bit older. But loads older. And married too. And you didn't even know about it.'

'That's what I mean. It will get worse.'

She gnawed her lip for a while. 'I know. But it's the thought that someone got away with it. That's what eats you up. Which is worse?'

'I'm not sure,' Breen said.

'Well, I am. I'm not like you. It's as if it's your natural instinct not to stir things up. All people your age are like that. Our generation want it all out in the open. I want everyone to know.'

'Who is he, anyway, James Fletchet?'

'Like I said, he's an earl or something. Owns a stonking great house about twenty miles from here. My father used to work for his family a while back before his father died. Has a farm. Bloody loaded and all. Fancies himself. Everyone I know thought he was a bit of a show-off.' Now the pianist had segued into 'Moon River'. 'I like this one, actually,' said Helen. 'He threw these big parties when he first turned up. I remember, went to one up at his place not long after he'd inherited it. It was wild. Barn dance for the hunt, it was. Big marquee on the lawn. Dancing and everything. Free booze. It's like he was working hard to impress us all. Mind you, I remember some lackey searched us all on the way out in case we'd nicked the cutlery.'

'Did Alexandra go?'

'I don't remember.'

'Do you still know Fletchet?'

'God, no. I never actually knew him. Mr High-and-Mighty.'

'Would he recognise you?'

'I don't know. Doubt it.'

Helen looked out of the window. The light was fading over the grey sea. 'God. This place is bad enough in summer. In winter it's a dump, isn't it?'

The piano needed attention. Keys clacked. When the tune finally ended, only one person was clapping: Helen Tozer, looking at the fragile old woman behind the keyboard, who smiled back at her out of the gloom of the hotel dining room.

SIX

The temperature was dropping fast. Large slate clouds hung over the moor.

A painted wooden sign had been knocked into the verge: 'Private Road'. Beyond, a long driveway led towards a distant grand house tucked somewhere out of sight. The English landscape, as dreamed, thought Breen.

With Helen behind the wheel, they paused by the open iron gates, the old Morris rattling gently as it idled.

'Go in, then?' she said.

Large, black-barked cedars were dotted around on either side of the pale drive ahead of them.

'We're crossing a line now. This is different from letting Freddie show you a few files, one copper to another.'

'I know,' said Breen.

'I mean, I don't mind. But then I'm not a copper any more. No skin off mine.'

'In for a penny,' said Breen.

'Right,' she said, putting the car into gear and heading through the gateway.

They edged down the driveway.

'Guernseys,' she said, nodding at the cows grazing on either side of the drive. 'Looks like they outwinter them. OK for some.'

Whatever that meant, thought Breen. In the distance, the large two-storey mansion loomed at the end of the driveway. For a stately home, it was an ugly one. A square building, the roof concealed behind a parapet that ran the length of it.

The house looked deserted. Helen pulled the car up on gravel close to the entrance. Breen got out and walked up lichen-covered steps towards a huge front door. To the right he found a handle on a chain and tugged at it, but if it sounded a bell, it would have been a long way off. He heard nothing.

He waited.

'No one in?' called Helen from the car.

Breen shook his head, banged on the door with the side of his hand. 'I don't think so.'

Helen got out of the car and, instead of coming to the front door, walked across a small strip of grass in front of the flower beds that spread under the house's immense windows.

'Bloody hell.'

Breen said, 'What can you see?'

'Get a load of this.'

Breen joined her on the grass, peering in through a large Georgian window. It was a living room, the sort you'd normally see in a stately home, with heavy velvet drapes hung around the windows and two large Chesterfields on either side of a vast marble fireplace. But instead of the usual oil paintings, the walls were covered by the mounted heads of animals.

A zebra, a warthog, gazelles, antelopes, some other deer-like creature with curly horns. Every available piece of wall was crammed full of staring animal heads. Some had mouths open, lips black and shiny, their eyes glossy and wide, in an eerie pretence of life. Breen shivered.

'It's like bloody *Daktari*,' Helen said.

Above the fireplace, stupidly large, was a lion, faced fixed in a roar.

'Hideous,' she said.

'They must be out,' said Breen.

'Imagine inheriting this lot. Jimmy Fletchet was born with a silver spoon up his arse.'

Breen looked at her. There was a darkness about her these last few days.

'Only, strictly speaking, all this was supposed to be his brother's. He was the younger one. But his brother was killed in a plane crash yonks ago.'

A huge blob of birds circled overhead, morphing into dark shapes, splitting into smaller ovals and rejoining.

'A plane crash, you said?'

'Can't remember much about it. I must have been about sixteen or seventeen at the time. Sometime after that, Jimmy came home – got the farms, the house, everything, fluky bugger.'

Gravel crunched behind them. 'Can I help you?'

They both turned. A tall, thick-hipped woman of about forty was standing about ten yards away with a pair of large pale brown dogs on leads. She wore a red coat and her long hair was held up in a bun.

'We were looking for James Fletchet,' said Breen.

'You are standing in my roses,' the woman said. She had a slight accent that Breen couldn't place and was too stylish and colourful to be English.

'I'm sorry. We were just trying to see if someone was here.'

'The tradesman's entrance is at the rear of the building,' she said, then leaned down and unhitched the leads from the dogs. The dogs bounded towards them, stopping a few feet short, barking.

Breen took out his wallet, pulled out his warrant card and held it up. 'I'm a policeman,' he said.

The woman stepped forward. She was middle-aged, but beautiful, with striking olive-green eyes under broad black eyebrows. 'Quiet,' she shouted. The dogs were instantly silent. She took the card from

Breen and leaned her head back a little to examine it. 'You are from London?'

'Yes.'

She turned her head towards the Tozers' car. 'And you came in that?' She seemed amused. 'Is that what British police drive now?'

'Is your husband here?' asked Breen.

The woman looked him up and down. 'Why are you asking?'

'I can explain that to Mr Fletchet. Is he here?'

'He is at the hospital.'

'Nothing serious I hope?'

'A worker injured himself on the farm this morning falling through the roof of our barn. James has driven him to the hospital.'

The dogs started barking again. Helen squatted on her haunches and held out her hand. The dogs approached cautiously, sniffing.

'Will he be back soon? We can wait.'

'No. That won't be convenient. I would prefer you to leave now.'

'Beautiful dogs,' said Helen, rubbing one of the dogs' heads. 'Otter hounds?'

The woman smiled. 'My husband's family keeps them.'

'You know this girl has ticks?' said Helen, ruffling the dog's ears.

The woman raised her chin a little and said, 'She does not.'

'Reckon she does.'

'Impossible.'

'Suit yourself,' said Helen. 'Only if you don't treat them there'll be a bunch of them, come summer.'

'Don't be foolish. Dogs don't get ticks at this time of year.'

'Depends where they been. You keep pheasants, don't you? I saw you had release pens down in the valley.'

'Yes. For the shooting.'

'If you don't believe me, come and feel for yourself,' said Helen.

76

After a second, the woman stepped forward. When Helen tried to take her hand, Mrs Fletchet snatched it back.

Helen said, 'I'm not going to bite.' Then reached out and placed her hand on the back of dog's head. 'See?'

The woman felt. 'I'll call the vet.'

Helen stood. 'You could do, if you like. Or I could do them. Wouldn't take a minute. I done billions of them. While we wait for your husband.'

The woman in the red coat paused, thought for a second, then said, 'I suppose you could come round the back.' Calling the dogs, she led them towards the servants' entrance at the left of the building.

Breen followed her down a flagstoned pathway at the side of the house. Behind him, Helen muttered, 'Never knew a toff that wasn't stingy.'

Breen turned and said, 'Don't let her know that this is about your sister.'

'In case I let slip that her husband was having sex with her?'

'Shh,' said Breen.

Mrs Fletchet stopped and looked back at them. 'Did you say something?'

'Just saying it looks like snow,' said Helen.

She frowned. 'Does it?'

The kitchen was huge. Heavy pans hung on hooks from the ceiling. A pot bubbled on a giant stove. Mrs Fletchet hung her coat on a rack while the two dogs left muddy footprints on the tiled floor.

'Got any tweezers?' said Helen. 'And alcohol.'

'I have gin. Will that do?'

Breen sat at a long kitchen table and watched as the two women held first one dog, then the other, Helen steadily picking off ticks and placing them in a glass.

'I don't understand what you two are doing here,' said the woman as Helen checked the second dog. 'You're not on official business.' She pronounced it 'oh-feesh-al'. 'You wouldn't be in that car if you were.'

'It's an old inquiry. I was in the area so I thought I would come and talk to your husband.'

'I'm his wife. Why not tell me?'

'It's confidential.'

Mrs Fletchet snorted, looked up from the dog. 'So it's something to do with one of his women?'

Helen looked up. 'What do you mean, "his women"?'

Mrs Fletchet tugged the dog away. 'You have finished. That is enough.'

Breen said, 'Is your husband a hunter? I noticed the animal heads on your walls.'

'You were snooping,' she said.

'I was just trying to see if anyone was in,' he said.

'James still chases after foxes and badgers and otters,' she said. 'I am less interested in that kind of sport. I always preferred bigger game.'

'You shot those animals?'

'Some. The elephant is mine,' she said. 'And the leopard. One of the buffalo, too, I think. We used Zimmermann's of Nairobi. The best taxidermist's in the world,' she said. 'Have you heard of it?'

'No,' said Breen. She seemed disappointed. 'I suppose it's hard, to shoot an elephant.'

'Harder for the elephant,' said Helen.

Mrs Fletchet shrugged. 'If you know what you are doing . . . and have the right gun. I got him with a Magnum .460. A shoulder shot. It severs the main artery above the heart.'

'You lived in Africa?'

'Kenya. For many years. Until James inherited this estate. Do you know Kenya?'

'I'm afraid not.'

'It was an exciting country. I loved it. England is so very dull in comparison. And so wet.'

There was the sound of tyres on gravel.

'I expect that will be him now,' Mrs Fletchet said. 'If you must talk to him, you had better come.'

They followed her out of the kitchen into a huge hallway, the dogs padding behind. A twelve-bore shotgun sat propped against the wall by the door, next to an ugly carved-wood umbrella stand.

Mrs Fletchet opened the door, letting in icy air. Outside, a tall man in a brown cap was getting out of a short-wheelbase Land Rover.

'Is he all right?' Mrs Fletchet called.

'He'll live.' James Fletchet approached his front door. 'Who's this?' He looked Breen up and down.

'This is a policeman,' said Mrs Fletchet. 'He wants to ask you some questions but he won't tell me what it's about.'

Breen stepped forward. 'I wonder if we could speak in private, sir?'

Fletchet hesitated. He looked at his wife.

'Well?' said Mrs Fletchet. '*Che cosa*, James? Have you been gambling again?'

'Haven't the foggiest, darling. They don't even look like police officers to me.'

Breen held out his warrant card and said, 'Do you know a police officer called William Milkwood, sir?'

'Milky?' said Fletchet. 'What about him?'

'I'm looking over the details of an investigation that he was part of four years ago.'

Fletchet hesitated.

'*Ha detto* Bill Milkwood?' said Mrs Fletchet.

'Bill's in London,' Fletchet told his wife. 'I have no idea what they're going on about.'

'Would you like us to explain a little more about the investigation?' said Breen.

Fletchet coloured. 'Get your superior officer to write to me. Right now I'm busy. I have a farm to run and thanks to some idiot injuring themselves I'm short-handed.'

'I just want to get a few facts straight. It will only take a few minutes.'

Fletchet raised his voice, 'If you don't get out of my house I'll have you thrown out. Please leave.'

Breen hesitated. He was about to give up and step onto the gravel when, behind him, came a voice.

'My name is Helen Tozer.'

Fletchet looked at her, startled.

'*Cosa?*' said his wife. 'Who is she?'

'I'll walk you to the car,' Fletchet said.

Mrs Fletchet stood at the door looking angrily at her husband as he followed them across to the car. Helen got into the driver's seat. Breen sat next to her.

'I'll talk to you,' Fletchet said quietly, leaning into Breen's window so he could speak out of earshot of his wife. 'But not now.'

'When, then?'

Fletchet hesitated. 'How did you get my name? I cooperated with the police fully. I told them everything I know.'

'I could ask your wife about Alexandra Tozer, if you'd prefer.'

'There's no point. She doesn't know anything about what happened.'

'Exactly,' said Breen. 'All I want is thirty minutes.'

Fletchet stiffened. 'That's a little grubby, isn't it?'

'Unlike sleeping with sixteen-year-olds,' said Helen.

Fletchet looked startled. 'OK. Tonight,' he said. He gave the name of a pub.

'Do you know it?' Breen asked Helen.

She nodded, started the car engine, then leaned across Breen. 'You might think about moving those cows down the bottom to higher ground. It's going to snow tonight.'

'Tonight, then?' Breen said. 'Seven?'

The clouds were blacker than before. The starlings wheeled in the sky above them. Breen leaned forward to watch them rolling above the car as they drove under them.

It was a long, grey building, low-doored. Cold in spite of a log fire burning slowly in the grate.

Above the fireplace was a fox, stuffed and mounted, grimacing its teeth.

'Why does everyone stuff animals round here?'

'They'd go off otherwise,' said Helen.

'No. I meant . . .'

'Look,' said Helen. 'Snow. The temperature's dropping. It'll turn to ice. It'll be a tough drive getting back.'

Beyond the window, flecks of white were starting to fall. Breen watched them settling on the road. 'I've got to get out of here. It's sending me doolally,' he said.

'See what I got away from?'

'Are you going to be OK? Meeting him. After all . . .'

Helen looked at Breen. 'You don't know what it's like, do you?'

'I was just thinking it would be upsetting. Even if he has an alibi, he's still a suspect. You'll be thinking that he could be the one.'

'What if I am? You think I'd sleep better not having tried?'

Breen looked at his watch. 'He should be here by now.'

'You could see he was scared when he realised who I was. What if he doesn't come?' He watched her biting a fingernail. 'Are we having a drink?'

So they sat and had a drink as the snow started to fall. And just as he was at the bar buying Helen's third rum-and-blackcurrant and she was starting to look relieved that he wasn't coming after all, the pub door opened and Fletchet came in, snow on his cap.

Fletchet was one of those people who made the chairs he sat on seem small. He was over six foot, tall and hearty in a way that city people never were. He looked at Helen across the table.

'I thought about what you said. You were right. I decided to move the cows. That's why I'm late.'

'Don't sound surprised. I've been working with cows since I was a girl.'

'You're Alex's sister, aren't you?'

Helen nodded, lips pressed together.

'I thought I recognised you.'

She didn't answer.

'I'm sorry,' said Fletchet, voice quiet. 'A terrible thing. I'd just like to say, I thought your sister was . . . amazing.'

Helen didn't speak for a while. Finally she said, 'My sister was sixteen.'

Fletchet hung his head. 'I didn't know. Not until later.'

'Of course you knew. How could you not know?'

'In other ways, she was very . . . mature.' He was blushing now. 'Besides, she told me she was nineteen. She told me all sorts of things. That her father was a film star. That she was born on an ocean liner. She liked to do that. It was always a show, you know? I broke it off as soon as she told me her real age. I don't suppose you believe me. But she really didn't look sixteen. She didn't act it.'

'Bet you were scared shitless when you found out. Any younger and you'd have been done for statutory rape.'

Helen was tipsy already, and angry, and Fletchet was the sort of man she would have hated even if he hadn't slept with her sister. Breen resisted interrupting her, telling her to keep her voice down. He wanted the opportunity to observe Fletchet. Fletchet was rubbing his palms against the top of his thighs as he tried to answer Helen. Were his nerves a sign he was lying, or was it just embarrassment that was making him squirm?

'If you give me a chance, I'll explain,' Fletchet was saying.

'I know the explanation already,' said Helen.

Fletchet dropped his voice. 'For God's sake. I am throwing myself on your mercy here. This was a deeply shameful and tragic episode of my life. I know that, OK?'

Helen looked at him. 'OK,' she said, finally.

Fletchet sat with a pint of stout in front of him. 'I met Alex that spring,' he said. 'At a point-to-point. I had a couple of horses. One was a grey filly that had just come third in a race that day. Alex came right up to me and told me how beautiful the horse was. She said she'd like to ride it. She was so confident I never imagined she was only sixteen.'

'She liked horses,' said Helen.

'And she was good with them, wasn't she?'

'Yes. She was.'

'I told her she should come up to the house. Try her out. And she did.'

'And one thing led to another,' said Helen.

'Please. You're making it sound like something it wasn't,' said Fletchet. 'My wife and I had taken over the house here the previous summer. Eloisa had never wanted to leave Kenya. We had a big estate there in the White Highlands. She's Italian. Doesn't much like it here in England. She liked all the servants and parties out there. The whole shebang. It was high society, really. But my brother died. I inherited the estate here. It was my duty to come home and look after the estate.'

'Poor lamb,' muttered Helen.

'What I'm trying to say, if you'll let me, is that Eloisa didn't like the change. We had rows. In 1964 it came to a head. She went back to her mother in Milan. For a while I thought that was it. And I was pretty down. I was finding it really hard to fit in back here. My brother had been popular and practical and had made a success of the farm. I was the unfortunate child they'd sent out to Africa. When I came back I was trying too hard, I suppose, trying to be the new lord of the manor. Out in Africa you had to be larger than life. The big bwana, you know? I suppose I carried that on a bit too much back here. I threw parties like we had in Africa. Went to all the races. Splashed out. Looking back, I realise everyone was just laughing at me. And then I met your sister. She was gorgeous. She was confident. There was something very pure and English about her. And she liked me. And looked up to me. And believe me, it wasn't me who took the first step.'

'She was a kid. Of course she was going to be impressed by you.'

'Are you going to make this public?'

'Why shouldn't I? It's true, isn't it?' said Helen.

'Oh, God,' said Fletchet, putting his head in his hands, fingers in his thick hair.

Breen decided it was time to speak. 'We don't need to tell anyone about this, Mr Fletchet. We're more interested in knowing the truth of what actually happened between the two of you. We need to know what you told the police.'

He looked up. 'How did you find out I spoke to the police?'

Helen said, 'That's what you're worried about really, isn't it? Because if we found out, maybe anyone could.'

'Enough now,' Breen said to Helen.

Helen folded her arms and looked away.

'And who are you?' Fletchet asked. 'Why are you so interested?'

'I'm a friend of the family.'

'So this is unofficial?'

'Yes.'

Fletchet looked relieved about that. 'OK.'

Breen said, 'If you tell us exactly what happened and don't hold back anything, we won't need to tell anyone else about this. We will agree to keep it to ourselves, won't we, Helen?'

Helen grunted, folded her arms.

'Won't we?' Breen said again.

'Yes. OK.'

'Right. When did you last see her, Mr Fletchet?'

Fletchet looked from one to the other, as if weighing them up, then said, 'The day before she died. I took her out for a drive. We broke up.'

'Why did you break up?'

'Because I found out she was only sixteen, believe it or not. We were having an argument. I had a car radio. State of the art. It was the bloody Beatles all the time. All that *yeah yeah yeah*. She always tuned the radio to Caroline and then called me names when I tried to tune it back to the Home Service.'

'The bloody Beatles,' said Helen. 'That was Alex.'

'And then I told her to grow up and act her age and she got into a real bate with me and told me what her age was.'

Helen closed her eyes, as if trying to picture her sister.

'How did she take it?' Breen asked. 'When you told her it was over.'

'Very well, I think. Better than I'd imagined.'

'You being God's gift, of course.'

'Say what you want,' Fletchet said to Helen. 'I did adore her. You have to believe me. She was beautiful. I think about her all the time. She told me I was too old for her anyway.'

'I bet she dumped you, only you don't like to admit you were dumped by a sixteen-year-old girl,' said Helen.

'You don't have to believe anything I say.'

'I don't.'

'Were you angry with her?' said Breen.

'I suppose I was,' said Fletchet. 'But I know what you're trying to say. And no. Not like that. I wasn't angry like that.'

'But you were worried that she would go round telling everyone she had slept with you,' said Breen. 'And that your wife would find out.'

'My wife was in Italy. She had left me, remember? You must think I'm a bloody monster. I did not kill her. I was nowhere around her when she was killed.'

'You made sure of that, did you?' said Helen.

'For God's sake. The police suggested that too at the time. Don't think they didn't.'

Breen sat and thought about this for a while. A car drove past outside. Breen could hear the tyres throwing up slush.

'I think about her all the time too,' said Helen.

From the bar, the elderly woman who ran the pub called, 'I'll close down if that's all you're drinking.' She wore glasses so dirty they seemed pointless. The single log in the fire cracked and shot a spark out onto the hearth.

'I'll have another drink,' said Helen.

'You've had enough,' said Breen. 'I can't drive.'

'I've barely begun,' said Helen.

Breen watched the old woman grope her way to the beer taps to pour Fletchet another pint.

'How did you say you heard she was dead?'

Breen stood and walked to the window. Snow had settled over the Morris, covering the windscreen.

'It was on the news. I was watching it at home. I knew it was her.'

'They kept showing that school photo,' said Helen.

'So I went out and phoned a friend I knew in the police.'

'Milkwood,' said Helen.

'I made a statement, there and then.'

'You made a statement to your mate Milky. Who happened also to be your alibi. I'm sure he gave you a hard time.'

Fletchet lit a cigarette. 'I came forward. I gave a statement.' He chewed on his lip. 'I was nowhere near poor Alex when she . . . died. Like it or not – and I do not particularly like it – because of my family, I was a well-known figure locally when this happened. Sometime in the autumn my wife, Eloisa, came back home. We both agreed to try and make a go of it again. It would not have been good for your family or for mine if our affair had been made public. Believe me, if I could find the man who did this, I would make him bloody suffer. I would dearly, dearly, dearly love to do that.'

'Man?' said Breen. 'How do you know that?'

'Well, it's obviously a man, isn't it? I mean . . .'

'You were worried that if news of your affair with a teenage girl got out, your wife would divorce you,' said Breen.

'I didn't want to hurt her,' said Fletchet.

Helen rolled her eyes.

'As time went on, and no one was found, they announced that some people from another county were about to come in and review the case. I became worried that somebody would go back to the files and turn up at my house unannounced. I mentioned my concerns to Milky. He said he could sort something out. As a favour. And he did. I swear on my heart that I would throw away my entire inheritance if it would help find the bastard who did that to her.'

'What was in it for Milkwood? Did you offer him money?'

'God. No. It wasn't like that at all. We were friends. We'd known each other for years. He didn't do anything wrong. I was absolutely cleared. One hundred per cent.'

'He removed the files. That's wrong,' said Breen.

'Well. Maybe technically, yes.'

'When did you last talk to Sergeant Milkwood?'

'He was transferred not long afterwards. To London. I hear he's in the Drug Squad now. He will tell you that everything I've told you is true, I promise,' said Fletchet.

'The Drug Squad? You sure?'

'He's a good copper. I expect he's very useful to them.'

'Do you keep in touch?'

'Christmas cards. His wife sends them. She's a bit of a social climber. She seems to like writing my full title on the address.'

'Your full title?'

'Lord Goodstone.' He grinned. Brushed his blond hair away from his forehead. 'Nobody calls me that. Ridiculous. This is 1969, for God's sake.'

Helen said, 'You two used to be big mates, I recall. You're not any more?'

'Time goes on. He moved away. I'm busy with the farm. I'm sure he's busy too. As policemen are. If you're planning on heading back home, you'd better think about it,' said Fletchet. 'The snow's getting thicker. I'd offer you a bed at my house, but . . . it would be hard to explain to my wife.'

'What about other boyfriends?' Helen asked. 'Did she tell you about any others?'

'No. But then I wouldn't have expected her to. From the way she behaved, I expect there were others.'

'What do you mean, "the way she behaved"?'

'I was not her first.'

'How did you know?'

He blushed. 'I'm afraid you'll have to use your imagination.'

'Did that disappoint you?' said Helen. 'That you weren't her first?'

Fletchet looked at Breen and said, 'I've come here to try to be helpful. There's not a single day when I haven't regretted what happened between myself and Alexandra. It was a mistake.'

'You must have had some idea of other boyfriends she'd had?'

Fletchet shook his head. 'You didn't know about me, did you? Alex was good at keeping things quiet. A girl who talks about these things gets a reputation. Alex was far too clever for that.'

'How very convenient for you,' said Helen.

Fletchet pulled at his cuffs. 'I should go. I need to check on the cows before it gets too late.' The window was obscured by spatters of snow now. 'I shouldn't try driving if I were you. I'm sure Dot here will put you up overnight if the snow's too thick.'

He held out his hand for Breen to shake, then said to Helen. 'I know you hate me, but please believe me. Your sister was a remarkable young woman.'

'I know,' she said.

'I miss her still.'

'Right,' she said quietly.

When he was gone, Helen said, 'Not staying in this dump,' and fumbled in her handbag for the keys to the old Morris.

*

89

His bare hands ached from the cold, brushing the snow off the windscreen in the darkness.

'You sure about this?' he said when they were both inside. 'You're drunk.'

The engine was cold. It whined before the engine finally started, stalled and started again.

'It wasn't him,' said Helen.

'How can you be so sure?'

'His alibi, for one.'

'He could have got someone else to do it,' said Breen.

'But why torture her? Why do all that stuff?'

'To make it look like the work of a madman?'

'No,' she said. 'I just don't think it was. Funny thing, but I think he meant it when he said he missed her. I mean, that's really weird. It made me so angry hearing him say that. How does he have any fucking right to say that? But I think he meant it. He was in love with her.'

She put the car in reverse and the wheels spun on ice.

'Crap,' she said. 'Maybe there was another boyfriend then?'

'Maybe.'

She revved the engine again. The car didn't move.

Breen saw the light go off in the bar where they'd been sitting. He jumped out and started banging on the door of the pub until the light came back on again.

SEVEN

It was an unheated twin room, under the eaves. She had given them two hot-water bottles and brought a ewer of water up for them to wash in. A small gable window that didn't fit properly let in blasts of cold air.

There were no street lamps around here. The light from the window only illuminated the snowflakes closest to it.

'Which bed do you want?' she asked, looking from one to the other.

'We could keep each other warm.'

'I'd like that,' she said. 'Tonight, at least.'

They lay in bed cramped together under a weight of old eiderdowns, his bare legs tangled with hers, Helen drinking whisky they had bought from the bar.

A mezzotint of a smug Victorian mother, her round-faced child and a kitten playing with a ball of wool hung on the wall next to their bed. With age, the print had turned a deep brown.

He reached out and switched off the bedside light. Under the blankets, she put her hand under his vest, running her fingers over his chest and gently across his bandage.

'Makes my sister sound like a slag, doesn't it?' she said.

'You're shivering.'

She clung onto him for warmth. 'I mean, whatever happened, it wasn't her fault, was it? She was just a kid.'

'Shh,' he said.

'You think he was being honest with us?'

'I don't know. In some ways.'

'All that "I've come to try and be helpful". Only 'cause we twisted his arm.'

'Maybe he was just ashamed,' said Breen.

'Scared more like. Scared about his reputation.'

'Both, perhaps.'

She turned to face him and he could smell the whisky on her breath. 'I don't believe anyone who cheats on their wife with a teenage girl is ever going to be honest with you,' she said. 'You can't trust a man like that to tell us everything.'

'Mind my arm,' he said. 'It's sore.'

The bed groaned and creaked as he tried to find a more comfortable position.

'I hate him,' she said. 'I would like to smash his bloody face in.'

'Are you crying?' he asked.

'A little.'

He held her. 'She always used to go on about how she wished her father was a film star,' she said. 'Or a pop star. Not a bloody farmer.'

He felt her chest rising and falling slowly as she sobbed. Eventually she lay still. They lay there together in the bed. 'Have you got socks on still?' She giggled.

The first time she had laughed, it seemed, in days.

It was only the second time they had ever made love. It wasn't easy or particularly satisfactory in this small bed with the sagging mattress. The sex was painful, not just for his shoulder, and hurried. She didn't seem to have enjoyed it much more than he did.

Afterwards, she untangled herself from the muddle of blankets, got out of bed.

'What are you doing?'

'I'm thirsty,' she said. 'Drank too much.'

In the dimly lit room, she poured water from the ewer into a glass and drank it. Breen looked at her long legs. They seemed to glow in the lightless room.

When she got back into bed, her body felt cold again. He wrapped his arms around her to warm her and leaned over to kiss her. But she was asleep already, snoring slightly.

She had been drunk, just as she had the first time. In the morning she would probably regret what she had done.

In the morning he would tell her he was leaving for London. He had a reason now. To track down Sergeant Milkwood and try to verify what Fletchet had said.

It was for the best that he go away.

He lay awake, trying to be still, so as not to disturb her, holding the moment. The world beyond this creaky bed was totally silent. It was as if they were on an island of their own in the middle of cold nothingness.

The toilet door had a small ceramic sign on it: 'Our Country Seat'.

'Helen?'

He banged on the toilet door.

It was at the far end of an uneven corridor. 'Are you OK?'

'Five minutes,' she said.

Breen went downstairs. The lounge was deserted. Last night's empties were stacked on the bar, and the room stank of beer slops and stale smoke.

He drew back the bolt on the front door and pulled it open. Snow tumbled onto the mat he was standing on. He blinked at the suddenness of white. The world outside was transformed.

Wind had sculpted the thick, clean snow. Waves of it ran along the narrow lane. It had pressed into the side of tree trunks and the red telephone box.

A set of dark animal paw prints made a line across the lane, from hedge to hedge.

In front of the granite wall of the pub, the Tozers' car had vanished. They would need to borrow shovels. Breen shivered, closed the door and went upstairs to wait for Helen to emerge again.

The journey home was long. Twice the car had got stuck in drifts. The first time a tractor had been nearby and had pulled them free of the thick snow. The second time Breen had had to push the car back into the road, struggling to shove with his bad shoulder.

They had slid slowly down gullied lanes, snow hanging from the hedges above them.

Sometime in the late morning they had rounded the corner to come across a horse lying dead in the road. Blood from a gunshot wound had melted the snow under its head.

'What happened?' asked Breen, as Helen drove slowly around, wheels skidding on the bloody slush.

She looked up at the broken hedge branches above the dead horse. 'It must have fallen into the road somehow.'

The feet-deep snow in the field must have hidden the hedges. The horse would have tumbled into the lane below and must have broken a leg in the fall.

'Couldn't they just have put a splint on it or something?'

Helen didn't answer, leaning forward into the windscreen, peering at the road ahead in the thin light. She hadn't talked much since last night.

'I was thinking of going back to London. I'll be fit for work again soon. I thought I'd track down Sergeant Milkwood. Find out what was in that report.'

'Right,' she said.

'Maybe you could come and visit some time, like I said. Get away from the farm?'

'Maybe.'

But that was all. She didn't try and encourage him to stay any longer, just gripped the wheel. Did she not care, or was she angry at him for going? He wasn't sure.

It was afternoon by the time they arrived home, edging slowly down the icy lane.

Snow rarely settled along this coast, but the next morning it made everything clear. Breen looked at the boot prints. There was a smaller set going into the henhouse. That would be Hibou, who fed the chickens every morning. The other prints were much larger. A size nine, at least. They came as far as the edge of the chicken coop but didn't go in. And then the bigger boots retraced their steps towards the estuary.

He followed them slowly down the hillside, each footfall creaking into the whiteness. At the estuary's edge they turned towards the town. It must be warmer here, thought Breen. The snow was mushier, the prints harder to read. There was enough of a trail to follow, though. Soon the path wound into the low trees.

He had gone about fifty yards when the boot prints disappeared. It was dark under the small oaks, so it was hard to see, at first, whether they had just petered out where the snow was thinner. Breen was puzzled. He lowered himself to look at the last boot print. Then as he squatted down, he caught the scent of woodsmoke. He stopped and listened. Nothing.

He stood again. 'I know you're there,' he said.

Silence.

He looked around him and noticed it, finally. A smaller pathway

95

heading into the woods had been obscured by a branch placed across it, but even in this light it was clear enough to see. Someone was trying to conceal themselves there. He lifted the branch and had only walked two or three paces when he saw the grey canvas tent in a tiny clearing beneath the low branches. In a circle of rocks a small fire smouldered, mostly ashes and embers. Placed among them was a small tin billy-can. He half expected to see a stolen egg boiling in it, but in the water sat an opened tin of baked beans.

'You in there. Hello,' he said, leaning down to the tent. 'Come out.'

He expected movement from within the tent; instead, there was a small crackling sound behind him.

He turned. From under a pile of twigs and leaves that he had taken no notice of, a man was emerging. One moment he had not been there, the next he was, as if he was some supernatural force materialising from the dark undergrowth. As he stood, Breen realised it was the man he had seen in the road. He wore a long, dark woollen overcoat. His hair was long and his beard was thick and matted, his skin tanned brown from woodsmoke and dirt. There were filthy woollen mittens on his hands.

Breen looked down at his fire. 'Have you been stealing this food?'

The man did not look him in the eye. His head was turned half away as if he was afraid. What Breen could see of the man's face was dark and greasy with soot and dirt. He looked old, but it was hard to tell.

'If you don't move on, I am going to report you to the police,' Breen said.

The man twitched. Breen was reminded of the chickens in the coop. He was not right in the head, Breen realised.

'Didn't steal,' whispered the man.

Afterwards, trudging back up the slope, Breen felt stupid. Hibou had been taking food to him; scraps from Mrs Tozer's kitchen. That was all.

Mrs Tozer tried to persuade him to stay, but Helen said nothing more about it. On Breen's last night at the farm they had a chicken as a special treat. Mrs Tozer roasted it until the skin shone like varnished wood.

They crowded around the kitchen table and ate until their bellies strained. Napkin rings and everything. A candle in the middle. Unusually, Helen only picked at her plate. She had not been the same since seeing Fletchet. Breen got the sense of something burning inside her, hollowing her out.

The snow had thawed suddenly, turning the yard outside to dark slush.

'Don't you want that potato?' said Hibou.

'We managed fine without you when you were stuck in the snow,' said old man Tozer. 'Didn't we, Hibou? Great team. All the milk in churns and out on the lane.'

Hibou smiled at him. Helen's mother didn't even scold her for using her fingers when she lifted the potato off Helen's plate.

'Just because you're not here doesn't mean everything grinds to a halt.'

'No, you didn't manage without me, Dad. There's barely enough forage for the winter. The cows are thin as sticks. That's why the yield's down.'

'Helen, enough,' said her mother.

'But it's getting better now,' said Hibou. 'There'll be new grass coming through once the snow's gone.'

Helen rolled her eyes. 'You saying I shouldn't have come back to help on the farm? And now I'm here everything's hunky-dory. I wish I hadn't bothered.'

'Don't spoil it, Hel,' said her mother. 'It's Paddy's last night.'

Helen glared at Hibou. Hibou put her head down, blushing, busy sawing away at the potatoes with her knife and fork.

'Besides. It wasn't right for you, the police,' said her father.

'How the heck would you know?' said Helen.

'It's not a woman's work.'

'And wading ankle high in cow shit is?'

'Language,' said her mother.

After Helen had left the room, banging the door behind her, her father had broken the silence by saying to Hibou, 'She used to be just like this with her sister. Jealous. Don't mind her.'

'Actually, I don't think it's anything to do with me,' said Hibou. 'She's all crotchety because Paddy's leaving, if you ask me.' She turned to see if Mrs Tozer was watching, and when her back was turned, she slipped what was left of the potatoes and a bit of her meat into handkerchief.

When she saw Breen had seen her doing it, she blushed, but didn't say anything.

That night, Breen lay in bed listening to the snow sliding off the roof above him, crashing down into the yard.

EIGHT

Big John Carmichael stood as he approached, arms wide, almost knocking the chair behind him backwards.

'Paddy. Paddy bloody Breen.'

Other diners stared, harrumphed, looked harder at their food. The restaurant was full of rich foreign tourists, Common Market functionaries talking in French or Dutch and cigar-waving captains of British industry showing off to guests.

This was a posh place to eat. A place of murmurs and starched napkins.

Across the round room, Breen smiled at his friend, walked towards him. John was tall and broad-shouldered. His hair was a couple of inches longer than when he'd last seen it, his waist a couple of inches thicker. John grasped both of Breen's arms, then said, 'Sorry,' as he saw Breen wince. He gestured at the windows, like the view was his own. 'Not bad, eh?'

London surrounded them. Even on this grey, dim day, you could see for miles.

'You are such a bloody lah-di-dah, John.'

'*Classy* is the word you were looking for, Paddy. This is a celebration. You've returned. When are you getting back to work?'

When he had called Carmichael to tell him he had returned to London, Carmichael had suggested the Top of the Tower, the restaurant at the top of the tallest building in London, the Post Office Tower. The whole seating area spun slowly around the tower, giving diners a view of the entire city. Waiters emerged from the lift in the centre always looking to the left and right, trying to see where the table they were serving had gone. The white heat of technology made concrete. Below them, banks of microwave antennas beaming radio signals across Britain.

'How the heck did you get a table here?' asked Breen.

'Friends in low places. Sit down, Christ's sake. Enjoy yourself,' said John.

A waiter in a red-trimmed jacket and bow tie took Breen's coat.

'How's the shoulder? How's Helen and all her yokel pals? Tell me everything.'

The place was decorated in swanky bright red and dark blue, as if it was a BOAC airline lounge at London Airport. A series of clocks showed the time zones around the world. Very international jet set. Below them, Regent's Park gave way to the distant terracotta pointy-ness of St Pancras Station. 'Beautiful, isn't it?' Carmichael said, looking past the other diners out of the window.

'Yes, it really is,' Breen said.

'So. What are you having? It's all in Frog. Why do they have to do that? Can't read a word.'

When the waiter arrived Breen ordered *Moules Normandes*.

'What's that?' said Carmichael.

'Mussels,' said Breen.

'What's *Escalope de Veau Holstein*?' The waiter disappeared and returned with a menu in English.

'I hate that,' muttered Carmichael. 'What about a bottle of red?'

'I'm not supposed to drink.'

'Bugger that,' said Carmichael.

'How's the Drug Squad?' said Breen.

Carmichael leaned forward. 'Busy. Always busy.' He grabbed a waiter. 'Got a light, mate?'

The stony-faced waiter reached in his pocket and gave him a black book of matches: *Top of the Tower*.

'Give us a handful,' said Carmichael. 'Souvenirs.'

The tables by the windows were all taken. At the one closest to Breen and Carmichael, a classy-looking woman with straw-coloured hair and red lipstick sat with a businessman, smiling at something the florid-faced man was saying.

'Look at her,' said Carmichael. 'God's sake. What's she doing with a wrinkled old arse like him? He must be sixty if he's a day.'

'When she should be with you?'

'And she would if I was as rich as he was.'

'Tell me, John, do you know a man called Milkwood?'

'Course. You know Milky. Everyone does.'

'Do I?'

'You must have met him at some point at New Scotland Yard.'

Breen frowned. 'I don't remember.'

'Don't know how you made detective, Paddy. You never notice anything. Why you asking?'

'Tozer wanted to know, that's all,' Breen said. 'Apparently he's from her neck of the woods.'

'Suppose he must be.' Carmichael frowned. The waiter arrived with a bottle of wine and offered it to Carmichael to taste. 'Four quid a bottle and you're not sure if it's any good or not?'

Other diners twitched.

'Just leave it,' he ordered, and picked up the bottle, holding it by the bottom, and filled Breen's glass to just under the brim.

'What's he like, Milkwood?'

Carmichael grinned. 'He's not one of her . . . you know?'

'Her what?'

'You know what she's like. Oh. I forgot. You've got a thing for her.'

'Milkwood must be twice her age.'

'Only joking, chum. Only ringing your bell.'

Carmichael was expansive, full of himself. Breen took the cigarette Carmichael was offering. First of the day.

'What's Milky like?' said Carmichael. 'Devoted to his missus.'

'Good copper?'

'Very good. Dedicated. One of the few straight ones in the squad.'

'You're not getting cynical, are you?'

Carmichael sighed. 'Drug Squad. We've got a reputation. You know.'

'What's happened to you? You used to say all that was bollocks.'

'He's a good man. I'll admit it. A lot of the lads on the squad just want to nick the stars, get their names in the paper. Milky's been working on importers. That's what we've got to go after. This last year, all the gangs have got into drugs. Big money. The game's changing.'

The large businessman stood up unsteadily and went to the bathroom. The woman was now on her own. Carmichael called over to her. 'Do you reckon if you paid them enough, they'd speed this roundabout up? It's a bit slow, isn't it?'

She smiled back at him. 'Who are you, Jack Brabham?'

He lifted up his glass. 'Might spill the vino though.'

She lifted her handbag from the chair next to her to look for a cigarette. Carmichael was standing in a second, holding a match from the matchbook at the ready.

Back at the table he whispered, 'See the way she smiled at me?'

Breen grinned. 'You're the one who used to be on Vice. She's a posh tart. See it a mile off.'

'You think?' said Carmichael, still looking at the woman, less certain of himself.

'Don't know how you made detective, John. You never notice anything.'

'Not really interested, anyway.'

'You're always interested.'

He tore his eyes off her. 'No. As a matter of fact, I'm spoken for.'

Breen's eyes opened wide. 'You've got a girl?'

Carmichael shifted in his seat. 'Kind of.'

'What do you mean, kind of?'

'It's complicated. Anyway, what's Milky to Tozer?'

'Don't try and change the subject. Are you seeing someone?'

'Maybe. Only she don't know it yet. Milkwood's still waters. Keeps himself to himself. Doesn't come out drinking with the boys. Bit like you only less ugly. Sup up,' he said, lifting his glass and draining it.

The woman's dining partner returned, scanning the room for his table. It was hard to remember where you sat when the room kept revolving.

Their plates arrived. Carmichael's eyes widened. Carmichael's had a large lump of meat on it, covered in a fried egg, with anchovies laid over it. 'Ruddy fantastic,' he said, lifting his knife and fork.

Through the window, Breen watched planes heading west, towards London Airport. Carmichael was talking about getting tickets for some jazz trumpet player. Breen nodded. OK. He would go out more. See some art. Hear some music. Be part of London as it woke up from the long dark half of the twentieth century.

'We should go to the movies. You'd like that.'

Opposite them, the woman whose cigarette Carmichael had lit and her dining partner stood. As she walked towards the lift, the older man's hand on her bottom, she turned and gave John another smile.

'See?' said Breen.

'I'm irresistible,' said Carmichael. 'That's all.'

They ate together until they had to loosen the buttons on their trousers. Afterwards Carmichael insisted on ordering brandies. Doubles.

'How you getting home?'

'Bus.'

'Stuff that. I'll call you a squad car.'

'You can't do that,' said Breen.

'Watch me.'

Breen hadn't drunk anything for weeks.

'You were the copper who was shot, weren't you?' said the young, spotty-faced policeman who arrived to drive him home, glancing in the rear-view mirror. As they sped eastwards through the streets, alcohol flooded his brain with a sense of connectedness. The nightmares would go; he was the copper who had survived being shot. Everything could begin again. He would get behind his desk again. Life would be better. Life would be great.

NINE

He woke at nine in the morning, mouth tasting of tin and his shoulder aching. He must have slept on the wrong side.

Yesterday's euphoria was blunted by a dull head. In winter, his basement flat was dark. The back bedroom was empty now and smelt damp and unused.

He ground beans and made a coffee, then sat at his table with it, looking around him. The living room had a small dining table, a couple of armchairs and a black-and-white TV. The room didn't look like it belonged to anyone in particular, certainly not to him. Some possessions seemed to make it look more like a home, but mostly these had been his father's. A mantelpiece clock; an ivory letter knife. Others had been acquired carelessly. The two mismatched armchairs with antimacassars. That brown rug. The last year's calendar, still on the wall, hung a little too high because the nail had been there when he had moved in. It was, he supposed, a woman's talent, making a home.

Maybe he should spend some money. New curtains. Maybe candlesticks. Buy a colour TV. Switch from mono to stereo.

He took out the copy of the pathologist's report he had stolen from the files in Devon and started to read it again, making notes. Whoever had carried out the autopsy had been thorough. There was the detail of the ligature marks on her wrists and ankles ('Thin rope. Possibly sash cord'). The detailing of the nature and position of each cigarette burn ('Left upper arm 1. Second degree. Left upper arm 2. First degree'). And so on. Though the assault with the egg was of a sexual nature, there was no sperm present. Was it the murder itself that was methodical, or just the way it was written about? He found it hard to discern. After an hour, he put the report aside and went to heat up the rest of the coffee.

Later, he would call Milkwood and ask if they could meet.

He was about to fry himself an egg when he heard someone walking down the outside steps. Then a knock at the door and a voice.

'Sergeant Breen?'

The coffee hadn't fully woken him yet. He realised he was still in his dressing gown and had not shaved.

'Just a minute,' he called, and went to the bedroom, where he began struggling to get his arm into yesterday's shirt.

'Sergeant Breen? You in there?' A young copper, helmet skewed, hair almost covering his ears, was peering in at his front window.

The police car swerved left and right round traffic. Breen sat in the back, sliding from one side of the car to the other, banging his bad shoulder against the door each time they cornered.

'Where are we going?' asked Breen, as the car crossed Blackfriars Bridge.

'Surbiton,' said the driver. 'Didn't they tell you?'

The tide was out. Barges lay unevenly on bright mud.

'Do you mind driving a bit slower?'

'Orders. They said I'm to get you there by ten. Supposed to be back at the Yard at ten thirty.'

Breen rubbed his unshaven chin. He hated leaving the flat like this. 'What's the hurry?'

'Think they'd tell me that? They just told me to get you there.'

'To Surbiton?'

No answer.

'They didn't tell you who had ordered this?'

'Just got a call to pick you up and take you there. Your day off, is it?'

'I'm on sick leave.'

'Lucky bleeder. Wish I was.'

Today the London he was driving through didn't look so miraculous. It just looked dirty, grey and cold. Rubbish blew around in the streets. South London still had almost as many bomb sites as the East End; buildings remained half demolished, their yellow bricks blackened by years of smog, precarious walls propped with timbers.

The traffic moved too slowly for the driver's liking. He pulled out in front of a startled motorbike, forcing it onto the pavement, then revved up against the oncoming cars.

London became leafier. The houses became tidier. They finally pulled up outside a semi-detached house in the calm of a cul-de-sac.

'That's the one,' said the driver, pointing. 'Number seventeen.'

A nice house, built before the war, with stained glass in the front door and a leafless cherry tree in the garden. Pebble-dash walls and recently painted metal windows. A milk-bottle carrier with two empties in it outside the front door. A small red disc set to 'Two Pints Today Please'.

A woman in her mid-thirties, woollen skirt, woollen cardigan, opened the door. 'Sergeant Carmichael?' she called, looking back over her shoulder. 'I think it's a man for you.'

Carmichael emerged from the living room, tie half undone. He glared at Breen for a second.

'John? What's going on?'

Carmichael ignored him. 'Sergeant Breen. This is Mrs Milkwood. Sergeant Milkwood's wife.'

She gave Breen a little smile. Breen could see from her eyes that she had been crying. He looked to Carmichael for an explanation.

Carmichael just said, 'Can we have a minute alone, Gwen?'

'I'll make a cup of tea,' she said, standing twisting the ring on her left hand.

'Right,' said Carmichael, closing the living-room door behind him and shutting Mrs Milkwood out. It was a nice, ordinary living room, with a brown velour three-piece suite with lace on the arms and a wood-effect TV set. A set of carved wooden antelopes on the tiled fireplace. Photographs in a cabinet.

Carmichael stood in front of the stone mantelpiece, arms crossed. 'Spill.'

'Spill what?' said Breen.

'Whatever reason it was you were asking about Sergeant Milkwood.'

'I don't understand.'

'No. You tell me. I want to know what you were up to yesterday. It's too much of a coincidence, you showing up and asking me about him on the day that he's disappeared.'

'Disappeared?'

Carmichael looked at him for a second, as if trying to gauge whether his surprise was genuine, then said, 'Milkwood didn't come home yesterday after work. He seems to have gone missing. So tell me what you were doing, asking about him. There's more to it than him being some old chum of Tozer's, isn't there?'

Breen sat down on the sofa, nodded.

'Jesus Christ, Paddy. I am supposed to be your mate. Sometimes I don't think I know you at all.'

'You didn't tell Milkwood I was asking after him?'

'God's sake, Paddy. Answer my questions before you start asking yours.' Carmichael was trying hard not to raise his voice, but not succeeding.

Breen asked, 'Did Tozer ever tell you about her sister?'

Carmichael shook his head.

'Helen's younger sister, Alex, was assaulted, tortured and murdered four and a half years ago. They never found the killer. Milkwood was part of the team who investigated her sister's murder.'

'Jesus. I never knew.'

'That's how she knew Milkwood. And it's why she got into the police in the first place in a kind of way.'

'Oh, she's just asking about an old pal. God's sake.'

Carmichael's big frame thumped down onto the sofa next to Breen. The springs sang.

'I'm sorry. She doesn't like telling people about her sister.'

'You must be pretty special, then.'

'She didn't want to. I made her.'

A cuckoo clock somewhere in the house struck the quarter-hour.

'And anyway, I thought I'd take a look at the investigation files while I was down there. As a favour. And there was a suspect folder missing. It had been removed from the files completely. So I asked around a bit. The missing suspect turned out to be a friend of Milkwood's. And it turned out that Milkwood had removed the papers.'

Carmichael whispered, 'You don't think Milkwood was . . . involved in the murder of Tozer's sister?'

Breen shook his head. 'I don't know. It's not likely. But there may have been something in the folder that might have been useful. I wanted to get Sergeant Milkwood to tell me his version of why he'd removed that evidence.'

There was a gentle knock on the door. 'Tea, Mr Breen?'

They both looked at the door.

'Just a minute, Mrs M,' said Carmichael. 'Christ.'

Breen said, 'You sure he's disappeared, then? He's not just run off on some investigation?'

'He's a steady bloke. If he wasn't coming home for a reason, he'd have called his wife.'

They looked at each other for a second.

Breen asked, 'So did you tell him I was looking for him?'

Carmichael shook his head. 'No. I don't think I even saw him yesterday afternoon.'

'And did you tell him you were meeting me?'

'I told a few of them in the squad. Don't know about him exactly. He was there, I suppose. You're my mate.'

'Did you say I'd been away in Devon? Did you mention Helen at all?'

'I'm thinking. I may have done. I can't remember.'

Breen wondered about Sharman. Or someone else in the Devon and Cornwall Police maybe? Would they have somehow told Milkwood that Breen was looking into Alexandra Tozer's murder?

'It's got to be coincidence, though, hasn't it?' said Carmichael.

'Your tea will get cold,' said Mrs Milkwood, outside the door.

Breen said, 'Maybe it's nothing. Milkwood was Drug Squad. He must have made a few enemies.'

Carmichael whispered, 'That's what people are most afraid of, back at the shop. This is all new ground for us. The drug gangs are growing faster than we can keep the screws on them.'

'I could make a fresh pot, if you like?' A tremor in her voice.

'No. Come on in, Mrs M. We're done.'

As she carried the tray past the cabinet, teacups rattling, Breen glanced at the photos in it. There was a black-and-white one of a younger Mrs Milkwood in a floral swimming suit, standing next to someone who must be her husband. On either side of her, a couple of men and another woman stood holding drinks. They were all laughing about something. The photograph must have been taken in the 1950s, probably somewhere hot and bright from the way they all squinted at the camera. She alone wore dark glasses. She was younger then; her hair was down and her skin smoother.

'How do you take it?' Mrs Milkwood asked. But when she lifted the china pot, her hands were trembling so much that tea slopped over the saucers and onto the tray, soaking the lace beneath the plates.

'Oh dear,' she said, and sat down suddenly on the floor and hung her head so that her hair covered her face, shoulders heaving.

Breen and Carmichael sat wordless, embarrassed, each waiting for the other to say something.

'You must think me such an idiot,' she said between sobs; she seemed unable to stand on her own. Spilt tea steamed gently.

Afterwards, they sat in Carmichael's car, smoking cigarettes.

'I mean, he wouldn't have just run off?'

Carmichael blew out smoke. 'Not likely. Not Milkwood.'

'Anyone he'd crossed?'

'That's what frightens me. Unlike the rest of the Drug Squad, who are running around posing for the papers, Milkwood has plenty of contacts in the drug trade. He was good. He was getting somewhere. At a guess, there were definitely people who were concerned about him. Serious people. He was tracking some gang that's been bringing drugs out of Spain.'

'You worried?'

Carmichael nodded. 'I've got a bad feeling about this. Coppers don't just go missing.'

'It's only been for a day. He'll turn up, probably.'

'It's not like him, though. One of the old-style ones. Short hair, you know?'

'Your mate?'

Carmichael shrugged. 'God, no. Too square. But he's still one of us, you know?'

Breen ground his cigarette into the ashtray and snapped it shut.

Carmichael asked, 'Tozer's sister was killed four years ago?'

Breen nodded. 'Milkwood moved up here about six months after that? Maybe a year?'

Carmichael wound down the window and threw out his butt. 'That's right.' Then leaned down and started the engine. 'What are you trying to say?'

'I wish I knew.'

They drove in silence back towards the centre of the city, heater up full against an icy wind.

Carmichael sat at Milkwood's desk, the floor around him surrounded by wood splinters from where he'd forced the locks. He was looking through wads of paper he had piled on the desk.

He looked up and said, 'What about checking his bank account?'

Sergeant Pilcher had been standing next to them. He snapped, 'Sergeant Milkwood isn't on trial here.'

'Who said he was?' Carmichael looked him in the eye. 'Might be worth it. Just in case.'

'I don't know what you're implying, Carmichael. But if I were you I'd shut up now before you say something stupid.'

'I'm just trying to help find him, Nobby.' Sergeant Nobby Pilcher. Golden boy of the Drug Squad.

When Pilcher had gone, Breen said, 'Anything?'

'There's nothing much here. Take a look at this.' He pushed a large black-and-white photograph across the desk.

A dead body, of course. A man, probably in his thirties, laid flat on a floor. He had been fit and healthy. There was something beautiful about his sinewy frame. Unshaven, longish-haired and naked, arms splayed out on either side. Like Jesus. Only instead of having holes in his hands, he was missing three fingers. His face was so badly swollen from being beaten that it was hard to tell what it would have looked like, and there was a clean bullet hole in the front of his head.

Breen turned it over. On the back was written: 'Estudio Fotográfico Alberic'.

'This isn't the first. Milkwood had another a couple of weeks before. According to that man's parents, he was on his way back from Marrakech,' said Carmichael. 'Milkwood got this from the Spanish police in Madrid. Morocco's full of hippies thinking they can make their fortune by bringing a bit of hash back from their holidays. Afghanistan too. Only, if you're bringing it back from Morocco you come through Spain, where half the criminals from east London now live. I was hoping for notes. Anything.'

'His fingers? Tortured?'

'It's not just a manicure, is it? The Spanish police have had half a dozen bodies of British hippies turning up in the last three months. Milkwood told me the Spanish Cuerpo General think it's some kind a honey trap. They meet the hippies on the way out. *Buenos dias*. Going to Morocco? Tell them they know this great guy up in the mountains who'll look after them. Talks up how cheap drugs are to buy, maybe. How easy it is to smuggle them back and make a fortune. Look us up on your way back, kids. Show us your holiday snaps. This great guy in the Rif Mountains sells them drugs to take back with them. Heroin. Marijuana. All that. So basically the gang get their drugs bought for them, get them over the Spanish border, then they think they'll go and look up their great new mates in

Spain. Both the bodies had bullets in the head. So these hippies are not only smuggling the drugs for them, they're paying for them too. They think this one must have hidden his gear somewhere. So they chopped his fingers off until he told them. Stupid arse. All you need is love, hey?'

'No other notes about who he was investigating?'

'No idea. I can't find anything. Milky didn't seem to keep notes. It was all in his head.'

'Who would you reckon?'

'I mean, take your pick. Half the gangs in London are winding up in Spain these days.'

Breen scratched his unshaven chin. 'So it could well be something to do with that? Nothing to do with Helen's sister?'

Breen gazed at the clutter on Milkwood's desk. A leather pot for pens. A typewriter. He leaned forward and pulled a single sheet of carbon paper out of the typewriter and held it up to the light in the hope he'd be able to read the last thing Milkwood had typed. But the carbon had been used many times. It was just an indecipherable blur of letters. Breen crumpled it and threw it into the dustbin.

Then he caught Carmichael's eye. Carmichael nodded, lifted up the dustbin and emptied it onto the desk. He shook cigarette ash off balls of paper and started unfolding them on the desk. 'You ever thought what you'd do if you quit the police?' he asked.

Breen said, 'I don't know. There's not much I'm any good at. Apart from this.'

'Who says you're any good at it?'

'What about you? You're not thinking of jacking it in, are you, for God's sake?'

Carmichael stopped, lit a cigarette. 'I just hate the way all the young people think we're such arses, you know? And I hate that half the time they're right.'

'Young people? Since when did you start caring about what they thought?'

Carmichael ignored him. He was making a pile of small torn-up pieces of paper.

Breen wondered what Helen was doing now. He hadn't called the farm since he'd gone. The snow that had started the night they had made love had not let up. It would be hard work down there.

There was a phone on the desk. He could call now. Only if he did, they'd think there was something wrong. Only the rich made personal calls during the daytime, unless it was urgent. Maybe tonight he would call. At home. In private.

He noticed Carmichael was holding up a piece of paper, noting the date on it.

'What's that?'

'Petty cash claim. Two hundred and fifty quid.'

Breen had pulled up one of the plastic chairs and was sitting opposite him. 'For what?'

'What do you think? Miscellaneous expenses.'

'Two hundred and fifty quid for miscellaneous? You're joking. That's not miscellaneous.' That was a couple of months' wages. 'Many more of them like that in there?'

Carmichael shrugged. 'A couple.'

Breen whistled.

'Don't look so shocked. It's just how we do it in the Drug Squad,' said Carmichael quietly, so that the man at the next desk wouldn't overhear. 'If we put down what it's really for . . .'

'Informers?'

'Yes. Miscellaneous arseholes.'

Breen shook his head. 'Nice work.'

It was a large noisy office, desks in lines. This side of the New

Scotland Yard building had clear views over towards Petty France and Buckingham Palace, even in the dwindling daylight.

Breen picked up the stapler and banged it so that a useless staple fell out of the bottom. 'I don't suppose he'd have kept a list of those informers anywhere?'

'You know how it works,' said Carmichael. 'He wouldn't have written it down.'

'I know how it works in the rest of the Met. Everyone's got informers, but they don't pay them two hundred and fifty quid.'

'This is drugs. It's a whole new world.'

Breen nodded. 'But perhaps he was on to something.'

'If he was, I can't see what it was.'

Carmichael was still picking through the debris. An empty biro. Mouldering apple cores. A broken light bulb. And two small, screwed-up pieces of yellow paper. Breen reached out and took them. They were both messages, written in the same rounded female hand, that must have been left on Milkwood's desk. One said 'Pilcher says meeting now at 10.30 a.m.' and the other said 'Your wife called. What time will you be home?'

Breen was screwing the pieces of paper up to put them back in the bin when he noticed the blue ink stains on the backs. He unwrapped them again and pushed them across to Carmichael.

'The message book.' Carmichael nodded. 'Worth a look.'

The notes had been written on sheets torn out of a duplicate book. The secretary who had left them for Milkwood must have kept a copy at her desk in case anybody called in for their messages. It might contain other messages Milkwood had received.

'It'll be locked up now. I'll see to it in the morning.'

The office was clearing. Lights were going out.

'Fancy doing something later?' he said.

'I'm tired. I don't sleep well with this arm.'

'I don't want to go back to the police flats. It's driving me crazy there. Come on. Please, Paddy. Tell you what. You like films. Want to come to the cinema?'

'What's on?'

'Some old silent movie.'

Breen frowned. 'I thought you were into Westerns?'

Carmichael stood. 'And how do you bloody know what I like and what I don't?' he said, suddenly angry for no apparent reason. He left the room, leaving Breen alone at Milkwood's empty desk.

TEN

It was late. A crowd was gathering outside the Imperial Cinema in Notting Hill, a mixture of hippies and bohemians, chattering students and swaying drunks from the nearby pubs. Breen felt conspicuously sober waiting with them in his mackintosh and light tan shoes. A chalked notice said, 'Tonight 11 p.m. Electric Cinema Club'.

Carmichael arrived with a panatella between his lips and a bunch of daffodils in one hand.

'For me?' said Breen.

''K off.'

'Any news of Milkwood?'

Carmichael bit his lip, shook his head. 'I just called up again. Nothing. I called his wife too. She's in pieces. Wanted me to go round. I couldn't face it.'

Policemen didn't just go missing. Especially not married ones.

They joined the queue. 'Who are the flowers for, then?'

Carmichael said gruffly, 'Someone.'

The box office was just inside the entrance to the cinema. When they reached the front of the queue a young man wearing a deer-stalker with a feather in it scowled and said, 'Oh. It's you again.'

Carmichael showed a membership card. 'I've brought a friend,' he said.

'I'm surprised you have any, considering,' said the young man, taking ten shillings.

'Considering what?' asked Breen as they walked into the cinema.

Carmichael looked around him. 'Well, it's like this. I started coming to this place undercover a few weeks back. We had a tip-off they were selling drugs here.'

'So how come they know you're Drug Squad?'

"Cause I raided it two weeks ago. Arrested six of them.'

Breen burst out laughing. 'No wonder nobody likes you.'

Carmichael, taller than most of the people coming in, was craning his neck around. Then he broke into a smile. Breen watched him pushing his way through the stream of cinema-goers.

'Amy,' he shouted.

The small entrance to the old cinema was packed with people. Breen struggled to see where his friend was heading. Then he saw her. A small girl, only around five foot tall. She was dressed in a black T-shirt, black cap, black hot pants and black-and-white striped tights, and was holding a silver torch.

'Amy,' he shouted again.

Breen realised she was supposed to be an usherette, something imagined from the 1920s. She was wearing thick kohl around her eyes, Clara Bow-style. She grimaced when she saw Carmichael charging towards her through the crowd, holding out the daffodils in front of him.

Breen couldn't hear what Carmichael was saying, but he saw the girl reluctantly accept the flowers. When she rolled her eyes in exasperation, there was a hint of a smile too.

A long-haired man in a windcheater shouted, 'Hey, Johnny Narc's back and he's got a girlfriend.'

The crowd stopped pushing past and watched. Carmichael stood, looking sheepish. The tiny girl took the flowers and started hitting the man in the windcheater with them. 'He's not my fucking boy-friend,' she shouted.

And then she turned to Carmichael and started beating him with the daffodils too. People stared, laughed. By the time she'd finished, the daffodils flopped out of her fist, broken-stemmed and shredded. She held them out to Carmichael and said, 'Here.'

Big John dropped them on the floor, pushed the mocking crowd aside to make his way back to Breen, who stood there, open-mouthed.

'Shut up,' said Carmichael.

'Didn't say a dicky bird,' said Breen.

The film turned out to be *Metropolis*.

The forty-year-old film looked strange and beautiful, the plot unfolding at a pace that seemed uncomfortably slow for the fast city it was being shown in. Yet these young men and women watching it seemed rapt at the heavily made-up people clutching at their hearts dramatically, the robotic workers, shuffling like dead men, in a totalitarian city. At the front, a piano player thumped a modernist soundtrack, full of clanging semitones.

The seats were old and uncomfortable. Breen noticed something moving on the floor by his feet. 'Are they mice?'

'Probably. What I don't get,' said Carmichael, 'is why they're watching it in the first place.'

'Shh,' someone behind hissed.

Carmichael turned. 'It's a silent bloody movie. It's not like you're listening to it.'

'Why are you watching it?' said Breen. 'That's the question. Who's that girl you brought the flowers for?'

'Amy,' said Carmichael. He relit his panatella. 'Did you like her?'

'I didn't exactly meet her.'

Breen looked around at the crowd lounging in the seats. A man to his right had hooked his legs over the empty chair in front.

This generation always seemed so keen on the past, dressing like eighteenth-century dandies or dark-eyed Twenties flappers and watching silent movies that had seemed so old-fashioned when he was growing up. They treated history as their playground. Perhaps they were losing trust in the future, in the white heat of technology and restaurants in the sky. Like Hibou, he supposed, who wanted to turn the Tozers' farm back into something ancient and primitive.

Was that something rustling in the old popcorn on the floor? Breen lifted his shoes and placed them on the chair in front of him. When he looked up, he noticed the usherette had squeezed herself into the seat next to Carmichael.

'Don't you ever come to this place again,' she hissed. 'It's embarrassing for me.'

Breen leaned closer to hear.

'Give me your phone number and I won't need to,' said Carmichael.

'I thought you bloody lot could find that out anyway,' she said.

Another voice from behind: 'Shh.'

'What about a meal? This is my best friend, Paddy. We could make a foursome.'

'Are you mad?'

'Tomorrow night.'

'I work Friday nights. Leave me alone.'

The girl called Amy stood and stamped away up the aisle and through the swing doors at the back.

Carmichael waited a minute, then stood and went to follow her.

Through the projector-lit fog of smoke, Breen watched the young couple kissing on screen, watched by the mad scientist with the strange steel hand. He stayed for another few minutes but Carmichael didn't return, so he followed him out of the cinema into the cold air.

Carmichael was sitting on the step at the front of the cinema, smoking. Breen put his scarf down on the cold step and sat next to him, shaking his head when Carmichael offered him a cigar.

Portobello Road was quiet. It was past midnight. The pubs were long shut.

'So yeah. We raided this place two weeks ago. We had word some people were smoking marijuana on the premises.'

'And?' said Breen.

'By the time we got past the door most people had had time to dump their gear on the floor. Only we caught one guy trying to leg it out of the emergency exit. We made him strip and he had this big bag of resin down his Y-fronts. We banged him up. Next thing Amy turned up at the station at two in the morning demanding we set him free.'

'He was her boyfriend?'

'Her cousin. Anyway. There was nothing we could do about him until the magistrates' court in the morning, so we spent a bit of time talking, her and me.'

Breen grinned. 'And you fell for her?'

'I wouldn't say fell for her, exactly,' said Carmichael, looking down at his feet.

Breen was laughing.

'I know. She's not even my type. But she's . . . I don't know. So alive.'

A taxi came past with its FOR HIRE light on, slowed when it neared Carmichael and Breen, then drove on down the cold street.

'She looked pretty alive when she was hitting you with those flowers,' said Breen.

'Do you think I'm making a twat of myself, Paddy? Only, I'm so bloody tired of hanging around with lowlifes. I want something different.'

'Yes. You're making a twat of yourself.'

'I better phone in. See if there's any news from Milkwood. Got any pennies?'

Breen dug in his pocket for change. The red phone box was lit up in the darkness. From fifteen yards away, Breen sat watching the big man fumbling the coins into the slot, waiting for someone on night duty to pick up the phone.

Then there were a couple of striped legs next to him.

'Give this to your friend.' Amy spoke in a quiet Scottish accent.

A folded piece of paper torn out of an exercise book. He stood to look around but the doors were already swinging behind him. Without thinking, he opened the paper, expecting to see some rude message. Instead there were seven numbers. Her telephone.

'Hey, John! Guess what?'

But now Carmichael was walking towards him, face white.

'I've got to go. They've found Milkwood.'

This was not the man who held out a bunch of flowers to the woman in striped tights. He moved slowly, shoulders slumped.

'Where?'

'Epping Forest. They found the body late this afternoon, but it was naked. Stripped. They didn't even figure out it was him until tonight though, apparently. Christ.'

'Shall I come?'

He shook his head. 'Watch the film. You're on leave, Paddy.'

Breen stood outside the cinema, watching Carmichael walk back down the street to his car, head down. He briefly considered going back to catch the rest of the silent movie, but his heart wasn't in it.

ELEVEN

Early on Friday Breen called Carmichael at Scotland Yard, but he didn't pick up. He would be busy. With nothing to do, Breen bathed, taking care to keep the bandage dry, then took the bus to an exhibition at the big new art gallery on the South Bank.

He never had the time to do this normally. Now he had nothing but time. Breen spent an hour walking around low sculptures of flat, industrial sheets of metal, some brightly coloured, welded at all angles. They had installed a few on the Hayward Gallery's concrete roof. Under a grey London sky, he walked around them, listening to an American in pale slacks talking loudly to his pretty, much younger girlfriend. 'Don't you see? This is sculpture that's about being alive. Alive to yourself.'

Breen looked at the sculpture and tried to understand what the American meant. The girl sucked on her hair but didn't seem any more moved than Breen by the works, though he wasn't sure whether this was the sculptor's fault or his own. Instead of trying to fathom the minimalist sculptures, he kept imagining Milkwood's pale naked body, lying in the woods. Or the photographs of the dead hippie he had seen on Milkwood's desk. And of Tozer's sister.

Nagging at his brain was the thought that he had somehow been responsible for what had happened to Milkwood. If he hadn't come to London asking after him, perhaps he would still be alive. There was little logic to the thought, but it had buzzed in his head all through the night.

'I think it's boring,' the seen-it-all girl was saying.

He decided he agreed with her. Like the concrete building itself, the art seemed joyless, disconnected from the chaos of the city around it.

He needed a coffee. There was no cafe in the new gallery, so Breen walked down a bleak concrete walkway to the South Bank Centre. The tide was low, the Thames reassuringly greasy and loaded with silt.

He sat down and lit a cigarette; his first of the day. He savoured the harsh taste of nicotine and coffee, still relishing the novelty of being back in London.

An elderly woman with a fox-fur stole sat down at the table next to Breen, filling in crossword clues with a fountain pen. She worked fast, as if this was something she did every day. In a matter of minutes she had finished it. She placed her pen back in her handbag and lifted the paper to read it. It took Breen a second or so to notice the front page.

DEAD POLICEMAN
WAS TORTURED

Two lines. Beneath that: 'London gang connection'.

And another second for the penny to drop.

Breen stood. 'Excuse me. I need to look at your paper.'

The woman looked him up and down and then said, 'Get your own.'

'It's important,' said Breen.

The woman raised the angle of her head a little, ignoring him.

Breen looked around for anyone else reading a newspaper. Upstairs, an orchestra was rehearsing for a concert. The sounds of strings leaked out of the large hall whenever someone opened the doors. The cafe was all but deserted.

'Could you keep an eye on my coffee?'

The woman didn't answer. Breen ran out of the building, trying to find a newspaper vendor. It wasn't until he was almost at Waterloo Station that he found one, standing with papers under his arm.

He walked back towards the Festival Hall reading the newspaper. 'Sources at Scotland Yard point to the probable involvement of London gang members in the gruesome killing.' The newspaper's crime correspondent had written a column titled 'New Gang Threat?': 'London police may have arrested the leaders of the notorious Kray twins' gang, and the Richardson Gang are on the run, but sources within the Metropolitan Police suggest that a more ruthless generation may be taking their place.'

Breen arrived back at the Festival Hall to find the woman with the fox fur gone. His undrunk coffee had been cleared away.

Back at home, he called Carmichael's desk at Scotland Yard, but there was no answer. Then he tried the section house. A man on the phone said he was at work, so he tried his office again, but there was still no one picking up. Then, even though it wasn't evening yet, he phoned the farm, but no one answered there either.

He felt unsettled. He did not like not knowing what was going on.

He walked to Abney Park Cemetery, looking at gravestones and angels with broken wings. On the way back he looked in at the Stoke Newington Police Station.

'Aye, aye. Bloody Paddy Breen. Back again like a bad rash on the bollocks.'

Though years ago he had worked with him, Breen was struggling to remember the name of the old copper at the front desk, so he just said, 'Morning, Sarge.'

'To what do we owe the pleasure?'

Breen closed the big blue front door behind him. 'Just thought I'd pop in and say hello.'

'What do you think this place is? A ruddy social club?'

'Might as well be, for all the work you do.'

The dirty old Victorian building was close to his flat. Rat-infested and freezing in winter, it had been the first station he had worked in and he had loved it here. Today, it looked worse than usual. One of the ground-floor windows had been broken recently. Someone had tried to tape a piece of cardboard over it.

'You're the one who's pulled sick leave, what I hear,' the sergeant was saying.

He missed the familiar banter. Men who insulted each other in place of having to say anything more familiar.

The sergeant lifted the hinge on the desk and beckoned him in. 'Anyway, what's this we hear about you getting yourself shot, you stupid pillock? Criminals these days. Can't even shoot a gun proper.'

Another younger copper emerged from the office behind the sergeant's cubbyhole. He had a plaster above his eye, probably from a fight.

'Fetch Paddy Breen a cup of tea. No, you never liked tea, did you? Fetch him a cup of coffee if we've got one.'

'Don't bother. Your coffee's worse than your tea.'

'Ooh. Bloody Paddy Breen has gone all West End on us. Spending too long in the Eyetie caffs.'

Breen joined the sergeant in the small space behind the desk. The man was sitting on a stool next to a paraffin heater that blared heat upwards but seemed to make no difference to the chill in the small room.

'You're off a while, I suppose,' said the sergeant.

'Six weeks,' said Breen. 'Maybe longer.'

'Jammy bastard.'

'I was bloody shot. Couple of inches lower and I'd have died. What's jammy about that?'

A short moment of embarrassed silence. A couple of frowns. Realising that there had been too much anger in his voice, Breen forced a smile. 'Still, you should have seen the other man.'

This time, a big laugh from the other two coppers. Breen turned away and closed his eyes. Behind lids, he saw the dead man, head like half an orange, flat on the tarmac. Bile rose in his stomach. Deep breath. Get a hold on yourself.

Other policemen crowded in. N Division had always been a rough patch; so were its coppers. Brawny, broken-nosed men who gave as good as they got. A couple of ex-dockers, tattoos out of sight under their sleeves. One with a bandaged hand, Breen noticed.

Cigarettes were passed around. Somebody found a tin of biscuits that one of the local shops had dropped by a couple of days before. The gloss paint on the walls dripped condensation. Idly, Breen riffled through the shoebox under the counter, full of lost belongings that members of the public had handed in. A wallet, probably empty; a watch with a broken strap; a sorrowful-looking knitted gollywog.

'Pretty quiet, I suppose?' he said. People round here would still be broke after Christmas.

'Quiet, my arse,' said the sergeant. 'Spent half the morning filling in the Occurrence Book. Six common assaults and two wilful damages last night.'

There was muttering. 'Where you been living? Haven't you heard?'

'What?' Breen looked around him and noticed the other men had marks on their faces too; scratches and cuts. One had a blackened eye.

'Bloody Scotland Yard everywhere yesterday, that's what's going on. Looking for them bastards that nailed that Drug Squad copper. They came through here last night on batting practice, stirring up seven kinds of shit.'

Breen said, 'Where?'

'The Rochester Castle. Broke all sorts of heads. Drug Squad are putting it about they're offering a monkey to anyone with information on what happened to their feller. Now every snitch in London is trying to get lucky. So some fibber said it was the Dalston firm's business.'

'Five hundred quid's just petty cash to the Drug Squad,' said the copper with the sticking plaster.

'Nobody talked to us, course. They just steamed in, closed the doors of the pub and started interrogating the regulars then and there. I mean, Christ. Shut this young guy's fingers in a door when he gave them lip. First we heard there was trouble was a car drove past here, chucked a brick in the window, last night. Next thing it was like Gallipoli round here.'

'OK for them. They bugger off back to Scotland Yard, leaving us to clear up the mess. We're not going to hear the last of it, neither.'

'There was bother all over the place, I heard. Not just our division.'

'Stupid buggers. We know what's going on round here. We got our snitches. We'd have known if it was one of our lot killed that copper. Certain.'

More muttering. 'They're just kids throwing stones at a wasps' nest.'

A thin, dark-eyed man belched loudly.

'You know what it's like round here, Paddy. You need the goodwill of the people. This area is dangerous. Everyone knows that.'

Breen nodded.

'So have they got anyone yet?'

People shook their heads. 'Not from round here, anyway.'

'I mean. Stands to reason they're angry. Specially after what they did to Sergeant Milkwood.'

People muttered. Shook their heads.

'What?' said Breen.

'A mate of mine who works in the Flying Squad heard they pulled his nails out.'

The dark-eyed man said, 'Shut up. Never?'

'They're keeping the lid on it, but there's all sorts of talk, isn't there?'

'Don't go listening to talk,' said the duty sergeant. 'That's what got us into this crap in the first place.'

The room went quiet for a moment.

'When you going back to work, Paddy?'

'I can't move my arm too well yet. Doctor says it'll be a few weeks.'

'Lucky you use the other one to wank with, then.'

Even Breen joined in the laughter. Stupidity. It dispelled the sense of fear that had settled on the small room, thinking about their tortured colleague. And for a second, it distracted Breen from thinking about Helen.

This time Carmichael picked up straight away. 'What's the news about Milkwood?'

Carmichael took a long time to answer. 'Not great.'

'Jesus. They tortured him. I read it in the paper. Coppers are saying they pulled his nails out. Any idea who it was?'

'I can't talk now. It's crazy here.'

'What's going on? The papers were saying it could be a gang thing.'

'Remember those photographs I showed you? That guy who had been tortured? We're working our way through every criminal who has a known associate who's holed up in Spain. Turns out there's a few. And it's not like they're the sort of people who take kindly to being questioned. Couple of constables got themselves beaten bloody in Camberwell just for asking. Listen, Paddy. I have to run. There's a meeting at the pathologist's office.'

'What if I was to come and . . . help out?'

A pause. Breen could hear the sound of a telex machine chomping away at a line of paper somewhere in the background. Eventually Carmichael said, 'Paddy. Put your feet up, God's sake.'

Only after he had put the phone down did Breen remember the piece of paper the woman at the cinema had given him. The telephone number. But when he called Carmichael's number back, it rang and rang and rang, unanswered.

Later, he tried the farm again. On a weekday evening, he knew they would be sitting round the dining table in the kitchen.

'Hello, Cathal. It is lovely to hear from you.' He had been itching to get away from the farm, but it was reassuring now to hear Helen's mother's voice. She was one of the few people to call him by his proper name now his dad was gone.

'How is Helen?' she asked before the conversation went anywhere else. The long-distance line crackled and echoed.

'Sorry?' he said.

'How is Helen?' she asked again.

It took him a second. Why would he know? 'I was about to ask the same.'

Now there was a long pause.

Mrs Tozer said, 'She is staying with you, is she not?'

Breen said, 'No.'

Another voiceless five seconds. Then: 'There must be a mistake,' she said. 'She told us she was going to stay with you for a couple of weeks.'

Breen gripped the phone harder, shook his head. 'No,' he said. 'I haven't heard anything from her.'

'She said you'd called and asked her to come and look after you.'

'When did she leave?'

'Tuesday, early.' Breen imagined Mrs Tozer in the hallway of the old farmhouse, holding the phone, a frown on her old face. He could hear a farm dog barking in the background.

'And she said she was coming to stay with me?'

'That's what I thought,' she said.

'Did she say why she was coming to see me?'

'Oh dear,' said Mrs Tozer. 'I thought she was coming to look after you.'

'Well, I'm sure she's OK, Mrs Tozer,' said Breen.

'Yes,' she said eventually. 'I must have made a mistake, then. I'm sure she's fine.'

Breen stood holding the phone for a minute after she'd replaced the receiver, unsure whether he'd understood what had just happened.

Helen had told her family she was coming to visit him. But she had not arrived. Had something happened to her on the way? The thought made his stomach lurch. He should have asked her what train she had caught.

The high-pitched warning tone coming from his handset startled him. He banged it down hard onto the cradle.

TWELVE

Saturday's pavements were crammed with people trying to get to the shops before they closed for the afternoon. He walked cautiously, trying to avoid women bustling along with their wicker shopping trolleys. He was just letting himself back in when he heard a call from the steps above him.

'Wait a sec. I've got something for you.'

A young woman with fair hair stood on the steps holding a shallow dish. He recognised her; she lived upstairs. Before Christmas, a couple had moved into the flat above Breen. They were young and with-it. They held parties. They bought furniture from the new Habitat shop on Tottenham Court Road.

They had got off to a bad start, playing their music too loud, parking their car in front of his window. But then they'd discovered he was a policeman and things had improved, from his point of view at least.

She smiled. 'I saw you were back,' she said, clacking down the stairs in sandals. 'Brought you this.'

When she reached the bottom of the steps he could see there was something dark and oblong on the dish.

'It's supposed to be a meat loaf,' she said. 'I made it myself.'

She and the man she lived with were slumming it, moving in around here. He was in advertising, apparently. He wore suede Chelsea boots and yellow shirts with long lapels.

'We heard you'd been . . . wounded,' she said.

She was wearing blue dungarees that had white paint on them; it was hiding a bulge. She was pregnant, he realised.

'You were in hospital,' she said, looking behind him at his flat. 'It must have been awful. Have you just come back?'

They would have heard about the shooting, he supposed. Word got around. They probably thought it frightfully exciting, living above someone like him. They'd have told all their rich hippie friends about it. Now she wanted all the grisly details, he guessed.

'I made it myself,' she said again, sounding less certain of herself when he didn't speak. 'I'm not much of a cook. It's a little burnt on the outside. But there's an egg in the middle.'

Eventually he reached out and took the meat loaf from her. She stood there a few seconds longer, as if waiting for him to say something. He didn't.

'Bring the dish back any time,' she said. 'Just knock.'

He closed the door on her and looked at the meat loaf. She was right. It was burnt. He could see where she'd tried to scrape away the worst bits.

The hours dragged. At midday, he took the meat loaf out of the fridge and tried a slice.

The end was too black and dry, so he put that into the dustbin and cut another slice. He cut another one and there was the egg she had talked about.

Yellow dot in a white circle. A boiled egg.

He felt nauseous. He went to the phone and dialled.

'Is Sergeant Carmichael there?'

'Not at his desk right now,' said a man's voice.

'Get him to call Cathal Breen when he gets back.' He spelled out the name automatically.

'Is it important?'

'I'm not sure,' said Breen.

'Well, either it is or it isn't,' said the man irritatedly.

He threw the meat loaf into the dustbin. The doctor had told him to try and move his arm a little each day so after he'd washed up the dish he stood in the kitchen swinging his hand backwards and forwards.

The day stretched out long ahead of him. He felt useless. He wanted to ring the farm and ask if there was any news of Helen, but if there wasn't, he'd only be alarming them more.

Carmichael didn't call back until gone two.

'I've got one minute, Paddy,' he said. 'What is it?'

'OK. I've got a question. Was there anything strange about Milkwood's body?' he asked.

Carmichael hesitated. 'What have you heard? We're not allowed to give out any details.'

Breen said, 'I know this sounds weird, but I've got to ask. I told you I heard a rumour they pulled out fingernails. Was there anything else . . . funny about it?'

Carmichael said, 'Funny?'

'Yes.'

'The whole thing was weird, if you ask me,' Carmichael said.

'What kind of weird?'

Carmichael lowered his voice. 'Not a word.'

'OK.'

'There was something . . . up his arse.'

'Christ.'

'I know.'

'What was it?'

'Please, Paddy. Leave it alone.'

A loud buzzing in his head. The image of Tozer's dead sister, naked in the copse. 'I know this is going to sound strange. But was it an egg?'

A pause. Breen could almost hear the gasp. 'Who the bloody hell told you that?'

It was strange how physically the body reacted, sometimes. Blood rushed to his head. He felt as if he was far above, looking down on himself, so perilously far above that he felt weak. He dropped into his father's old armchair, the telephone cord stretching across the room.

'Paddy? What's going on?'

Breen said, 'I think you better stop trying to round up gangsters in London. It's not them.'

'What do you know?' demanded Carmichael.

He lay his head on his knees, phone still clamped to his ear.

'Give me ten minutes,' said Breen. 'I'll call you back.'

'No,' Carmichael was saying, 'stay on the line,' as Breen stood, strode across the room and put his finger down on the cradle, cutting the call.

The spiral cord tangled and twisted. Breen held the end nearest the telephone up and watched the handset spin, as the kinks in the wire unwound. When it had slowed and he had caught his breath, Breen put the handset to his ear and dialled the farm.

Old man Tozer picked up the phone before Breen had heard it ring, which was unusual in itself.

'Hel?' he said.

'No. Sorry. It's me. Cathal,' said Breen.

'Paddy?' Old man Tozer hardly ever touched the phone. 'You heard anything from our Hel?'

'Who's that?' Another voice in the background: Mrs Tozer. She took the phone from her husband.

'What's going on, Mrs Tozer?' said Breen.

'We've still not heard anything from Helen. Though I'm sure everything's fine,' she said.

'She left the farm shortly after me. And you've not heard from her since?'

'You know what she's like, Cathal.' But he could hear the anxiety in her voice.

'And you have no idea where she may have gone?'

'Like I said last time, she said she was coming to visit you.'

'Is Hibou there? Let me speak to her.'

He could hear Mrs Tozer shuffling away, opening a door, calling Hibou's name. She would be out somewhere on the farm.

It was at least two minutes before the girl came to the phone; she was panting. 'Paddy? What is it?'

'What is going on?'

'I don't know, Paddy. She just upped and went.' She whispered into the phone, as if she didn't want the Tozers to hear what she was saying. 'They're really upset. It's like it's happening all over again. You know. Like Helen's sister. Her dad's been going down to the spinney, poking around in there like he's looking for her. It's weird.'

'And you have no idea at all where she's gone?'

Hibou was quiet.

'You know something? If you do, it's vital you tell me.'

'Thing is, I can't.'

'Why not?'

'It's a promise.'

'No, Hibou. You have to. This is really, really important. Whatever she made you promise, believe me, you have to tell me.'

Hibou said, 'Sorry, Paddy. I can't. She's the one who looked after me back in London. The only one.'

Breen held his breath for a minute. Closed his eyes.

'I have to go, Paddy. I'm cleaning the milking machine.'

'Wait,' he said. 'Please.'

'I've got to go. Honest.'

'Are Mr and Mrs Tozer with you?'

'No. They've gone into the kitchen.'

'Listen to me. Remember I told you I didn't love her?'

'Yes.'

'You were right. I wasn't telling you the truth. Of course I do.'

'Knew it,' Hibou said.

'And I think she's in real trouble. Really, really serious trouble. She may have done something . . . stupid. I'm the only person who can help her. Honestly. You have to believe me. But I need to know where she was going.'

'She never said that,' said Hibou. 'Just said she was going and she'd be in touch.'

'If she didn't say where, what did she say, then?'

Hibou sighed, then said, 'She made me promise to look after the farm on my own for a few days. She didn't know how long she was going to be. She said she was going to do something –' she lowered her voice – 'bad.'

'What?'

'She didn't say exactly.' She whispered, 'Something bad. Something that would make you angry with her. So she had to do it on her own.'

Breen felt panic.

'Paddy? You still there?'

'Did she say anything else?'

'No. Nothing.'

'She must have said something.'

'Don't shout at me.'

138

Had he been shouting? 'I'm sorry. I just really need to know where she is.'

'That's all she said. I promise. Sorry.'

Breen shut his eyes tight. His head was buzzing. 'It's not your fault.'

'I have to go,' she said. And she put the phone down without saying anything else.

The phone started ringing the moment Breen put it down. It would be Carmichael, Breen knew, desperate to find out what he knew about Milkwood's murder.

He didn't answer for a while. Just sat there listening to the phone ringing and ringing, head in his hands, thinking of what to do. Then he picked up the phone.

'I need to talk to you, John,' he said. 'In private.'

THIRTEEN

Breen made it to Joe's All Night Bagel Shop just before the rain started. There was a new sign up: 'Buy Our Bagels. We Knead the Dough.'

A young woman with thick, pale arms beneath her rolled-up sleeves was frying onions behind the counter. It was Joe's daughter.

'You look rubbish,' she said. 'Have you lost weight?'

'I've been off sick,' said Breen.

'Something serious?'

Breen said, 'Not really. How's your dad?'

'Not too good,' she said, pushing the browning onions around the pan. Joe had had a stroke in November. He sat at home now talking angrily in sentences no one could understand.

Breen ordered a coffee though they only served instant. She took the pan off the heat and opened the big tin and spooned the brown powder into a cup.

'I thought you hated this place,' said Breen.

'I do,' she said, putting the mug under the urn. 'It's a dump. I'd sell up if it was just me.'

'It's not so bad.'

'What about you?' she said. 'You been seeing that girl, I heard. The policewoman.'

Breen shook his head. 'I don't think it's working out.'

'Oh,' she said. 'Pity.'

Carmichael burst in through the door, dripping. It must have started raining hard. He shook out an umbrella on the doormat.

'Aye, aye,' he said.

'Thanks for coming,' said Breen.

Carmichael looked around the cafe and grunted. He had never liked this place. 'Coffee still rubbish, Paddy?' he asked.

Breen looked down at his cup. 'Terrible,' he said.

'Charming,' said Joe's daughter. 'Anything to eat?'

'Not likely,' said Carmichael, sitting heavily at one of the small yellow Formica tables.

The cafe was quiet, this time of day. They were the only customers. The radio was playing 'Ob-La-Di, Ob-La-Da'. Joe's daughter filled another cup.

'Come on, then,' Carmichael said. 'I haven't got all day.'

Breen sighed. He'd both hands around his mug to soak the heat from it.

'It's about Helen.'

'Tozer? 'K sake, Paddy. I thought this was going to be about Milkwood. I've just run halfway across London.'

'It is about Milkwood too,' said Breen. 'That's the point.'

Carmichael looked confused.

'You know we were talking about Helen's sister?' said Breen.

'The one who was murdered?'

The radio played its ridiculous, sing-song tune. 'Before she was killed, she was tortured,' said Breen.

'Fuck. I didn't know.'

Joe's daughter glanced up from the sink, where she'd started washing plates, frowned and then went back to her work.

'Listen to this.' And Breen pulled out a notebook from the pocket of his mac and started to read out details he'd copied from the pathologist's report. 'Victim had had a boiled egg inserted into her vagina. Reddened tissue of the dermis of the inner labia indicates the object was hot when inserted into the victim.'

Breen looked up and watched his friend's face as he absorbed the horror of it. The widening eyes, the falling jaw.

'An egg?' he said, shaking his head slowly. 'You're not serious?'

Breen closed his eyes for a second. A wave of nausea, caused by more than just the image in his mind.

'Is he OK?' said Joe's daughter.

Breen opened his eyes, took a breath and turned the page in his notes and read again. 'Breasts mutilated with sharp instrument. Victim's nipples had been entirely removed and were not present.'

Carmichael looked shocked. 'They cut Milkwood's chest too.'

'I thought so,' said Breen. Again he read, 'Burns to abdomen with cigarettes. Burns to buttocks with cigarettes.'

'Jesus. I don't get it. That was four years ago, yes?'

Breen explained how he'd gone through the murder files at the small Devon police station and made the connection between Milkwood and Alexandra Tozer. 'Alexandra was going out with an older man. A friend of Milkwood's. Milkwood had all the references to this man being a suspect removed from the file. Milkwood was trying to protect him, but it's not clear why. It may have been just to keep his name out of the papers. Or . . .'

'Slow down, Paddy. So you reckon the same person who killed her sister killed Milkwood? And in exactly the same way?'

Breen shrugged. 'You can't jump to conclusions. All I know is that they were killed in the same way. Either it's the same person, or someone trying to make a point about the first murder.'

'What about Helen?' said Carmichael.

'What do you mean?'

'Where is she? Is she OK?'

Breen didn't answer.

'Is there something wrong with him?' asked Joe's daughter. 'I've been thinking he doesn't look right.'

The bell above the door rang and a group of young Jewish boys in long coats entered talking loudly, laughing. They had dark springs of hair on each side of their faces, small black skullcaps on their heads.

Breen took a gulp of his coffee and put the mug back down on the table. He took a breath. 'I called Helen up just now to tell her about all this. Only she's not there. Apparently, the Tuesday after I left the farm, she left too. She told her mother she was coming to see me. She never arrived.'

'Christ.'

'Helen was lying, I think. She'd have called me if she was coming to see me.'

'Why was she lying?'

'I don't know.'

The Jewish boys had pulled out a box of dominoes and were shuffling them noisily on the table next to theirs, tiles clattering on the Formica.

'So have I got this right? Tozer disappears two days before Milky turns up dead. And whoever kills him is either the same person as killed her sister . . .'

'Or someone who's copying the way her sister was killed.'

Breen could see the ugly thought working its way through Carmichael's mind, his eyes getting wider.

'Wait. Did she know the details of her sister's murder?'

Breen nodded. 'Yes. I told her.'

'Jesus,' Carmichael exhaled.

'Exactly.'

'All the details? And the . . .' He pointed to his nipple.

Breen nodded. 'She read the pathologist's report. I had them in my room. She read them, yes.'

Carmichael was shaking his head now. 'You do know what I'm thinking?'

'Yes. I've been thinking the same.'

'You think it was revenge?'

'You can't just go jumping to conclusions like that,' said Breen.

Carmichael was silent for a while. He stared at Breen. 'Helen Tozer?' he said eventually. 'With the beanpole legs and everything? She couldn't do that. I mean, Milkwood was strong.' Breen thought about the darkness that had settled over Helen. 'Could she?' said Carmichael. 'She wasn't like that. Was she?'

'Like what?'

'Did she ever talk about taking revenge on whoever killed her sister?'

Breen shook his head. 'She just wanted to know who did it,' he said. 'That's all.' But as he took one of his own cigarettes out of his pocket and held it in his hand, he remembered Helen telling him how she admired a woman whom Breen had once investigated; a woman who had calculatingly arranged the murder of the man who had killed her brother.

'And whose idea was it that you go digging around into her sister's murder?'

'Mine,' said Breen. 'It was mine.' And as he said it, he knew that wasn't really true either. It had been Helen who had arranged for him to go and look at the case notes. His skin felt cold.

Carmichael nodded. 'I'm just thinking aloud, you understand? That's all. Doesn't everyone who's had a family member killed dream of this? Getting their revenge?'

Breen didn't say anything. But it was possible. Violence had its echo.

'And you've no idea where she is now?' Carmichael said.

'She said she was coming to London, to visit me. But I don't even know if that's true.' Rain streamed down the window at the front of the cafe. 'I don't even know if she's in London. She just told her mum that. Do you really think she set this whole thing up, so that I could lead her to Milkwood? That would be . . . fantastical, wouldn't it?'

'No. God, no,' said Carmichael, though he didn't sound certain either. 'All the same, I'll have to tell this to CID, won't I?'

'Yes.'

Carmichael chewed on his tongue; a habit when he was thinking.

'Or you could wait?' suggested Breen. 'Just a couple of days. It's going to kill her parents if the police arrive at the farm and start asking about all this. Maybe she'll turn up.'

Carmichael breathed out heavily. 'You know I can't do that, Paddy. I've got to tell them.' Carmichael's voice had the tone of someone visiting a hospital bedside.

Breen looked away.

The boys clacked dominoes onto the table.

Carmichael frowned. He dug in his pocket for some change and put it on the table. 'Let's get out of here. I don't know why you hang round in these places.'

Outside, it was still raining hard.

'Don't go fucking weird on me,' Carmichael said, opening the passenger door to his police car, then running round to his side.

'I'll be fine,' said Breen.

Carmichael slammed his door shut, wiped rain from his face with a handkerchief. 'You'll be fine, chum. No question.'

It was an Escort with no police markings. The ashtray was full and the floor on the passenger side was covered in empty Rothmans packets.

'Thanks, John.' Breen sat in the car seat, feeling like a drowning man. 'Just take me home, will you?' Carmichael sat there for a minute, thinking, still chewing on his tongue, saying nothing. 'To be honest,' said Breen, 'I don't feel that great.'

'Sitting around isn't going to fucking help,' said Carmichael.

'Somebody will probably need to interview me formally, I suppose.'

Carmichael snorted. 'God's sake.'

'I don't suppose it's a Drug Squad investigation now, anyway,' Breen said. 'It'll be CID. You better let them know.'

'Course it's a fucking Drug Squad investigation. Whatever you're saying, there might still be some drug-gang thing going on. Besides, try stopping us. Milkwood was one of ours.'

'And what if he was involved in the murder of a teenage girl?'

Carmichael said, 'All the more reason.'

Breen's head went down, chin on his chest. 'I'm tired.'

Carmichael turned to him. 'Paddy. You don't need to bloody sleep. You need to wake up! This is no time to give in.'

Breen blinked.

'Jesus, Paddy. Sometimes I don't bloody know you,' Carmichael said, putting the key in the ignition. 'You're such a fucking homo. There's work to do. Serious bloody work.'

'You going to call CID and tell them?'

'In a minute.'

Carmichael turned to look out of the rear window, one hand on the wheel, pulling the car out into the street in front of a taxi. Leaning forward to peer through the rain-smeared glass, knuckles white on the wheel, he looked huge.

FOURTEEN

Mrs Milkwood sat by the gas fire, dressed in a black skirt and black cardigan. 'I mean, how can I plan a funeral when they won't tell me when they'll release the body?' she said.

Carmichael nodded. 'I know.' There were cards on the mantelpiece. 'In deepest sympathy'. 'Thinking of you at this sad time'.

'You think all this is going to take long? He's my husband, after all. Why won't they let me have Billy back, Sergeant Carmichael?'

Breen looked at Carmichael; Carmichael looked at the carpet. 'I'm sure they will release the body soon, Gwen,' he said. From the evasive way he said it, Breen realised, they had not told her the details of how her husband had been tortured. As with the Tozers, they were trying to save her from the hurt. This British reflex to conceal.

'He wanted to be cremated,' she said. 'I was against it. My family are always for burial,' she said. 'You've let your tea go cold, Sergeant Breen,' she said. 'Shall I pour you another?'

Despite everything, she seemed oddly calm. Coping, thought Breen. He shook his head. 'I'm fine, thank you.'

'Anything at all, Gwen,' said Carmichael. 'Just say the word and we'll help out. All the boys want you to know that.'

'My mind's a blank,' she said. 'I keep thinking about who I should invite to the funeral. I've never liked funerals.'

Carmichael turned to Breen. 'What's the name of that man who Milkwood was friends with in Devon?'

'Fletchet,' said Breen. 'James Fletchet.'

'Oh yes.' Mrs Milkwood smiled. 'James. He's a lord now, of course. I'll have to invite him. I expect if he does come he'll give a speech. He's an excellent speaker. And he did admire Billy very much, I think, in his way.'

'What about children? Did you and Bill have any children?'

She shook her head. 'No. We never did.'

Breen looked at her. She had found someone she presumably loved and now that certainty had been obliterated. He thought about Helen. Tried to imagine her in this sort of setting, the wife of a policeman, but couldn't. Then he tried to shut her out of his head; best not to think about Helen.

Carmichael sat in the armchair with a half-eaten iced-ring biscuit in his hand. A proper armchair, upholstered in a sturdy floral fabric. It would have been Milkwood's chair, with a footstool and the best view of the TV. 'How did they know each other, Gwen, Fletchet and your husband?'

'They worked together in Africa,' said Mrs Milkwood. 'Great pals, they were in those days.'

Carmichael looked at Breen and said, 'Fletchet was a copper?'

Mrs Milkwood's laugh was high and thin. 'Heavens, no. Not Jimmy. He was a farmer. A gentleman farmer.' She laughed again. 'When his father, Lord Goodstone, died, the family estate in Devon went to his older brother. The family sent Jimmy out to run the farm in Kenya instead. That's where we met him. Kenya was full of people like that. The also-rans of the British aristocracy.' She laughed. 'That's what he used to call himself. An also-ran. As if. The younger brothers used to wind up there and they'd get set up with a coffee farm or whatever. We moved in pretty grand circles in those days, Bill and me.'

'You were in Kenya?'

'Bill was in the Kenyan police. CID as a matter of fact. We went out after the war. It was an opportunity.'

'And Fletchet?'

Mrs Milkwood lifted the plate of biscuits to offer them round. 'I am sure they would have ended up knowing each other anyway. Kenya society was quite small, really,' she said. 'Quite exclusive. And they were such good pals, Jimmy and Bill, but it was the Emergency that brought them together, really.'

'What Emergency?' said Carmichael.

'The Mau Mau of course.'

'The Mau Mau? He never talked about that,' said Carmichael.

'I wouldn't expect him to,' said Mrs Milkwood. 'The point is that it was a crisis. And the British all pulled together. That's how they knew each other.'

Breen tried to concentrate, to engage his brain in what Mrs Milkwood was saying. It felt so hard to think at all right now. 'The Mau Mau was an independence movement,' he said.

Mrs Milkwood slammed her cup down into her saucer. 'It was evil, barbaric superstition. Those people were savages.'

'I'm sorry. I only know what I read in some of the papers.'

Mrs Milkwood quivered with rage. 'Precisely the problem, Sergeant. You people back home . . . you didn't have a clue what was happening out there. We were stationed in Nyeri. The White Highlands. You'd have known what was happening if you were out there, I'll tell you that.'

'I didn't mean to offend you,' said Breen.

Mrs Milkwood sighed. 'It's not your fault, I suppose. Even the bloody Governor didn't have a clue. How would he, stuck in Nairobi? Nobody understood what it was like for us.'

Carmichael leaned forward in the armchair to have enough space to dig into his pockets for his packet of panatellas. 'So how did they end up together?'

'When the Emergency started they stationed us in Nyeri. They set up little police stations all over the Highlands to try and keep a lid on it. And sent out the soldiers too. Lancashire Fusiliers. But half the time they didn't know what they were doing. It would have been chaos if it wasn't for landowners like Jimmy. It was people like him who really got things going while the government was still sat on its behind. Back in '52, when the murders started, the farmers were the only ones putting up a fight. After all, they were the ones being murdered in their beds. The monsters were breaking into farms and killing men, women and children. The landowners were the ones with the local knowledge. They worked with the blacks. They spoke the lingo. Jimmy and Bill ran the screening station, weeding out the malefactors.' She paused. Glared at Carmichael. 'Do you mind not smoking those, Sergeant? I don't mind cigarettes, but cigars do linger.'

Carmichael muttered an awkward apology, put the cigar back into the packet.

Breen stood up and walked over to the cabinet, and pointed at the photograph he had noticed before. He bent down and peered at it, and realised that Fletchet was there, in the picture. 'That's the two of them in Kenya?'

She smiled. 'Yes.' Mrs Milkwood followed him to the shelf of photographs, opened the glass door and took out the silver-framed picture. 'I was a little thinner then, I suppose,' she said, as if waiting for a denial.

She handed the picture to Breen. Breen tried to understand what he was seeing. Three men and two women standing in the sunshine, smiling, holding drinks. He recognised Fletchet. Though he stood to one side, he clearly seemed the important person in the photo. He stood a head above them in height, with his arm around Bill Milkwood's shoulders. They were in a garden, surrounded by roses and more exotic-looking flowers.

'And Mrs Fletchet?' She was standing to the side, in a black swimming suit and dark glasses, holding a martini glass.

'Yes. Eloisa. She's Italian, you know. I always found her a bit of a snob. Not like Jimmy. He was one of us. One of the white community. But she did throw great parties. We used to drink such a lot in those days.' She giggled.

'Where was this taken?'

'At Jimmy's house. We had a lovely house too. One of the cottages on his estate. Nowhere near as grand as his, but I loved it. Servants. Everything. I've got a photograph of that somewhere. It had this beautiful balcony which we used to eat our supper on. Beautiful bougainvillea everywhere. It was quite splendid for a while. It all feels like a dream, now.'

'So . . . you were friends with James Fletchet too?' said Breen.

'Great pals. We knew him back here at home too. But Africa was the highlight. If it wasn't for the Mau Mau it would have been such fun. Then again, I suppose that's how we knew each other in the first place.' A high laugh.

'But you knew each other in Devon too?'

Mrs Milkwood poured hot water into the teapot. 'Jimmy left Africa first. His brother had died, you know, so he came back to run the estate in Devon. We moved back to Nairobi after the Emergency. Billy had a job with CID there. Then by '59 it became pretty obvious that Kenya was about to go down the pan with Kenyatta all lined up to take over, so we started making plans to come home. Some of them stayed on, but God help them. We thought we'd better get out while we could. We still kept up with Jimmy, so we thought, why not go and find a place near him? So we jolly well packed our bags and left. I do miss the heat in Africa, but we were right to go. But it was never the same when we came back here. We were never as close, obviously. Eloisa in particular, now she was a lady. Did you want more tea?'

Breen looked at the photograph. In the floral swimsuit, Mrs Fletchet looked a different person. There was something come-hithery about her smile; she was enjoying the company of men.

'That would have been 1955, I expect.' She smiled. 'Somewhere round there. They were back from one of their expeditions. That was at the end of the worst of it. They'd be gone into the bush for a fort-night and then when they'd come back we'd always have a party.'

'What were they doing?'

'Fighting the Mau Mau of course. With the Home Guard. Local black fellows. Useless mostly. The Mau Mau were worse than fighting the Germans, Bill always said. The Germans wore a uni-form. You never knew who was Mau Mau and who wasn't. They were a secret society. That was half the problem. Swore a blood oath. So you never even knew whether the Home Guard were loyal or not. Savages, really. Barbarous in the extreme. The thing about Africans. You have to understand that there is no real culture there. No depth of thought. Some of them were wonderful. Our servants were the sweetest people you could wish to meet. A little lazy sometimes but devoted to us. But people like that, their whole lives are governed by superstition. And fear. And that made them prey to any vicious agitator there was. You'd hear these awful stories of people whose servants turned on them and murdered them in the night. It was terrifying, really. I remember one particular story. This one family had lovely servants. One day their little boy fell off a horse and broke his ankle. One chap carried him miles to get him home. A few nights later the same servant hacked the whole family to death with a machete, mother, father and the same child whose life he'd just saved. Blood everywhere, so they said. The horror. There was no logic to it at all, you see?'

She stood and looked at herself in the mirror above the mantelpiece. Adjusted her hair.

'And now their lot is in power. Place will go to the dogs. Everybody's sucking up to that awful man Kenyatta these days, but everyone knew he was a leader in the Mau Mau.'

She paused. Looked at the photograph. 'Funny. So much horridness going on, but when I look back, I always remember it with such fondness. If I'm honest, I was always quite scared on my own when Bill was away just in case something happened. And now he's gone for good,' she said.

Breen peered at the photograph. 'Who's the third person?' he asked. A man, in big serge shorts, cigarette in hand, his smile less certain than the other two.

'Nicky, Jimmy and Bill. The three musketeers. Nicholas Doyle. A police constable. Jimmy was a farmer. Bill was a CID man. Nicky was just an ordinary fellow, really. He'd never been outside England until then. But they all came together to fight the Mau Mau. Didn't wait to be ordered to. Nobody back home ever knew what it was like. They just wanted rid of the problem. But out there it brought us all together. Nicky was always the quieter one. You have to understand, they saw terrible things. The Mau Mau would slaughter families of anyone they thought was a collaborator. Anyone who had broken the oath they forced people to swear. Once, Bill saw a baby that had been boiled alive in a pot. Some people aren't as strong.'

'Where is he now?' Breen asked.

She took the photograph from his hands. 'He was younger than Bill. They didn't have that much in common.'

'Doyle, you say?' said Carmichael.

'Yes, why?'

'Do you have an address for him?'

Mrs Milkwood laughed. 'Oh no. I don't think Bill kept in touch with him at all. He didn't think much of him. Sergeant Carmichael, do you think a weekend is better for a funeral?'

'I should say,' said Carmichael. 'Definitely a weekend.' There was an uncomfortable pause. 'Can we borrow this photograph? We'll make a copy and give it straight back?'

She frowned. 'What is all this? What's this got to do with the people who killed Bill?'

Carmichael said, 'I worked with your husband for three months, and I admired him a great deal, but I didn't really know him, I suppose. I'm just trying to find out a little about him. We're going to need to talk to James Fletchet.'

'We haven't seen so much of Jimmy recently. I mean, it was different back here at home anyway. In Kenya we whites were all together. Just because his family were lords and sirs didn't mean a thing out there. I used to invite Jimmy and Eloisa round for dinner. I rather miss that. Back here it's more us and them, if you know what I mean. Jimmy and Bill still got along like a house on fire. But when I asked Jimmy round for dinner when we were back, he didn't even reply. It was like I was no longer part of the same set. Bill was. Not me, though.'

Suddenly her lip wobbled and Mrs Milkwood burst into tears. She sat on the smaller of the two armchairs for a second, shoulders heaving, while Carmichael and Breen watched her cry.

'I'm sorry,' she said, when she'd found her breath. 'I'll tell you what I miss most. It's the smell of the place.'

'Sorry?'

'Africa,' she said. 'You know when rain hits hot soil? There's nothing like it. England has always seemed so grey in comparison.'

'Did he bring work back here at all?' asked Breen.

'Some.'

Breen looked at Carmichael. 'Were there any files. Any folders?'

She hesitated. 'Why?'

'We've been through all his files at the office,' Carmichael said. 'Just to make sure we've got everything covered.'

'I'm not sure. He never used to let me anywhere near his desk. If I so much as moved a bit of paper, he'd be upset.'

'We'll be as careful as we can.'

She looked anxious.

Carmichael reached over and took her hand. 'We want to catch the bastards who did this,' he said. 'All of us do.'

It was a small spare bedroom. A small bookcase full of Westerns by Zane Grey and Louis L'Amour. A small oak desk. On the wall above the desk, a photograph of him as a Metropolitan Police Cadet at Hendon, some time just after the war, Breen guessed.

The desktop was empty, save for a blotter, a souvenir ashtray from Windsor and a box of pencils.

Breen tried the drawers. They were both locked.

'I don't have the key,' she said.

'Did he spend a lot of time in here?'

'Half an hour or so when he got home after work. He didn't like to be disturbed, he said. He used to lock the door behind him. I never liked that.'

'Mind if we look around?' said Carmichael. 'Maybe he kept the key somewhere safe.'

'I don't know if I want you to do this,' she said, toying with the hem of her cardigan.

'Don't worry,' said Carmichael. 'We won't disturb anything. We promise.'

'Bill wouldn't like it.'

The doorbell rang. She hesitated, but it rang a second time. 'Don't touch anything,' she said.

'Absolutely not,' said Carmicahel.

The moment she was gone, Carmichael took a Swiss Army pen-knife from his pocket, took out a spike, and began digging in the lock hole of the top drawer.

Breen started at the shelves, pulling out the books to see if there was a key concealed anywhere. It was wrong to be sneaking behind her back this way, but it felt good to be doing something, at least. It took his mind off Helen. He could hear Gwen Milkwood downstairs, talking to someone at the door. A neighbour?

Her voice rose up the stairs. 'I'm not sure when the funeral is going to be. It's terribly complicated. I have a lot of notices to send. It's very wearing.'

There was a loud crack behind him. 'Bugger,' said Carmichael.

Breen looked round. Trying to force the lock, Carmichael had slipped and gashed it. He spat on his sleeve and started rubbing at the mark. Breen turned back to the shelf, pulled out another slim book and a small dark key flew out and fell on the floor, bouncing under the spare bed.

On his hands and knees, he retrieved it, then passed it to Carmichael.

The top drawer was full of odds and ends. Pens, rubber bands, a bottle of ink, a book of matches from the Playboy Club.

'Are you all right up there?' called Mrs Milkwood.

'Coming down now,' shouted Carmichael, putting the key in the second drawer and turning it.

Inside was a pile of magazines. The one on the top was called *Busty*. Carmichael pulled it out and flicked through it. There were pictures of naked women sitting in awkward poses on beds and sofas, single and in pairs, smiling at the camera. 'So that's why he locked the door.'

He reached in and pulled out the whole pile to see if there was anything else in there.

'Put that back.' Mrs Milkwood was standing at the door, face pale. Carmichael was holding a picture of a woman in white suspenders and a bra, legs wide apart. 'Right this minute.'

Shocked, Carmichael spilled the pile, sending the magazines across the floor. *Kolor Klimax. Lark. Natural Women.*

Breen and Carmichael looked at each other. Breen wondered briefly if his own face looked as appalled as Carmichael's did, before dropping to his knees, scooping up the magazines without trying to look too closely at them.

'I think you should go now,' she said, not looking either of them in the eye.

On the doorstep, Carmichael said, 'Well. We better be off then.'

'You must have a lot to do,' she replied.

'Yes.'

'It's Saturday, isn't it?' she said, looking back towards the kitchen. 'Usually I cook steak and kidney for Bill. I'm not sure I can be bothered any more.'

It was as if they'd never been upstairs. She held out her hand, to shake.

Carmichael drove in low gear, high revs, overtaking when he could, swerving around cars. He wasn't familiar with south London, peering up at street signs, trying to figure out the best route.

'Oh, Christ.' Carmichael burst out laughing. 'Your face.'

'What about yours?'

Carmichael shivered. 'It's not my scene. Widows.'

Breen looked at his colleague. 'Your scene? What does that mean?'

'I don't know,' said Carmichael.

Carmichael braked, then swung left onto Kew Road. 'Drive more slowly, can't you? I'm only just out of hospital.'

Carmichael slowed to well below the speed limit. 'Better?' he said.

Now he drove so slowly that the cars behind started to honk.

'Much better.'

Carmichael sped up again.

'Are you going to tell them about Helen?'

Carmichael nodded. 'Yes.'

Breen thought about asking to stop to ring the farm to warn them what was about to happen. That there would be police, coming to question them about their daughter. Would that make it worse? Breen dug into his pocket and pulled out a sheet of paper and tried to peer at it.

'What's that?'

'It was in the pile of magazines. I stuck it in my pocket when she wasn't looking.'

'What's in it?'

Breen unfolded it and peered. The car was bouncing around too much. 'I can't see. It seems to be just a list of numbers.'

It was getting dark now; there were lights on in the shop windows. Breen put the paper back in his pocket to look at later.

'Doyle,' said Carmichael. 'Thing is, I think I remember the name from somewhere.'

'Where?'

Carmichael frowned. 'Or something like it, at least. I'm trying to remember. Something I saw.'

'It's a pretty common name.'

Carmichael didn't answer. If it was Breen, he'd at least be able to flick through his notebooks. Carmichael had never been much for note taking. Carmichael's mind was like his car: empty cigarette and sweet packets everywhere.

'Come and have a drink with me. It's Saturday night. You'll only stew on your own. It won't do you any good.' Carmichael pulled up outside the section house near Paddington Station where he had lived for years.

'I'm not good company.'

'That'll be a change then,' Carmichael said. 'I'll sneak you into an empty room. You can stay over.'

Breen hesitated.

'You'll drive yourself nuts thinking about it if you go home. Until she turns up, there's nothing you can do.'

Most single policemen lived in section houses; married men in police flats. The rents in the section houses were cheap. Carmichael preferred to spend his money on clothes and bars. Besides, he enjoyed the company of men. His section house allowed you your own room, so it was better than most.

'What if she doesn't turn up?'

Carmichael didn't answer.

Breen waited in the billiard room while Carmichael went to pilfer the keys to an empty room. Exhausted, he flopped down in one of the old armchairs, fabric almost shiny from grease and cigarette ash.

Helen Tozer had lived in the women's section house not far from here in Pembridge Square. She had shared a room with another WPC, annoying her with her records and untidy habits. Where else did she know in London? Where else could she be staying? If she hadn't been involved in Milkwood's killing in some way, why was she not getting in touch?

A constable Breen didn't know put his head round the door and asked, 'You using the tables?'

Breen looked up, shook his head. A red-headed copper joined them, racking up the balls on the table. He watched the younger men playing pool, joking and laughing, just as he had done on the evenings he wasn't working. These were the dead hours. Their shift had finished but the pubs wouldn't be open until seven.

'Missed! By a mile.'

'It didn't. You weren't even looking. The white kissed the red.'

'Kissed my arse.'

It seemed to take Carmichael a long time finding a bed for Breen to doss down in. They had played two frames by the time he joined them.

'Johnny!' the younger men shouted.

'Fancy a game, Paddy?' said Carmichael. 'Us against them?'

'With my arm?'

'Excuses!' shouted the redhead.

'No. Serious. Paddy's got a bad arm. He was shot a few weeks back, trying to arrest a man.'

The two men went silent and looked at Breen, suddenly respectful. 'You the one who was shot back in January? Up in Holloway? Where that other copper was killed?'

The two younger men looked at him, open-mouthed, awed. The redhead called out of the door, 'Lads. You'll never guess who we've got in here.'

Men drifted in from the TV room next door. Breen sat, embarrassed at the attention, as the younger coppers told the others who he was.

'I heard you shoved the other guy off the building. Killed him.'

'It wasn't like that,' said Breen. 'It was an accident.'

'Course it was, mate! Whatever you say.'

'You must be bloody brave, taking on a man with a gun like that. I'd have shat myself.'

'Did it hurt?'

'OK, lads. Enough.' Carmichael muttered, 'Course it fucking hurt, you knob.'

As he led Breen out of the room he turned to the pool players and said, 'We'd have beaten you anyway. One-handed or not.'

In the corridor which Carmichael's room was on, a policeman stood in his underpants, ironing the serge of his uniform as he listened to the transistor.

Carmichael's room was small, but it was private, at least. In some of the section houses all you had were partitions between you and the next copper. He knelt on the floor and dug out a bottle of Bell's from a box hidden under his bed.

'When you were in the billiard room, I called up the CID man,' he said. 'Told them what you said about Helen's sister.'

'Right,' said Breen. It's what he would have done himself. It was better that the police were looking for her, he supposed.

'They want to talk to you tomorrow.'

'Sunday?'

'Murder investigation, Paddy.'

'Right.'

'I'll give you a lift in. In the morning.' He left the room with a glass, returning a minute later with it full of water. 'I'll tell the Drug Squad tomorrow, too, when I go in,' he said. 'I told CID to talk to Devon and Cornwall and to dig out the pathology report and forensics from 1964.'

Breen said, 'Two-to-one they'll be down at Helen's farm tomorrow asking them what they know about it.'

'Tonight, I'd guess,' said Carmichael. 'They won't mess around.'

He imagined Helen's parents watching the police arrive, trying to understand what was going on. Old man Tozer was just starting to emerge from the catastrophe of losing his youngest daughter. It would tear them to pieces.

Carmichael poured two glasses of whisky, diluting his with water, passing one to Breen. A drink would be good tonight.

'Can't be helped,' said Carmichael. 'It's put the wind up everyone, Milkwood being killed like that. Nobody touches the Met. Not like that.'

Someone out in the corridor 'Ac-cent-tchu-ate the positive . . .' in a thin, tuneless voice.

'Do you believe she used me to track down Milkwood?'

Outside the door, somebody shouted, 'Stop that bloody singing. I'm trying to sleep.'

Carmichael put a finger into his glass of whisky, stirred it around, then sucked it for a second. 'You're the one who always used to say we should see where the evidence leads us.'

Breen balanced his glass on a pile of motor magazines. 'It doesn't make sense.'

'Who says it has to make sense?' he said. 'She's a dark horse. Always has been. There was something running deep in there.'

'You hardly knew her,' said Breen.

'Keep your hair on,' said Carmichael. 'Of course I knew her. We were mates. True, though, isn't it? She always had something hidden.'

'You would too if your sister had been killed.'

Carmichael wiped a dribble of whisky from his chin with the back of his hand. 'That's my point.'

'Shut up, John, now. I've had enough of this.'

'Only saying.' He downed his whisky. 'Drink up,' he said.

'Oh,' said Breen, and pulled his wallet out from his trouser pocket. 'I'm sorry. I forgot. The girl from the cinema. When we were leaving, she slipped me this.' He handed Carmichael the note. 'You had to go. So I never had a chance to give it to you.'

Carmichael looked it it. 'She gave you this? For me?'

'I forgot about it. What with one thing and another. Are you going to call her?'

Carmichael was staring at the paper. 'I don't know. I mean . . . A bit late now, isn't it?'

'Only ten.'

He shook his head. 'I mean, she'd probably be at work, wouldn't she? Maybe I'll do it tomorrow. No big deal.' But he placed it on the table in front of him, trying hard not to look pleased.

It took an hour to finish the bottle. Afterwards, they crept downstairs to an empty room on the floor below, taking care to avoid the Warden. Carmichael unlocked the door and let Breen in.

That night Breen lay in a narrow bed in his underpants and vest as the walls spun around him.

He had lived in section houses like this for years. When he left he had missed the male camaraderie of it. But tonight the room was airless and the cast-iron radiator would not switch off. Drinking too much whisky had only amplified his misery.

He tried to picture Helen as a killer. She was so skinny and light. However hard he tried, he could not see her abducting Milkwood, torturing him to death. But then, he was not sure whether this was just a failure of the imagination.

In the morning, when he'd folded the blanket, he sat on the bed for a while gathering his thoughts while the familiar hubbub of the section house played out beyond the door. From his jacket pocket he removed the sheet of paper he'd stolen from Bill Milkwood's desk.

It was a list of letters and numbers, just as he'd said in the car:

N	55	C7	486 520
	2B	18	089 646
D	96	3A	853 979
	1H	4F	970 441
J	22	B9	633 611
	L8	56	213 640

He stared at them for a while, then copied them into a notebook, carefully checking the numbers back against Milkwood's hand-written version.

At a quarter to eight, Carmichael was banging on the door, hissing, 'Hands off cocks, on socks,' as if there was nothing wrong with the world. Even on a Sunday morning, the corridor outside was full of the bustle of coppers preparing for their shift.

FIFTEEN

The CID sergeant was all smiles. 'We've heard a lot about you, Sergeant Breen. All good. Tea? No? Water? Nothing? OK.'

His name was Dixon. Breen was offered an orange plastic chair to sit on. Dixon sat on the corner of a desk, legs crossed, closer than was comfortable. He wore neatly ironed slacks and a pale cardigan, a yellow tie and Hush Puppies. Breen thought he looked like he should be modelling for a knitting catalogue.

'So, tell us all about this notorious girlfriend of yours,' Dixon said.

'Did you send someone to her home?'

'Local plod went there last night. The family told him she'd left home four days ago and they haven't heard from her since. Do you know about that?'

'I tried calling her the day before yesterday. Her mother told me she wasn't there.'

Dixon nodded, pursed his lips. 'So I understand. They confirmed that.'

The desk was tidy. A typewriter under a loose grey vinyl cover and a single box of index cards. Another policeman sat behind it, with a pad and biro on his lap, as if he was ready to take notes, though he didn't seem to be writing anything. Instead, he played idly with a red anglepoise lamp, pulling it slowly one way, then the other.

Breen said, 'So you're treating her as a suspect?'

Dixon grinned wider. 'Well, you've got to admit. She

disappears and our guy turns up dead. We'd be foolish not to assume there's some kind of connection. It's just process, obviously. We may be able to rule her out quickly. I mean, she used to be one of ours.'

Breen nodded.

'Obviously it would have been helpful if you'd contacted us yesterday and let us know she'd gone missing.' Smile.

'I don't think she's involved.'

Dixon exchanged a glance with the other policeman. 'Sergeant Carmichael said you showed Miss Tozer the pathologist's report on her sister.'

'I didn't show it to her. She found it in my room and read it.'

The man held his palms up, smiling again. 'OK. I'm not blaming you. Mistakes happen. We try to do a pal a favour and one thing leads to another. But you know for sure she read it. And she knew the details of her sister's murder?'

'Yes.'

'Have we had a copy of that yet?' Dixon asked the man behind the desk.

The man batting the anglepoise from side to side shook his head.

'So we've got a girl who knows exactly how her sister was killed. And a few days later she disappears and a man connected to the case turns up with exactly the same . . . injuries. And you don't think she's connected?'

Breen didn't answer.

'Give me some idea of what she's like, then, Miss Tozer.'

Breen said, 'I thought she had the makings of a good copper.'

'A good plonk,' said Dixon. 'What's she like as a person?'

'Well, she's clever but doesn't like to show it. Doesn't like being told what to do. Likes a drink. Doesn't like doing things by the book. She knows her mind. Likes pop music—'

Dixon interrupted. 'Would you say she was affected by the death of her sister?'

Breen said, 'Of course. Anyone would be. The whole family was affected.'

The sergeant slowly rotated one of his shoes in circles in the air. 'She talked about the murder to you?'

Breen looked at him. 'Not much, no, as a matter of fact. She found it quite hard to talk about it. I made her talk about it once, because I was concerned that what had happened to her was affecting her ability as a copper.'

'Really? So you were concerned about her?'

Breen nodded. 'I was concerned. But wrongly, I think. She was very dedicated. In some ways I think it made her better at what she did.'

'Dedicated,' repeated the man.

'Yes. We worked on a nasty case together last year. She knowingly put herself in danger to try and help catch a dangerous killer.'

'I don't doubt that, Sergeant. It's her state of mind I'm interested in. She didn't discuss the killing with you again?'

'Only in terms of her family and how it affected them. Her father especially. He had some kind of breakdown as a result of it, I think.'

'So it affected them pretty badly, you'd say?'

'Of course it did. As I said.'

He wished Dixon would stop smiling at him. 'Right.'

'You said you weren't her boyfriend?'

'That's right.'

'So what were you then? Did you have sex with her?'

'Once. No, twice.'

The sergeant smiled. 'Wasn't she much good?'

The other copper laughed very quietly, the first noise he'd made since Breen had entered the room.

'That's just the way it worked out.'

'My goodness, Sergeant. Sounds like you'd have liked a bit more of it?'

Breen didn't answer.

'OK, then. What about other men? Did she have other boyfriends?'

'No one steady. There may have been others.'

Dixon nodded, pursed his lips. 'I've got you. She played the field, so to speak.'

'That's not what I said.'

The man held his palms up again, laughing. 'Keep your hair on. No offence meant. But you fancied her, would you say?'

Breen said, 'I don't see what that's got to do with anything.'

'It's pretty simple, Sergeant. Would you say you've been influenced by your feelings for her?'

'In what way?'

The man shrugged. 'I don't know. Just asking. It's my job. You know. You're in the same job as me. Maybe she persuaded you to do things for her. Like investigate her sister's murder. Like get her the pathology report.'

'I didn't get it for her,' said Breen. 'I got it for myself.'

'Right. Right. But she was the one who arranged for you to come down to Devon?'

'I'd been shot. She suggested her family could look after me while I recovered. I don't have any family myself.'

The sergeant tutted. 'But she was the one who persuaded you to go and look into her sister's death.'

'She suggested it. She didn't persuade me.'

Dixon got up, walked, stretched and sat down again. 'What about any other friends?' he said.

'She had friends at the women's section house where she lived. And John Carmichael in the Drug Squad.'

'We've got those covered. Anyone else?'

Breen shook his head.

Dixon pulled out a pen and wrote something on a sheet of paper. 'My number. You will get in touch the moment she tries to contact you, won't you?'

On the floor below, Carmichael and a half a dozen other Drug Squad officers were sitting in a windowless meeting room around a table covered in pieces of paper and half-drunk cups of tea.

'How was that?' asked Carmichael.

Breen looked around the room. All the chairs were taken. 'What's going on?' he asked.

'We just want a word,' said Sergeant Pilcher. He turned to his left and slapped the head of a young plain-clothes copper sitting in the chair next to him. 'Stand up, you cunt. Paddy here's a hero. He's been shot while going about his duty as a copper.'

Silently the man stood and made way for Breen.

'How are you, mate? Recovering? How's the wound? Always a place for you here when you want it, Paddy, you know that.'

'Thank you,' said Breen quietly.

'Now then,' Pilcher said. 'Carmichael says you had some information about the death of Sergeant Milkwood.'

'I've just been talking about it to CID.'

Taking his time, Breen sat down opposite Carmichael. People in the Drug Squad dressed differently. They were smoother, flashier than other policemen. Young men in gaudy Tommy Nutter jackets with wide lapels. Another with checked trousers and two-tone shoes. Carmichael had gone for a pale paisley shirt. Among them, Pilcher was the least showy. A dark jacket and a white tie.

'I'm sure you wouldn't mind filling us in too, then,' said Pilcher.

Breen said, 'Won't they brief you?'

Pilcher smiled, rubbed his palms together. 'Obviously. Though I just want to make sure of all the facts myself.'

Breen looked around the room. 'What's wrong? Aren't CID working with you on this?'

Pilcher sucked his front teeth with a loud click, then said, 'Let's put it this way. We don't always see eye to eye with CID about our objectives. That has created certain obstacles.'

The copper to his left smirked.

'What about some coffee?' Breen said.

Pilcher nodded at the red-faced young man who had stood for Breen. 'Fetch him one, will you, lad?'

There was an ashtray in the middle of the table piled with a pyramid of fag ends. Breen pushed it away. He said, 'You've heard then? I think Milkwood's murder may well be connected to an investigation he was involved with when he was working for Devon CID. He was killed in the same way as that victim.'

Pilcher nodded. 'Carmichael said you'd been asking after Milkwood before he was killed.' His lips twitched into a small smile. 'Which would indicate to me that you thought something was up even before Bill was murdered.'

Breen looked Pilcher in the eye. 'Milkwood had investigated the original case. There were some notes that had been lost from the original files. He knew what they were. So I wanted to know what he knew.' He was conscious that everyone apart from Carmichael was watching him. Carmichael seemed to be looking uncomfortably down at the table in front of him, fingering a folder. 'What is this about?' asked Breen.

Pilcher's laugh was loud, high-pitched and abrupt. 'We want you on our team for this one, that's all.'

The young man came in with a mug of instant coffee.

Pilcher said, 'Show him, John.'

Carmichael looked up. He opened a folder and handed Breen a sheet of typed paper.

'What is it?'

'Remember when you suggested we should check the message log book?'

It was a list of people who'd called Milkwood. Two items had been circled. Both were the name 'Nick Doyle'.

'It didn't mean anything to me at the time,' said Carmichael, 'but when Mrs Milkwood mentioned his name yesterday I knew I'd heard it before.'

'So?'

He opened the folder again and passed a large black-and-white photograph across the table. It was a copy of the photograph that had been in Mrs Milkwood's cabinet.

The original had been blown up to eight by ten inches. It had lost a little focus, but it was still clear enough. Bill Milkwood and his wife, Jimmy Fletchet, and the third man, Nicholas Doyle. But in red biro, someone had scrawled longer hair onto the third man's head. The drawn hair came to the man's ears and was parted in the centre.

'We know him,' said Carmichael. He pointed at Doyle. 'He's one of ours.'

'He is an informer,' said Pilcher. 'We know him as a colourful chap named Afghan.'

'After I recognised the name, I thought I should take another look at that photo Mrs Milkwood had given me. That photograph is almost fifteen years old. He had a police haircut then, so I didn't recognise him in it at first.'

Pilcher smiled. 'Never knew his real name, but he was on the payroll. One of ours. A drug dealer turned helper. And very useful too. Only he's disappeared.'

Breen looked at the photograph. 'And the hair?'

'That's what he looked like last time I saw him. I met him just the once,' Carmichael said.

A couple of the coppers sniggered; Breen wasn't sure why.

Pilcher said, 'He's an interesting fellow, by all accounts. They call him Afghan because that's where his connections get their drugs. Afghanistan. The Magic Bus. You heard of that?'

Breen shook his head.

'It's a kind of Thomas Cook for hippies. Goes to India through Turkey, Afghanistan and Pakistan. Places where heroin poppies and hemp grow like daisies. And he went to Morocco regularly, apparently. Only Afghan's a better name, I guess.'

'Where's Doyle now?'

Pilcher looked at Carmichael. 'That's sort of the point. We don't know,' he said.

'With Milkwood dead, you don't have any idea where this man Doyle is, or any way of getting in touch with him?'

Pilcher said, 'In a nutshell, yes.'

The younger copper who'd brought the coffee said, 'Most of us haven't even met the guy.'

Breen took his coffee and sipped it. He said, 'You met him, John. You're the one who recognised him.'

Everyone apart from Pilcher burst out laughing. Even he smiled a little.

Breen looked round him. 'What's funny?'

'Big John pulled him in one night.'

Carmichael said, 'It was a nightclub. A place called Middle Earth. Heard of it?'

Breen shook his head.

'Psychedelic music. Loads of drugs there, always. So I raided it, first week I was on Drug Squad. Afghan was a regular there and had some cannabis on him. I arrested him, not realising he was one of Milkwood's contacts. How was I to know?'

'Very keen, Big John was, when he first got stuck in.'

'That could be a bit of a problem for you lot,' said Breen. 'Telling the drug dealers and the snitches apart.'

Pilcher shrugged. 'Hazard of the trade.'

'And Big John couldn't tell his elbow from his arse.'

'Enough,' shouted Pilcher. The room was instantly quiet.

'So there's a man who may be involved in the death of one of your officers in some way, or at least know something about it, only you don't know where he actually lives?'

'Precisely,' said Pilcher.

'So tell CID. That's their job.'

'Use your nut, Paddy. Doyle was one of our informers. We may not exactly want CID to start crashing around looking for him. If word got around that we passed the names of our men over to CID . . .'

Breen had drunk half a mug of the police coffee. He couldn't face the rest. He said, 'So you know he's involved, but you're not telling CID about it?'

'May be involved,' said Pilcher. 'We don't know that, do we?'

'Same difference,' said Breen. 'Have you considered the possibility that this Doyle man is dead too? Like Milkwood.'

Pilcher nodded. 'Always possible,' he said.

Breen shook his head. 'And have any of your other informers heard anything?'

'The hippies on the scene wouldn't tell us where Doyle was even if they did know. They don't know he's one of ours. That's the whole point. They think he's one of them. Which he is, in a way.'

Breen said, 'I'm not sure why you're telling me this.'

'So we have a problem,' said Pilcher. 'We're not having any luck finding Doyle ourselves. And our informants are not telling us anything, because, well, we're the pigs.'

Another laugh went round the room.

'We can't just go round asking, "Where's Doyle?" without them wanting to know why. On the other hand, if we tell CID about Doyle and get them to look for him, then we'll blow his cover and every other bloody narc in London will stop trusting us. Our options are limited.'

Pilcher's concession to being flashy was smoking Lucky Strikes. He banged his pack on the table until a filter emerged, then raised it to his mouth and pulled it out.

'When Big John here came and told us that you had linked Milkwood's killing to the murder of the girl in Devon,' he said, 'and that CID had kindly arranged for you to come and visit, an idea occurred to me. You do it. You go and look for him.'

Breen blinked. 'You're pulling my leg.'

'Nope.'

Breen shook his head. 'I'm on sick leave.'

'Precisely. You're not even a copper, officially. You don't have to report what you're doing to anyone. Our hands are clean. Just go and find him.'

'Why doesn't one of your boys do it, undercover?'

'Too risky,' said Pilcher. 'Lots of people on the hippie scene know who we are now. We're almost as famous as pop stars these days, ain't we, boys?'

A small laugh.

'We've got a golden opportunity. Middle Earth's on tonight. If we don't go to this one, it'll be at least a week before the next.'

'So you want me to look for Doyle?'

Pilcher leaned forward. 'I know you, Paddy. You wouldn't mind getting stuck in, would you? That's why you found out about Milkwood in the first place. And it would be doing us a big favour, wouldn't it, John? We're talking about a copper killer.'

Breen sat in the chair, his undrunk coffee in front of him.

Pilcher looked at his watch. 'Almost lunch, then?' he said, and stood.

Carmichael came outside to the corridor with Breen. 'I told him I didn't think you'd do it. Pilcher said he'd bet me a tenner you would.'

The other Drug Squad officers were putting on their coats, ready to go out to the pub. Breen looked at the black-and-white photograph of Doyle with his hair coloured in in red biro and said, 'Doing nothing is driving me mad. Besides, everyone's convinced Helen is involved. Only one way to find out.'

Carmichael looked at him. 'And what if she is? You know, involved?'

Somebody called, 'You coming for a pint, John?'

'You go on. I'll catch you up.' He nodded his head towards the other end of the corridor. 'Come with me, then,' he said. 'We'll kit you out.'

'Kit me out?'

Carmichael led him down towards a door on the right of the corridor. He pulled a key out of his pocket and unlocked it.

It was a small room; more of a large cupboard. On both sides were racks filled with clothes on hangers. Lined up on a shelf above were shoes.

The clothes were not the sort you'd normally see the Scotland Yard officers in. There were big army coats and shaggy sheepskins; bright paisley shirts and flared jeans. Old grandad shirts with the collars off. Tie-dyed cotton waistcoats and short-sleeve T-shirts.

'Jesus. Pantomime,' said Breen, picking up a pair of pink-tinted glasses from a box on the floor.

'It's for undercover,' said Carmichael.

'You're just a bunch of bloody kids, aren't you?'

Carmichael said, 'You know the Roundhouse?'

'The old engine shed?'

Up at the north end of Camden, the circular brick house had once contained an engine turntable. In the days of steam they had serviced the trains there. Over the last few years, British Rail had phased out the last of the coal-fired engines, leaving the building to become derelict.

'They've been using it for parties. It's where tonight's concert is. Odds are someone there will know if Afghan's been around. It's a small scene. Everyone knows everyone. You never know. He might be there himself.'

'Tonight?'

'We even bought you a ticket.' Carmichael grinned. He opened his wallet and pulled out a small printed piece of paper. 'Middle Earth', it said. 'Admit one. £1/-/6'.

'I know, I know,' said Carmichael. 'Fucking hippies. Here. Try this one on.'

He pulled out an embroidered sheepskin coat.

'No bloody way.'

'Keep your hair on. What about this?' he said, offering a heavy grey army coat. 'NVA. East German army. Very trendy, I've heard.'

He held it up for Breen to put on. It was too big.

'Perfect,' said Carmichael. 'You look like a twat already. We got some wigs too, if you like.'

'Not in a million years,' said Breen. He reached into his jacket pocket. 'By the way. This is the piece of paper I found at Milkwood's house yesterday.'

'God, I was embarrassed standing there in front of Mrs M with all those wank mags. "Sorry about your husband, Mrs Milk." ' He took the paper from Breen.

'Any ideas?' said Breen.

Carmichael frowned. 'What is it? A code of some kind?'

'I don't know. But I suppose it was something he wanted to keep safe. That drawer was his secrets. What do you think it is? Bank accounts?'

'No.'

'National Insurance numbers?'

'Too many digits.'

Breen left the room with the army coat, a woollen check shirt and a pair of flared jeans.

'Fancy a quick one in the pub before you go?'

Breen shook his head and left, carrying the clothes in a large brown-paper parcel. He wanted to get home.

SIXTEEN

The bus back into town was full of giggling Girl Guides. They disembarked noisily at Tottenham Court Road, satchels swinging. He changed at Angel but on Sunday only a handful of buses ran. He had to wait an hour in the cold for another to take him towards Stoke Newington.

When he arrived the milk bill was lying on the mat inside the door. Door still open, he picked it up. That's when noticed another note lying underneath, written in blue biro on the inside of a torn-up packet of Player's No. 6.

His eyes took a while to focus on it.

Where are you? I am in London. Need to explain. It's V V important!!

I am at the YWCA. H.

Helen? She had been here. She had been looking for him. If he hadn't stayed at the section house last night he would have found her.

Just seeing her handwriting made him grin. She was alive and she was in London. Whatever she had done or been involved with, she had tried to seek him out.

The phone book had been propping the kitchen door open. He picked it up and flicked through until he found the Young Women's Christian Association. They were in Portland Place.

'All our guests have left. They have to be out by nine thirty a.m.,' said the woman.

'When are they allowed back in?'

'We are not an introductions agency, sir.'

'It's important. I am a policeman.'

'I can check the register for her name, but she is no longer here, sir.'

The milkman usually dropped his bill round with the Sunday delivery. Helen's note must have been put through his door before that. Breen ran upstairs and knocked on the door.

The young woman opened the door. 'How was the meat loaf?' she asked. 'Was it awful?'

'Was there a young woman knocking on my door yesterday?'

'Aren't you the lucky one?' She smiled at Breen. She was dressed in an orange trouser suit and was holding a pair of crochet hooks with some wool. 'Is she your girlfriend? Yeah, she knocked here yesterday afternoon.'

He would have been with Carmichael, in Surbiton.

'She wanted to know where you were. She was trying to call you, she said. I wasn't sure how I was expected to know. Did you not come home last night then?'

'How did she look?'

She shrugged. 'She just asked if I'd seen you. I told her to come in and wait, but she didn't want to.'

When she'd closed the front door, Breen stood on the step for a few seconds.

Downstairs in his flat, he put on the pan for coffee and paced around the living room as he waited for it to boil.

The phone rang.

Breen ran from the kitchen, grabbing at the handset and knocking it to the floor, wrenching his bad arm as he bent to pick it up.

'Helen?'

A pause on the line. 'Why did you think I was . . . ?' It was Carmichael. 'Have you heard from her?'

'Yes. She left me a note.'

'She's in London?'

'She was at the YWCA last night. She tried to come and see me but we were out.'

'You should call CID now,' said Carmichael. 'Let them know.'

'Why did you ring?'

'I just wanted to say, you don't have to go through with it tonight if you don't want. Just because Pilcher wants you to. Fuck him, you know?'

Breen stood in front of the full-length mirror in his father's old room dressed in the full outfit.

He felt ridiculous.

He tried one of his father's woollen caps on to hide his hair, but it made him look even older than he felt right now. He growled at himself in the mirror. These people dressed in hand-me-downs as if they owned nothing but they were wealthier than Breen had ever been at their age.

He tried running his hand through his hair to mess it up a little, but even with a month's growth in Devon, it still looked too orderly.

It would have to do. It wasn't his idea, anyway.

He put on the greatcoat. It smelt of mothballs.

He looked around the cul-de-sac. He was wondering if CID had put a plain-clothes copper on surveillance in case Helen turned up, but he couldn't spot one. Which was something at least.

Before leaving the flat, he pinned a note to his front door:

Helen. I will be back. PLEASE wait for me. Important.

He was about to leave the cul-de-sac when he had second thoughts and returned to knock on the front door of the flat above.

The young pregnant woman opened the door again.

The first thing she did was laugh. 'Are you going to a fancy dress?'

She had changed, now she was wearing a yellow kimono, tied just above the bump on her belly.

'It's a long story,' he said. 'I was wondering if you could keep an eye out for the lady who knocked on my door yesterday. If she comes while I'm out, will you give her my spare key?'

'Oh, my God,' she said, hand on mouth. 'Are you supposed to be, what, undercover?'

Breen looked away. 'As a matter of fact, yes.'

'What are you supposed to look like?' she said, giggling.

Breen sighed. 'I am supposed to look like someone who would be going to a concert at Middle Earth.'

She put her head on one side. 'This is priceless. I'll tell you what you look like.'

'What?'

'A bloody copper trying to pretend to be cool. They'll spot you a mile off.'

'Thanks,' he said. He held out his front door key. 'Will you give it to her?'

'Are you going to bust it? For drugs or something?'

'No. Nothing like that. It's complicated. There's someone I need to find. Somebody who may have some evidence about a murder. And I know no one will talk to me if they think I'm a . . .'

'A pig.'

'If you like.'

'I'm sorry,' she said. 'I can't stop laughing. You look so funny.' She frowned. 'Tell you what. Come on in. I can do stuff like that.'

'Thanks. I'll be fine.'

'No, you won't. You look ridiculous. Besides, it'll be fun.'

'Where's your husband?' Breen asked.

'Boyfriend,' she said. 'He's out.'

Breen hesitated on the doorstep.

'He'll be cool,' she said, holding the door open. 'Come on. I'm getting cold.'

He followed her inside, down a corridor that they had wall-papered with pages from the *Beano* into a living room. She scooped a magazine off one of the two huge beanbags and dropped it onto an ashtray on the floor to cover it.

'My name's Elfie. Short for Elfrida. What's yours?'

When he told her, she said, 'That's an unusual name. Sit down. I'll get some stuff.'

'What stuff?'

'Stuff to stop you looking like an undercover narc.'

They had painted the living-room walls a dark yellow. He chose the old Chesterfield covered in Indian cloth, rather than the white fibreglass armchair or a beanbag.

A reel-to-reel tape recorder played some fluty jazz through a pair of huge Wharfedale speakers. From the ceiling rose hung a huge white paper lampshade. A large art nouveau poster of a half-dressed woman on a bicycle was Sellotaped to the wall, one corner hanging down.

She returned with what looked like a black pencil and a bottle of dark red nail varnish.

'Give me your hand,' she said.

'No.' Breen put his hands behind his back.

'Don't be so sissy,' she said, sitting on the floor in front of him.

'The whole place will be full of freaks. Nobody will look twice if you look like one yourself.'

'I can't wear that,' he said.

'That's precisely why you should. Zen logic. No copper would paint his nails. Hand,' she said.

He gave her his right hand, and she started painting the nails one by one.

'You have nice hands,' she said. 'You should be an artist.'

Elfie concentrated, chewing on the inside of her cheek as she painted his nails. As she worked, legs bare on the carpet, he realised her kimono was slightly open at the top. He looked away.

'What about my shoes?'

Knowing that his brogues would look too polished, he had taken an old pair of his father's plain boots that he hadn't thrown out yet.

'They're OK, I reckon,' she said. 'It's crazy you're a policeman, living right underneath us.' She blew gently onto his hands.

'Why's that crazy?' he said.

'Because you're the man,' she laughed. 'You know. Authority. Other hand. Don't smudge it until it's dry.'

He looked at his hand. The nails were all painted so deep a red it was almost maroon. She started on the other one.

'I'm not authority,' he said. 'I'm just a policeman.'

'Really?' she said.

'I'm just doing a job that needs doing.'

'So when you came and knocked on our door and ordered us to turn the music down, you weren't being the man.'

'I'm not the man,' said Breen. 'I just wanted a good night's sleep.'

'Course you're the man. That time you came to our door about the noise, you flashed that police thing with your photograph in it.'

She held his fingers now, keeping them steady.

'Only because I'd asked you before and you didn't do it.'

'Play your own music loud. We wouldn't care. It's cool.' He was looking down again at the ripe curve of her pregnant belly when she looked up. 'Right. Hold still.'

She took the pencil she had brought into the room and licked the end.

'What are you doing now?'

She put her knee on the couch and leaned over him, her face close to his.

'Your eyes,' she said. 'Don't move or I'll end up poking one out.'

'Christ's sake,' he said.

'Shh.'

Staring at the ceiling, where someone had drawn small stars, he felt her thigh press against his as she concentrated.

Standing in the queue on a dark Camden pavement a man in a big black felt hat said, 'If you got any weed on you I'd ditch it, 'f I were you.'

'Sorry?'

The man said, 'Don't look now. Pig. Right behind us.'

When Breen did look he saw a man wearing an embroidered suede sheepskin coat. It was the young red-faced copper who had been at the meeting with Pilcher, trying to look casual, pretending not to notice Breen. He looked hot and uncomfortable in his wig.

The man in the felt hat leaned closer. 'I heard a rumour they're going to raid tonight. You clean? If you're not, I'll help you swallow it, man.'

'Yes,' said Breen. 'I'm clean.'

'Bummer,' the man giggled. 'Worth a try, man.'

At the turnstile a long-haired ticket man said, 'Bands start at midnight.'

The circular engine hall had been stripped bare and seats had been added around the outside of the room. There was loud music playing, strange and modal, all guitars and drums. Globs of coloured water and oil were being projected onto the ceiling.

Breen joined the groups of people milling around. Some were sitting on the floor against the walls, eyes closed. A girl with a round silver spot on her forehead was soundly asleep on the floor next to him despite the music. Were these people on drugs, Breen wondered? Was this what being on drugs looked like?

Despite the fears of the man in the queue on the way in, the air was thick with the oily smell of what Breen guessed was marijuana. The room was dirty too. Old cigarette packets, many torn, lay everywhere. People left empty bottles against the walls, hoping that others wouldn't kick them over.

Upstairs there was a bar. Breen bought a bottle of beer so he would have something to do with his hands besides leave them in the coat of his pockets. One of the rooms off the walkway that surrounded the main floor was offering massages for five shillings. Another was selling cakes. A sign read: 'These are NOT hash cakes. DON'T EVEN ASK.'

Breen asked the woman running the stall, 'Do you know a man called Afghan? I'm supposed to find him here?'

She looked him up and down and said, 'Never heard of him.'

At around midnight a band came on and started playing long, complicated songs on keyboards and fuzzy guitars.

Breen came across the man in the floppy hat sitting on a blanket on the main floor, nodding his head to to the music. 'Amazing,' the man said.

Breen squatted down and asked, 'Have you seen Afghan anywhere?'

'You looking to score? There's a guy backstage selling some green tabs. They're good.'

Breen had no idea what he was talking about, but nodded anyway.

'I just have a message for Afghan.'

'Haven't seen his arse round here in a while. Maybe he's on the road. Wasn't he going to Morocco?'

A group of young women who were dancing together at the back said they thought they'd seen him, but they didn't seem sure. A bearded man dressed in a black leather jacket said, 'Afghan? Why would I know him, man?'

'I was just asking if you'd seen him tonight.'

'I don't know who the fuck you're talking about,' he said, and turned away.

Breen gave up for a while and just observed. A young man was sitting on the floor, against the old brick wall of the building, licking cigarette papers. A woman sat next to him saying something in his ear as he concentrated, carefully attaching the papers together. From a tobacco tin, he pulled a lump of something dark and held it above a lighter for a few seconds. Breen looked around. Nobody else seemed to think what the man was doing was out of place. The woman was large, with heavy eye make-up. She looked a little bored, if anything, watching her boyfriend carefully rolling the joint.

Helen Tozer would probably love it here. She would be one of those dancing in the space in front of the stage, lit by the lamps which projected coloured blobs of oil through the haze of smoke. Moments like this made Breen feel utterly disconnected from this new world.

The boy lit the joint and sucked. The pale smoke drifted around his head, then he blew out of his mouth slowly. Breen half expected him to slump into a narcotic coma, or perhaps leap up, wild-eyed. But he looked much the same as he did before he'd smoked the drug; he just passed the long cigarette to the woman.

★

There was a phone near the box office. He put one finger in his ear and dialled the number for the YWCA.

'Is there a Helen Tozer staying there tonight?'

'I can't hear you,' complained the woman on the other end of the line. 'There's too much noise.'

A thump of drums drowned out everything.

'Helen Tozer,' he said again. He spelled out the letters, one by one. 'It's very urgent.'

After he'd put in another pile of pennies, she came back on the line and said, 'No. No one of that name.'

It was after two in the morning that the main band came on. By now the place was full, the floor was crowded. The band were all very thin and had beards, but dressed more neatly than the crowd who were now standing on the floor in front of them. They seemed to be playing music that was caught between a Californian trippiness and a kind of very cartoonish Englishness. It was so loud Breen wanted to put his fingers in his ears but he knew he'd look out of place if he did, so he stood, nodding his head and wishing the music would finish.

Someone was tugging at the back of his coat. He turned. The man in the floppy hat was swaying slightly, a goofy look on his face.

'I'm so stoned,' he said.

Breen nodded.

He said something else.

'I can't hear,' shouted Breen.

The man pulled Breen by the lapel of his coat and said, right into his ear. 'I said, the General is looking for you.'

'Who?'

'The General. You know, friend, the General.'

Breen looked around. All the other people's eyes were fixed on the stage, faces changing colour in the lights.

'I don't know him. Who is he?'

'The man who has soldiers all over him.'

Breen looked at the man. He was giggling now, his pupils like saucers.

'Right,' said Breen.

'Little soldiers marching up and down. Left right, left right.'

Breen left him idiot-grinning, waving his fingers in front of the lights. So that's what someone on drugs looked like. Breen knew what it was like to feel out of place; it was something he had lived with for as long as he could remember. But he had never felt as out of place as he did here. None of this was his world.

There were flashing lights. A squeal of feedback filled the hall. People cheered. Some annoying saxophone was playing the same phrase over and over again. The voice of the thin man on the stage had a strange tremolo that was getting to Breen.

He rubbed his forehead. This morning's headache had returned. The entire front of his skull throbbed. He should head home. He had tried, at least.

'This one's called "Hey Mr Policeman",' said the singer.

A huge cheer went up. The guitarist was trying to tune his guitar, crouching down by his amp. A squeal of feedback emerged.

'Do we have any policemen in the Roundhouse tonight?'

Now the hall was full of boos.

Breen looked around the crowd to see if there was any sign of any other undercover police from the Drug Squad, but he couldn't see any, not even the red-faced boy he'd spotted earlier.

The band had started playing a drawn-out, bluesy riff. How long could these people endure this noise? There seemed to be no end to their enthusiasm for it.

If Breen listened to any music, it would be jazz. As a younger man he and Carmichael had gone to see the Jazz Couriers or Charles Mingus on his rare London visits. Though these blaring electric chords shared the same kind of ambition, to make something entirely new, they seemed too leaden, too deliberately simple. It was as if they were saying, 'Anyone can do this. Anyone can be part of this.' An ideological statement of the age of Aquarius. The line between performer and audience was blurring. Everybody was an artist now. He hated this idea. It seemed so dull, so unambitious.

A tall young woman in front of him moved her hands in the air in strange, expressive shapes that reminded him of someone trying to walk through cobwebs. Was she audience or performer? Or was she just on drugs? Were they all on drugs? How could you tell?

A man in an army coat walked past. It seemed to be covered in matted fur. Breen looked again and realised that the coat was adorned with little bits of plastic. He looked again, closer, and saw toy soldiers. Hundreds upon hundreds of small plastic toy soldiers, carefully attached to his coat with small safety pins.

It took him a second.

By the time he had made the connection, the man had pushed into the crowd closer to the stage. Breen went after him, shoving his way between the swaying hippies. A young man with a woollen hat over his long hair glared at him. 'Chill out, man.'

Breen ignored him, looking to the left and right. He was there, talking to a woman with a long, flowery dress on.

He reached out and grabbed the man's coat. 'Excuse me,' he said. 'You're the General?'

The man saluted. Breen now saw that the front of his coat was covered in medals too.

He leaned towards him, shouting above the roar of music, 'I was looking for Afghan.'

'I heard.' The man tugged him away to one side of the hall. He had one of those faces where smooth skin sat tightly on the skull. Small crow's feet by each eye deepened as he peered at Breen. 'Who are you?'

'Just a friend of a friend. I need to find him. I need to get a message to him.'

'Afghan's long gone, man. Long gone. On the road. What's the message?'

'He was here?'

'No. He's gone. *Disparu*.'

The riff they were playing was getting louder and louder.

'Left London?'

'Maybe. What's the message?'

'I'd tell you if I could, but I can't. I have to speak to him face to face. It's important.'

The General looked him up and down, then said, 'How important?'

'Life and death.'

'Crazy.'

Breen shook his head. 'No. I'm serious.'

The General nodded. 'His old lady's kind of been looking for him too.'

'His mother?'

The General was laughing now, all his little soldiers shaking. 'His girlfriend. Penny. You know Penny?'

Breen shook his head. 'I'm not from round here,' he said.

'If you were from round here, I'd know you,' said the General. 'So you have this message for him. Is it about the cops?'

'The cops?'

'They're always after him, man. They're crazy.'

Breen said, 'No. A friend of his is dead. I need to tell him.'

190

The General nodded. 'You should tell Penny. She's freaking out about him already.'

'Freaking out?'

'You know Afghan. Sometimes he just goes places. On the road. He's always on a journey, right? Only she has these bad vibes about him.'

'Vibes?'

'You know. She does the *I Ching*. Tarot. Something like that. I don't know. Want to split?'

'What?'

'Now. We'll go and see Penny.'

'At this time of night? Will she be awake?'

'It's early, man. Besides, Penny doesn't sleep much since Afghan disappeared. And she's always got some gear on her.'

Breen looked at his watch. It was approaching three in the morning.

The General's car was parked by Camden Lock. He drove an Austin A30, painted to look like camouflage.

'Want some speed?' he said, holding up a small packet of neatly folded paper.

'No. I'm fine.'

'Suit yourself.' They were parked off the road on a piece of derelict land that was used on Sundays as part of the market. The General started the engine, but instead of driving away, he reached across to Breen's side of the car, opened the glove compartment and pulled out a mirror, which he set on his lap.

He tipped a little of the white powder onto the mirror and produced a razor blade and started chopping at the powder.

'Can I borrow a quid?' he said.

Breen pulled a pound note from his wallet and the General rolled it carefully into a tiny tube, then leaned over the mirror and sucked up the first of two neat lines he'd made into his nose.

Breen watched, appalled and fascinated, trying not to look as if this was the first time he'd seen anybody do this.

The General held out the pound note towards him.

'You sure you don't want some?'

Breen shook his head.

'I understand. Want to stay mellow, right?'

'Right.'

The General leaned down again and sniffed the second white line, then wiped his nose with the back of his hand and passed the note back.

As Breen unrolled it and returned it to his wallet, the General crunched the car into gear.

'Let's go then.'

Breen looked ahead, anxious not to betray any reaction to watching a man take drugs so openly. He knew nothing of this world. But the man who called himself the General seemed to assume that he would find this behaviour perfectly normal.

The man jolted the car into motion and set off down Camden High Street, driving straight across Parkway even though the lights were still red.

SEVENTEEN

The General was right. She was still awake.

She opened the door of the house off Ladbroke Grove barefoot, in a long dark cotton dress.

'Oh. It's you.' She leaned forward and kissed the General on the cheek.

'Who's this?' she asked, looking at Breen. She was young and blonde and wearing a strange oily scent that reminded Breen of damp earth.

'A messenger,' the General said. 'I don't know his name.'

'Cathal,' said Breen.

'You got any hash, love?' asked the General. 'I'm speeding my socks off. I need to come down. Urgently.' He giggled.

She opened the door wide and they walked inside.

The flat was messy, but in a comfortable way. An old bicycle, painted yellow, scuffed the wall it lay against. A huge poster of Humphrey Bogart was pinned above it. She led them through to a large kitchen at the back of the house. There were scarves draped over lampshades to keep the light low in the house. The air had the thick, sweet scent of burnt-out incense mingled with the smell of cooking.

'You hungry? I made some soup,' she said.

The General shook his head. 'Too much whizz,' he said.

The kitchen was somewhere she clearly spent a lot of time. There were shelves full of rice and lentils. Strange Buddha figures, embroidered onto brightly coloured cloths, hung from the wall above a large cooker. Strings of cotton flags crossed the ceiling. At the back of the room was an old pine table, surrounded by mismatched chairs.

She opened a drawer in the table and pulled out a silver tin and handed it to the General. Inside was a lump of what looked like brown stone. He sat at the table, then pulled it out and sniffed at it.

'Nepalese?' he said. Digging in his pocket, he pulled out a small glass pipe and started crumbling pieces into it. 'Put some music on, Penny. It's too quiet.'

'No,' she said. 'Not now. I like it quiet.'

Breen stood awkwardly, watching. Penny looked at him and said, 'Who are you?'

'Cathal,' Breen said again.

'You said that already,' Penny said. 'I meant what are you doing here?'

The General said, 'He was at the Roundhouse, telling everyone he was looking for Afghan.'

From his coat pocket, Breen pulled out the photograph of the three men and handed it to the woman. The General held a lighter above the pipe and sucked hard.

She took the photograph, looked at it and sighed. 'Who was on?'

'Family,' the General said, his voice pitched higher as he held in the smoke.

She wrinkled her nose, as if she didn't like them. 'Haven't been there since Jim Morrison played. Where did you get this?' she demanded.

'Bill Milkwood's wife gave it to me,' said Breen. 'I'm looking for Nick.'

'He's dead now too, isn't he?' she said, looking at the picture. 'Bill, I mean.' She didn't seem particularly concerned.

'Who's dead?' said the General, passing the pipe to Penny, who pulled out a chair and sat down beside him. She didn't answer.

'An old friend of Afghan's,' said Breen. 'What do you mean, "too"?'

It was Penny's turn to suck. She held the smoke in her lungs a minute. 'He wasn't a friend of Nicky's,' she said, as she exhaled smoke through her nostrils. 'Nicky hated him. Just someone Nicky knew. From the old days.'

'You heard about him being killed?'

'Killed?' said the General, coughing. 'Wow. Bummer.'

'It's OK. He's been reborn.' She held out the pipe to Breen.

He shook his head. 'I'm OK, thanks,' he said.

'Take some. It's good.'

'Really, I'm fine.'

She handed the pipe over to the General and smiled at Breen. 'You don't fool me,' she said. 'That make-up and those nails.'

'Don't I?' said Breen.

'You're not on the scene.'

'I'm a policeman,' he said.

The General had just taken a long pull on the pipe and erupted into coughing. 'Bloody hell.'

Penny leaned over and thumped him on the back. 'I thought so,' she said.

Breen said, 'I'm trying to find who killed Bill Milkwood. Nothing else. I'm not here about drugs. I'm not even here officially.'

'Christ. I thought there was something funny about you. Jesus. Jesus. Jesus.'

Penny just stood and said, 'I'm going to make some tea.' She switched the electric cooker on and went to fill a kettle.

'I can't believe I brought the bloody fuzz to Afghan's house. What a fucking moron. He'll kill me.'

'Where is Nicky?' asked Breen.

Penny said, 'Why? Why do you want to know?'

'Because he may know something about who killed Bill Milkwood.'

She nodded.

'Nicky's dead too,' she said simply.

'I mean, you don't actually know that for certain,' said the General. 'You don't really know it, do you? What if he's just lying low? Sometimes he just, you know, vanishes.'

'He's dead. I know.'

Breen looked at his watch. It was very late. 'Are you his . . . lover?'

'Yes. Was his lover, I suppose. He left. Went. Never came back.'

Breen was puzzled. 'Did he pack a bag or anything? Did he leave a note?'

'I don't really know,' she said. 'He may have done. He came and went as he pleased. He was never here that long. But he always came back.' She stretched up and took a tin from the shelf. 'Chamomile or lapsang?'

Breen looked around the kitchen. It was messy, but not chaotic. 'How can you not notice whether he packed a bag or not?'

'I was in Afghanistan,' she said. 'It was getting towards winter so I came home. When I came back he was gone. No note. Nothing. He'd been planning a trip to Morocco.'

'A fucking policeman.'

She leaned down to the General and said quietly, 'It's OK. Stay calm. You're peaking. Nothing bad is going to happen.'

'Right,' said the General, reaching for the pipe.

She took it from his hands. 'Not now. Later. You need to chill out. I'll give you some tea.'

'OK.' He nodded. 'Tea. Sounds nice.'

The kettle began to bubble. She spooned black tea into a large

196

pot. Even if it was in a city, something of the warmth of the kitchen reminded Breen of the Tozers' farm.

'This was when?' he asked.

'It would have been back in November, only I got ill in Afghanistan. They said it was dysentery, but I don't think it was.'

'The shits. Oh, God,' muttered the General.

'I was so sick I spent two weeks holed up in a freezing shed in an olive grove near Herat hallucinating, so I didn't make it back until a few weeks ago. By then he was gone.'

'He's probably still on the road,' said the General. 'Morocco. Goa. You know.'

The tea steamed in mugs. Breen took one and put his hands around it.

'I don't think so,' said Penny eventually. 'He's moved on.'

'Moved away.'

'Moved on to another existence.'

Breen sipped the tea. It was rich and smoky. He didn't normally like tea but this tasted good. 'Did he have another girlfriend?'

She laughed suddenly. 'You're quite beautiful, for a policeman,' she said.

The General snorted. 'Look out, piggy. She likes you.'

'Moved on to another life,' she said.

'Why?'

'Have you read *The Tibetan Book of the Dead*?' she asked.

The General giggled. '*The Tibetan Book of the Dead*. It's an acid trip.'

'In Herat I was close to death. My soul left my body for a while. I met Nicky in the afterlife.'

Breen said, 'What do you mean?'

'I met his soul. I saw him clearly surrounded by light. He was passing on.'

'Wow,' said the General. 'You saw Afghan?'

'It's just like it said in the *Book of the Dead*. His soul was free. He was emancipated. He could go anywhere. He came to me. I was blessed. I tried to talk to him but he was talking in another language.'

'You dreamed you saw him?'

'It wasn't a dream. It was real.'

Breen said, 'But you don't know he's dead. Not for certain.'

She was still smiling, but tears were coming down her cheeks now. 'I do,' she said. 'I know for certain. He always came back. Or sent a message. There has been nothing.'

Maybe it was the fumes of whatever they had been smoking getting to his head. Could you inhale them just by being in the same room? Breen's brain was fizzing. If Nick Doyle was dead, he had disappeared in November, then.

'He stared at the sun, man. Afghan stared right into the sun. I saw him do it.'

'Hush, baby,' said Penny. 'You need to rest now.'

The General sighed. 'One more pipe?'

'You've had enough, baby.'

'Just a little bit?'

'Shh,' she said.

'Maybe I could sleep. Can I crash here, Penny?'

She stood. 'I'll find an eiderdown. You can sleep on the couch in the front room.' She told Breen, 'Pour yourself another cup of tea.'

When she was gone, arranging a bed, Breen stood and walked to the shelf. There was a picture in a frame, draped with a string of faded dry marigolds. Penny stood with a bare-chested man in front of a temple. Between them stood a bearded sadhu in an orange robe. Penny was smiling. The bare-chested man was Nick Doyle. In contrast to Penny's bright smile, his expression was serious, his gaze almost vague, as if he was looking beyond whoever was taking the picture.

Seeing him tanned, dressed in loose cotton trousers, a pair of leather sandals on his feet, he looked very different from the photograph he had already that had been taken at least a decade before. His face was much thinner and wore an intense, serious expression.

Penny came back into the room.

'Is this your house?'

'My parents' house. They're dead,' she said.

'I'm sorry,' said Breen.

'Best thing they ever did was die,' she said. She pulled up a chair next to him and sat cross-legged on it. 'So,' she said. 'Tell me what you know about Nicky. I miss him. I like to hear anyone talking about him.'

'But I don't know anything about him,' said Breen. 'I was hoping to find out.'

'He was amazing. He had an ancient soul. You know what that is?'

Breen shook his head.

She said, 'Have you got any cigarettes? I'm out.'

Breen offered her one, and took one for himself. He had already smoked his ration for the day but anything this late counted as tomorrow, he supposed.

'When did you meet him?'

'It was in the Amir Kabir in Tehran. It's a hotel, of sorts. A doss-house, really. I was heading out to India, but our bus needed fixing. Tehran's such a dump. The city's full of Yanks. They run the place. Nicky was just on his way back from Kashmir. I fell in love with him there and then. He was different. All the other travellers were all talk, talk, talk.'

Tehran and Kathmandu. Breen realised that he hadn't even made it as far as Ireland, yet these people, only a few years younger than himself, were travelling the world.

'Travelling was like a competition with them. They'd talk about rat-infested beds they'd slept in, or cockroaches in their food, like they were boasting. "I was beaten up by Turkish police." "I ate rat in Delhi." Nicky was different. He didn't talk much at all, in fact. It's like he was on a higher level.'

'But he was smuggling drugs?'

She shrugged. 'What's so bad about that? Besides, he didn't take drugs himself any more. He didn't need to,' she said. 'But he turned lots of people on.' She was talking about him in the past tense, he noticed.

'He didn't take drugs?'

'No. He was already there. He had been stripped to the bone. We only get a glimpse of the light sometimes. He saw the light all the time.'

She picked up the pipe and the lump of dope and started breaking small pieces of it with long fingernails.

'I shouldn't be here if you're doing that,' said Breen.

'Arrest me, then,' she said. 'I don't really care. I don't care about anything.'

'What do you mean, stripped to the bone?'

She licked small pieces of the hash from her fingers. 'He only talked about it the one time. In Cappadocia I think it was, a bunch of American draft dodgers started talking about how the Viet Cong tortured their victims. They made them watch while they killed their children and raped their wives. This was the war they escaped by leaving America. Nicky just said, "I have seen that."'

'He said that? When? Did he talk about that?'

'He didn't have to say when. We all knew it was true. "I have been to the Gates of Hell," he said. You read William Blake?'

Breen shook his head.

'Blake is beautiful. He talks about the Gates of Hell. Meeting the devil. Anyway, it was obvious Nicky was telling the truth. We all believed him.'

Breen blinked. 'Weren't you curious what he meant?'

'Of course we asked. But he didn't say any more. Like I said, he didn't need to. His soul had been scoured clean. That's what he was like. What about the *Book of the Dead*? You read that?'

'No.'

'You should. Then you'd understand. Nicky had already been right to the edge of experience.'

Breen blinked. 'I don't understand.'

'I don't expect you would,' she said.

'What did you like about him?'

She smiled. 'Do you know why we went travelling? We were looking for knowledge. It's why we take drugs. Why we study religion. You just had to look at Nicky to know he had the knowledge.'

'Do you have any idea why he disappeared?'

'Why?' She shook her head slowly. 'But then I don't really understand why he appeared, either. Or why he stayed. Why? Why do you need to know about him?'

'Because Sergeant Milkwood was killed. The police don't know why. I'm trying to talk to anyone who knew him.'

She laughed gently. 'So you put on make-up and did your nails.'

Breen had forgotten about the eyeliner. There was a small Indian mirror in a hand-painted frame propped on the shelf. He stood up and looked at himself in it. The black around his eyes had leaked onto the surrounding skin, giving him a demonic look.

He tried wiping it with the back of his hand.

'Don't,' she said. 'It looks sort of cool. I like it.'

It was late. He didn't know what he was doing here any more. Nothing she was saying seemed of any use to him.

'And you think he's dead just because you had . . . this dream?'

She shrugged. 'Some heads I know met up with him in Marrakech around Christmas. I found that out a couple of weeks ago. They had a big party. I wish I'd been there. Last thing I heard, he was heading back after that, through Spain. From what people are saying they got him there.'

Breen remembered the photographs from Milkwood's desk at Scotland Yard. Had he recognised the dead man?

'They?'

'Whoever killed him. It's dangerous there. A few people have disappeared this winter. Not just Nicky.'

'Was he bringing drugs back?'

'Probably. People think he was murdered there. He just disappeared, you see. Nobody's heard of him for so long. It's like a network. If you just live in one place you wouldn't understand.'

'Did he ever talk about Kenya?' Breen asked. 'Was that where he had seen suffering?'

'I knew he'd been there, but he didn't ever talk about it.' She lit the pipe and drew on it, closing her eyes.

'Did he ever mention James Fletchet?'

Two streams of smoke blew from her nostrils. She shook her head.

'He didn't really talk about people. He talked about experiences. How to make consciousness-expansion endure in ordinary life. And he didn't need drugs to do it.'

She held out the pipe to him. He shook his head.

'You should. You need to open yourself up. I can tell. I can see right through you. Under the make-up, which is nice by the way, you're just a frightened boy hiding under the bed.'

'What experiences?'

She flicked the lighter and took another pull.

'"The road of excess leads to the palace of wisdom." That's William Blake, too. You need excess.'

'I thought excess just led to the hospital.'

She laughed, smoke bursting from her lungs.

'Oh boy. You're a long way away from where Nicky was. Nicky read a lot of Blake. "If the doors of perception were cleansed every thing would appear to man as it is, infinite,"' she said.

'What kind of experiences?' Breen persisted.

'You want to know? He had been with the devil. Just like Blake said. You could tell, just by being with him.'

Breen said, 'He had been with someone who was the devil?'

'No. The devil himself. He went on journeys all the time. Sometimes he went with his body. Sometimes he went without.'

Breen said, 'Don't get me wrong, but was he mentally ill?'

She laughed again. 'Jung says that if you enter the world of the soul, you are like a madman. Of course people like you might think he was mad. You think all visionaries are mad.'

'What about Alexandra Tozer? Did he ever mention her?'

'Who's she?'

'Someone who died.'

Again she shook her head. 'No. Was it someone Nicky knew?'

'I don't know,' said Breen. 'I'm just trying to make connections.'

'We're all just trying to make connections,' she said.

They sat in silence for a while. She didn't seem to mind. He thought about getting up to go home.

'What about you?' she said, unsmiling. 'What are you really looking for?'

The question annoyed Breen. He was looking for whoever killed Helen's sister. But that was not what she meant. Besides, it wasn't the answer he wanted to give, right now. Why wasn't it enough any more just to answer the obvious questions?

'I'm not looking for the same things as you,' he said.

'Maybe you will be some day. Everybody comes to it in the end.'

He thought about Helen. He thought about the smarmy sergeant who had interviewed him at Scotland Yard: 'So we've got a girl who knows exactly how her sister was killed. And a few days later she disappears and a man connected to the case turns up with exactly the same . . . injuries. And you don't think she's connected?' He was here because he was looking for a way to prove to himself that it couldn't be her. That's all.

He stood. 'I really should go,' he said.

'It's OK,' she said, reaching out to his arm. 'You can stay if you like. Talk some more.'

Breen remained standing. He wanted to be home; had Helen visited again? He wondered if there would be any taxis at this time of night. If not it would be a long walk across London.

She tugged at his arm. 'Please stay. I don't like to be alone. I'll be OK in the morning.'

Breen said, 'That other man's asleep in the living room.'

She let go of his arm. 'No. You're right. I'll be fine.'

'I'm tired,' he said. 'I need to sleep.'

'Sleep with me, if you like,' she said, looking up at him. 'I don't mind.' Suddenly she seemed less like the confident traveller, hitching a ride from Tehran to Kathmandu. She looked lonely.

'I could stay, I suppose,' he said, sitting down again. 'But I'm OK on the couch.'

She reached out a hand and touched his face.

'I could cook you something,' she offered.

'I'm fine,' he said.

She dropped her hand down to his lap and squeezed his thigh, then rubbed.

'Relax,' she said.

He flinched away from her, pushing his chair back.

'Suit yourself,' she said, withdrawing her hand. Instead she turned to the table, picked up the lump of resin and crumbled some more into the pipe.

She said, 'I'm not like this usually. I don't just have sex with people because they're there.'

She smoked her small pipe while Breen sat in silence in her kitchen. The tang of tarry smoke filled the air. Breen wasn't quite sure whether he was just exhausted, or whether the smell of it was making him high as well. His head swam.

'Did you have sex with Nicky?'

She shook her head. 'A few times. But he wasn't very interested. Not like you. I can tell you're interested. You're just too afraid.'

There was a wailing noise. Outside, behind Penny's kitchen, cats fought in the wet alleyways.

He tried to put Helen Tozer out of his mind. Instead he thought of hot countries, far away. Of travelling through them, away from cold, dark London. Unless you were in the army, travelling in foreign countries had never been an option for his generation. Even if they'd had enough money, exchange controls meant you were only allowed to take a few pounds with you out of the country, anyway. It had been impossible for most people. But it would have been good to see temples and minarets, to look at snowy mountains and wide deserts.

After about ten minutes, she laid her head on his shoulder and started to cry. 'It's just I miss him,' she said.

★

He closed the front door as quietly as he could, not wanting to wake her. On the outside of the door there was painted an orange lotus flower which he hadn't been able to make out in the darkness the night before.

On the Central Line, a young woman with a baby in her arms looked at his fingernails, then curled her lip into a sneer and whispered to another woman next to her.

The train was full. It was Monday morning. Breen had taken one hand out of the army coat pocket to grab the strap-hanger that hung from the ceiling of the carriage. Breen glared back at her. Took the other hand out of his pocket.

He must look like some old queen, returning from a night on Piccadilly. Breen had done his best to wash the make-up from his eyes in Penny's bathroom. The water had been cold and the towel was greasy with dirt. But the paint on his nails wouldn't wash off. He felt unclean. He hated being unshaven. His hair was uncombed and his clothes were dirty and slept in, making him feel like a tramp. He closed his eyes.

He had slept fitfully in a small bedroom on the first floor, covered in eiderdowns. The house had been silent, Penny asleep next to him, fully clothed.

He had untangled himself from the bed and roamed the house in the dark early morning. It was large and full of junk. Old wind-up gramophones, dusty drapes and Victorian furniture, sometimes repainted in bright greens and blues. He had looked for any sign that Nicky Doyle, a man in his mid-thirties, a traveller, drug dealer and mystic, a police informer and constable, had ever lived here, but apart from the photograph in the kitchen he had seen the night before, Doyle had left no trace.

He thought about what having sex with Penny would have been like. Underneath the hippie clothes her body would have been good to hold. He would have hated himself for it, but these chances didn't come around often.

A chance for all that pent-up anger at Helen Tozer, for her not being here, to be released. But instead he had held on to it.

When he opened his eyes in the underground train, both women were looking at him now, disdainfully.

And then.

He was just struggling with the key in the front door of his flat, exhausted and wanting to lie down and sleep, when he heard a voice, high and loud.

'Paddy.'

He looked up and blinked.

Helen Tozer. Blue minidress and cup of tea in one hand, big smile on her face.

EIGHTEEN

'Where the hell have you bloody been?'

'Nice to see you, too, Paddy.'

He went up the stone stairs as she came down from the flat above. 'I was worried. Everyone was worried. Have you talked to Scotland Yard?'

She drew her head back and frowned. 'What about?'

'You haven't heard?'

'Heard what?'

'Where were you on Wednesday?'

Helen frowned. 'What's this about?'

'Just tell me where you were first.'

She glared at him. 'Jesus, Paddy. Is that nail varnish you have on? What's been going on?'

Elfie came out of the door after Helen, and explained how she had arrived the night before. When Breen hadn't answer the door, Helen had gone upstairs and knocked.

'She crashed at ours.'

'Crashed?' said Breen.

'Slept.'

'Just tell me where you've been?'

'No need to bloody shout, Paddy. What's so important about Wednesday?'

Elfie said, 'Will you be OK, Helen?'

'We need to talk,' said Breen. 'Now.'

'The look of you and them nails, I think we probably do,' said Helen.

'You don't have to go with him,' said Elfie. 'You can stay at ours if you like.'

'I'll be fine, thanks,' said Helen.

'Please. Where were you on Wednesday evening?' Breen asked again.

She was leaning on the cast-iron railings. 'What is this obsession about Wednesday? Why are you acting so weird?'

'Just tell me.'

'I was in hospital.'

Breen blinked. 'Is there something wrong with you?'

'Oh, thanks for asking, Paddy.'

'Why did you need to go to hospital?'

She folded her arms. 'I'm not going to go discussing . . .'

'A hospital in London?'

'Paddington.'

'Why would you come to London to go to hospital?'

She looked away, down the cul-de-sac. 'Can we talk about this inside?'

'You sure you're going to be all right with him?' said Elfie.

Breen put his key into the door to unlock it. 'And the hospital will confirm that you were in there?'

She stopped halfway down the stairs to the basement flat. 'Why do you want to know that? Why all these bloody questions? I thought you'd be pleased to see me.'

'God, Helen. For once . . .'

'I'm just asking.'

'Tell me.'

'No, actually. They won't be able to confirm that I was there on Wednesday evening. I signed myself out.'

'Were you with anybody after that? Anybody who can confirm that?'

Helen said, 'Not unless someone on the Circle Line recognises me. I went round a few times.'

All three of them stood there, Breen with his key, Helen with a dark look on her face, Elfie looking down at one, then the other. Breen considered for a second, then spoke. 'You,' he called up to the young woman. 'Do you mind joining us down here for a while?'

'You want me to come down there?'

'Please. Just for a few minutes, I am going to need a witness.'

'Is he OK?' Elfie asked Helen.

'All you have to do is be there with us. Just in case the police suspect me of colluding with Miss Tozer.'

'What in bogging hell is going on, Paddy?'

'You haven't spoken to your parents yet, either?' Breen demanded.

Hesitantly, Elfie was descending the stone stairs.

'My parents? No,' said Helen. 'I was meaning to call them but I didn't get around to it yet. Explain, Paddy. Bloody hell.'

'Come in,' he said, opening the door. 'Both of you.'

Elfie stood looking around Breen's room.

'Who are you phoning?' asked Helen.

'The police,' Breen said.

'Why? What's all this about colluding?'

The phone at Scotland Yard was ringing now.

'Paddy. You're behaving very weirdly. What's the nail varnish all about? Have you been wearing make-up?'

Breen held his hand over the mouthpiece. 'Give me a couple of minutes. I can't explain anything until I've done this. Trust me, Helen. Please. You'll understand.'

Breen was relieved to find Carmichael at his desk at Scotland Yard.

'Helen's here,' said Breen.

'And?'

'She has an alibi for Wednesday. But it's not a good one. Will you call CID?'

'An alibi for what?' said Helen. 'This is really making my head hurt. Get off the bloody phone, Paddy What's been going on?'

Breen had his finger in her ear, trying to hear what Carmichael was saying.

'Don't let her go anywhere,' said Carmichael. 'What about last night? Did you find Doyle?'

'Doyle's missing,' he said, and put down the phone.

Helen looked at him. 'So? What?'

Breen said, 'You're a suspect in a murder case.'

'Me?'

Elfie's eyes widened.

'And Scotland Yard CID are going to come and interview you.' He looked at his watch. It was just past 10 a.m. 'I'd guess they'll be here in twenty minutes or so. The less you know about it, the more obvious it'll be that you know nothing about what's happened. For your sake it's best if I don't say anything.'

'Jesus fuck, Paddy.'

'That's why I've asked Elfie to be here. It's for your own good. So we have a witness to say I didn't tell you anything about the case, or tell you to say anything.'

'What bloody case?'

'You know how it works, Helen. I can't tell you any details.' He looked at his nails. Needed a bath. 'What about your parents? Did you tell them you were going to hospital?'

Helen paused. 'You don't actually believe I did anything, do you, Paddy? Whatever it was?'

Breen sighed. 'Of course not.'

'So I've just got to wait here until they come?'

'Bummer,' said Elfie.

'Can I have a cup of real tea? Elfie here makes the most disgusting tea I've ever tasted in my life. Earl Grey. Have you ever tried that? It was like drinking old women's drawers.'

Elfie giggled.

Breen said, 'You told your parents you were coming to stay with me, didn't you?'

'Oh,' said Helen. 'So you spoke to them, then?'

'Yes.'

'Why?'

'Call them now.' He picked up the receiver and held it out to her. 'Tell them you're OK.'

For the first time, she stopped looking angry and started looking worried.

'What am I supposed to have done?'

'Tell them you're OK. Please.'

Breen went into the kitchen with Elfie and put the kettle on while Helen talked to her mother.

'No. I'm at Paddy's now. I was . . . with a friend, that's all.'

He leaned his head against the closed door of the kitchen, trying not to listen.

'I'm so sorry, Mum. I didn't mean to frighten you . . .'

The kettle started to groan and fizz as the water heated. He looked for teabags. There were some old ones in a tin that he kept for guests.

'What's all this about?' asked Elfie.

'Did Helen say anything about where she has been all this time?'

Elfie blushed. 'Yes. But it's private.'

Breen nodded. Another boyfriend? Why not. He looked at his shoes.

When Helen had finished the call he brought her tea on a tray.

'Mum was crying,' said Helen, looking shocked. 'They were questioning her for at least an hour. Why were the police trying to find to me? What the hell do they think they're doing?'

Breen put the tray on the dining table and said, 'I can't say anything.'

She frowned at him. 'Were you something to do with all this, Paddy? I'll bloody kill you if you were. You know what kind of effect that is going to have. The police going round and asking them, of all people, "Where's your daughter, Mr Tozer?" Jesus.'

Breen said, 'I'm not the one who disappeared and then lied about where she was.'

Helen looked stung. She opened her mouth to say something, then closed it again.

Elfie stood by the old mantelpiece puffing away at a cigarette, as if pretending she wasn't in the room.

'Did you actually do these drawings?' Elfie asked.

Helen joined her, leaning towards the sketch Breen had pinned on the wall. He had done it last winter, after she had left the police.

'That supposed to be me?' Helen said, peering at it. A picture of her naked back, in bed, drawn from memory. A long curve, with the shadow of a spine. Next to it, another of her face. Breen felt the colour rising to his cheeks.

'Christ. Is my nose really that big?'

'Quite good, actually,' said Elfie. 'I said you should be an artist.'

Helen stood next to Elfie, putting her cup down on the mantelpiece. 'My face is all squished up. I look like a Chink.'

'I think it's beautiful,' said Elfie. 'You're gorgeous.'

Helen shrugged. 'You need specs.'

'The hospital, Helen. It's important,' said Breen eventually. 'What were you doing there? I need to know what this is about.'

Helen took her tea, looked up at the ceiling. 'If you really want to know, I went to hospital to have an abortion.'

'Oh.'

'Yes. Oh,' Helen said quietly.

Elfie pretended to peer even harder at the drawings.

Breen said, 'You were pregnant?'

'That's usually why you have abortions.'

'With our . . .'

'Who says you've got anything to do with it?'

Breen sat down with a thump on a dining chair. 'Christ. Why?'

'Actually, I can't explain anything,' she said, deliberately mocking Breen. 'Not now.' She glanced at Elfie. 'I don't want to talk about it yet. OK? I'll talk about it later. What the hell did you do your nails for, anyway? Are you on the turn?'

'I was undercover,' he said.

'Undercover? You're on sick leave.'

'It's complicated. I'll explain after . . .'

'I know, I know,' Helen said, holding up her hands.

'I did them, actually,' said Elfie. 'I thought they looked pretty cool.'

'You?' said Helen, looking from her to him and back again.

'She was just helping out,' said Breen.

'I did his eyes too.'

Helen grimaced and said, 'Well, if CID see you with your nails like that, your career is over.' She pulled out a second dining chair and took Breen's hand. 'Pass me my handbag, Elfie,' she said.

'So I just have to wait here?' Elfie said. 'Until what?'

'Until the police arrive.'

'He needs you to tell them how well behaved he was. That he didn't tell me anything about this case. So that when they interrogate me and I say I don't know anything, I'll be telling the truth.'

'A murder.' Elfie was open-mouthed. 'Wow. I mean, you didn't do it, right?'

'Oh, Elfie, don't you bloody start.' Helen took a small bottle of nail polish remover and upended it onto a chunk of cotton wool. 'Stay still,' she said to Breen.

She started dabbing at his nails.

Breen said, 'I can't believe you went and had an abortion without even being decent enough to ask me about it.'

'Keep your voice down,' Helen hissed. 'I've got a headache.'

'Besides. I thought you were on the pill.'

'I was on the pill. It was before Christmas. I was leaving London. There were a lot of parties. I may have been sick or something.' She kicked off her shoes, moved to the next fingernail.

'Without telling me. Without even discussing it.'

'Look. I wanted to talk to you about all this. I know I owe you it. Only . . .' She paused in her work, picked up the cup of tea. 'This isn't really how I imagined the conversation was going to go, you know?'

A car was pulling up outside.

'That'll be them, I expect,' she said, putting the lid back on her nail varnish remover and returning it to her handbag. 'And I've only done half of one hand.'

NINETEEN

Breen sat at Carmichael's desk.

'She'll be fine,' said Carmichael. 'They're just talking to her, that's all. Nobody's going to think she did it. She's a copper, after all.'

Helen was somewhere else in the building, still being questioned by CID. 'And Doyle's bird. She good-looking?'

'Not your sort,' said Breen. 'Trust me.'

'Did she have big bosoms?' asked Sergeant Pilcher.

'I suppose,' said Breen.

'She's John's sort, all right.' Big laugh.

Carmichael said, 'But she thinks Doyle is dead?'

'That's what she says. She thinks he was murdered in Spain. Though she has no proof.'

'So potentially we're looking at three murders.'

'Potentially. Yes. The other two bodies were hidden in woods. Could that be a pattern? Torture and then dumping the body?'

Carmichael said, 'Really, we're no closer, are we?'

'No, we're not.'

Breen waited downstairs for Helen Tozer. People scurried around the lobby looking important. Breen had spent his career working in old Victorian buildings; this place felt more like an advertising agency or a stockbroker's office. It didn't feel like a police station at all.

Helen came out of the lift looking small and tired, fiddling in her shoulder bag for a packet of chewing gum.

He stood. 'Was it OK?' he asked.

She nodded.

'They asked me the same thing over and over. They said I'm to stay in London a few days. They might want to talk to me again.'

'You know how it works.'

'I told them I'd be at yours. I hope that's OK?'

Breen smiled and said, 'I'd like that. Let's ask for a car. They can drop us home.'

She shook her head. 'I've had enough of the ruddy police. Can we catch a bus? I want to feel like I'm in London while I'm here, at least.'

So they walked down Victoria Street, side by side towards the station, where they caught a 38, sitting at the front like schoolkids.

'Will they be OK on the farm, without you?' said Breen.

She nodded. 'They don't even need me there, with Hibou,' she said. She sounded petulant, like a child. 'The CID. They told me about Bill Milkwood,' she said.

'How much did they say about how he died?'

'Not much. Got a cigarette? I'm out.'

She lit it. The bus was mostly empty this time of day. A couple of women sat behind, clutching nylon shopping bags.

'I'm not ruddy stupid,' she said. 'I know there's got to be something that connected me to him. They wouldn't say. You can tell me now, though, can't you? They've interviewed me. Took my statement. It's all done proper, like you insisted,' she said.

'I had to,' said Breen.

'Where would we be if we didn't have procedures?' she said.

'Don't be like that. It was to protect you.'

She lapsed into sulky silence for a while. The British Museum looked oppressively grey ahead, the columns of the portico almost black with London grime.

'Well?' she said eventually.

'He was tortured, just like Alexandra.'

'Just like? How can it be just like? She was a girl, fuck sake.'

The women behind stopped their chatter. Drew in breath.

'The wounds were the same,' said Breen.

'How much the same?'

'Cuts to his . . . nipples. Cigarette burns.'

'But . . .'

'And he had an egg in his . . . rectum.'

Silence now, from behind.

'Up his arse?'

'I know.'

The bell dinged and the bus jerked forward. They were nose to tail with a bus in front; the back of it read: *Typhoo puts the 'T' in BriTain*. They sat together silently for a while. The women behind resumed their chatter.

'So you obviously thought it was me? That I'd read that report and jumped to some conclusion?'

'I never thought it was you.'

'Why not?'

'I just didn't. You wouldn't have.'

She turned her head away from him. 'Maybe you don't know me at all,' she said.

'You wouldn't.'

At Gray's Inn Road, the pavements below were suddenly full of gowns and wigs. People stood on the pavements, files under their arms. Helen turned to him and said, 'You know what this means, Milkwood being killed?'

'Of course.'

'He's alive. Whoever it is. He's around. Maybe even in London still. Somewhere.' She took a huge lungful of smoke and blew it out through her nose. 'This is amazing.'

'Amazing?'

'I mean, for the last four years we've heard nothing about who killed my sister. I don't know what you've done but you've stirred something up. Things are finally moving, at least. There's a chance of finding out what happened. I'm sorry if that sounds callous. I mean, I'm sorry for the guy. But . . .'

She shook her head, still taking it in.

'OK. You gave me a surprise. I got one for you too,' she said.

He looked at her. 'What?'

'I didn't have the . . . you know, procedure.'

'The . . . abortion?'

'I was meaning to. Right up to the day I was booked in. But I couldn't go through with it. That's when I walked out. I went and sat on the Circle Line going round and round until they closed it. I went back the next day, only they didn't have a bed for me any more.'

Breen opened his mouth to speak, but then the bus braked hard and his head banged against the glass at the front. An old man had walked out to cross the street in front of the bus. The bus driver pressed the horn, but the old man just turned and flicked a V-sign at the driver.

'Go on then,' she said. 'Say something.'

'So you're still . . .' He lowered his voice.

'Still what?'

'You know . . .'

'Up the duff? That would be the logical conclusion.'

Breen sat, looking ahead, at the smeary window. 'Why didn't you go through with it?'

'Can we get one thing straight? Right now, I don't want to have to explain anything,' she said. 'OK?'

'Right.' He nodded. 'Only . . .'

'Only nothing,' she said, folding her arms. 'My decision. No one else's. I don't want to explain it to you. To my parents. To anyone.'

His mind started to unfog. She hadn't gone through with it. There was something thrilling about her sitting next to him, pregnant. Like she had tattooed his name beneath her skin. He looked down at her, trying to discern anything beneath the coat she was wearing, beneath those tightly folded arms.

'I don't know why you're looking so fucking happy. Technically speaking, it might not be yours, anyway.'

'What do you mean?'

'Just saying,' she said. 'God. I'm so hungry. I didn't have a proper breakfast.'

Breen cooked for her, then enjoyed watching her eat. Double egg, sausage, beans, fried bread and mushrooms. Three sugars in her tea.

'I'm starving,' she said.

'Eating for two.'

'Will you just shut up?' But she smiled as she wiped egg yolk up with fried bread.

'What are you going to do?'

'I said, I don't want to talk about it. I spoke to Mum. She says I'm OK for a few days. Hibou's coping fine.'

'She's only seventeen.'

'She loves it. It's the making of her. Can I have your toast?' she asked, then sat back in her chair, closed her eyes and belched.

He put an electric fire in the spare room to make it feel less damp and put fresh sheets on the bed. Maybe he should get some flowers, he thought.

She was still sitting in the chair when he came back into the living room. 'So you reckon it was the same person that killed Alex killed Milkwood?' she said.

Breen nodded. 'It looks like it.' He went to his desk and pulled out his notebook. 'And we know that Milkwood and Fletchet were connected. And then there's more.' He liked this. Talking to Helen about a case as he used to. 'This fellow called Doyle. He's a friend too. It's possible he's dead as well.'

'Who?'

Breen flipped the pages. He turned to a sketch he had drawn of Doyle. It was from a copy of the photograph at Penny's house. A muscular, intense-looking man. Breen explained about the third member of the group who had worked together in Kenya.

Helen was leaning over him now, asking questions. 'He became a drug dealer?'

'Yes.'

Helen stared at the drawing. 'So what's all this about?'

Breen said, 'I don't know. But I don't think it's just about your sister. I think it's more than that.'

Helen chewed the inside of her cheek. 'Are they interviewing Fletchet again?'

'They'd be stupid not to.'

They sat in silence for a while. It was frustrating not to be able to do anything.

That night, they lay in Breen's small bed together.

'Just tonight.'

He had his pyjamas on, she had on the prim flannel nightgown she'd taken to hospital.

'You don't even have any decent books to read,' she said. It was true; he had never been much good at reading.

'I was thinking,' he said. 'There's not much we can do until we hear anything from CID, or from Carmichael. I could borrow a police car. We could go for a drive.'

'Where?'

'I don't know. Kew maybe?'

She leaned over the side of her bed and picked up her handbag. 'I've got an idea,' she said, scrabbling around inside it. She pulled out a crumpled envelope.

Breen looked at it, puzzled. 'Where did you get that?'

'You left it behind in the bin in your room at the farm.'

'You went through my dustbin?' It was the envelope Hibou had thrown away. The one addressed to her parents in rain-smeared ink. The unwritten, blank letter was still inside it.

'Yes.' She reached for a cigarette. 'Don't look so offended. If you didn't want me to find it you shouldn't have put it there. Besides. You didn't even tell me about her never writing that letter. I'm the one who should be angry. She never posted it, did she?'

'I found it stuffed into the hedgerow. The letter was blank.'

'Weird. It's like whatever has happened was so bad, she can't even let them know she's all right. God. I've eaten too much,' she said. She lit the cigarette, then looked for somewhere to put the spent match. Breen never smoked in bed. He got up, walked to the living room and returned with an ashtray for her. She was looking at the address on the envelope. 'Why do you think she's so afraid of writing to them?'

'I don't know,' he said, getting back in the bed.

'Why do you think a teenage girl runs away from home?' she said.

'She meets a man from the motor trade,' said Breen. A Beatles song Helen had played him once.

'Think about it, though. She's too bloody scared to even write home,' said Helen. 'What do you think all that is about?'

He switched off the light. Her cigarette glowed in the darkness. The springs creaked as he moved to lay his head on her stomach.

'What's she saying, the baby?' said Helen.

'She?'

'It's a girl. I know it.'

'There you go. Jumping to conclusions again.'

'I'm usually right, though.'

'A girl. Trouble,' said Breen.

'Indeed.'

Breen heard nothing but the soft gurgling of her full stomach.

'Have you told your parents yet?'

'No way.'

'You're going to have to.'

'Stop telling me what I have to do. How do you know I even want to keep her? She'd be better off being adopted, maybe, poor mite.'

'Don't say that.'

'It's OK for you. A bloody baby, God's sake. I can feel her insinuating herself. I can't even keep a decent drink down any more.'

'Why did you want to get rid of it?'

'I don't want a baby. They take over your life.'

'I think I'd like something to take over my life,' he said.

'I know, Paddy.' She kissed him on the cheek. 'Believe it or not, I know. But it's not me.'

He lay on the bed, feeling her fidgeting. He'd been thinking about how he'd say this for a while. 'I'll marry you, if you like.'

She stopped moving. 'Did I just hear you right?'

'You heard.'

She snorted. 'What kind of proposal is that?'

223

'I'm serious.'

'I'll marry you, if you like,' she mocked. 'It's kind of insulting.'

'What do you want then?'

'Because you've got a bun in the oven.'

'I mean it.'

'Leave me alone now. I'm tired.'

He pulled away from her. 'Your trouble is, you're afraid of commitment.'

'Paddy. You don't know what it's like being me.'

'So why did you decide to keep it?'

She didn't answer.

'I can buy you a ring and do all the kneeling business if you'd prefer.'

'Oh, shut up.'

And within seconds she was asleep. Breen lay awake thinking, trying not to disturb her. Was he relieved she hadn't said yes? Or angry? Nothing was ever certain with Helen Tozer. She was like the weather.

Breen bathed twice a week. He lay looking at his body in the warm water. Pale undefined skin. He should exercise more. But his wound was healing well. The long black crust of scab left where they'd opened up his skin to fix his broken bone would fall off soon, leaving just the scar. He was getting back on top of it. A fresh start. A fresh life.

He was going to be a father. He would win Helen round. She would see it was the only real choice she had.

In his dressing gown, Breen rang D Division to ask if he could borrow a car for the day.

'For you, Paddy. Only don't wreck it.'

'Were you singing in the bath?' asked Helen.

'Was I?' said Breen.

He made cheese sandwiches and wrapped them in waxed paper.

'Got any pickle?' asked Helen.

It was the first time he'd been back to the Marylebone station since he'd been shot.

'I'm just going in to say hello,' said Breen when they got there. 'You going to come?'

'I had enough of that lot to last a lifetime,' she said. She waited outside in the late winter sunshine.

The CID room went quiet for a second when Breen walked in. It was Constable Jones who spoke first, glaring. 'Bloody hell. Paddy bloody Breen.'

No love lost.

Breen looked around the room. It was different. All the old dark wood desks had gone, replaced by newer, lighter ones. The buzzing neon tube that they'd all got used to had been replaced. The walls had been repainted for the first time since for ever.

As for the men, he didn't recognise any of them, apart from Jones. The new boss, Inspector Creamer, had cleaned the place out, bringing in his own officers.

'How are you, Jones?' said Breen.

'Been better,' Jones said quietly.

A phone rang. One of the CID men answered it. 'I had been hoping to get sergeant,' Jones told Breen, 'on account of I need the money with the babies coming, only somebody snitched about that dead bloke we found in the cells and now there's an investigation, so that's my chips pissed on. Don't suppose you know anything about it?'

'About what?'

'About why I'm not going to get sergeant because of the investigation.'

'You said babies?' said Breen.

'Doctor says it's ruddy twins.'

Jones's wife was expecting; she was due in May. Breen had to resist the urge to say he was going to be a father too.

'Not sure we can bloody afford them now. Thanks a bunch to someone not a million miles . . .'

Jones had beaten up a prisoner; the man had died. Breen had just made sure the death was properly investigated. But before he could say anything, the door to the inspector's office opened. 'Paddy Breen,' said Creamer, smiling. 'As I live and breathe. Coming back to work, are you?'

'Not quite. I just dropped by to see how the place was falling apart without me.'

'Don't expect you recognise it, do you? New faces. I've ordered new typewriters for everyone too. They're coming next week. Modernising, Paddy. Modernising.'

They offered him tea and biscuits and told Creamer's secretary, a prim young woman who wore a gold crucifix around her neck, to bring it. She switched off her new electric typewriter and went to the kitchen to put the kettle on.

'Frigid,' one of them said, when her back was turned.

'Turned you down, did she? She polished my broom handle nicely the other day.'

'Liar. She wouldn't touch your prick if it lit up and sang "Jerusalem".'

'You should see a doctor about that, pal.'

The office looked busy. He wondered how well he would fit in when he came back to work.

The secretary returned with mugs of tea and a piece of paper. 'Sergeant Breen?'

'Yes?'

'I forgot to say. This woman called in for you. A darkie. I told her you were on sick leave, but she left a message.'

Breen took the piece of paper and unfolded it.

It was a name and a phone number: 'Izzie Ezeoke. 01 242 4344.'

'Anything wrong?' she said.

'No. Nothing.'

'Funny name, isn't it?' she said. 'All them zeds.' Then she turned away back to her electric typewriter. It whirred into life again.

'Thought you'd been shot in the arm,' the man in charge of the cars said. 'You sure you're OK to drive?'

Breen manoeuvred the car out of the garage, round to the front of the station, where Helen was waiting.

'Shunt over, then,' she said.

'I better drive a little way, in case somebody sees.'

'Don't be such a scaredy-cat.'

He handed her the piece of paper. She read the name on it; it took her a second. 'Bloody hell. Where d'you get this?'

Izzie Ezeoke was a ghost from a case they'd worked on together. She was the daughter of a murderer and the lover of the victim; trying to solve her lover's murder was how he and Helen had met.

'She wants me to get in touch,' said Breen, putting the paper back into his jacket pocket.

'What about?'

Breen shrugged.

They drove out of London on the A40, Helen at the wheel, the road clear and the light thin and bright. The odd fleck of green was already bursting into the hedgerows. Breen felt good.

For him, this was something new. The sense of moving forwards after years of being still made him feel he was finally joining the world. Black tarmac empty ahead of him as Helen drove west.

'I called Mum again when you were in the bath,' Helen was saying. 'Don't mind, do you? They're OK. Hibou is taking the cows out of the byres this week. Weather's good enough to save on the fodder bill by putting them in the fields. She and Dad are doing it all themselves.'

'I meant it, what I said yesterday, in bed.'

She said, 'Dad was worried there wasn't going to be enough pasture but now he thinks it's going to be OK.'

'I said, I'd marry—'

'I heard,' she said.

They were almost at Gerrards Cross when she said, 'I'm not marrying nobody just because I'm pregnant.'

'Well, what are you going to do, then?' he said. 'You can't have a baby on your own.'

'Why not?'

'Because . . .' He trailed off. He should be used to this by now, he thought, smiling.

It was an old farmhouse that had been swallowed up by the suburbs. Now it had become grand: a weeping willow by the pond, cherry trees blooming along the pathway.

'Posher than I thought,' Helen said.

People from the city lived around here. Wealthy people who sent their children to public school and gave their girls ponies for Christmas.

'What are you going to learn from being here?'

'I just want to know why she ran away from a nice place like this. She's still frightened of something.'

'It's her business.'

Helen didn't answer. They had parked the police car about a hundred yards away so they wouldn't attract attention. Helen was peering over the hedge. Breen was worried that someone would come out of the house and ask them what they were doing.

'If she didn't post the letter, she wouldn't want us to be doing this,' he said.

On her toes by the hedge, Helen said, 'Why's she so scared of what happened to her here?'

'Sometimes people just run away.'

'Not without reason,' she said.

'All the same. If she doesn't want us to look into it, it's not fair on her.'

'It's not like I'm barging up to the front door or anything,' said Helen 'I just want to see. That's all.'

A woman in tweed came past, walking a Labrador. She called 'Good morning' at them brightly. Ten minutes later she was back, frowning at them this time. It wasn't normal just to linger around here.

'We've seen it. Now what?' said Breen.

'I want to see them. Mr and Mrs.'

'Why?'

'Why is she so frightened of them?'

Breen said, 'I don't know. Isn't everybody a bit frightened of their parents?'

'I was never frightened of mine,' she said. ''Sides, you didn't exactly have a normal childhood, did you? You and your dad.'

Breen said, 'But children run away all the time.'

She turned on him and said, 'Why do children do that? You never thought about that?'

'Because they're kids. Because they don't know better. Because they read *Five Run Away Together*.'

'You're such an idiot, Paddy.'

'You better hope it's not hereditary, then.'

'Not funny, actually.'

The day was bright but cold. Breen's toes were starting to ache. He stamped up and down on the grass, trying to warm them. More people walking dogs. A postman on second delivery, brown bag mostly empty.

'I don't know what you're hoping to see.'

'You're the one who taught me this, you know. You're the one who says you have to look at things for so long that something emerges.'

At around two o'clock a dark-eyed woman in a headscarf emerged from the front door. Helen tossed a coin and won on heads, so she followed her while Breen waited.

The house seemed dead. There was nobody in. Breen tried to imagine the hippie girl from the farm growing up here. It looked so perfect. What was there to run away from?

Nothing happened.

After an hour and a half, the woman in the headscarf returned – Hibou's mother. She was holding the hand of a smaller girl.

Hibou was walking twenty yards behind. 'Oh, my God. Hibou's got a sister,' said Helen when she'd rejoined Breen.

'She looks just like her, doesn't she?'

The smaller sister must only be about twelve or thirteen, but she was already willowy, like Hibou. Helen watched the woman putting the key into the front door. 'Imagine leaving a sister behind as well.'

After that the house was quiet. A light went on downstairs. Gradually more lights came on.

'I don't know what we're expecting to see,' said Breen. His shoulder was starting to ache in the cold.

'What if the same thing that happened to Hibou was to happen to her sister?'

'We don't know if anything happened to Hibou. She's never said anything about it.'

'Come on. Of course something happened.'

'You've got an overactive imagination,' said Breen.

'I was a policewoman, remember?' she said. 'We get to see stuff that happens that you men wouldn't believe.'

'I thought you complained that you never got to do anything when you were a policewoman.'

'The crap that men don't want to do. The family things. You hear all sorts. You men wouldn't touch it with a bargepole. That's why nobody ever hears about it. Ask me, the worst stuff that happens to kids happens behind their own doors.'

'Like what?'

She looked away, then said, 'Like daddies who fuck their kiddies. Or hit them. Women police see that kind of thing all the time.'

Breen said, 'I'm not saying it hasn't happened. But saying it goes on all the time . . .'

'You wouldn't, would you?'

Breen knew better than to carry the conversation on.

'Give it half an hour,' said Helen. 'I mean, we came all the way here. We might as well stay a little longer.'

It was dark by the time the man of the house came back. He saw Breen and Helen first, walking down the tarmac pavement with an old brown briefcase in his hand. 'Can I help you?' He smiled at them. 'Are you lost?'

Helen nodded towards their house and said, 'Is that your house?'

'Yes. Why?'

'Have you always lived there?'

'Yes.'

Helen smiled. 'I've got a younger sister. I was just saying to my friend, I seem to remember coming to a birthday party with her once.'

The man smiled. 'I suppose you may have done. We have birthday parties every year for our daughters. Well . . . used to have.'

'It must have been winter because there was snow, I think.'

'What's your sister's name?' asked the man. 'Perhaps I remember her.'

'Alex,' said Helen. 'Alexandra.'

'We should go,' said Breen, starting to feel anxious. He pulled at Helen's coat.

The man frowned. 'I'm afraid I don't remember her.'

'Is your daughter OK? I'd like to say hello.'

The man coloured. 'She's away,' he said. He looked from Breen to Helen and back, squinting now. 'Who did you say you were?'

'Just a friend of your daughter's,' said Helen. 'She had a younger sister, too. What if I spoke to her? It would only take five minutes.'

'I don't think so. Who are you? Have you seen my daughter?'

Breen tugged at Helen's sleeve. 'Come on. Leave the man alone.'

The man looked rattled. There was a little blob of spittle on his lip as he spoke. 'Actually, I don't recognise you at all. Who are you?'

'I was younger.'

'What's my daughter's name?'

Helen opened her mouth. Closed it again.

'You don't know her,' Hibou's father said, suddenly angry. 'What do you think you're doing, hanging around here?'

They were walking away now, back towards the car. When they reached a curve in the road, the man was still standing there, brief-case in hand, glaring after them. 'Come back here and explain yourselves,' he was shouting.

Helen pulled chewing gum out of her handbag and started munching on a stick of it.

'I'm calling the police,' the man shouted.

'What the hell were you doing?' said Breen, exasperated.

Helen didn't answer. She just marched on ahead to the car and sat in it, waiting for him to catch her up.

TWENTY

Carmichael was in a suit and tie, jacket straining at the buttons. He had arranged to meet them at the Feathers in Westminster. Close to Scotland Yard, it was crammed full of coppers celebrating the guilty verdict in some court case.

'Just a lemonade?' said Carmichael. 'You're pulling my leg?'

'I've got an upset stomach,' said Helen. 'Can't keep nothing down.'

'Miracles never stop. What's wrong with Paddy? He looks like he's swallowed a wasp.'

'He's just in a bate with me about something. So. Tell me about this girl you're going out with,' said Helen. 'Is she nice?'

'I'm not going out with her. It's just a date. That's all. The Rib Room.'

'You sure that's the kind of place she'd like?'

'It's posh. Best restaurant in London.'

'That's what I mean,' said Helen.

'You don't think she'd like it? Oh, God. Here's trouble,' Carmichael said.

'What?' said Helen.

'Pilcher is here,' he said.

Before he could say anything else, Pilcher was sitting down with a pint of mild at their table, in a pale brown suit, side parting carefully Brylcreemed.

'Hello, Paddy. I hear you dressed up all pretty for us the other night,' he said, smiling. 'One of the lads saw you there. Apparently you were quite the looker.'

Helen said, 'Oh, here we go.'

'Oh, hello, Tozer. Back so soon? Thought you'd gone to live down on the farm,' Pilcher said in a mock-yokel accent.

'Know what?' she said. 'You should try a bit of make-up some-time yourself. Anything to make you less ugly.'

Pilcher mock-winced. 'Back in the knife drawer, Miss Sharp,' he said.

'To what do we owe the displeasure?' she said.

'I just need a word with Paddy here,' he said. 'I want him to tell me about this Doyle bloke.'

Breen took half an inch from his lager, then said, 'Like Carmichael told you, I found his girlfriend. Went and talked to her. Apparently he disappeared on his way back from Morocco. She thinks he may be dead.'

'And do you actually believe what this woman says?'

Pilcher offered around his Lucky Strikes. Breen didn't take one; Helen refused one too.

'Why wouldn't I?' said Breen.

Pilcher shrugged, lit his own cigarette with a match. 'Think about what she's got to protect. Her boyfriend is a drug dealer. You're a policeman. Very convenient if he just disappears, isn't it?'

He held the match upright until the flame burned out.

Breen said, 'I don't know if Doyle is dead or not, but I believed her when she said that she thought he was.'

Pilcher blew smoke out through his lips. 'We knew about Doyle's girlfriend. She's a known liar and a drug addict.'

'Known liar?'

'Customs caught her at Dover last year.' He put on a girlish voice. '"Oh my. I was just carrying that shoebox home as a favour to a man I met in Istanbul. I had no idea it was full of cannabis resin." Milkwood fixed it that she got off as a favour to Doyle.'

'That's different,' Helen said.

'But it doesn't make her the most reliable of sources. Maybe he took the money and scarpered.'

Helen said, 'So, let's get this straight . . . The CID are looking into Milkwood's murder. But you haven't actually told them what Paddy says about Doyle, have you?'

'Of course we will,' said Pilcher. 'We just haven't yet.'

Helen snorted. 'You don't like the idea of other coppers digging around in your business, do you?'

Carmichael was talking now: 'What if Milkwood and Doyle, together, were on to whoever had been killing drug smugglers? And that's the reason they're both dead. The Spanish stuff . . . That photograph of the dead guy that the Spanish police wanted us to identify. It squares with what she was saying.'

Pilcher nodded. 'Maybe.' He turned to Breen, 'Sonny Jim here –' he pointed at Carmichael – 'tells me I spend too much time going after users. He says we need to tackle the suppliers. I'm all for that. But I'm more of an economist, see. If you just try and cut off the supply, you'll only increase the price of drugs and make the trade more profitable. The best way to kill the demand is to scare the shit out of the drug addicts. Johnny feels different. But maybe he'd be happier in Customs and Excise.'

Carmichael scowled, but didn't answer.

Helen said, 'I thought you just busted pop stars 'cause you like getting your picture in the papers.'

'Nice to be noticed by the grateful public,' said Pilcher.

'We need to figure out whether Doyle is one of the bodies that turned up in Spain,' said Carmichael. 'We can't find dental records for him. Even if we had them, it could take weeks.'

Pilcher sucked his lip for a while, then reached inside his wallet and pulled out a ten-bob note. 'Here, John. Buy your friends a drink. On me.' And he stubbed the half-smoked cigarette out in the ashtray and stood.

'Is Pilcher always such an arse?' said Helen when he'd gone.

Carmichael looked at his watch. 'Maybe I should go.'

'There's ages yet,' said Helen.

Breen said, 'I can't believe he's still not telling CID.'

Carmichael nodded. 'He's convinced they'll steam in and start to pull in dealers, scaring the horses.'

'Ask me, he doesn't want anyone poking around and finding out how many bungs Drug Squad takes off half the dealers in London,' said Helen.

'That's a total lie,' said Carmichael.

'Slightly under half, then,' said Helen.

'Come on, Helen. It's not like that,' said Breen.

Helen shook her head. 'I don't know which of you has your head further up your own arse, sometimes,' she said. 'It's not exactly a secret. Every bloody hippie in London knows about it.'

'So young. So cynical,' said Carmichael.

''K sake,' muttered Helen.

'Have a drink, why don't you?' said Carmichael.

'I'm off the booze.'

Carmichael said, 'Come on. Have one at least. Right now you're as much fun as a wet toilet seat.'

Helen made a face. 'You should slow down a little. You don't want your girlfriend thinking you're a soak.'

'She's not my girlfriend,' said Carmichael, looking at his watch again.

When he stood to leave, Helen stood too. 'Wait,' she said, and loosened his tie. Then she reached up and mussed his hair. 'You'll be fine,' she said.

Watching them, Breen found himself feeling a little jealous of Carmichael, going out to meet a new girl. New relationships were so much less complicated.

TWENTY-ONE

Helen was in the spare room, fast asleep.

He was in his bed, awake, wishing she were in here with him.

He did not fall in love easily, he thought. It never went well. Once, three years earlier, he had fallen in love with one of the women who came and looked after his father. Her name had been Sarah and she had been round-faced and jolly. Unable to leave his failing father alone, they had spent evenings at his flat playing cards and drinking Madeira, which she loved.

But it turned out she had been stealing cash from him. Small amounts at first, but then more. At first he hadn't wanted to believe it was her. And when he confronted her, she denied it, though there was no other possible explanation of how the money had gone missing.

So he had sacked her. It made him sad to think about it now. He understood so little of other people.

There were several African-looking women in the Students' Union canteen in Bloomsbury. He wouldn't have recognised her from the family photographs he had seen – she had been much younger in them – but she waved at him as he walked through the glass door. He was clearly more conspicuous here as a policeman than she was as a black woman.

Ijeoma Ezeoke sat with a half-drunk cup of black coffee in front of her. She had her mother's height and her father's looks.

If it had been the other way around she would have been beautiful; instead she just looked big-boned. Her black hair formed a large globe around her head. She had a Bic biro stuffed into the tight Afro curls, as if her hair was simply a useful place to leave it.

'You're Detective Breen?' she said.

'Detective Sergeant,' he said.

'You're the one who arrested my father last year?'

He nodded warily.

'No. I'm glad,' she said. 'He deserved it. I hope they put him away for a long time.'

Breen introduced Helen. 'Helen worked on the case at the time.'

Izzie held out a hand without standing. For all her African looks, she spoke in a polite, English public school accent. Breen sat down opposite her.

The student canteen was loud and busy. It seemed to be full of all the nations. Indian women in bright saris. Young African men in suits. Radicals in army fatigues, covered in protest badges. Ijeoma Ezeoke was dressed in a loose African-print shirt and jeans.

'How are you coping?'

'As well as can be expected,' she said.

'I'm sorry about your . . .'

'Girlfriend. My lover,' she said steadily.

He nodded. 'Right,' he said. 'You're a student here?'

'No. I just like it here. I have rented a flat around the corner. I feel less out of place here than in the rest of London. People here don't question who I am.'

Breen looked around at the other students. They were talking loudly, self-confidently, sitting on the edge of tables, clutching folders covered in stickers and doodles.

'How is your mother?'

'I don't see very much of her. She wants to go back home to Biafra, but the war is dragging on.'

'So what was it you wanted to talk to me about?' Breen asked.

'I need to know what happened to Wenna. My father refuses to see me or my mother,' she said. 'My mother doesn't want to talk about it.'

'I understand,' said Breen. Ijeoma had not been in the country when her father had killed her lover.

'He's pleaded guilty. So nothing's going to come out in court about what happened. I feel cheated by that. I don't know how else to find out.'

'Right.' So Breen thought back and tried to sort the details of the case in his head. It already seemed an age ago. Then he started to talk, telling her what he knew. It had been a difficult case. He had got so much wrong. But he tried as best he could to tell the young black woman how her father had killed the girl she loved.

For the bare three or four minutes it took, Ijeoma sat perfectly still, not wiping away the tears that trickled down her cheeks. At one point, a young man in a beret and army jacket came up and said, 'Is he bothering you, Izzie?'

But she just shook her head, cheeks shiny with tears. The young man hesitated, then left, still looking over his shoulder at them as he walked away.

Finally, when Breen had finished, she asked about whether her girlfriend would have suffered.

'I want to be honest with you. I don't know. The only person who could answer that is your father.'

'Yes,' she said.

Breen said, 'That's all I know, I'm afraid.'

She sat in silence for a few seconds, then said, 'Thank you. I appreciate it.'

Helen leaned forward and asked, 'How are you coping?'

'Coping? I'm a lesbian,' she said. 'I'm black. I have a thick skin.'

'I know what it's like,' said Helen.

'Really?' said Izzie, looking her in the eye. 'I very much doubt that.'

Helen looked right back at her. 'I know what it's like when someone you love is murdered. You wake up every day with that burning in your chest. It never goes away,' said Helen quietly. 'But you carry on. Because people do.'

Izzie held her hand out across the table. Helen took it.

Breen looked away. They sat there together for a while in the bustling room, the two young women holding hands across the table.

Eventually Breen said, 'I wonder if you can help us.' Izzie frowned, let go of Helen's hand. 'Do you know anything about Kenya?'

'Why would I know anything about Kenya?' she said. 'Because I'm black? Because I've an African name? I grew up in London. My parents sent me to Cheltenham Ladies' College. I don't know anything about Africa.'

'It was just a thought.'

Helen's hand was still there, halfway across the Formica table. 'Paddy's working on a case,' she said. 'It involves some people who lived in Kenya in the 1950s.'

There were two types of students at the School of Oriental and African Studies: young white people who mostly dressed scruffily in denim and T-shirts, and Asians and Africans who, on the whole, dressed more conservatively – some in suits, others in their local costumes and cloths that made them look like the kinds of dolls you'd find in a gift shop at London Airport. An Indian girl at the next table wore a sari in startling green. The black man talking to her was dressed so formally, in a white shirt and black bow tie, that you might have mistaken him for a waiter.

'What about here? Are there any Kenyan students here?' asked Breen.

Izzie thought for a moment. 'I know a law lecturer from Nairobi who teaches here. He says he wants to sleep with me. I told him I wasn't interested in men, but that only made it more of a challenge to him.'

Helen snorted. Izzie smiled at her.

'Would he talk to me?' Breen asked.

'I can ask,' she said, standing to leave, offering a hand to shake. 'I'll tell him you have a pretty assistant.'

Helen laughed.

After she'd gone, Helen stood to leave, but Breen stayed seated for a moment longer, relishing the strangeness of the place.

'You never wanted to go to university, Helen?'

She said, 'Never was an option, really.'

Breen had not gone to college or university. Instead of waiting for National Service, he had signed up for the police. His father had always wanted him to have a proper education, but he doubted that this was what his father had imagined an education to be. There were posters on the wall: 'Study Group on *I Ching* 2 p.m.'; 'Bakunin vs. Marx: National Conference on Workers' Control'.

A couple put down their trays, sat next to him without asking, and started talking loudly. The boy had long hair and spots. He was earnestly telling the girl, 'The Reynolds Tobacco Company has already patented the brand names of every variety of pot, no shit. Acapulco Gold. Congo Brown. They're building vending machines. Like bubblegum. Just you wait. Capitalism cannot resist profit. In a year they'll be selling pot like Coca-Cola.'

The girl just drank her tea and looked bored.

TWENTY-TWO

Helen was lying on the living-room carpet in pants and bra, looking at her stomach. It was pale and smooth, sinking under the line of the elastic of her light blue knickers, which stretched from bony hip to bony hip. 'I know you're not supposed to see anything there yet,' she said, pinching at her skin, chin on her chest. 'But I feel like a whale.'

Breen looked at her as casually as he could, as if it was normal to have a half-naked woman in his living room.

'You look beautiful,' he said. Skinny as a stick, though.

'Shut up,' she said. But at least she smiled.

'Anybody call?' he asked.

'No one. So I tried phoning Carmichael. I was wondering how his date went. Don't you want to know? Only he wasn't there. Nobody's telling us nothing,' she said, sitting up. 'Was it OK to use the phone? I'll leave some money if you like.'

Breen said, 'Would you like me to take you out to a fancy restaurant, then?'

She frowned. 'Why would you do that?'

She walked into the kitchen, still in her knickers, and started pulling things out of the cupboards. 'Anchovies. Yuck. Got any proper food?'

'Let's get out. There's no point waiting for the phone to ring.'

She stretched up on her toes and pulled down another can. 'What the heck are chickpeas?'

'Let's go to Joe's. I'll buy you lunch.'

'Is that your idea of a fancy restaurant?'

Breen stood in the corridor of Joe's All Night Bagel Shop at the payphone.

'Any news about Doyle?'

'Nothing,' Carmichael said. 'We're working in the dark here, Paddy. I called my mate in CID. He said he's not allowed to talk to me any more.'

'Not allowed? What's going on?'

Helen was standing next to him, grinning. 'Have you asked him about his date yet?'

'Seems like CID think about as much of Drug Squad as Helen Tozer does,' Carmichael was saying. 'They reckon we're too close to our snitches. But I get the feeling they're on to something. I don't know what.'

'They're worried if they tell you anything it'll get back to the drug gangs.'

'That's my guess too. They're sure Milkwood was killed over some deal that went wrong and they're still hauling in every known drug dealer in London. It's killing us. Pilcher is doing his nut.'

'Go on. What's he saying?' Helen mouthed.

Breen put his hand over the receiver. 'Nothing. No news at all.' Then, to Carmichael, 'What about James Fletchet?'

'You don't understand what it's like now, Paddy. CID don't trust us as far as they could throw us.'

'God's sake, go on. Ask him how his bloody date with that girl went,' said Helen.

'I heard that,' said Carmichael.

Breen could hear Carmichael lighting one of his panatellas. There was a dirty old brick wall on the other side of the road. Someone had graffitied 'Just let it burn down, baby' in dripping white paint on it.

He could hear Carmichael blowing out smoke. 'And?' said Breen. 'How was Amy?'

'Helen was right. I shouldn't have taken her to the Rib Room. It was too posh. They wouldn't even let Amy in 'cause she had them stripy tights on.'

'Oh. I'm sorry,' said Breen.

'No. It was fine. We went for chips instead. We had a great time.'

'So? What did he say?' said Helen afterwards.

Breen shook his head. 'Nothing. Absolutely nothing. CID aren't telling him anything because they think the Drug Squad are up to their neck in the drug gangs.'

'Not about that, you idiot. About Amy.'

She laughed when he'd told her. 'I said the Rib Room was all wrong. What a prannock.'

They sat in silence for a while. Breen picked up a pencil and started doodling.

'I feel we've got to be close, haven't we?' said Helen. 'I mean, something's got to happen. Don't you think?'

Workmen in overalls from a nearby building site came in with dirty tea mugs, every other word a 'fuck' or a 'cunt'. As they were leaving two loud Cockney girls entered. 'Turn up the tranny, love. We like this one.'

Joe's daughter turned up Joe's old valve radio. Breen looked round. One of the girls wore a huge pair of dark glasses and a big floppy hat. Both were in miniskirts, and the one with a hat had a large *I'm Backing Britain* badge on her pale blouse. She was not wearing a bra.

'Eyes,' hissed Helen. 'Back in your head.'

Breen turned to his paper, picked up his pencil again.

She leaned over and whispered, 'I bet you're drawing Titty Girl, aren't you? Another of those pervy drawings, like the one you did of me.'

'It wasn't a pervy drawing.'

'Will you still draw me when I'm big and fat and ugly and pregnant?'

'Stop it.'

'Come on. Give us a look.'

'No.'

'See?' she said. 'I knew you were.' She leaned over and snatched at the paper. Breen tried to hold it down. It ripped. 'Ooops.'

But when she held the two pieces of torn paper together, all that Breen had drawn was a big black triangle, the pencil going over and over the same lines.

'Sorry,' she said. 'I didn't mean to be a bitch. I just can't help it sometimes.'

At the corners were the names James Fletchet, William Milkwood and Nicholas Doyle. And in the middle was the name Alexandra Tozer.

When they got home, walking side by side, Breen saw a uniformed copper squatting down at his letter box. 'Hello?'

The policeman said, 'I was looking for Sergeant Careful Breen.'

'What did you call him?' Helen asked.

The constable looked at his notebook. 'Careful?'

'Cathal,' said Breen.

Helen laughed. 'Careful Breen. I like that.'

Even from the top of the stairs they could see the young copper was blushing. 'Sorry. Superintendent asked me to call you. Inspector Creamer from Marylebone was trying to get in touch. Said you weren't picking up your phone.'

They clattered down the stairs, pushing past the constable, and Breen fumbled with the lock.

'What do you think he wants?'

'We seem to be your answering service while you're away,' Creamer said. 'I had a phone call from Lord Goodstone. He was trying to track you down. Hobnobbing with the aristocrats while you're away?'

It took Breen a second to remember that Lord Goodstone was Fletchet's title.

'He seemed like a nice fellow,' said Creamer. 'He a pal of yours or something?'

Creamer was a Rotarian, easily impressed by titles. Though Fletchet pretended to be embarrassed by the title when they met, he clearly didn't mind using it if it got him attention.

'He left you a contact. Got a pen?'

Breen wrote it down: it was a seven-figure number.

'A London address?' Breen said, surprised. But there was no reason why James Fletchet shouldn't be in London, he supposed.

'I imagine he's at the House of Lords or something,' Creamer answered. 'Going to meet up? You must come into the station again, Paddy. I'll take you out for lunch.'

When Breen rang the number, a man answered with, 'Good afternoon. Pratt's.'

A gentlemen's club, Breen realised. Not one of the newer, fashionable ones. The more ancient, creaky sort. 'Is there a James Fletchet there?'

'I shall enquire.'

After a minute, Fletchet came to the phone. 'Breen. I need to speak to you.'

'What about?'

'I've had CID turning up mob-handed down in Devon to

interview me about Bill Milkwood. My wife was furious. They wouldn't tell me what was going on.'

CID would have played their cards as close to their chest as they could; he'd have done the same. 'Are you a suspect?' asked Breen.

'God, no,' said Fletchet. 'Bloody hell. Am I?'

'Not as far as I know.'

'Christ. But I've just got back from seeing Gwen Milkwood. To offer my condolences. She told me there was funny business with his body. She didn't seem to know much, but it all seems very . . . strange. What the hell is going on, Sergeant?'

He sounded rattled. Drunk maybe?

'It's not my case,' Breen said. 'I can't say.'

'I wouldn't dream of asking you to speak out of turn, but I have a right to know what's going on,' Fletchet said. 'Don't you think?'

Breen considered. 'I can be there at six,' he said, looking at his watch. He replaced the handset.

'See? I told you something was going to happen. Shall we get a taxi?' Helen hadn't taken her coat off. Now she was holding up a small powder compact and putting on lipstick with her other hand, eyebrows raised slightly.

Breen said, 'It's just me, I think.'

She stopped, lipstick half done. 'Did he say that? He didn't want me to be there.'

'No. But he wants to meet at a gentlemen's club.'

She thrust her compact back into her bag. 'So?'

Breen shuffled his feet uncomfortably. 'Men only.'

Helen rolled her eyes. 'Welcome to the Space Age. Christ. He knows something. I know he does. I feel it in every bloody limb. Don't you? I mean, I should be there.'

'I'm sorry.'

'God's sake, Paddy. You could have said we have to meet some-where else. You could have insisted.'

'He sounded nervous. I thought it would be best to meet on his terms.'

She thumped down into his armchair. 'So what am I supposed to do, then? If he wants to meet, why can't it be on our terms?'

'We're not the investigators on this one. It's not our case.'

'"It's not our case." Why are you always so cautious, Careful Bloody Breen?'

Breen was at the door now. He opened his mouth to reply, but said nothing. He just left her smoking, dropping ash on his upholstery.

From the address in St James's, Breen imagined a grand house. And it was. The club, however, was just two rooms in the basement. It was a simple arrangement. In one they served drinks; in the other they served food. Fletchet was sitting in the dining room at a small table. He had been eating. There was a bottle of HP Sauce on his table, cap off, with a dribble of brown running down the outside. From looking around at the other diners, all they seemed to serve was bacon, eggs, sausages and chops, even at this time of evening.

'Breen. Take a seat,' said Fletchet.

It was an ordinary-looking place, slightly grubby even, which probably meant it was very exclusive, Breen guessed. A nouveau-riche establishment would be showier. These red-painted walls, covered with mediocre etchings of politicians and boxers and a few stuffed birds, spoke of that very English sense of class you couldn't possibly buy. Breen imagined that a senior common room at Eton would probably feel like this, serving the kind of meal a nanny would cook for a child. The British aristocracy had never quite left the nursery.

'George, bring this man a drink. Fix him some eggs or something.'

'I'm fine, thanks.'

Fletchet noticed cigarette ash on his tie and brushed it off. A club tie of some kind. He said, 'I don't mind admitting I'm seriously bloody concerned.'

'Why?' asked Breen.

'I don't like having the police turn up at my house. It's not good.'

'They are investigating a murder.'

Fletchet picked a piece of meat from his teeth. 'How was Billy Milkwood killed? I need to know.'

'Why?'

'Because the whole bloody thing is creepy. Seriously strange. He was tortured, wasn't he?'

Breen nodded warily. For all sorts of reasons, the police never liked to give details of a murder away. Especially one like this. Sensationalising a case always made it harder to bring it to trial, and keeping the public in the dark gave investigators leverage. Not to mention that in this particular case, the force wouldn't like to admit that they had let one of their own down so badly.

'I asked Gwen Milkwood how he had been hurt, she didn't seem to know. Why is that? What's bloody going on, Breen? Tell me. Why is it all so hush-hush? I mean, who goes around torturing police officers in England? What were they trying to find out?'

'If CID didn't tell you, why do you expect me to?'

'Oh, come on, Sergeant. You're not one of those bloody stuffed shirts, are you? Sorry. I'm a bit drunk already. Been at it since I came back from Gwen's. The whole thing gave me the heebie-jeebies, to be honest. It stirs you up.' He picked up the bottle of claret and poured Breen a glass. The label was faded and stained, which Breen guessed meant expensive. 'Obviously you know best. But you must have some lead on the suspect, for fuck's sake.'

'It's not my case,' said Breen.

'Of course not. But they must know bloody something,' said Fletchet.

Breen looked him in the eye. 'Why are you so keen to know the details?'

'He was a friend, for God's sake.'

'And?'

'And nothing. Isn't that enough? Let me explain something. I don't know if it's the same for a man like you. I'm sure it is, you being a policeman. It's not just personal. I grew up with a sense of duty. Duty to my country. Duty to my family. Duty to my fellow men. It's sort of bred into you, and it's no bad thing. Not so fashionable these days, I know, but it's something I'm sure you understand.'

'Duty to your family?'

Fletchet pushed his fair hair out of his eyes. 'I've said my piece about sleeping with that girl. That was a mistake. I let myself down. Mea culpa. But Bill Milkwood is an excellent man. Was. We served together in Africa. When he came back home we stayed pals. Solid as a bloody rock. And I refuse to let a man like that die the way he did without doing my best for him. Do you understand that?'

'And I'm sure CID are doing their best to find out who killed him and to bring him to justice,' said Breen. 'Why did you go and see Gwen Milkwood?'

'Why shouldn't I? She's the wife of an old pal. Why did the police want to interview me about Milkwood's death?'

'As you said, you're an old pal.'

'Come off it. Billy had dozens of old pals. I know for a fact they haven't gone round talking to everybody. What made me so special?'

'You tell me,' said Breen.

Two crabs circling each other at the bottom of a bucket, thought Breen. Fletchet wanted to know something. For Breen, the question was what.

Breen looked around the club. The men here were of a kind. They wore tweeds and blazers. The upper classes at rest. The old prime minister, Macmillan, was a member here, he had heard. Then he looked back at Fletchet.

'I was thinking about that girl you brought to see me the other day. Alex's sister,' said Fletchet.

'Helen,' said Breen.

'She didn't like me at all. No surprises there, I suppose. But I liked her,' said Fletchet. 'You could tell she had it. You know? A sense of duty to her sister. She was still angry about what had happened to her. I respect that. That's what I'm on about.'

An elderly man at the next table had started playing patience, dealing out rows of cards.

'Perhaps I should offer to help their family in some way. It must be an awful thing to have gone through. Do you think they'd be offended?'

'Almost certainly,' said Breen.

Snap-snap-snap, went the playing cards.

'Right. Me speaking out of turn, I suppose,' said Fletchet. 'Just a thought. What about drugs?'

'Drugs?'

'Milky was in the Drug Squad. All these dreadful drug pushers I'm hearing about. All over the newspapers. Was he on to something? Could that have been it? Revenge.'

'It's certainly one line of investigation.'

'Just one? So you're confirming there are others?'

Breen was trying to work Fletchet out. He seemed like a

straightforward man. A decent chap, as they'd say. But something was definitely rattling him. He was determined to dig; and the more determined he was to sound Breen out, the keener Breen was to know why he needed to know. Keep him talking. Breen tried another approach.

'What were you and Milkwood doing in Africa together?'

'The Emergency in Kenya. It was bloody brutal, I'll tell you that. We saw things you would not believe. You needed men around you you could trust. Milky was that kind of man.'

'You were a farmer, not a policeman or a soldier.'

'Yes, but it was the farms they were attacking, the Mau Mau. They wanted to drive us off our land. To be fair to the Kikuyu, there was a land shortage. It was an issue that needed addressing, but this lot were terrorists. They forced ordinary decent black folk to commit the most ghastly atrocities. They used all sorts of ju-ju to scare them into taking part. Forced them to swear an oath. A disgusting ritual involving drinking blood. They had to eat sheep's eyeballs. Honest to God. Once they'd got them, they forced them to do anything. Sounds incredible, doesn't it, sitting here in St James's? But these things really went on. A man I knew, owned a farm nearby, hacked to death in the night by his own servants. His son and wife too. Perfectly loyal one minute – the next . . . The servants did it because they were terrified of what would happen to them if they didn't. Terrorism, pure and simple.'

'And you and Milkwood . . . ?'

'The Mau Mau tried to enforce secrecy. That was their weapon, if you like. Of course, lots of the poor people didn't want to be part of it at all. They loved us. Respected us, at least. The only way the Mau Mau could operate was by terrorising people. The Kikuyu are weak-minded people. Superstitious. Easily led. The trick was getting to the ringleaders before they got to you and protecting the locals from them. Milky and I, we ran what was called a screening station.'

'Screening?'

'Standard investigative procedure. A series of interviews designed to flush out members who had taken the oath. Target the right suspects. Find out whether they were or were not Mau Mau. If they weren't, fine. If not, they were sent to prison. It wasn't just about protecting our land. It was about protecting the people who worked for us. And Milkwood was a very good investigator.'

'So I've heard. So how did you meet Milkwood?'

'It was all hands on deck. Milkwood was a policeman, but he wasn't from Kenya. He'd been seconded out to Nyeri before the Emergency started. In the early days, when the violence first started, most of the Colonial Office johnnies were way out of their depth. He came round in a Land Rover one day. Milkwood was much smarter than most. He knew he needed local knowledge. Someone who knew these people, who understood the way their brains worked. Understood the subtleties. The Kikuyu are different. Different values. Cattle men. They have a web of family loyalties that it's hard for an outsider to understand. I had worked alongside these men. I knew them. So Eloisa suggested he moved into one of the bungalows on our estate.'

A round man in a Norfolk jacket came in and called to the waiter, 'George, any kidneys today? I'm starving. Evening, Jimbo.' He waved at Fletchet.

Fletchet waved back, smiled, then said to Breen, 'Look. Why are you interested in Kenya? Milkwood's murder has nothing to do with that, surely? Are you on to something?'

Breen ignored his question. 'Would you say you worked together closely?'

'We were a good team and we ended up spending a lot of time

together under trying circumstances. Remember, I had a farm to run too. But terrorism is a cancer. It spreads fast and drags everybody down with it unless you find the cancerous cells and cut them out first. It's about using intelligence to take out the leaders.'

'And that's what you were doing? Cutting out cancerous cells?'

Fletchet frowned. 'Always within the law, obviously. It was a mixture of interrogation and intelligence.'

'Paid informers?'

'When necessary. Look. I'm not actually very interested in talking about this stuff right now. Why are you so bloody interested in Kenya? What's that got to do with it?'

'I'm just curious because you both spent time there.'

Fletchet was quiet for a second. Then he said, 'Right. I've told you about my bit of it. What about yours? Surely you can tell me something.' He reached forward to fill Breen's glass, but it was still full. 'Drink up, man,' he said. 'It's good stuff.'

Breen paused.

'Where were you when Milkwood was killed?'

'Oh, for Pete's sake. Don't you start. I already told that to the police who interviewed me. I was on the farm all day. I'm not stupid, you know. There's a reason why you're so interested in me. I have a right to know what it is. Am I in any danger?'

A servant's bell rang somewhere. The room was stuffy, overheated and smoky. Breen wondered what he was doing here anyway. This was not his investigation. It was not his place to ask these questions. But he made up his mind to take a risk. It was Helen's 'Careful Breen' taunt that did it. First he leaned forward, took a sip from his glass of red wine. It was dark and rich and unlike any wine he had tasted before.

'Tell me about Nicholas Doyle,' he said quietly.

'Nicky?' Fletchet's head jerked back a fraction of an inch. 'Why do you want to know about him?'

Breen observed Fletchet, trying to assess his reaction. 'You and Milkwood served with him in Africa, didn't you?'

'Absolutely. How did you . . . ?'

'I saw a photograph of you with him at the Milkwoods' house. I asked who he was. When did you last speak to Doyle?'

'Me? I don't know. Not for bloody yonks, I don't expect.' A pause. Apart from that small twitch of the head when he had first mentioned Doyle's name, Fletchet's face was a mask again, fixed into a small smile. 'Would you prefer a brandy? I expect they've got some beer, if that's more your thing. George?' He beckoned the waiter.

'How long ago?' said Breen.

'Give this man a large brandy. One for me too.'

'Doyle,' nudged Breen.

'I probably haven't spoken to him much since we left Africa. We didn't rub along so well.'

Fletchet's calm was too studied. Breen felt that almost childish thrill. He had believed Fletchet had something to hide. Now, at the mention of Doyle's name, he was surer of it than ever. He asked, 'Did you know Milkwood was still in touch with him?'

'Was he? I had no idea. Why are you interested in Doyle all of a sudden?'

George arrived with two huge balloons of brandy. Fletchet seemed to be thinking. Eventually he looked at Breen and said, 'What's bloody going on, Breen?'

Breen shook his head. 'As I said, it's not my case. But I wouldn't be surprised if CID wanted to interview you again.'

'That's their choice, obviously.'

Breen said, 'What did Doyle do for you out in Africa?' The tiniest flicker of the eyelid again. 'Was he part of your intelligence gathering operation?'

'I wouldn't have invited you to my club if I knew you were going to be such a . . . bloody copper.'

'I believe something happened in Africa and Doyle was involved. What was it?'

Fletchet raised his voice. 'Tell me. What's fucking Doyle got to do with this?'

The round man who had greeted Fletchet looked up, frowned at the sudden outburst.

Breen persisted. 'Where was Doyle when you last heard of him?'

The smile returned. 'Sorry. Bit worked up. Too much wine, probably. And all this beastliness. But you have to tell me, old man. What's he got to do with all this? It's crucial I know.'

Breen had said too much already, but he had no choice but to press on. 'I asked you just now if you had met Doyle since you'd been in Africa together. When did you last see him?'

'I'll give it some thought.' Fletchet looked at his watch. 'Damn. Promised to call my wife. Short leash and all that. Excuse me.'

And he stood abruptly and held out his hand to shake.

'You're going?' said Breen.

'Sorry. Yes. Please, stay as long as you like.' Fletchet called to another of the club's servants, who was collecting empty plates. 'George, look after this man, will you? He's my guest.'

'He's called George too?' said Breen.

'Oh yes. All the staff at Pratt's are George,' Fletchet said, as if it was perfectly normal. 'It's a sort of tradition. That's right, isn't it, George?'

'Yes, sir.'

After he'd gone, Breen sat alone with his wine and the untouched brandy in front of him.

'Pal of Jimbo's, are you?' said the round man.

'Acquaintance.'

'Been to his estate?'

'Just once.'

'I hear the shooting's very good,' said the elderly man, who was still playing patience. 'Wouldn't mind going there myself.'

'I wouldn't know,' said Breen.

'More of a fishing man, are you? It's always either one or the other in my experience.'

Breen sat thinking. The man in the Norfolk jacket hummed a snatch from the 'Radetzky March' to himself.

'Balls,' the man playing patience said. 'I think I'm going to have to cheat.' And he lifted up a card and put it on another pile.

'Nothing wrong with cheating,' said the round man. 'That's a game in itself.'

'Very true,' said the other.

A large, badly-varnished wall clock struck quarter to and then the hour. Breen took a gulp from the brandy glass, angry at himself. He had the feeling he had given away something of value but was not sure what. Nor was he sure he had received anything in return.

'Well? What?' said Helen.

She was sitting in his father's armchair with an open packet of digestives, crumbs in her lap and on the floor around her, and the TV on loud. 'Yes, it's Number One! It's *Top of the Pops*!' The set was up much louder than he usually had it. He went to turn it down.

'So? What did he have to say for himself?'

Breen took off his mac and put it on a hook. 'Not much, actually.'

'What d'you mean?' She prised her eyes from the television to look at Breen.

'He wanted to know why the police were interviewing him about Milkwood. He kept asking me about it. But when I mentioned Doyle, something spooked him. He tried not to show it, but there was definitely something. And then he just sort of ended the conversation and left.'

'Because you mentioned Doyle's name?'

'I don't know. Maybe.'

She picked up another digestive and chewed on it thoughtfully. 'Perhaps you were right, then,' she said, looking back at the long-haired man in a polo neck and silver chain, introducing the songs. 'Fletchet, Milkwood and Doyle.'

'I may be,' said Breen. 'But I'm just not sure what I'm right about.' He pulled out one of the dining chairs and sat next to her. Cliff Richard sang, 'Boom boom boom, now the whole world's singing, good times!'

'I hate Cliff Richard,' said Helen. 'That smile. He makes my skin crawl.'

Breen had never watched a whole episode of *Top of the Pops*. The cameras lingered on a girl in a black fringed bikini top who was bending at the knees as she danced, arms swinging in tandem. He hated the vacuousness of it. Helen wasn't enjoying it either. A middle-aged man came on to sing a ballad and she snorted. 'Why's it always so rubbish? There's Marvin Gaye, Nina Simone, Martha Reeves, Sam and Dave in the charts this week. I bet they don't play any of them. It's crap, that's what it is.'

'I suppose some people like it,' said Breen.

'They're idiots, then. Another thing. CID phoned. I'm allowed to leave London,' she said, eyes fixed again on the TV. 'I can go home.'

'Oh,' said Breen.

'Good news, eh?' she said.

'Any idea why they've said you can leave London now?'

She shook her head. 'Don't think I didn't ask. I got the idea something was going on, but they wouldn't say what.'

It meant she would leave soon. He wished they hadn't called. What had happened, he wondered, that made CID so sure that it couldn't have been her?

He watched her as she pulled out a cigarette and lit it, then blew out the match and put it down on the arm of the chair. Breen went to the sideboard, picked up an ashtray in the shape of an Irish harp and put the match into it, then put the ashtray down beside her.

She said nothing, just watched the TV, volume still too high.

'I was bloody right. They didn't even play Canned Heat,' she said as the credits rolled. 'They didn't play anything decent at all.'

She lit another cigarette.

At 10 p.m. she was still in the chair watching the ITV news. She had slumped right down, legs spread wide, feet sprawling onto the carpet. Breen went back to washing up. He had cooked omelettes with tarragon and cheese; Helen had carefully picked out what she called 'the green bits'.

'Paddy, come quick,' she shouted from the living room.

By the time he had dried his hands and reached the television set she said, 'You missed it.'

'What?'

She was sitting up now. 'I was bloody right. Look. They gone and bloody arrested someone for Milkwood's murder. There was something going on.'

'Who?'

'A Chink.'

'A Chinese man?'

'I think they said gang. I don't know.'

'A Chinese man from a gang?'

'Something like that. It was halfway through before I realised what they were saying, then it was over.'

The weather forecast had already started. Breen picked up the phone and called Carmichael, first at Scotland Yard, then at the section house, but he wasn't at either place. He left a message instead.

'I don't get it,' said Helen. 'I was sure Milkwood's killing was going to be something to do with Fletchet.'

Breen stood, dripping washing-up water on the carpet. 'We don't know anything yet. It's just a report on the news.'

'I know, but . . .' She slumped back down and felt for her cigarette packet. 'I just thought . . . God. I don't know what to think any more.'

'I'm going to bed,' he said.

She didn't answer.

Everything felt wrong, thought Breen. The odd conversation with Fletchet; the man arrested for Milkwood's murder. Nothing fitted.

And Helen was free to go now, back to the farm.

TWENTY-THREE

That night she slept in the spare room again. She said his bed was too small for both of them.

At eight in the morning she was still asleep. Breen looked in on her, opening the door as quietly as he could. She lay on her back, mouth open, one foot dangling out of the bed.

She was still asleep when he returned from buying an early edition of the *Standard*. The report started in a small box on the front page and was continued inside, but it didn't say much. A member of a Chinese gang had been arrested in Limehouse 'on suspicion of the abduction and murder of Police Sergeant William Milkwood'. The arrest had been made 'following a tip-off'. There were no details.

'I don't know any more than that,' said Carmichael on the phone later. 'But everybody here has been going nuts. CID cracked out a couple of Party Sevens and a case of Bell's last night. They were up till three.'

Breen said, 'You think it's kosher?'

There was a pause.

'Why?' said Carmichael.

'Does it feel right to you?' said Breen.

Another pause.

'It doesn't, does it?'

'Let's talk about this later,' Carmichael said.

*

They had arranged to meet Ijeoma Ezeoke at the School of Oriental and African Studies that afternoon. There was a demonstration outside. Three students were asking for signatures. One held a banner reading: 'ALWAYS CREATE ART AND DESTROY PROPERTY'.

Helen had been uncommunicative all day. She had read the report in the paper and said nothing. When Breen said she didn't have to go home until she was ready, she could stay in the flat for as long as she wanted, she just shrugged. She had sat listening to Radio 1 all morning, drinking tea and smoking more cigarettes. By the afternoon, he'd been grateful they had a reason to get out of the flat.

'If the Chinese bloke killed Milkwood, I don't see the point of all this anyway,' said Helen.

'Don't give up now.'

'But that means the police think they know what happened. They're not going to connect it to Alex.'

'I know.'

'I'm not giving up, anyway. I'm just frustrated. I'm tired now. I thought we were getting somewhere.'

'You're . . . you know. Expecting. It's bound to affect you.'

'Will you shut up, Paddy? Please. You're giving me a headache.'

Ijeoma appeared out of the crowd and walked past the demonstrators, ignoring them. 'Come this way.'

Breen and Helen followed.

'His name is Sam,' Ijeoma said as she walked them up the staircase. Inside the building, every single inch of the walls seemed covered in posters and cards advertising events, shared rooms or second-hand books. 'He's very earnest. Except when he's drunk, and then he's very boring.'

She knocked at a plain white door in a corridor and then opened it.

'Izzie.' He greeted her with a kiss.

Sam wore a white shirt and a tie with no jacket. He had a young, round face, and sat in a small study with books piled haphazardly on shelves. There were several chairs, presumably for students, stacked against the wall.

'You are the man who arrested Miss Ezeoke's father?' he said, unsmiling.

'Yes.'

'It's OK, Sam,' said Ijeoma. 'He did the right thing. I'll tell you about it one day.'

'If you say so.' Sam gestured to the chairs. 'So. Miss Ezeoke says you want to know about the Emergency? Would you like tea?'

'Do you have coffee?'

'I'm a Kenyan. Of course I have coffee.'

'Izzie, do you mind? You know where our kitchen is.'

Ijeoma left the room. There was a black-and-white portrait of a bearded African leader on the desk, a man with a patterned kofia hat holding a fly whisk in his hand: Jomo Kenyatta.

'So. What do you want to know?'

'There's an investigation going on into the murder of a London policeman. I believe it's connected to another murder that happened four years ago.'

'I don't understand what this has to do with Kenya.'

'It may be a coincidence, but both murders are linked by three people, all of whom worked together during the Emergency. One of them is definitely dead. Another probably.'

'I repeat, what does this have to do with Kenya?'

Breen said, 'Honestly? I haven't any idea at all. That's why I wanted to speak to you.'

The man called Sam put his fingers together and leaned across the desk. 'I don't understand. Why are you asking me? Why don't you ask the High Commission? Or the Kenyan Embassy?'

Ijeoma came back with a tray with four cups on it and some coconut biscuits.

'Because I'm not officially connected to the investigation. I'm just an interested party. Besides, going through official channels takes time. I just want some background.'

'I am an academic, not a policeman. Why should I help you with this?'

The young man was acting like some court barristers; policemen and barristers never got along at the best of times.

'If you don't have time, I understand,' said Breen.

'It's nothing to do with time. I just want to understand why you're interested.' He held out a cup to Breen.

'Because he's investigating the death of my sister,' said Helen. 'She was murdered.'

Ijeoma spilled coffee on the carpet. 'I'm sorry,' she said, lowering her eyes.

'You can clean it up later,' said Sam.

'It wasn't you I was saying sorry to, you pompous idiot,' said Ijeoma fiercely. She put the coffee on the floor and sat next to Helen. 'Was it one of these men that killed your sister?'

'We don't know. That's what we're trying to find out.'

Ijeoma nodded. 'Stop pretending you're all high and mighty, Sam. You're only a junior lecturer. Just tell them what they want to know.'

Sam picked up his own cup and sipped it. Then he asked, 'I assume these are all white men, yes? Do you know what they were doing during the Emergency?'

Breen closed his eyes and tried to remember what Mrs Milkwood had called it. 'One minute,' he said, and pulled a notebook from his jacket.

Ijeoma caught Helen's eyes while he was flicking through the pages. Helen looked away.

'They were screening people to find out if they were members of the Mau Mau.'

'They ran a screening station?'

'Yes. That's it.'

'Where?'

Breen checked his notes again. 'Nyeri.'

Sam nodded. 'Tell me, what do you think "screening" means?' he said.

'I haven't any idea. James Fletchet described it as interrogation and intelligence.'

'What's so funny?' said Helen.

'Screening. It was such an innocent word. The men you are talking about were probably torturers.'

'Torturers?'

'That's what screening was. The British like to pretend otherwise. But it's a fact. Especially in the screening stations in Nyeri.'

Breen looked round at Helen, who was seated slightly behind him. 'Torturers?' She was chewing on her lower lip. 'How do you know this?' she asked.

'Everybody knew it. How aware are you of the background?' He didn't wait for an answer. 'By and large, during the course of the first half of the twentieth century, the Kikuyu people were evicted from their land by white farmers. Instead of being farmers, they became tenants with few rights, or landless labourers. This suited the white settlers, because they didn't understand the land they had taken. They needed the local Kikuyu farmers to help them make it productive. Without labourers and people who understood the land, their farms would have inevitably failed.' The young man smiled, leaned back on his chair until it almost touched the wall behind him. 'The Mau Mau was a secret organisation that vowed to fight until they got their land back. It started with a few assassinations. A pro-British Kikuyu chief. A settler. A black policeman. But it quickly grew. When the whites finally realised that the Mau Mau meant business, they created a system of mass arrests, mass internment, to isolate them. They rounded up every black man in Nairobi. Every single one. But the British had a problem. How could you tell who was Mau Mau and who wasn't? They called it screening.'

Breen tried to imagine the blue-blooded gentleman he had met in a darkened cell with a victim at his mercy. Here, in an office in Bloomsbury, the idea seemed ridiculous.

'The Mau Mau were well known to be a fanatical underground movement,' said Breen. 'Presumably you would expect the government's response to be harsh.'

Sam smiled. 'As an Englishman, how harsh would you have expected them to be?'

'Don't get Paddy started,' said Helen. 'He's always going on about how he's Irish, even though he grew up in England.'

'An Irishman?' smiled Sam. 'Well, you would know about how the British are.'

'Were you arrested?' Helen asked Sam.

'I was detained. But I am not Kikuyu. I am a Luo. I was set free within two days. It was fine.'

'What about him?' Breen pointed to the picture on the desk, Jomo Kenyatta.

'Of course. They thought he was a leader of the Mau Mau. It was never about leaders. The Mau Mau was like a virus. A fanaticism that spread through the people. But he was a politician. They didn't torture him.'

Helen said, 'Are you actually, genuinely, truthfully saying that these people we are talking about were torturers?'

'I would be extremely surprised if they were not. You don't

believe me, do you? I knew you would not. You have to understand what they believed they were up against. They thought the people were savages.' Sam laughed. 'Maybe they were savages. Do you know how the Mau Mau recruited people? The Mau Mau would arrive at night and force the squatters to swear an oath of secrecy. And if they didn't take the secret oath, they would kill them. In front of everybody. Men and women. Even children sometimes. And then they would make friends and neighbours mutilate the body. Sometimes they would come back, dig up the rotting body and make them hack it apart again with knives and spears. Savages, you see?'

Ijeoma had been silent through all this. Now she said, 'When you are faced with superior weapons, you use the only weapon left, which is fear.'

'You think that is how people should behave?' said Sam.

'Maybe they had no choice,' said Ijeoma.

'Sometimes they forced people to rub the rotting flesh on their hands and their lips. To show people they were not afraid to kill the enemies of the Mau Mau.'

'That's disgusting,' said Helen.

'I'm just saying,' said Ijeoma. 'Imperialist brutality creates brutality.'

'Spoken like a true Maoist.'

'I'm not a Maoist. I'm not anything,' said Ijeoma.

'It was efficient, at least,' said Sam. 'People were more afraid of them than they were of the British. Which was an achievement, I suppose. So people like your friends responded in kind. They knew they had to make people more afraid of them than they were of the Mau Mau.'

Helen wrinkled her nose and said, 'The British tortured hundreds of people during the Emergency? This is only, what, ten, fifteen years ago? And we'd never heard of it? I'm sure there were some, but . . .'

'It wasn't hundreds. It was thousands,' said Sam. 'Thousands and thousands. I don't expect you to believe it. Many of the British who were there didn't believe it at the time. But if your friends were at a screening station in Nyeri, that's what they would have been doing. Prisoners could be there for months, being processed. I was a young legal student then. You heard people talking about what went on in these places.'

Helen said, 'I just find it pretty hard to believe, that's all. If anything happened on that scale there would have been records. Reports in the newspapers.'

'I'm sure there are records,' said Sam. 'The British always kept good records. But there were also a lot of bonfires in the days before independence.'

Breen sipped his coffee and looked at the man. He said, 'Say I believe you. What kind of torture?'

'The usual. Torture is always the same. How do you hurt someone to make them say things they do not want to say? The first job I had was with some Indian lawyers in Nairobi. They defended people who had confessed to taking part in atrocities. The defendants had had their fingernails pulled out. They had been electrocuted. Some had been burned with cigarettes, or had the soles of their feet whipped. Sometimes the lawyers won. Sometimes they lost. If they lost, the men were hanged. But in every single case I was involved with, the judges refused to believe the men had been tortured.'

Ijeoma asked, 'Why did none of this come out when you got independence? Why didn't you bring Britain to justice?'

'It is an inconvenient memory. The torturers were not just white men. They had helpers too, who profited. Kikuyu tortured Kikuyu. Other Kenyans tortured Kikuyu too. But we all knew what was happening. The violence was everywhere. A friend of mine, his father saw his own two-year-old boy beaten to death with the butts of guns, right in front of him. Everyone has a story. It wasn't just men. It was women. Children. Everyone. You don't believe me, do you? I can see from your face that you don't.'

Helen said, 'There are always some people who will go too far.'

'This was not "some people". It was the British system. This was how they ruled us. I will tell you a story. There's a nightclub in Nairobi I used to go to. The Starlight. We used to go there to listen to Congolese music. Do you like music, Mr Breen? I love it. The Congolese are the best musicians in the world. But mostly I went there for the girls. There was one girl I fell in love with there. She was so beautiful. Beautiful hair. Beautiful face. Beautiful bottom. Her name was Mukami. In Kikuyu it means "the one who milks the cows". But everyone called her Tusker. You know what Tusker is?'

Breen shook his head.

'It's Kenyan beer. They say it drives men crazy. She certainly did that. But she was also cold and hard as glass. Like a bottle of beer. But that just made men crazier. That's why we called her Tusker. She loved to dance, but she was cold and hard and she drove us crazy. Me at least. I was in my twenties. I was single. I was a senior clerk in a legal practice. I was going somewhere. And I was determined I should have her. Everyone talked about the lucky man who would eventually get Tusker. So I danced with her every night. I was a young man earning lots of money in a legal practice. I bought her gifts. I bought her perfume. I wore her down, bit by bit.'

'I hope there is a point to this story,' said Ijeoma.

'I thought you would appreciate a story about a pretty girl,' said Sam.

'I'm just feeling sorry for her already,' she said.

'You should. I have known many shy girls, but Tusker was the shyest. How could such a beautiful girl be so shy? It was like a challenge. When I finally won her trust I persuaded her to sleep with me. So one night I took her back to my apartment. She said she would sleep with me on one condition: I kept the lights off. I agreed. I wanted to undress her, but she insisted on getting into bed fully clothed, taking them off herself under the covers. And when I tried to touch her, she kept pushing my hands away. It was driving me mad.'

'God,' said Ijeoma.

'Yes. You know what's coming? Eventually my hand landed on her buttock. I had always wanted to touch her buttocks. You, Izzie. You like to do the same, don't you?'

'You disgust me, Sam.'

'I'm sorry. I am just telling the truth. The globes of her arse had always looked so good under her dress.'

'That's enough, Sam,' said Ijeoma. 'I get your point. I know what you're going to say.'

'When I put my hands there I felt how they had cut her bottom. Her buttocks were just scars. And my erection simply faded away. She cried a lot. She had scars on her back too. And on her thighs. And her breasts. She told me that when she was seventeen they had thought her father was a senior figure in the Mau Mau. They held her in Athi River Camp, one of the screening centres. He was held too. They tortured him but he wouldn't talk. So they tortured her too and said they would rape her unless he became an informer. But he didn't say. I don't know if he was really a Mau Mau or not. If he was, I despise him for letting his daughter be mutilated like that.'

'*One* of the screening centres?' said Breen.

'There were many, many, many. Athi River Camp was just one near Nairobi but there were many, many more. In Central Province there were dozens. Nobody knows how many.'

'I feel sick,' said Ijeoma.

'She put on her dress and left my apartment. I never saw her again after that. She was too ashamed to come back to the Starlight. Imagine that, Mr Breen. Are you sceptical still?'

'They cut her breasts?'

'They tortured many women like that,' said Sam.

'But these were black men torturing them?' said Helen. 'Black men, yes?'

Sam shrugged. 'You don't think white people would do this?'

'It would have been in the papers.'

'You're a fool.'

Helen said, 'I think you're exaggerating, that's all.'

'They gave the torturers names. Like code names. I heard of one they called Kiboroboro. In Kikuyo it means "The Killer".'

'A white man?' said Breen.

'Yes. There is a friend of my mother's. She told my mother she was beaten by a man they called Karoki. A white man. This man put banana leaves inside her.'

'Inside her?' said Ijeoma.

'In her anus and her vagina. And they mutilated her breasts with pliers. It's well known they used pliers on the testicles of the men too. Anything you can imagine, they did. There is a man who begs at Donholm Station in Nairobi, close to where my mother lives. The skin on his face is all scarred. Sometimes I've caught the young boys throwing stones at him. He was skinned by a white man, he says. They literally peeled skin from his face. Do you want to hear more?'

Breen opened his mouth. Closed it again.

Sam said, 'Shall I ask Izzie to fetch you more coffee? Yours is cold, I think.'

Breen looked down. He had not touched it. He felt cold too.

'I don't feel well,' Helen said as they walked down the stairs to the front of the building. 'You think what he said is true?'

Ijeoma looked at her. 'Why wouldn't you, of all people?'

Helen said, 'I mean, was there some kind of justification for that kind of behaviour? There had to have been.'

'Why do you find it so hard to believe?'

'Because if it's true, then . . .'

'Then what?'

She didn't answer.

'I have to go now,' Ijeoma said, holding out her hand to shake. 'Did you get what you wanted?'

Breen shook her hand and watched her walk away across Russell Square. There were purple crocuses struggling through the grass, heads blown by a north wind. The temperature was falling. He should have worn a scarf.

Helen shivered. 'I think he enjoyed it, didn't he, telling us all that?'

'But don't you see? It connects the three men, Fletchet, Milkwood and Doyle, to torture.'

'Of course I see,' she said. 'It just wasn't what I expected, I suppose. And maybe it's not even relevant any more.'

'We don't know that,' said Breen. 'And just the mention of Doyle's name spooked Fletchet.'

'I think I'm going to go home, Paddy. I've had enough.'

'You're not giving up, are you?'

'Don't,' she said.

In spite of the cold, they walked round the outside of Russell Square twice. Then they went inside and sat on a bench. He pulled out an address book from his jacket pocket and started flicking through it. After a minute he stood and walked to a payphone on the corner of the square, outside the iron railings.

'What are you doing?' said Helen.

'I have to make a phone call.'

The last few months, he realised, had brought him face to face with people in power. Once he would have been intimidated by them. But as London was changing, so was he. He opened his address book at the name Tarpey. He was the private assistant of a Labour minister; Breen had done him a favour in the past, though Breen suspected Tarpey would not have seen it that way.

'Mr Tarpey?' said a voice. 'One minute please.'

Breen had to put in two more shillings while he waited.

The man came to the phone, finally. 'Breen,' he said. 'What a pleasure. I heard you were wounded. I was hoping for worse, of course.'

'Of course.'

Tarpey was a Welshman. A Labour diehard, loyal to the party, always disappointed by England. 'To what do I owe?'

'Where would all the justice records from Kenya's colonial administration have ended up?'

'Why are you interested in them? And why do you think I would know?'

'I'm sure you know better than I do.'

'Don't you policemen have proper channels for this kind of thing?'

'I'm on sick leave still. But I need to find out whether a story I've been told is true or not,' said Breen.

A woman with a dog came up and stood next to the door, impatient. She pulled open the door. 'You've been on the phone for five minutes,' she said, tapping at her watch.

Breen tried pulling the door shut from the inside. He fed another shilling into the slot.

Tarpey was saying, 'If it's at the Public Records Office, you probably won't be able to get at it under the fifty-year rule. Is it important?'

'I wouldn't be asking if it wasn't,' said Breen.

'What's it about?' asked Tarpey.

'Counter-insurgency measures in Kenya during the Mau Mau Emergency,' said Breen.

Tarpey was quiet for a moment, then said, 'You'll be lucky. Tell me why you want to know.'

'I'm interested in some British citizens who may or may not have tortured suspected members of the Mau Mau.'

'I doubt they'd let you have it, then,' said Tarpey.

'You don't think so?'

'If such evidence even exists, and I'm only saying if, it would be buried for years.'

'So there's no chance of corroborating it?'

'Why are you so interested?'

'Would you think a story like that could be credible?' asked Breen.

Tarpey said, 'Put it this way, what is stopping you from believing it's true?'

Breen said, 'If you asked to see files on it, would they confirm that they existed?'

'I couldn't ask, myself. You'd have to do it.'

The pips went again, sooner than Breen expected, and he was left feeling in his pocket for change while the woman rapped on the door to the phone box. By the time he'd got another coin out, he'd been cut off anyway.

TWENTY-FOUR

Breen called to book a taxi.

'Spendthrift.'

'You're pregnant,' he said.

'I hate being pregnant,' she said.

'I'm not having you going on public transport.'

'You're not having me going on public transport! Who are you to decide how I travel?'

'Look. Catching a taxi is fine. I keep getting this money from the Police Benevolent Fund. Don't know what else to do with it.'

'Worth getting shot, then, was it?'

'Like I said, you don't have to go, anyway,' he said. 'I'd like it if you stayed.'

'I've been away too long. Besides, I have to go and tell my mum and dad about . . .' She looked down at her stomach.

'Will they be OK?'

'Dad'll be hopping. Mum will worry what everyone will say. A baby out of wedlock. There will be lots of wagging tongues.'

'Stay here, then.'

'No. We're bloody losing, Paddy. I thought we were winning, but we're not. If they're not connecting Alex's death to Milkwood's any more, we're back to square one.'

He went with her in the taxi to Paddington. Helen didn't have much in the way of luggage; just a duffel bag and there wasn't a lot in that. It was true. They could have caught the bus. Breen liked

London taxis, though. It seemed to be the most civilised way to travel in the capital, even if it was one of the old ones; an empty space by the driver for the luggage and a ticking meter that crept round. Springs that dug into your behind in the seats.

Helen was biting her fingernails. She took her hand from her mouth and said, 'My dad'll want me to marry you. And he's got shotguns and everything,' she said. 'Joke.'

'Don't say I didn't offer.'

'I know.'

'It still stands.'

They were on Marylebone Road. Their old turf. Where they had first met. There was a queue of tourists outside Madame Tussaud's already. He had not liked Helen at all at the beginning. He had found her brash and mouthy; they were the things he liked about her now.

'Paddy, don't think you're going to change my mind. I'm not getting married to anyone. Least, not all because of a mistake with the pill.'

The taxi driver was watching them in the rear-view mirror, listening in.

'Think of the baby,' said Breen. 'You don't do that, just bring up a child on your own. Nobody does that.'

Helen leaned forward and shut the glass window to the compartment in front.

'It's my baby. Nothing to do with you.'

'Something to do with me.'

She didn't deny it, at least. At Paddington, she wouldn't let him buy a platform ticket. She stood by the barrier at Platform 1 and said, 'You will call me up? Tomorrow evening. After milking.'

Breen said, 'I'm not the one who disappears for several days at a time.'

279

'Don't be angry,' she said. 'I'm just a bit fed up. I'm not myself any more. I don't mean to take it out on you.'

'Sorry.'

'I'll call you,' she said.

And she leaned forward, stretched up and kissed him on the cheek and then turned, lifting her ticket for the inspector. He stood, waiting for her to wave before she got onto the train.

When Breen arrived at the old snooker hall in Marshall Street, Carmichael was already there playing against himself, knocking the balls around the table. The room was in the windowless basement of an old factory building.

Breen arrived at the bottom of the stairs and stood in the dark corner of the room, watching Carmichael for a moment. He was leaning across the table, cigarette in his mouth, trying to pot an awkward ball in the far corner, the weight of his belly flat against the baize. Smoke disappeared up into the large lampshade above the table.

There were four tables. The other three were empty. They would be closing the building down soon. They were demolishing it to build new shops and offices. Soho was on the up. Now it was all film companies, advertising agencies and pop impresarios. American tourists wandered the streets trying to find the new pizza restaurant on Wardour Street.

They had played in this hall as sixteen-year-olds, him and Big John, sneaking in despite being underage, talking in deep voices and swearing to try and seem as grown up as they could until they figured out that nobody there seemed to mind much anyway.

Carmichael fluffed the ball and it bounced off the cushion, knocking the white into the pocket.

'It's something to do with Fletchet,' said Breen. 'I'm sure of it. I don't know what.'

Carmichael looked up. 'I told CID all that. They're not interested now. They've got a case against that Chinese bloke and they're happy with that.'

Breen told him about the university lecturer he'd talked to.

'A politico,' said Carmichael. 'A red. Someone trying to stir it up against the British. The world is full of them. None of that ever happened. We weren't like that. Maybe the Belgians in the Congo. But not us.'

'Maybe,' said Breen.

'All those academics love to stir it. They'd rather be living under Ho Chi Minh or Mao. Fuck them, I say.'

'But the details of torture are too much of a coincidence.'

'Torture is torture,' said Carmichael. 'Even if these men did it, which I don't believe for a minute . . . Think of the vilest, most degrading thing you can do to someone. You're going to end up doing the same things. Pliers? The Richardson Gang use bolt cutters. Same effect. And they did the electrocution thing too. Stuck the old Tucker Telephone on their balls and electrocuted them. About as logical as saying Dr Mengele did it.' He picked up a frame and placed it on the table. 'Amy's been in touch. She sent me a note. Invited me to the theatre.'

Breen broke, scattering the balls with a loud crack. 'That's good.'

'I know.' He grinned. 'But theatre. I've never really been. I'm a bit bloody worried about that.'

Breen hadn't played pool in months, but it felt good, hearing the clack of the balls again. 'Milkwood and Alexandra Tozer were tortured before they were killed,' he said. 'And if Doyle is one of those bodies, he would have been tortured too.'

'You're saying this person, whoever it was, travelled to Spain to kill Doyle.'

'I don't know. But nobody's looking into it.'

'She wants me to see some political play. It's called *Strike*, for God's sake. Alternative theatre. Alternative to what, exactly?'

'I'm thinking of going back down to Devon,' said Breen. 'Helen's gone back.'

'I thought you hated the place.'

'I do. She's pregnant,' said Breen.

'Christ.' Carmichael fluffed a ball and knocked the white into the pocket again. 'Two shots,' he said.

'Thing is, John. I want to marry her.'

Carmichael stood up straight, lifted the cue, put the end of the shaft on his shoe and looked at Breen. 'You want to marry her? Or think you ought to because she's up the duff?'

'I love her.'

Carmichael nodded slowly. 'Love? You sure?'

'I think so. I've been thinking about her all the time.'

'Jesus. I mean, that's serious.'

'But you're in love, aren't you? With Amy?'

'I am nuts about her. But I'm not ruddy proposing or nothing. Christ sake.'

They had known each other since they were kids, but they never talked about stuff like this.

Carmichael said, 'But you think you could actually get along with her?'

Breen laughed. 'Not really. But.'

Carmichael laughed too. 'Your funeral, mate. I mean, good luck to you. So when are you going to ask her?'

Breen said, 'I already did. She said no.'

Carmichael looked genuinely shocked. 'She never? You're a sergeant. You got your own flat and everything.'

'She doesn't want to get married just because she's pregnant.'

Carmichael turned the edges of his mouth down. 'Thought that was the only reason anyone did it.' He leaned over the table again with his cue, missed the pocket. 'Your shot.'

Breen picked up his cue, knocked a spot ball into the corner pocket. And then another into the side pocket. And a third.

Carmichael sighed. 'I thought you had a bad shoulder.'

'I have,' said Breen. 'Still beating you, though.'

'Maybe that's for the best. I mean, you and her. She's a bit nuts. And you're . . .'

'Conventional.'

'I wouldn't say that, exactly.'

Breen's last shot tucked the white behind two of his balls.

'I'm sorry,' said Breen. 'I didn't mean to talk about all of this.'

Carmichael said, 'Forget it.'

The rest of the evening they played without talking much, concentrating on the game. It was better just to play. Breen won the first two games. Then they played best-of-five. Breen won the next two as well. Carmichael was usually the better player. Breen had never won so many games against him in his life.

When they were younger, he would have been elated at the victory. But tonight he felt oddly flat. Helen had gone. He understood nothing. All he had was a head full of nightmares.

It was dark outside. They walked east, still not talking. The streets were quiet; the pubs were full.

They reached Charing Cross Road. London's shops were usually all shut by 5.30, but there was one still open: a bookshop that had neon lights blazing. They crossed the road to look at what was happening there.

It was different from the other dusty booksellers along Charing

Cross Road that sold rare bound editions or piles of cheap paperbacks. This one seemed to be selling mostly pamphlets and comics. A sign in the window read: 'POETRY TONIGHT! LIVE.'

Breen placed his face against the glass. Inside, under the bright lights, dozens of people were sitting cross-legged on the floor. Some had brought cushions. Others sat with their chins on their knees, arms wrapped around their legs.

At the far end of the shop, a thin, gaunt-faced man with a wispy moustache was reading something from a typed sheet of paper, stalking across the floor as he read, grinning like a madman. A younger man in a mac was next to him, squeezing notes from a soprano saxophone.

Without asking Carmichael whether he wanted to go in, Breen pushed open the door. A bell rang. Momentarily distracted, some of the audience looked round, glared.

'I'm not going in there,' hissed Carmichael. 'I hate bloody poetry.'

'I bet Amy likes poetry,' said Breen, grinning, and went inside.

Reluctantly, Carmichael followed. Breen found space at the back next to the sales counter. There was a burst of laughter. Applause.

'A class society so tight and proper / Such accents, clipped and kempt. Assholes!' shouted the poet.

The audience whooped and cheered more at the profanity. A girl with a bandanna round her head shouted, 'Right on.'

From his accent, the poet was an American. He wore a fringed suede jacket, the type that bikers sometimes wore. 'He needs a hot poker up his ass / Before he'll feel a think,' he recited.

'Profound,' said Carmichael, joining Breen on the floor.

'Shh,' hissed the girl in the bandanna.

The poet continued, dropping pages as he finished them. As the saxophone wailed higher and higher, the poem climaxed with the shouted line 'A nation of gardens, surrounded by fences', which several in the audience seemed to know and shouted back at the poet.

People stood, clapped. The poet did a little dance.

'Call that poetry?' muttered Carmichael. 'Anyone could do that. Even me.'

Afterwards, as the crowd surrounded the performer, Breen stood and walked to the counter. There was a young man in a waistcoat covered in badges standing behind it reading a book.

'Do you have something called *The Book of the Dead*?' Breen asked the young man.

The man looked puzzled at the question. 'We have several editions. Do you mean Timothy Leary's?'

'I don't know. What is it?' asked Breen.

'It's instructions for how to die. How to pass over to the other side so you can be reincarnated as a pure soul. Which edition do you want?'

'I don't know,' said Breen.

The man pushed past them to the other side of the room.

'What's wrong with you?' hissed Carmichael. 'Can we go now?'

The girl with the bandanna was talking earnestly to the poet, nodding at whatever he was saying. The bookseller returned with three books. One had *The Tibetan Book of the Dead* in big letters on the cover. The other two were called *The Psychedelic Experience*; one of those was a comic. Breen stared at them, unsure which he wanted.

'The first one is the original translation of the Bardo Thodol. The second is Timothy Leary's translation. Basically, it riffs on the concept that the three stages of transition to the dead are the same as when you trip on LSD. You can reach enlightenment without having to, like, die.'

'Fuck sake,' muttered Carmichael.

Breen pulled out a pound note and bought the book called *The Psychedelic Experience*.

'Can we go now?'

They meandered back west again.

'What was all that about?'

'Something Doyle's girlfriend mentioned, that's all.'

Soho was on the move again. In the cramped roadway of Lisle Street, a couple of Chinese restaurants had opened just in the last couple of months, hanging red silk lanterns outside. They looked gaudy and exotic, out of place, in the dark London evening. Until now, the Chinese had always lived around the docks. Even the bombs hadn't shifted them. Ducks hung in the window of one restaurant, their skins roasted shiny and darkly gelatinous.

'Well, look who it is,' said Carmichael.

The Chinese waiter, dressed in black suit and bow tie, looked up and caught Breen's eye. There was a definite flinch. His eyes darted to the kitchen door behind him. Breen held up his hands and smiled. It's OK. You're safe. After a second, the man relaxed, smiled back.

'Ask him,' said Carmichael. 'After all. He owes you one.'

It was true. The man was a criminal; a thief. Breen had saved him from a beating a few months earlier, letting him go when the other coppers had wanted to see his legs broken at the very least.

'You reckon?'

'Why not?'

Breen turned to his friend. 'It's just that it might not be what you need to hear.'

Carmichael nodded. 'I know.'

The restaurant was nearly empty. The interior smelt rich and sweet. There was a hint of seared onions. Sat beneath a gaudy picture of a dragon, an elderly Chinese couple were bent over bowls of watery noodles.

'Do you have a minute?' asked Breen.

Without saying anything, the man nodded towards the swing door at the back of the tiny room. Breen and Carmichael followed him there. The first thing Breen saw were the huge knives hanging on meathooks. He stopped in the doorway, gripping the edge of the door.

The Chinaman grinned. 'Don't worry. The knife is not for you this time.'

Breen tried not to look at the blades. They made him feel nauseous. The kitchen was hot and cramped. Tins cluttered the shelves. Ugly-looking dried fish hung from a string, white blots where eyes had been. A tiny man, less than five foot tall, was holding a huge rounded dish over a gas flame. The Chinaman said something incomprehensible. The small man shouted back angrily, but eventually turned off the gas, picked up a dishcloth, wiped his hands and left the room for the cool of the alley behind.

In the fetid, thick-smelling air, Breen felt sweat breaking out on his face. The waiter pulled out a cigarette and lit it. Breen said, 'Have you heard about a Chinese gang who were arrested recently for the murder of a policeman?'

The waiter's smile vanished; he looked from Breen to Carmichael and back again.

'Well?'

The man nodded, slowly, sucked deeply on his cigarette.

'Do you know them?'

Another hesitation. His nostrils blew streams of smoke. 'A little, maybe.'

'Did they do it?'

'Why does it matter if they did it?' said the waiter. 'The police say they did.'

'It matters to us.'

The Chinaman snorted.

'Well?'

'These men. They are shit,' said the Chinaman. 'They deserve it, anyway. Nobody is crying apart from them.'

Breen looked at Carmichael. 'But they didn't kill Sergeant Milkwood?'

The man shook his head. 'Everyone talking about it. One day before the arrest, some people arrive at their house with search warrant. Nobody understands why. Next day different police arrive and find photographs of dead man there.'

'The police planted the evidence?'

'Of course.' The man shrugged. 'Only a fool keeps a photo of the man he kills.'

'Who planted the evidence?'

'They say they were looking for heroin.'

'The Drug Squad?' Breen said. 'You know anything about this?'

Carmichael said, 'A few days back, Pilcher picked a couple of the lads for a raid in the East End. I was surprised. He doesn't normally bother with lowlifes like that.'

'Did they find any drugs?' asked Breen.

The Chinese man shook his head. 'They were not looking for drugs,' he said. 'They could have found plenty. Heroin. Everything.'

Outside Breen was grateful for the cool air. The smell of spices and meat had made him feel sick. 'My bus will be along in a minute,' he said.

Carmichael was deep in thought

'Well?' said Breen. Carmichael didn't answer. Breen said, 'It was a stitch-up. Drug Squad framed them. Why?'

'Why would you believe a man like him?' said Carmichael. 'You'd stick up for a guy like that before your fellow coppers. Always.'

Breen could see his bus, coming up Charing Cross Road.

'You're the one who said I should ask him.'

'I know.'

'You call sticking up for your fellow copper letting whoever killed him go free?'

'Fuck off. You know I didn't mean that.'

'Your lot are bent, John. Something's going on.'

'I know,' Carmichael said, shaking his head. 'It's all shit, isn't it?'

On the bus, he looked for Carmichael on the crowded pavement to wave goodbye, but he had gone already. He opened the book he'd bought in the hippie bookshop and read two or three pages, but couldn't make head or tail of it. He was never much good at reading at the best of times.

TWENTY-FIVE

Breen couldn't sleep.

The flat suddenly seemed too empty, too quiet.

He got up at four and sat by the electric fire, smoking a cigarette.

He was at the reference library when it opened at 8.30.

'Do you have *The Times* for 1953 to 1955?' he asked.

He found a space at a desk and sat with the pile of wide volumes, bound in green leather. Fifteen years ago the Kenyan violence had been in the newspapers almost every day: assaults on farmers, calls to extend emergency powers, settlers demanding executions. The heat and the violence seemed contained in the neat, orderly newspaper prose. It was all very dry. Very English. He made the occasional note in his notebook, but he was not sure what the purpose of those notes was.

He worked through the huge bound pages, piling the volumes on the desk. He remembered little of it. It was not his world. He would have been sixteen or seventeen when this had been going on, bunking off school, which he hated but which his father insisted he stay on at, to hang around Soho with Carmichael.

He struggled to concentrate on the articles. Time and time again, one colonial government spokesman after another would reassure journalists that the situation was coming under control; appeal court justices would complain about the 'softening up' processes being used in the screening camps, but there was little detail about what those were. Meanwhile, the anger and frustration of settlers seethed through in their demands for 'swifter justice.'

He found an article about how they were setting up new police stations in the Kikuyu areas, staffed by local white police reservists, and how they'd rapidly recruited hundreds of new white policemen, 'mostly untrained, and from England'. Doyle would have been one of those, Breen supposed. Milkwood would have been more experienced, but again, nothing would have prepared him for this world.

What would it have been like to arrive there, young and idealistic, into an ugly, violent war? Everything would have been unfamiliar.

His mind drifted. He found himself reading the classified adverts for small hotels and charities, and the marriage and death notices that had filled the front page of the newspaper back then. When had they started putting the news there instead of adverts? The newspapers seemed so much stuffier than they were now. Had so much changed since he was a boy? He turned a page. A butcher fined for buying meat coupons. Rationing seemed so far away now, but he had grown up with it as part of everyday life. There were so few large advertisements in those days too, which made the pages even more lifeless.

In the afternoon, the librarian woke him, a thin man in wire-framed glasses. Breen lifted his face from the open volume. A dark spot of drool had soaked into the newsprint.

'You were shouting,' said the librarian.

He looked around. Everyone in the library was staring at him.

'Was I?'

He tried to remember. He had been dreaming of men with knives again, cutting skin. Only this time he realised he was one of the men with the knives, doing the cutting.

Other library visitors looked at him warily now, as if he were some escaped lunatic.

That evening he called Helen.

'Last night, I dreamed I gave birth to a fish,' she said. 'It was horrible. You think that means something? I think I'm going bananas.'

'Mine was a nightmare too,' said Breen. 'Listen. I've been thinking. We have to at least try to speak to Fletchet again. He's the only real lead we have.'

'You still think it's worth it?'

'Yes.'

'That mean you're coming down?' she said.

'Why? Don't you want me to?'

There was a pause. 'Yes. I would like that.' Then she whispered, 'Don't say anything, will you?'

'What?'

'I've not told them yet. About the baby.'

'Jesus, Helen. When are you going to?'

'They were still upset about the police being here. I thought I'd better wait.'

'What about Hibou? Did you tell her we saw her parents?'

'No. I shouldn't have gone there. You were right.'

'Really?' he said.

That night Breen didn't sleep any better. He lay awake listening to the noise of the streets outside, wondering whether it was a mistake going down to Devon.

When he finally fell asleep it was past five o'clock in the morning. The first post woke him a little after that. He walked in his slippers to the door, but it was only a bill from the GPO and a letter from D Division. The doctor had informed them he would be fit for work again in a week.

The train to Devon was full of Marines returning to base in Plymouth. They drank bottles of cider and put their feet on the opposite seats. But when a woman got on with a boy of nine or ten and took the last remaining seat in the compartment they all fell quiet and hid their bottles.

'Want a cigarette, ma'am?' one of them said, holding out a packet of No. 6's.

She shook her head.

When the child began looking bored with his copy of the *Beezer*, one of the soldiers pulled out a pen and drew a face on his hand, turning the joint of his hand and his thumb into a mouth and using it to talk to the boy.

'What's the difference between an evil baker and a brave soldier?' said the hand.

'Don't know.'

'A brave soldier darts into the foe and the evil baker . . .'

The boy started laughing. The woman smiled.

'Give over, Smiler,' said one of the squaddies.

'Sorry, ma'am.' Big laugh all round.

Breen tried to imagine these people torturing anyone. He couldn't. But perhaps it didn't take much to turn men into monsters.

There was a generation of men a little older than Breen who had come back from the war, who had served in France or Germany, North Africa or Italy, and talked about their war all the time in pubs. The same stories over and over.

Others stayed quiet. Was it because they didn't like to discuss what they had seen, or because they couldn't bear to talk about what they had done?

Helen was waiting outside the station in the Morris. He leaned over to kiss her as he got into the car but she moved slightly to one side, so he ended up kissing air.

'Still not told them?' he asked.

She shook her head. 'Not yet. I'm not ready.'

The car smelt as if they'd been keeping chickens in it.

'How's Hibou?'

'Happy.' She crunched the ancient gears.

'You sound like that's a bad thing.'

'Being on the farm makes her happy. She loves it. She's a bloody natural.'

'And how are you feeling?'

'Fat,' she said.

'You look good. Glowing.'

'Do I?'

The farm looked different. A bright, new sheen of green covered the hedges. Winter was sliding into spring. The cows were in the fields, eating the new grass.

Mrs Tozer had cooked dinner, but Hibou and Mr Tozer stayed out until it was completely dark. 'Dad's teaching her how to plough. You were never so good at ploughing, were you?'

'Bully for her,' said Helen.

Breen stared at the hunk of greasy lamb in front of him and watched Helen tuck in.

'I wasn't that bad. I was better than Alex, anyways.'

There was cabbage too. This time of year, cabbage was about the only green vegetable left. Mrs Tozer had put a mound of it on Breen's plate. She was glad to see Breen back. She sensed something was in the air. The lamb was a treat.

Breen was still carving small pieces of his meat and chewing them slowly when Hibou and old man Tozer returned. Mrs Tozer stood and removed their hot plates from the range.

'How's the ploughing?' Helen asked.

'Super,' said Hibou.

'How can ploughing be super?' said Helen.

Hibou ignored her. 'Want some more gravy?' she said to old man Tozer. He nodded and she poured some over his plate.

Helen rolled her eyes.

'She done great stuff,' said Mr Tozer. 'You should have been out there too, Hel.'

Helen shrugged. 'I told you, I don't feel well,' she said.

Breen raised his eyebrows.

'No need,' said Hibou. 'I can do it fine anyway.'

Breen watched the slight young girl tucking into her meat.

'What's this I heard about you having a boyfriend?' Helen said.

The eating stopped. Mrs Tozer looked at Helen. 'Is that right, dearie?'

Hibou blushed, didn't answer.

Helen said, 'My friend Val said she'd seen you down by the river with this bloke. Holding his hand apparently, she said.'

Breen remembered seeing her disappear on walks. Hibou said quietly, 'Just somebody I met.'

'You should bring him round, love. I'd like to meet him,' said Mrs Tozer.

Mr Tozer grunted, put another piece of meat on the end of his fork and ate it.

'Is that who you've been going to see some evenings?' said Mrs Tozer. 'When you go on your walks?'

Hibou, still blushing, shook her head. 'It's nobody. Honest.'

'It's Spud, isn't it? He had his eyes all over you.'

Hibou looked at her plate.

'Is that true?' said old man Tozer, frowning.

Hibou shook her head. 'No. I don't know what they're talking about.'

Mr Tozer stared at her for a couple of seconds, then grunted. He tipped his plate forward to catch the gravy, using a spoon to scoop it all up.

That evening, Breen helped with the washing-up. Afterwards, they washed jam jars. Mrs Tozer had hundreds of them in the shed, ready for the fruit picking at the end of the year.

'Hibou's sneaky, that's what she is. She hides things from us. Like the letter. Like Spud.'

Helen was driving, cigarette in her mouth.

'Alex was seeing a bloke too, wasn't she? And then what happened? Besides, Hibou's choice in men hasn't been exactly great.' The man she lived with in London was the person who'd introduced her to heroin. Breen opened his mouth to speak but Helen turned to him and said, 'Don't you go saying I told you so. I mean, she knows what happened to my sister.'

'You shouldn't have brought it up, though. At dinner. She was embarrassed. You should speak to her on her own.'

'I'm not like you. You're the one who always wants to keep stuff bottled up. I say bring it out into the open. It's all these secrets that I can't stand.'

'What if she doesn't want it brought out into the open?'

Breen thought of the time he'd seen her walking across the fields, down to the estuary.

'Do you have to drive so fast?' he said.

'I know these roads.' But she was gripping the wheel, white-knuckled.

'One thing, though. We don't know that Fletchet is even involved in this. It's just a guess, still,' he said.

'I know that,' she said. 'What do you take me for?'

'I just don't want you to get your hopes up.'

'Hopes?' she said, and braked hard. A pair of cyclists, startled by her sudden approach, were cowering close to the hedge.

Spring made the Fletchet estate look even more English. The leaves were bursting on horse chestnuts, almost absurdly green.

Helen pulled the bell chain.

There was a red Riley parked by the door, but Fletchet's Land Rover wasn't there. Nobody answered so Breen banged on the door with his fist while Helen walked round to the side. Still nobody came. Breen followed Helen, walking down an alleyway of sandstone flags.

'She's in here,' Helen called to Breen.

Mrs Fletchet was in the dining room at the back of the house, shortening the stems of some daffodils. Breen entered through the kitchen and joined Helen.

'He's not here, apparently,' said Helen.

'As I said, he's gone to Africa,' said Mrs Fletchet, secateurs still in hand. 'It would have been a courtesy to call first. I don't like being ambushed.'

'Kenya?'

'One would assume so. It's what he told me, at least. We still own a farm out there. Apparently some business cropped up.'

'Very sudden,' said Breen.

'Yes,' she said, standing back from the vase and looking at it, head cocked. 'Wasn't it?'

'When was this?'

'Last Thursday. He had gone up to London. Instead of coming home, he went off to London Airport.'

Breen did a quick calculation. That was the day he had met Fletchet at Pratt's. He asked, 'Did he tell you what it was that was so urgent?'

297

'The farm manager had resigned, so he said.'

Breen paused. 'You sound as if you don't believe him.'

Again, a smile. 'Why should I not believe him? Of course, there was no need for him to go to Kenya whether a manager resigned or not. He hates the place. But maybe the farm manager has resigned. It's possible.'

Breen looked at Helen. 'What are you saying?'

'Oh. Use your imagination. Why do you think husbands say they are going away on business suddenly?'

Helen said, 'A woman?'

She said, 'I didn't say it, anyway.'

'When do you expect him back?'

'I don't know and I don't care.' And she snipped the end of the daffodils sharply.

'He didn't give you any idea?'

'No. He said he may be some time.'

She turned on her heels and marched out of the dining room as if she expected them to follow. Helen made a face and then left the room.

Mrs Fletchet was in the sitting room now, picking up an old newspaper from a pile by the fireplace, then laying it flat onto a coffee table beneath the head of a gazelle. The grotesque animal heads around the walls seemed to be glaring at Breen.

'Did he sound worried?'

'Yes, he did, as it happens. I don't know why. That makes me think the whole farm thing is an excuse. He's never that bothered about what happens there. Why do you want to talk to him?'

'Did the police come and interview him about Sergeant Milkwood?'

She looked up. 'Yes. Poor Sergeant Milkwood. Not that I liked him that much. I found him rather dull. His wife was awful. What was her name?'

298

'Gwen.'

'Was it? What a horrid name that is. They said he was murdered. I don't know what is happening to your country.'

'How did your husband seem, after the police interviewed him?'

'What is this about, Sergeant?'

'Tell me. Please.'

'Yes. He did seem upset. Obviously he would be. He worked closely with Sergeant Milkwood during the Emergency. And they just barged in and said he'd been murdered.'

'How upset?'

'He became quite drunk, as a matter of fact, after they'd gone. More than usual, anyway. He was on the Martel. I left him to it and went to bed. In the morning he had gone up to London, on business, he said.'

Helen said, 'What time did he leave?'

'We sleep in separate bedrooms,' said Mrs Fletchet, 'so I wouldn't know. I know the fashion these days is to share the same bed but I find I sleep better in my own room.'

She took a vase full of faded tulips and removed the flowers, laying them on the paper.

'Do you know exactly what your husband and Sergeant Milkwood were doing, during the Emergency?'

She jerked her head back a little, as if surprised by the question. 'Of course not. I wouldn't have dreamed of asking him, either.'

'Why not?'

She paused, looking down at the dead flowers. 'It was the one time in my life I have been very proud of Jim. I know he was doing important work. I know it was not easy, either. When such awful things are going on, it's important that normal life continues. The meal was on the table. The servants were properly dressed. It's not like you can say, "Did you have a nice day at the office, darling?" I'm sure it was quite horrid. But necessary.'

'Your husband ran a screening camp.'

'He was doing something useful in those days.'

'Useful?' said Helen.

'Of course.'

'So you had no idea what his work involved?'

'I'm a woman,' said Mrs Fletchet. 'It was not my business to ask.'

Helen said, 'I think you do know. But like his girls, you don't talk about it.'

Another of those tight smiles.

'You never even wondered?' said Breen.

'Sometimes he and the other men would come back to our house for drinks. They talked a little then.'

'What about?'

'We all used to drink a great deal in those days. It was one of the things I loved about Africa. Out there, we weren't so prissy. The English love gin. Me, not so much.'

'Did you know he was torturing people?' Breen asked.

She didn't seem shocked by the question. She simply said, 'It wasn't torture. It was interrogation. You should know the difference.'

'What is it?'

'I'm surprised at the question, Sergeant. Torture is carried out by evil people. And if that is too nice a point for you to appreciate, then what would you have preferred him to do? Let the country descend into chaos?'

'So he never discussed the details of what he did?'

'Not really. What kind of man do you think he is, for goodness' sake?'

Breen said, 'What about Nicholas Doyle?'

'Nicky? Is that what this is about?'

'I'm not sure,' said Breen. 'What do you mean?'

She went to the window. A long view out over rolling Devon countryside. 'I haven't thought about Nicholas for a long time. I always rather liked Nicky. At first anyway. He was always so very sweet. And very, very handsome. We used to invite them all to dinner once a week. Sergeant and Mrs Milkwood. And Nicky Doyle. He was only a boy, really, but so good-looking. I think he was very much in awe of us. He may have even been a little in love with me, I think.'

Behind Mrs Fletchet's back, Helen rolled her eyes.

'But he'd grown up in London, of course. He'd never been in society. It was all very new to him. I think he said his father was a docker. The first time we offered him cocktails, he got terribly drunk and started singing awful music-hall songs. There was one about a rat catcher. It was simply terrible. Quite funny, though. He came and apologised to me the very next day, though I didn't mind at all. But that was before he went native.'

'He went native?' said Helen.

'Poor Nicky went a bit mad. You have to understand the enormous pressure the men were under. They had to question hundreds of men, women, even children. It was a matter of urgency.'

'Question them?'

'Of course. To find out if they were Mau Mau. That was the whole point. I felt sorry for Nicky really. It was a difficult time and he was so very young. No experience of the world. He fell in love with a native girl. Poor silly boy. And then he and Jimmy fell out and he stopped coming to our parties. Not long after that, Jimmy said he had simply stopped turning up to work. He was sacked fairly shortly afterwards. It was inevitable. And that was the last anyone saw of him.' She wrapped the tulips in newspaper and picked them up. 'Is that all?'

'When is your husband coming back?'

'He didn't say.'

'When we came here the first time, do you know if your husband contacted Bill Milkwood immediately after we'd been?'

'I have no idea. Have you finished? I've had enough now. Can you leave?'

'He did, didn't he? What did he say to Bill Milkwood? Was he concerned that I'd been here?'

She went to the door and opened it. 'I've wasted enough time.'

'What frightened him, Mrs Fletchet?'

'You will leave now,' she said. She pushed Breen out of the door into the hallway.

Helen followed them. 'Your husband. Have there been many women?'

Mrs Fletchet glared. 'I don't think that's any of your business.'

'What about in 1964?' said Helen. 'Do you know who he was sleeping with in 1964?'

'Helen,' interrupted Breen.

'What?' And she looked at Breen, head slightly cocked, challenging him to stop her. Careful Breen.

Breen met her eye. 'Nothing. Go ahead,' he said.

Mrs Fletchet said, 'I don't like you being here and I don't like your questions. I shall report you.'

Helen said, 'In 1964, he was sleeping with my sister. She was sixteen. Did you know that?'

Mrs Fletchet didn't flinch. She simply looked Helen in the eye. 'Well, she must have been a bit of a whore, then.'

Breen wondered if Helen would try and hit her, but she just stood there, glaring at Mrs Fletchet, who strode to the front door and opened it.

'Why do you put up with it? All the women?' said Helen.

'Get out,' she said, not looking them in the eye.

She pushed the big front door shut behind them.

They stood on the doorstep. They could sense Mrs Fletchet on the other side of the door, listening for the sound of them departing.

'What a cow,' said Helen, loudly enough to be heard.

They drove back towards the farm more slowly than they'd come.

'What if he killed Alex because he was scared of her finding out?' she said. 'What if Milkwood was covering up for him all that time? All that alibi thing was concocted?'

She paused at a crossroads.

'It adds up, doesn't it?' she said. 'And then he'd be worried that Milkwood would spill the beans, so he killed him.'

'Why torture him?'

'I don't know. Because he's a sadist? Because he wants to throw the police off the scent?'

'The trouble is there's no way of proving it. And if they've arrested someone for Mikwood's death that investigation is at a dead end. If he goes to ground in Kenya, there's no way we can get at him.'

She accelerated, filling the road behind with black exhaust smoke.

Breen walked up the steep lane towards the farm gate.

Hibou was working on the hedge in the top field. Breen checked his watch. He had a few minutes before the bus. He worked his way across the grass, careful not to put his shoes into any dung.

Hibou moved slowly along the hedge, hacking at loose branches and saplings that had grown too tall. He watched her for a while. Her moves were confident and strong.

She turned, smiled at him. 'You off?'

'Just going into town. I need some clothes.' A lie. He wanted to go somewhere to use a phone that would be out of earshot of the Tozers. 'Do you want anything?'

'Does Helen hate me?' said Hibou, holding the billhook in the air, ready to strike.

'No. I think she's just having a hard time. And she's thinking a lot about what happened to her sister. She's not normally like this, I promise. Is it true you have a boyfriend?'

Hibou blushed, just as she had at dinner. 'No. I wish everyone would shut up about it.'

'What's his name?'

'I'm not going out with anyone, OK?'

'Just pulling your leg,' said Breen.

Hibou started hacking at a sapling, bringing the hook down diagonally onto the stem, half cutting it through. She knocked the stem sideways, down into the mass of the hedge. She looked like she'd been doing it all her life.

Breen said, 'Helen just gets worried. Her sister had a boyfriend she didn't tell anyone about.'

Hibou turned, billhook in the air. 'Helen thinks she owns me. Just because she helped me get off drugs.'

'She means well.'

'Does she?'

Whack: into the hedge went the hook.

'Yes. She really does.'

'I know. Tell you what, if you really want to do something for me, can you go and get me a postal order for eight and six?'

She put the hook down, handle up, and leaned on the head of it. 'I'm joining the Biodynamic Agricultural Association. I know you think all that's rubbish, but old man Tozer doesn't.'

'Doesn't he?'

She shook her head, smiled.

'No. He listens when I talk about it, at least. Unlike Helen. She thinks she's so clever.'

Old man Tozer would do anything she asked. She was his second chance.

'What the hell's that noise?' asked Carmichael.

'Sheep.'

'What?'

It was market day in Newton Abbot.

'Fletchet has gone,' he said.

'Gone where?'

'To Africa. I can't stop thinking it may be him. That the first investigation fumbled it.'

'Why? Because he has gone?'

'He slept with Alexandra. His wife was jealous. Maybe Milkwood was blackmailing him. I don't know. He was acting so suspiciously when I saw him at Pratt's. And now he's disappeared.'

'I thought you said he had an alibi.'

'He did. But maybe it was all a cover-up by Milkwood.'

'It would have had to be a pretty elaborate cover-up.'

Sheep crowded around the phone box, driven by old men in caps and worn jackets. They held their arms out, shouting strange words. To Breen it looked tribal.

'No, there's been nothing this end,' said Carmichael. 'Since they arrested someone for Milkwood's murder it's been quiet.'

'Whoever really did it is going to get away with it, John,' Breen shouted above the noise.

'I can't hear you,' said Carmichael.

Breen put the phone down and waited in the telephone box until the tide of animals passed on down the street, towards waiting lorries.

Pushing the door open, he picked his way through small piles of droppings, fresh and shiny on the tarmac.

'Did you get my postal order?'

Hibou, spooning down stew and dumplings at the dining table.

Breen said, 'In my coat. I'll fetch it.'

He didn't mind putting off eating Mrs Tozer's stew. The liquid in the pot was covered by a thick layer of animal grease. He returned with the envelope and handed it to Hibou across the table.

'What's the postal order for?' said Helen.

'I'm joining the Biodynamic Agricultural Association.'

Helen rolled her eyes.

'Leave her alone,' said her father. 'At least she's interested in farming. Like your sister was.'

'She was never. Alex hated farming.'

'No, she didn't.'

'First chance she got, she was going to leave this place. She told me a million times.'

Mrs Tozer tutted. 'Don't talk about your sister like that.'

Hibou looked down at the envelope, trying not to meet anybody's eye.

'Fine,' said Helen. 'Whatever you say.'

Before, they never even used to talk about Alexandra.

'Well, it's about time I said it,' said Mr Tozer. 'I'm going to fill in the dip in the spinney. Always meant to do it.'

Helen put down her knife and fork. 'You can't do that,' she said.

'Farm isn't big enough to let land go to waste like that,' he said. 'Way things are going now, we're having to compete with bigger

306

and bigger farms. We have to use all the land we have or we won't survive. Going to level it and drain it. Digger's coming next week.'

'You can't,' said Helen again. She looked pale.

Mrs Tozer said quietly, 'It's five years now. We've got to move on.'

'What if I don't want to?'

They ate in silence for a minute. Across the table, Hibou opened the envelope and pulled out two sheets of printed paper.

'They're pretty, aren't they?'

One for five shillings. One for three and six. Delicately engraved patterns to discourage forgers. Breen looked down at the postal orders too.

'Give me them,' he said, reaching out his hand.

'They're mine,' protested Hibou.

Breen stretched across the table and took them from her, staring at them. He hadn't looked twice when he bought them at the post office in town. Now he was frowning at them.

'What's wrong?' said Helen.

Breen looked at one, then the other, and back again.

'Paddy?' said Helen.

'Nothing,' he said, and handed them back.

As he dug at a bit of beef floating in his stew, Breen was conscious of people around the table looking at each other, raising their eyebrows.

'What exactly is biodynamic farming, anyway?' he asked, to change the subject.

Hibou said, 'It's about harmonising the life forces within the farm.'

There was silence.

'It's sort of about going back to the old ways,' said Mrs Tozer.

'Mum!' said Helen. 'Don't say she's got you involved in this mumbo-jumbo as well as Dad.'

'It's not mumbo-jumbo!' shouted Hibou, turning red.

'Load of superstious crap,' said Helen.

'Don't you get it, Hel? They're using DDT everywhere. That kills everything. The same chemicals they're pouring onto the Viet Cong, they're persuading us to buy for our farms. They're putting chickens in big sheds to get eggs cheap. Listen to what people are saying. They're saying how these chickens are pecking each other to death. Everything is out of balance. In a few years there won't be farms any more, there will just be factories. People think nature is there to be exploited.'

'That doesn't stop putting a load of old bones in a field and planting by the moon being a load of bollocks,' said Helen.

'I don't bloody care what you think,' said Hibou.

'We'll have no language in this house, my dear,' said Mrs Tozer.

There was silence for a second and then Helen said, 'And by the way. I'm going to have a bloody baby.'

This time the silence was even deeper.

Eventually her father said, 'What? You're expecting?'

'You heard what I said,' said Helen.

The rest of the supper was pauses and embarrassment.

'Is it Paddy's?' said Hibou.

Helen glared at her.

'Would anyone like more cabbage? No? Save a space for tinned peaches,' said Helen's mother, as if nothing had happened.

Helen's father muttered something.

'I think it's great, don't you?' said Hibou. Nobody answered her.

Mr Tozer pushed away his wife's hand when she tried to ladle more food onto his plate. 'I'm not hungry!' he shouted, then slammed down his knife and fork on his plate. Hibou looked shocked.

Helen held out her hand towards her father, but he didn't take it. Breen had the sense Helen's mother was glaring at him, as if this was all his fault, but didn't turn to look.

They ate tinned peaches with custard for pudding. Left on the cooker too long, the custard had a hard film of skin on the top.

As soon as supper was over Breen excused himself, glad to be away from the family. Nobody was talking. He went to his bedroom and started flicking through his notebooks until he found the copy he'd made of the note he had found among Milkwood's drawerful of pornography.

The lists of numbers and letters. The numbers were postal orders.

And from there, he realised that the letters in the left-hand column were the months. N, D, J: November, December, January.

They were monthly payments by postal order, and, assuming they'd been paid this year, the last one had been made not long before Milkwood's death. Why had he made them? Who had he made them to? And why had he hidden them in his drawer?

There was a knock on his door. It was Helen.

'It's like the whole house has gone bloody nuts.'

'You can talk. You picked your moment to tell your family the news.'

'I couldn't help it. She's driving me mad with all that muck-and-magic guff. I can't believe Dad has fallen for it.'

'You're jealous it's her who's brought your dad back, not you.'

'Oh, shut up.' She sat on his bed, laid back against the wall and lit a cigarette. 'You're right, though. I gave up everything to come back here and look after my dad. But I needn't have bothered, need I?'

She kicked off her shoes and they clattered onto the ancient boards.

'You should be pleased he's working again.'

'Course I am,' she said. 'But I didn't bring Hibou down here so they could bloody forget about Alex. That's what they're doing. It's like she's replacing her. Erasing her. They're bloody bulldozing over where her body was.'

'You brought her down here to try and help her. It's worked. She's happy here.'

'Well, I'm not bloody pleased. I'm pregnant.'

He shuffled next to her, back against the wall too. 'Do you think they're happy about the baby, though?'

'Mum says I have to bring it up here.' For the first time, Breen realised she was crying. Her cheeks shone. 'I'm never going to get away from this bloody farm. I'm going to be buried here alongside Hibou's bloody cow horns.'

Breen reached out and put his left arm around her shoulder. She leaned into him. They sat there for a while, together.

'What's that you're looking at?' she asked. Breen had the notebook open in front of them. 'They're postal order numbers. I only just realised when I saw Hibou's postal order.'

'What are?'

He explained how he'd found the list hidden in a drawer of men's magazines at Milkwood's house.

'Men's magazines?'

'Pornographic magazines.'

'Dirty perv.'

'They must have been important, mustn't they? Why would he hide it unless it was important? I was thinking, we could find out when they were cashed. And where. If they were crossed we could find out who cashed them. They'd need to have countersigned the orders.'

'It's just clutching at straws, Paddy.'

'No, look. The last one was in January. So if it's this year he was issuing these postal orders right up to a few weeks before he died.'

'Paddy, it could be anything. Maybe he was paying a mistress. Maybe he had a gambling habit.'

'Come on, Helen. Don't give up now. I've not seen you like this before.'

Helen said, 'Giving up what? Tell me? I'm so unhappy, Paddy. Everything's gone wrong. I was going to go and see the world. I was going to be so cool. Now I'm going to be stuck here with a bloody baby. I hate being a bloody girl.'

'Stop it, Helen. Please.'

'I can't bear it any more. Maybe Dad's right after all. We should just bulldoze over the whole thing and forget Alex. I'm going to live on a farm and raise babies.'

She wiped her eyes with the back of her hand.

'I didn't think you were like that, Helen.'

She pulled away from him. 'What am I like, Paddy? I'm like a pregnant woman whose life is over.'

He looked at her and said, 'When I first met you, I was scared of you.'

She laughed, clapped her hand over her mouth. 'Really? Don't be ridiculous.'

'Seriously. I didn't know what to make of you. You were so fierce. So determined.'

She dropped her hand down to her lap and peered at him. 'Was I?'

'Remember biting my head off that time in the police station? Mr Popularity Contest, you called me.'

'Did I say that? God. I'm sorry.'

'Another day you were so angry with me you just drove off and left me to walk back to the station in the rain.'

She was laughing now. 'God. It's true. I really hated you. I thought you were a stuck-up old fogey.'

'Don't give up, then. You were amazing.'

'I was pretty fab, wasn't I?' She leaned against him again. 'I'm just tired, now, Paddy. So fucking tired. I've been carrying this thing with Alex around for too long. It wears you down.'

The weight of her head against his shoulder. 'So don't stop. Help me . . .'

She lifted her head away and nodded. 'OK.'

He leaned over the edge of the bed and picked up the notebook again, showing her the list of numbers. 'If these are postal orders, I need to find out who cashed them.'

She slid off the bed and knelt on the floor, looking at the page in his notebook on the bed. 'Long shot, though, isn't it?'

'Do you reckon you could get Sergeant Sharman to do it?'

She shrugged. 'Course I could. I could get him to do most things,' she said.

Breen shook his head. 'Will you ask him?'

'You actually think this has something to do with Alex, don't you?' she asked.

'It may not be. But it's worth a go, isn't it?'

'I don't know why you keep going at this. Nobody else bloody cares.'

'Yes, they do.'

She exhaled. It was a long breath. As if she was trying to keep hold of that fury. Breen leaned forward to kiss her, but just before his lips met skin, there was another knock on the door.

A cough, then: 'Mr Breen?' Helen flinched away. It was her father. The door handle rattled.

'One minute,' said Breen.

Helen held her finger up to her lips and whispered, 'Don't let him know I'm in here.'

'I think you and me need a word.'

312

'I'll come downstairs,' Breen called through the door. 'Give me a second.'

They listened to him walking back downstairs.

'He'll be wanting to know what your intentions are,' said Helen.

'It's not my intentions that matter, is it?'

'Nope,' she said, turning her head away from him.

Downstairs in the kitchen Mrs Tozer busied herself tidying a shelf, lips pursed tightly, pretending not to notice Breen as he walked through to the living room to talk to her husband.

TWENTY-SIX

It the first warm day of the year. Above the new grass, there was an undulating haze of small insects.

Breen sat on a chair in front of the house with a sketchbook on his lap as a chainsaw buzzed at a tree at the front of the house. The water in the estuary looked oddly blue, the grass frighteningly green.

'There she goes.'

There was a splintering sound, then a groaning, then silence.

Breen left his sketchbook and went round to the front of the house to see what had happened.

One of the ash trees in the copse lay on its side, bare branches still bouncing up and down from the impact, buds like big, black, dirty fingernails.

Hibou was in the tractor seat in a tatty bright red jumper that was frayed at the neck, looking back at the trunk, while old man Tozer was bent over it, unhitching the chain. She was grinning. 'Ruddy great,' she said.

The tree looked absurd lying on its side, trunk split. It had cracked through the old rusty fence he had crawled through that time when the weather was colder, when he had fallen into the dip.

But old man Tozer wasn't looking at the tree. He was looking beyond it, up at the hillside. 'Ma!'

There was something in the urgency of the voice.

Breen followed his eyes. A police car, blue light spinning, slowly coming down the track from the main road, sump scraping on the rise in the centre of the track, wheels bumping into potholes.

'Ma! Come quick.'

When it was close, Breen made out the shape of Sergeant Sharman hunched over the wheel, a uniformed officer in the seat next to him and another in the back.

Three policemen and a light still flashing. Sharman got out of the car, looking around him.

'Where's Helen?' he said.

'Why?'

The other two policemen were out now, alert, waiting for some kind of instructions.

'What's going on?'

Old man Tozer had come down the path, out of breath, anxious. Hibou had jumped off the tractor and was running to the house now too, spooking cows that scattered, bucking hooves and snorting in the warm air.

'Where is Helen Tozer?' Sharman looked flushed, agitated.

Breen, Mr Tozer and Hibou looked at each other, waiting for someone other to answer.

'What you talking about, Fred?'

'She didn't do the milking this morning,' said Hibou. 'I did that.'

Mrs Tozer arrived, a dishcloth in her hands.

'These gentlemen want to know where Hel is,' Mr Tozer said.

'She went to the doctor's,' said her mother. 'She's having a baby.'

Sharman blurted, 'A baby?' There was an embarrassed pause before Sharman said, nodding at Breen, 'I need a word with him, then.'

'OK,' said Breen.

'In private. We'll need to search the house too.'

'What is it, Freddie?' Mrs Tozer was asking. 'What's all the fuss about this time?'

'Please let us look round the house, Mrs T,' said Sharman. 'We won't be a minute.'

'You don't have to let them if they don't have a warrant,' said Breen.

Sharman's lips tightened but he nodded.

'I don't mind,' said Mrs Tozer. 'No skin off mine.'

Sharman glared at Breen, then said, 'Thank you, Mrs Tozer. OK, boys.' The two constables moved hesitantly towards the front door. 'Sergeant Breen. In the car please.'

Breen got into the front passenger seat of the car. Sharman got in beside him.

'All that bollocks about a warrant,' said Sharman.

'She looks after me. I had to tell her.'

'Fuck sake, Breen. This is serious.'

'What's so serious that you need to frighten the life out of an old woman? You know what she's been through.'

'A few days back you and Helen went to see Mrs Fletchet. Yes or no?'

'We went to see James Fletchet. He wasn't there.'

'Why?'

Sharman gripped the steering wheel, knuckles tight. Whatever had happened, Sharman was rattled, tense. Breen began to feel less sure of himself. 'Look. We believe there is a connection between James Fletchet, the death of Sergeant Bill Milkwood and the possible death of a second man, Nicholas Doyle. I think there's also a connection between their killings and the murder of Alexandra Tozer.'

'Oh, Jesus. Did Helen know this?'

'Yes.'

'Did she suspect that James Fletchet may have been involved in the death of her sister?'

'Yes. We both did.'

Sharman breathed out through his teeth. 'I hope to fuck she is at the doctor's.'

'Why?'

'Eloisa Fletchet may have been abducted this morning.'

Breen felt the blood rush to his ears. The world seemed to slow. 'What do you mean, abducted?'

Sharman considered for a minute. 'She was seen getting into a grey Mini van this morning. A guy driving the milk lorry saw it. He went to pick up the churns from their farm. He may have disturbed the kidnapper as she was taking her away.'

'She?'

'He said it was a woman. He thought Mrs Fletchet appeared to have a cloth bag on her head. It was a bit of a way off, so he couldn't be sure. He didn't report it for half an hour.'

'Jesus. Why the hell not?'

'Because he was an idiot. It was early. He thought he must have been seeing things. Or it was a prank. Then he had trouble finding a phone box. A bobby went there, first thing. There were signs of a struggle inside the house. Mrs Fletchet's dogs were dead. We think they were poisoned. We've got a vet looking at them now.'

'A woman?' Breen's head was spinning. There was no way he had ever thought that this was a woman's crime.

'Longish hair, and thin. Wearing a khaki skirt or possibly shorts. The driver was a way off, so he couldn't see her properly.'

'And you think that's Helen? She doesn't even have long hair. Seriously?'

'Of course I fucking don't, Sergeant,' Sharman snapped. He turned to Breen, hands still on the steering wheel. 'You twats at the Met. You think we're all yokels down here, don't you? But I know someone has been kidnapped and I have to look where I can. And when I asked if they've seen anyone strange coming to the estate these last couple of weeks, the first person they think of is Helen Tozer. And you. We've a record of Mrs Fletchet calling us up to complain about you two.'

Breen looked out at the estuary. 'A woman, though?'

Sharman calmed down. 'And she would have a motive, wouldn't she? And we have no other ideas. Have you got any?'

'What about signs of entry?'

'Nothing. The front door was open.'

'Do you think she let this woman in?'

'Possible.'

'Someone she knew.'

'Xactly.'

'No note. No hint of ransom?'

'We're contacting her family in Italy to see if they know anything but that may take a while.'

Fletchet wouldn't kidnap his own wife, Breen thought. He said, 'Twenty-four hours.'

'What?'

'Whoever kidnapped Alex tortured her for twenty-four hours before they killed her. The same with Bill Milkwood. Twenty-four hours and when he, or she, had finished, whoever it was killed them. We know that for a fact in those two cases. It may have been the same with Nicholas Doyle, we don't know yet.'

'Oh, Christ.'

'I know. What time was she taken?'

Sharman looked at his watch. Just gone quarter to twelve. 'At around six. You think this is the same person?'

'Don't you?'

'Jesus. Things like this don't happen down here.'

'They did once before.'

'Oh, Christ,' he said again. The two constables arrived back,

318

shaking their heads. They had searched the house. No sign of Helen.

One of them opened the back door, to get into the car. 'Not now,' said Sharman. 'We're talking.'

'If not Helen, who?'

'I have no bloody idea,' said Sharman. 'But it all started here, didn't it?'

'I think it may have started before all that. Fletchet, Milkwood and Doyle all met each other in Africa. And I think Fletchet may have been involved in torturing people in Kenya. Milkwood and Doyle worked with him during the Mau Mau Emergency. I've been starting to think that all this may be connected.'

'You're shitting me?'

'I keep coming back to this. Alexandra was tortured. Milkwood was tortured. There's at least one dead man turned up in Spain, possibly Doyle. He was tortured, too . . .'

Sharman took out some matches and a cigarette.

'You told Scotland Yard about this?'

'I tried to. They didn't believe me.'

They sat in the car, side by side, thinking. A crow landed on the drive in front of them, watching them with a shiny eye.

'Are you the father?' said Sharman.

'I think so.'

Sharman nodded. He rubbed a little ash off the end of his cigarette into the small ashtray under the police radio. 'You know she and I were hitched once? I thought the world of her.'

'I know.'

'I'm married now. Lovely woman. Great mother, you know? It would never have worked between Helen and me.' The radio crackled. 'You should marry Helen, then, if she's expecting.'

'That's what I told her.'

'And?'

'She's not bothered.'

'You and me both, then.'

They smiled at each other for just a second.

'I was supposed to give Helen this,' he said. He pulled out a piece of folded paper. Breen took it and opened it. It was the list of postal order numbers; next to each number was a date and the location of the post office where it had been cashed.

But Breen had been hoping for more. 'No name?'

'No. The postal orders weren't crossed, so anyone could cash them. Usually it takes the Post Office weeks for them to get back about these things. I told them it was important. Is it?'

'I was hoping it would have showed the identity of someone Sergeant Milkwood had been making payments to.'

Sharman nodded. 'Sorry it wasn't more useful. Come on, lads,' he called. 'We can't mess around. Tell Helen to get in touch the moment she's back.'

They left, all three policeman, revving up the hill, the extra weight grounding the car on every bump and pothole as Sharman gunned the engine, blue light on again.

On the gravel Breen noticed a single blue egg, spilled from a nest that had been in the tree Hibou and Mr Tozer had just brought down.

Breen packed up his sketchbook and went inside to the kitchen.

'Why were they after Helen?' said Mrs Tozer.

'It was a mistake,' said Breen. He checked his watch. If he was right, Eloisa Fletchet would have only eighteen hours to live. She would be being tortured, just as Mrs Tozer's daughter had been.

'What kind of mistake?'

'They just needed to check where she was. A woman has been kidnapped,' said Breen.

'Oh,' said Mrs Tozer, quietly. The whisk stopped in her bowl.

He unfolded the piece of paper Sharman had given him and stared at it for a second. Frowned. 'Have you got an *A–Z*?' he said.

'What's that?'

'A map of London.'

'Don't think so. Maybe Helen's got one.'

'When's she back?'

But just then there was the sound of a car pulling up outside and of a car door slamming, and then Helen was screaming, 'No!'

'It's only a tree.'

'It was not only a fucking tree.'

'Oh dear,' said Mrs Tozer, still holding the bowl.

Breen looked out of the window. Helen was standing next to the felled ash, shouting at Hibou.

'Christ.' He ran into the hallway and out of the front door.

'You stupid bloody cow!' Helen was still screaming at Hibou.

Hibou stood, wide-eyed and pale, a little frightened.

'Doesn't what I think count for anything round here?'

'I'm sorry. It was your dad's idea,' said Hibou.

'It's where my sister was,' screamed Helen. 'You may not care about your sister, but I still bloody care about mine.'

Rooks circled above the copse, unsure where to land.

'Sorry,' said Hibou, again. 'I was only trying to help your father. He wants to take them all down.'

'Well, I don't.'

'I didn't want to hurt you, Hel. Not you. But you should let go. Our souls are just passing clouds. You have to learn to detach yourself.'

'Oh, shut up. Just shut up, you stupid bloody hippie.'

Hibou flinched, then said, 'And the police called in. They were after you.'

'What? The police?'

'It's Eloisa Fletchet,' said Breen. 'She's been taken. Kidnapped by someone.'

But then Hibou said quietly, as if she'd just understood what Helen had said, 'What was that you said about my sister?'

Breen looked at Helen. She stood open-mouthed. He was not used to her looking embarrassed.

'I never told anyone I had a sister.'

Helen looked at the ground. The shouting had stopped; their voices were quiet.

'How did you know I had a sister?'

Helen floundered. 'I . . . We . . . We went to see your house. Where your mum and dad lived.'

Breen turned to Hibou and said, 'I found the letter you never posted. It had the address.'

'You went to my mum and dad's house?'

She stood there in her tatty pullover, mouth open, eyes big.

Helen nodded. 'Just to take a look. What's been going on, Paddy? Why were the police here?'

'Did you tell them where I was?' said Hibou.

'Course we didn't.'

'Promise?'

'Your dad,' said Helen. 'He wanted to know where you were. We didn't say.'

She nodded. 'So you saw my sister and my mum and everything?'

'Only for a sec.'

'They OK?'

'They looked fine. I'm really sorry, Hibou,' said Helen. 'I shouldn't have gone. I was just worried about you.'

Hibou nodded again, looked away. 'I think I'll just go and check on the heifers.'

They watched her trudge up the track towards the path. He realised he still had the piece of paper in his hand.

'Can you drive me to a library?' he said. 'It's urgent.'

'Fuck sake, Paddy. What is it? A dangerously overdue book? And what's that about Eloisa Fletchet? What was she saying about the police?'

Mrs Tozer emerged at the front door, a dishcloth in her trembling hand. She was looking older, suddenly, the wrinkles around her eyes deeper. A woman had been kidnapped. It was happening again.

TWENTY-SEVEN

They stood on the small tarmac square in front of the farmhouse. Breen said quietly, 'Eloisa Fletchet was kidnapped this morning. If I'm right, she'll be being tortured now, just like your sister. She was spotted being led away from the house by a woman. Because Mrs Fletchet had made a complaint about us being there, they had to come and check it wasn't you.'

Helen said, 'A woman? Christ. I've never for a second imagined that.'

She went to her mother and put her arms around her, and squeezed tightly. Mrs Tozer stood there, arms by her side, embarrassed.

'Everything OK at the doctor?' said her mother.

'Fine, Mum. OK?'

'Yes.'

Her daughter released her. 'There's something going on. I need to speak to Paddy. We need to go somewhere. Will you go inside?'

'Yes, dear. But what about lunch?'

'Not today, Mum.'

Obediently, Mrs Tozer went back inside the house.

'So?'

'I was hoping for a name to be on the postal orders where they'd been countersigned, but there wasn't one. But Sharman had made a note of where they'd been cashed. I didn't notice it at first, but the first one was cashed in London, all the rest were cashed down here at the post office in Newton Abbot.'

'Shit. When?'

'Between October and February. If this was done by a woman, I've a hunch about the address in London. I need to look at a map.'

The air was still full of the noise of rooks, cawing over their broken nests.

Helen drove down the narrow Devon roads, horn blaring. When they reached the town, the streets were quiet. Helen pulled up right outside the big, grey, granite building and they ran out, leaving the car half on the pavement.

'Where's there a map of London?'

The reference library was on the first floor; the librarian was a thin, elderly man who explained that the maps were kept under lock and key. 'People steal them, otherwise,' he said.

The man had spider-like fingers, and spent a long time going through his desk drawers, one after the other, before his hand emerged with the right key. At the cabinet on the far side of the room, he spent just as long struggling to fit the key into the lock. Tucked in among the atlases was an old street map. Breen flicked through it until he found the street: St Helen's Gardens.

Breen pointed at the small street that ran north from Oxford Gardens, close to where they they had demolished buildings to make space for the new Westway. 'Look.' Breen took a pen from his pocket and drew a circle around them on the map. The circle intersected Ladbroke Grove. The post office was about five hundred yards from it.

'You can't do that,' protested the librarian, who was still standing over them.

'What does that mean?' asked Helen, ignoring him.

Breen blinked. Checked the map again. Breen was struggling to remember where Penny's flat had been. It had been dark when he arrived. He had been exhausted at the time.

'A woman called Penny lived somewhere around here. She was Doyle's girlfriend.'

'Do you think she's . . . ? Bloody hell.'

'There,' he said. 'I'm sure of it.' The post office would have just been a street away. They ran back down the stairs, map in hand.

'Come back! That's library property.'

'Why her, though?' said Helen, panting as she ran.

'I don't know.'

Helen pulled up right outside the police station doors. Sharman had his coat on and was about to go out when Breen and Helen ran up the stairs into the old building.

Torquay Police Station was deserted, save for a couple of people on the phones. Cups of tea, half drunk, gone cold. Fags stubbed out in ashtrays. Papers that had slipped onto the floor, trodden on.

Sharman led them up to a small office on the second floor. Small force, thought Breen. Everyone would be out looking for a grey Mini van. They didn't have the resources. They were overwhelmed by a crime like this. It showed.

At a desk, Sharman leaned over the map with Breen, Helen behind them, straining her neck to see.

Breen said, 'I think these were postal orders paid by Milkwood to Doyle. His girlfriend lives here. This is where he'd have gone to cash it. But also, maybe she cashed them. Maybe he was already dead by then. I don't know. But I think Milkwood was paying Doyle off about something using Drug Squad funds. Large sums once a month. The rest of the postal orders were cashed down here.'

'His girlfriend. She got long hair?'

Breen nodded.

'You met this woman? You think she could have done it?'

'I don't know her well. I went back to her house. I spent the night there.'

'Sounds like you know her well enough to me,' said Helen.

Breen tried to remember his strange evening with Penny. The drugs. The bizarre conversations about death and *The Tibetan Book of the Dead*. 'I don't know. Maybe. I asked her if she knew Sergeant Milkwood, but she said she didn't. Yet it's possible that she cashed at least one of the postal orders he made out. And the last five were cashed down here in Newton Abbot.'

'What's her address?'

Breen struggled to remember a house number. 'This road. Just off Ladbroke Grove.' Then: 'There was a lotus flower painted on the door.'

'Last name?'

'I have no idea.'

Sharman looked faintly appalled. 'You say you spent the night with this woman?' He shook his head and picked up the phone. Breen listened in. He was calling Scotland Yard now, passing on the details, requesting that they tear the flat apart looking for clues about where she might be.

Talking to the Metropolitan officers, Sharman was deferential, calling them by their ranks. 'Yes, Sergeant. One of your fellows here. He's down on sick leave. Suggests this woman could be a suspect. If he's right, the woman won't be at home so you'd need to break in.'

Breen looked at his watch. One o'clock. If he was right, Mrs Fletchet would be being tortured, a knife cutting flesh.

Helen stood by his side, pale. Yet still the world seemed to be moving at such a cautious speed, the minutes slowly ticking on the big electric clock.

★

The desk sergeant came in, panting from the stairs.

'Had a call from Constable Toohey. Milkman up Bovey said he thinks he saw the grey Mini van on his round this morning. Noticed it because he thought there was a scarecrow in the passenger seat. Thought it was someone messing around.'

'A woman with a hessian bag on her head,' said Breen.

'He get a good look at the driver?'

'Don't know, sir. He wanted to speak to you, only you was on the phone.'

Sharman rolled his eyes. 'Keep him on the bloody line next time he calls.'

When the sergeant had clattered back down the stairs, Breen said, 'Visual confirmation.'

Sharman nodded.

'Shouldn't you call all the officers together for a meeting?' asked Breen.

'Please put a bloody sock in it, Sergeant. We do it our way down here.'

They had set up a room in Plymouth to coordinate the search. Sharman was on a call to them now. Breen gathered they were calling in support from surrounding areas. They were going to flood the place with police.

'Christ,' said Helen. 'By the time they get here . . .'

'I know.'

There was a map on the wall. Breen found the scale of it terrifying. All this empty territory.

Other phones rang. Rang off again. Were the calls important?

'Want me to get that?' he mouthed at Sharman, pointing at a ringing phone.

Sharman shook his head. With everyone scouring the district, the station was oddly still, considering the drama that Breen supposed must be going on somewhere. Pliers, he thought, and knives. And he felt sick.

'What do we do now?' he asked when Sharman had finished his call.

'We?' Sharman looked up. 'You go back to the farm. Stay there so we know where you are in case we need you.' And then he was back on the telephone to the Newton Abbot post office. 'That's right. A woman. Longish hair. Tall. Anybody remember her? I'll hold.'

Breen blinked. He was not used to this. There was no reason why he should have a part in this investigation, of course. Technically he was a civilian; a man on sick leave. He didn't know the local territory or the local coppers. He was limited in how much he could do. As for Helen, she wasn't even a policewoman any more.

Breen stood. There was a large one-inch Ordnance Survey map on the wall. With his finger, he traced the road from the farm to the Fletchets' estate.

'Where's that Bovey place?'

'Down a bit. Left a bit. Just there,' said Helen.

Breen lifted his finger. Then moved it back towards the place where the van was last headed.

'What if she was coming in this direction?' said Breen.

Sharman put his hand over the receiver. He shouted, 'Do you mind? I'm trying to talk.'

'We should go,' said Helen, tugging at Breen. 'They don't want us here.'

They walked out of the building, back down to the car.

Helen was shaking her head. She stopped dead in the pavement, closed her eyes. 'I can't see it. In my head it was always a man. No woman would do those things.'

'You can't know that,' said Breen.

329

She opened her eyes again, fumbled for the keys in her handbag.

'This is horrible,' she said. She got in and started the engine. The exhaust was going in the ancient Morris. You had to shout to be heard over the noise if the car was driving uphill. 'The first day Alexandra was gone, this is what was happening to her.' She was chewing on her lower lip. 'I didn't like her much, Mrs Fletchet, but Christ. What do we do?'

'We have to wait,' said Breen. 'Think.'

Helen drove out of town. The world seemed ridiculously normal. Someone had a flower stall by the side of the road. Daffs one shilling a bunch. A crocodile of schoolgirls walked up the pavement, hand in hand, brown satchels swinging.

Away from the town, she accelerated, but then, rounding a corner, had to slap on the brakes. There was stationary traffic ahead. The Morris's pads were old and soft and the car seemed to take an age to slow. Breen closed his eyes and braced himself for a collision with a shiny new Zodiac in front, but when he opened them he saw that their car had slid to a stop less than a foot away from it.

'Jesus,' said Helen. 'If you're right, she could be taking chunks from her now.'

Breen's heart was beating fast.

The traffic was backed up on the hill approaching the town. Helen pressed on the horn. Others were doing the same.

'Stop,' said Breen, hands over his ears. 'There's no point.'

The queue crawled forward and when they eventually reached the next bend, they saw what was holding up the traffic. It was a roadblock. Policemen were leaning into the cars, asking questions, then waving them on.

'At least they're doing something this time,' said Helen.

This time, thought Breen. The car inched forward again. He looked at his watch: almost two now. Neither of them said it, but they were thinking the same thing. Was the woman taking Eloisa Fletchet to the same place where Alexandra Tozer had been tortured and killed?

The traffic crawled forward at an agonising speed. Neither of them spoke in the twenty minutes it took to reach the front of the queue.

The young constable who leaned in through Helen's window had a boil on his neck and a chipped tooth.

'Helen Tozer, isn't it?' he said. 'I know your dad.' She nodded. 'Only we're stopping people to ask if they seen a suspicious-looking grey Mini.'

'Mrs Fletchet,' she said.

'You heard, then? Well, if you or your gentleman friend see it anywhere . . .' said the copper.

'How many roadblocks are there?' asked Helen.

'Least half a dozen now. They're sending men from Somerset an' all,' he said, waving them on.

'No news?'

'Not yet.'

Breen was chewing on his lip, anxious, unsettled.

The farm looked strangely normal, too, cows placidly chewing on grass. But there was no work going on.

Mr and Mrs Tozer were sitting in the living room, holding hands, looking pale.

'Anything?'

They shook their heads.

Breen went to his room, pulled out his notebooks and laid them on the eiderdown. He knelt down by the bed and started looking through the pages, over and over.

There was a knock on the door. 'It's me, Hibou. Are you busy?'

'Yes, as it happens.'

She had changed out of her farm clothes into one of Alexandra's old dresses. She sat on the end of his bed, next to the notebooks and scraps of paper. Away from London she had become so much more confident. But now, sitting in his room, she looked more like the shy girl he had seen peeking out of the window at him at the squat in London.

She looked at him kneeling by the bed. 'Are you praying?'

'Something's wrong. I'm just trying to look at . . . Never mind.' Breen's head was humming. Why would Penny be doing this? He had the sense that if he could only concentrate on the facts, something would emerge – a pattern, an anomaly. But he was not in his flat, or at his desk. He was in a small, cramped bedroom.

Hibou said, 'I won't be a sec.'

He sighed. 'All right.'

'I wanted to ask. You spoke to my dad, you said.'

Breen nodded. 'Helen did.'

'Was he, you know, OK?'

Breen said, 'It's OK. We didn't tell him anything.'

'Promise?'

'What did he do to you, Hibou?'

She looked shocked. 'Why would you even think that?'

The phone started ringing in the hallway downstairs. He could hear Mrs Tozer downstairs. 'Oh, hello, Freddie. You again,' she was saying. 'Yes. He's here. Is everything all right, Freddie?'

Hibou said, 'What if it's nothing to do with him? What if it's something I did? Would Helen still like me then?'

'Give me a minute, Hibou, OK?' And he was pushing past her, out of the door and down the narrow staircase.

Mrs Tozer was still on the phone, saying, 'You must come round for tea sometime, Freddie,' as if there was nothing out of ordinary happening.

'Sharman?' said Breen, taking the phone from her.

'Wild bloody goose chase. Your Penny woman was in London all the time. It can't have been her after all. We've been wasting our time there. And she doesn't know anything about postal orders.'

'You sure?'

'That's what the Met said. They gave me an earful. I know you're trying to help, but . . . just leave it to us, OK? I have to go.'

Before he could say anything, Sharman put the phone down. The large grandfather clock ticked in the hallway.

'What's wrong?' said Helen.

'The woman wasn't Penny.' He turned away, puzzled. He walked back through the kitchen and up the small staircase to his bedroom, turning the pieces of the puzzle over in his head.

By the time he got back to his room it was empty. Hibou had gone.

He knelt back down and returned to flicking through his notebooks. The second fell open at the sketch he'd done of the photograph of the three men in Africa: Doyle, Milkwood and Fletchet.

He stared at the sketch of the photograph. It wasn't particularly good. And then he opened the drawer, picked out one of his drawing pencils and added longer hair to Doyle, just as Carmichael had done to the original a couple of weeks earlier.

He had a copy of the photograph somewhere. Where was it? He riffled through the envelopes but couldn't find it.

He stepped out of the bedroom into the hallway. 'Helen,' he shouted. 'Come quick.'

People weren't used to shouting in this house.

Helen came running up the stairs. 'What's the matter?'

Hibou reappeared. 'Hel. I want to talk to you. It's important.'

333

'Not now,' said Helen. 'Pete's sake.' They went into Breen's bedroom and closed the door behind them.

Breen held up the sketchbook, saying, 'It wasn't Penny. I think it was Doyle. He's alive.'

'What?'

It hadn't been a woman kidnapping Eloisa Fletchet. It had been a man; a man with long hair. Helen snatched the notebook out his hands and peered at it.

'Doyle was Milkwood's snitch. Milkwood was paying him as an informant. That's what the postal orders were. He would have been living with Penny when he cashed the first one.'

'I thought you said he was killed in Spain?'

'That's just what Penny thought. Maybe it was a way to hide, getting Milkwood to pretend he was dead, laying a false trail. I don't know. But look.'

'You think he could have been mistaken for a woman?'

'It was just the long hair. Long hair and thin, the man said. And he was living down here. He cashed the postal orders. The last one was just a few weeks ago. He's down here.'

Helen stared at the drawing as if waiting for it to talk to her.

'We should call Sharman,' he said. He looked at his watch. It was past three in the afternoon now.

Helen nodded, still holding the notebook. 'You should give his picture to the local police so they know who they're looking for.'

Breen thought he heard Hibou, still outside the door, but when he opened it, she had gone.

The light was already starting to fade. Clouds were building over the moors to the north.

Breen phoned Newton Abbot; Sharman was not there. He had

334

gone to the incident room in Torquay. Breen called there but nobody seemed to know where he had gone. A constable told them to call back in half an hour.

'There isn't time,' said Breen.

'Sorry, sir. We're up to our necks right now.'

Sharman didn't call back till a little before four. 'If this is another runaround, we don't have time for it.'

'It's not. He was Penny's boyfriend. It explains why the first postal order was cashed near her flat. I think he was being paid off by Milkwood in some way.'

'We're looking for a woman.'

'This guy had long hair. The milk-lorry driver was some distance away, wasn't he?'

'Well, yes . . .' Another phone rang somewhere in Sharman's office. Sharman sighed. 'If I find someone free, I'll send them for the photograph,' he said.

Helen was sitting on the stairs, head in her hands. 'You can't imagine what this is like for me,' she said. 'You can't bloody imagine.'

Mr Tozer emerged from the living room. He stared at the hall carpet in front of him for a second. 'Any news?'

Breen shook his head. The man's fingers trembled. He turned and went back into the darkness of the living room.

The house was changed. Everything that had happened in the summer of 1964 was vivid again. The past and the present had come together.

Mrs Tozer was standing at the door looking out at the fields, as if expecting to see something there. 'I heard it on the radio too,' she said. 'They're looking for this woman. They say she's been abducted. But they said another woman did it.'

'Paddy thinks it's a mistake. He thinks it's a man called Doyle. They're coming for a photograph of him that Paddy's got.'

335

'But the news says it's a woman,' said Mrs Tozer, as if that meant Breen must have got it wrong.

Breen stood next to her, smoking a cigarette. He watched her hands. They were clutching each other, but constantly in motion, fingers twining and intertwining, like a bucket of eels.

'Poor woman. I mean, she stands a chance, though, doesn't she, at least? Unlike Alex.'

When a loved one is murdered, it eats away at the families. Breen had seen it happen many times. Even good people like the Tozers absorbed some of the darkness.

The grandfather clock whirred and chimed.

'Where's that copper, for the photograph?' said Mrs Tozer.

'They'll be here soon,' said Breen.

Clouds hung low, turning the estuary water slate grey.

At five, the light broke from under the clouds that hung over Dartmoor. Gold light made the fresh green of the fields greener, the red of the soil redder.

The police car was here, finally. A big-eared young man in a uniform that looked too loose on him stood at the front door. Breen had hoped that Sharman himself would come so he could ask about progress, so he could explain his theories. Instead, the young man said, 'Bugger to find this place. I drove past three times. Should have a sign or something. I'm here to pick up some photo.'

'Any news about Mrs Fletchet?'

'Not that I heard.'

Breen went upstairs and looked around again. He had been sure the photograph had been on his bed.

'Helen?' he called down. 'Do you have the photograph?'

Helen emerged from the kitchen. 'I only saw the drawing. Mum? Did you move a photograph from Paddy's bedroom?'

336

'What photograph?'

He searched his bedroom a second time. He turned out each envelope, flicked through every book. He pulled out the bed and looked behind it, under it. No. It wasn't there. He went downstairs again.

Helen's father emerged from the front room dressed in trousers and a vest. 'Have they found her?'

'Did you take a photograph from Paddy's room?'

'I thought the policeman had come because they'd found her.'

'Dad? The photograph.'

'What you on about? Didn't see no picture.'

Breen said, 'It must have been Hibou. She was in my bedroom when I was looking at it.'

Helen barged past her mother to run upstairs now. She was down again within a few seconds. 'Where's Hibou?'

'I thought she was in her room,' said Breen.

'No, she's not. Mum?'

'Bloody waste of time,' said the copper. 'You got the photo or not?'

'Maybe she's out milking,' said Mrs Tozer. 'I saw her getting her boots on a while ago.'

'We'll find the photo. Wait,' said Breen.

'The milking's already done,' said Helen. 'Can't be that.'

'Why would she take the photo?' said Breen.

'Hibou!' shouted Helen, hands up to her mouth.

She walked a few yards, to the edge of the fields. 'Hibou!'

'I should head back,' said the copper.

'Please wait,' said Breen. 'We'll find the photo. It's important.'

The policeman stood awkwardly at the front door. Breen understood his unease. The copper would be thinking he should be out there looking for the kidnapped woman. And Breen felt exactly the same.

'Hibou!' Mrs Tozer was shouting now, too.

No answer. Just the caw of crows above the cow fields.

They were still shouting when the police car drove back up the rutted road.

By seven there was still no sign of Hibou. Mrs Tozer hadn't made supper, so Helen cut some sandwiches. She was hopeless with a bread knife so the slices were thick and uneven. Breen didn't feel like eating anyway. None of them did.

'Could have just gone off for a walk, of course. She does that sometimes,' said Breen.

'Maybe she's gone to visit her young man,' said Mrs Tozer, hands still wringing.

'How bloody irresponsible,' said Helen.

'Language,' said her mother.

'But she knows what will be going through our heads. Especially with what's happening. I'll kill Spud when I see him.'

Breen thought back over the first time Helen had told him about her dead sister. It had been in a pub in Stoke Newington. As he fed her rum-and-blacks, she had told the story about how Alex had disappeared, how her dad had roamed the local pubs demanding information. How Helen had been in school when her headmistress had taken her out of class to break the news.

'Stupid bloody cow,' said Helen.

'Helen,' said her mother quietly, as if she didn't have the energy to scold her any more.

The sky was almost black. If he was going to look for her there wouldn't be much time before the last light went.

He went round to the back of the house and started picking through the box of boots before he found a pair his size.

Helen came around the house. 'You going to go and look for her?'

'Better than sitting here.'

'Paddy. It was the photograph,' she said. 'It has to be. Hibou recognised him.'

'Jesus.'

With horror, Breen realised Helen was right. She must have seen the photograph he had left out and recognised Doyle. The thought chilled him.

'It was never Spud.'

'My God.'

Doyle, he thought. He said the name aloud.

'It's like he planned all this,' she said. 'He's been here, watching us all along. That's how he met Hibou.'

'We have to tell Sharman.'

Nobody had put the chickens in the coop yet. A pair of hens walked around the yard, as if looking for somewhere to roost.

'Not that he'll believe anything we say any more.'

'He'll listen to you, won't he?' said Breen. 'Where would he have met her? In the pub?'

'Maybe. I don't know.'

'If we knew where . . .'

'She might have caught the bus. She might have gone any-where.'

'She ever talk to you about him?'

'No,' said Helen. 'We haven't been getting along that well, be honest.' The same as with Alexandra. 'Christ. It's all my fault, isn't it? I should never have gone to see her mum and dad. You were right. Now I've gone and scared her off and she's gone running into his arms. Oh, shit.'

'What about your mum? Would she have talked to her?'

They went round to the front of the house to find Mrs Tozer.

'She ever tell you about her boyfriend?'

'No. She didn't say nothing. She knew Dad wouldn't like it, I suppose.'

They went into the front room. Mr Tozer had the TV on, loud. He was staring at it but Breen didn't think he was actually watching. Helen went to the telly and turned down the volume button.

Mr Tozer lifted his eyes off the screen and looked at his daughter. His eyes were mournful.

'She's dead, isn't she?' he said.

For a second, Breen wasn't sure if he was talking about his youngest daughter, Hibou or Mrs Fletchet.

'You don't know that, Dad,' said Helen.

'I do. I know it. Have you looked in the copse yet?'

'Listen, Dad. Did Hibou ever tell you about her boyfriend?'

'She didn't talk to us about him. Scared what I'd have said, I suppose. My fault.'

'I'm talking about Hibou, not Alex. Please, Dad.'

He blinked. 'Hibou. Yes. Boyfriend. I could tell. She had that same thing Alex had. That look. Oh, God,' he groaned.

'Did she say anything about him?'

'She won't leave the farm, will she?' said Mr Tozer. His lip was trembling.

Breen backed out of the room.

He hadn't thought to check the copse before the light was completely gone. There was no reason she should be there, was there?

He ran across the drive, fumbling with the gate latch.

'Wait,' said Helen.

But Breen didn't. He pushed through the gate, past the fallen ash, and then squeezed his way under the barbed wire. His sweater caught, pulling a thread. He didn't stop, though he could feel it unravelling behind him.

Branches flapped into his face. Spring had made the copse denser. New tendrils of dog rose scratched at his hands and tore at his clothes.

Breen paused, tried to make out shapes in the gloom, but he could see nothing. More gingerly now, he moved forward again. He was getting to the place where he had slipped last time.

His feet began to slide again. He reached out a hand and grasped for anything, hand wrapping around a stem.

He cried out in pain. Thorns were digging into his palm. He must have grabbed hold of a bramble.

But it had steadied him, at least. He let go slowly, feeling the curve of the thorns still clutching at his flesh, reluctant to let him go.

The hand tore free and he stumbled down towards the bottom of the hollow, half expecting to fall over a body.

Nothing. He leaned down to feel in the blackness in the place where Alex's body had been discovered.

His hand felt only earth at first, a few pieces of vegetation, slimy with rot. And then there was something harder. A stick? He picked it up, palm still stinging from the bramble cuts.

It was smooth, cylindrical, about eight inches long. Plastic? A piece of discarded farm equipment perhaps? He was about to throw it away when the new leaves above him were lit by torchlight.

'Paddy?'

Helen's voice, pushing through the undergrowth.

'Careful. It's steep.'

'I know.'

Then the torchlight was on him, blinding. He looked down at what he was holding. It took him a second to realise it was a candle, plain and white.

'Shine the light down here,' he called.

The light moved down to his feet.

The red earth was covered in dead daffodils. They hadn't grown here; somebody had brought them. And half a dozen candles, two still forced into the soil, half burned. He knelt lower and felt in the ground around where the two remaining candles still stood.

There had been a circle of them, roughly where Alexandra's head would have lain.

'Like some shrine,' said Helen. 'Hibou?'

The photograph of Alexandra's body had shown the roots of trees. He tried to remember the details.

Helen was lowering herself down the slope. Now the torch was no longer shining from above but from the same level as Breen, he could see the bottom of the dip more clearly. That hand-like root had been in the photograph, he remembered, close to her head. The position of the candles was exact.

'I don't think it was Hibou. It was someone who knew precisely where your sister's body had been left.'

'He's been here,' said Helen. 'The fucking bastard has been here, hasn't he?'

She switched off the torch and under the canopy of leaves they were in total darkness now. Her voice was oddly calm. 'Doyle is alive. He has been here. He has been talking to Hibou.'

'He faked his own death,' said Breen, panting. He was thinking: he may even have killed those young men in Spain, or maybe he just came across the reports of their murder and used them to construct his story.

He reached out his hand in the darkness and found hers. 'He's a monster. He persuaded Milkwood to collude in the story of his own disappearance. And then he bloody tortured Milkwood to death anyway.'

Helen pulled at Breen. She was moving now, climbing back up

the muddy slope. Together, they scrambled out of the dip, Breen pushing Helen, then Helen reaching down to tug him up.

The consequences of Doyle being alive, being close by, being the person who had killed Alexandra and dumped her body here, spun around his head. Until that meeting at Pratt's, Fletchet may have even thought Doyle dead too. It was when he had mentioned Doyle's name that Fletchet had panicked and fled the country. Fletchet had understood the truth of it long before Breen had. He had known what a monster Doyle was all along, but had said nothing.

'He's close. He would have to have been close to bring Alex's body here. He has always been here.'

'I know,' said Helen. 'She's close too, isn't she? Christ. Do you think he's got Hibou too?'

'I'll phone,' Breen said.

'It's my fault. I brought her down here. I'll do it. Sharman doesn't trust you. I know how to talk to him.'

Breen had to agree. They stood in the hallway while Helen dialled the station. The call was answered almost instantly.

'I think the person who kidnapped Eloisa Fletchet has been on my farm.'

Mrs Tozer was there now, eyes wide.

'I'll hold,' said Helen.

'You need something for those cuts,' Mrs Tozer told Breen, and she scurried off to the bathroom for TCP and plasters.

Helen was speaking. 'No. I haven't seen her. We found some signs that the person who murdered my sister has been on the farm again. If so, it's almost certainly the same person that kidnapped Mrs Fletchet . . .'

'Come in the kitchen, dear,' said Mrs Tozer, tugging at Breen's coat. 'The light's better there.'

343

He sat on the bench in the kitchen while Helen's mother dabbed his stinging hand.

'What did you find?' she asked.

'It was like a shrine,' he said. 'Where Alexandra's body was found.'

'Hold still,' she said.

In the hallway, Helen's voice was louder now, frustrated, urgent. 'No, it's not a woman you should be looking for, it's a man. Name of Nicholas Doyle. Didn't you get our message? It's a bloody man. Where's Sergeant Sharman? Please.'

'Let me clean that. It'll get infected else,' said Mrs Tozer quietly.

'Fuck sake, listen to me,' Helen was saying. 'Please. Listen. Get Freddie Sharman, please. He has another woman with him. A girl. No. Listen.'

'I'll just fetch the scissors for the plaster,' said Mrs Tozer. 'Tell me, Cathal. Is he here? The man who killed Alex?'

'I think so.'

Hibou had barely left the farm since she arrived here. It must have been somebody she had met nearby.

Jesus. The tramp, thought Breen.

Helen was struggling on the phone. 'I know he's busy. Of course he is. But this is important. Can't you raise him on the radio? Or get a message?'

Breen tried to recall the hermit's face, but hadn't he turned his head away when Breen had tried to talk to him?

Mrs Tozer returned with a large pair of scissors and cut off a length of pink plaster.

'I'll hold. I don't care how long it takes.'

Breen stood. Mrs Tozer said, 'I haven't finished, love.'

'I'm fine,' said Breen.

'You'll bleed.'

But Breen was already in the hallway. Helen put her hand over the mouthpiece.

'They don't believe me. They think I'm some nutter.'

'There was a a man living rough by the water, down by the path. I thought it was just a tramp. It was Doyle, I'm sure.'

'You think she went down there to find him?'

'Stay on the line until you get Freddie,' he said.

'What do you think I'm doing?'

He was here somewhere. Had he been watching them all the time?

'What if you went along the road?' said Helen. 'He must have hidden the van somewhere.'

'No time. Get them to send cars. You have to make them come. Do anything to get them here. I'm going down to the estuary. That's where she used to walk.'

'Wait for the police, please,' said Mrs Tozer. 'Don't go out there on your own.'

'No,' Helen said. 'He's right. There's no time to wait. Go.'

Breen said, 'Lock the door until the police come. Get your dad's shotgun loaded and keep it with you.'

'OK. I'll come as soon as I know the police are on their way. Hurry.'

He was out of the front door, striding down the hill.

'Mr Breen,' called Mrs Tozer. 'You'll need a coat, at least.'

TWENTY-EIGHT

The clouds were moving fast, occasionally making way for a half-moon. When they covered it again, the countryside vanished into blackness.

Breen walked slowly, with his hands out in front. Another few yards. Then he fell, tripping on a tussock of grass. He had been in this kind of darkness before, but that had been in a city, where there were solid walls and pavements. The countryside lacked predictable geometries. Here he stumbled on every thistle and hummock.

He had seen Hibou disappearing down the track that led to the estuary below the farm to meet the tramp.

Had Doyle persuaded her to collude with him? Had the secrecy been his idea, or hers? She was used to secrets, he knew. The idea that she had been sneaking him eggs from the henhouse made his stomach lurch.

His foot dropped suddenly and he fell forward again, into shallow, cold water. The mud stank. He recoiled, shoving himself up and staggering backwards.

There was a pond, he remembered. Falling in at this time of year would be lethal. Which side of the path was it?

The cloud parted again briefly and for a few seconds he got a clear view of the land around him and the water. The dark hump of the bridge that carried the path over the railway was to the right of him.

He looked back. The lights of the farmhouse still looked close. He had not come far. Had Helen managed to get through to Sharman yet? He doubted it. The local police were in chaos. Even if she did, she had to persuade him to divert resources here. That would not be easy. They were still convinced they were looking for a woman.

He trotted now, partly to warm himself after the coldness of the water, partly because he knew the cloud would cover the moon again soon.

At the railway, the tracks shone below the bridge for a few seconds and then the thick darkness returned. But he felt more confident of his route now. The estuary below seemed to glow slightly, even when the moonlight was not there.

He could hear the lapping of the water on the land now.

He tried to think. Doyle was an ascetic. A man who lived on little and who had survived below the radar for years, living rough or in other people's houses. He might be keeping Eloisa Fletchet in the van still, but Breen guessed he would need somewhere more remote to hide in. A Mini van would be too cramped for him to torture someone in.

Finally he reached the water's edge. Which way would Hibou have walked? Right would be upriver, towards the town, towards where Doyle had pitched a tent. Left would be out towards the sea.

The tide was high. Helen seemed to know whether it was rising or falling just by looking at it. Breen had no idea.

Which way?

Right? Breen had walked back from the town this way once, along a muddy footpath. Doyle would know that Breen had already seen him here. Breen peered into the blackness but could see nothing. He turned around. There was just darkness between him and the lights of the town at the mouth of the estuary, three or four miles away.

The air smelt dank and rotten. The stink of mud and dead water. A tang of salt too.

He chose left, calculating that Doyle, if it was Doyle, would always pick the remoter zone.

But the shoreline was narrow. After a few hundred yards it seemed to disappear completely. In its place, a steep, artificial bank made from rocks.

He climbed the bank and near the top saw, through the stubby trees, a faint orange light in the distance. A hurricane lamp maybe? It was something at least. A house, perhaps, that he'd never noticed before. Or a shed? He started to work his way along the bank towards it.

It was hard work. The bank was at an angle of roughly forty-five degrees, made of carefully laid stones. At low tide it would be easy to walk this way, along the mud and mussel beds below, but now they were covered in water. Instead he edged slowly forward, bent double to avoid the low branches above, always worried that he'd lose his footing and slide into the cold seawater.

He stopped and tried to spot the farmhouse on the hillside above, to see if there was any activity there, but it was hidden behind the bank now. He could still hear nothing beyond the splashes of the water hitting the stones beneath him. Even if Helen had managed to get through to the police it would take them a little while to reach the farm, wouldn't it?

What if they didn't come?

A click somewhere above him startled Breen.

A gun?

In the panic, he almost lost his footing, sliding off the bank.

Was someone watching him? If there was someone on the bank above him, Breen would be clearly silhouetted against the water.

Heart clattering, he shrank slowly to the rocks, trying to make his profile harder to see. He pressed his face against the bank, listening for any noise, waiting for the gunshot. The rocks were cold and rough against his cheek.

But instead of a gunshot, another noise. A rumble, building fast from a distance, then coming closer, until it was a roar.

A rush of wind too. And long flashes of light, illuminating the slapping waves below. The shock of it was so great he lost his grip on the rocks and slid downwards. At the last second, his feet inches from the water, his left hand managed to grab a rock that protruded from the wall, yanking his sore shoulder but stopping his fall.

A train, he realised, after what seemed an age. A diesel heading towards London at what seemed, at this close distance, a ridiculous speed.

The bank was the edge of the railway line, he surmised, snaking alongside the water.

He pulled himself back up the bank and lay against the rock, panting, trying to recover himself.

And then he heard the click again.

He looked up. The light that had been amber was now red. He laughed. Stupid, stupid, stupid. It had been the noise of the cable, changing the signal up ahead.

The train was now far down the valley, a line of light outlining the course ahead.

The house he had thought he was going towards was just a railway signal. Other than that, there was only the blackness ahead.

Should he go back or carry on?

There was no sign of anyone behind him. No torchlight. No other searchers. He edged on again, the cold beginning to make his fingers ache.

Another train was coming, this time in the other direction. In the strobe of lights as it passed, he tried to make out the shape of the route ahead. There seemed to be a dark lump of land jutting into the estuary.

Ten yards later he almost fell into a culvert cut into the bank. Water from some hillside stream bubbled underneath him as he cautiously edged his way around the top of it. If he fell in here, he would never get out.

Forced upwards, he was now squeezing under the hanging branches at the top of the slope. They scratched him, flicking into his face.

There was a sudden scrabble ahead of him and a bird flew out, wings scraping face. Quacking in alarm, a duck moved low over the water to his right. The noise faded as the creature travelled further across the estuary. Just when his heartbeat had slowed again, a second bird shot out, repeating the same quacking. It sounded absurdly loud.

He had cramp.

Something about the position he was crouched in and the cold in his limbs was making the muscles in his left foot seize up. The pain grew. He should move on. If he could reach the land ahead he would be able to stand up properly and stamp out the pain.

He moved less cautiously now, keen to make it to flatter ground.

Was that another light?

He was shivering slightly now. It was harder to hold his gaze. Another small, pale, orange-ish glow in the distance.

Was it just a distant sodium light? Or something closer?

And then it was gone.

He stopped and looked, straining his eyes.

There. Again. It was not far away at all, on the dark land ahead. Yes.

He stepped forward.

And fell.

His foot sliding into nothingness, his head cracking against something hard and then his body engulfed in coldness. An iron fist around his chest.

Down into a churning current.

TWENTY-NINE

He sucked cold water as he sank, arms flailing, into the black.

The cold seemed to invade him completely, filling his body with its icy weight.

He was still travelling downwards, bumping along rocks and weed. With so little air in his lungs, this would not take long.

At school they had made him swim in pyjamas. To dive to the bottom of a pool and pick up the rubber brick. The memory of being told to remove clothes. In panic, he realised it was the wellington boots that were sucking him down. He had to take them off.

Bending, he struggled with one, but it was tight and he was weak now. The boot seemed to suck onto his foot just as hard as he tried to push it off.

He thrashed his arms more desperately, trying to work against the downward pull. For a fraction of a second, striving with all his might, his face emerged from the water and he sucked in a mouthful of air, but there was not time to shout for help before the water pulled him down again.

Stupid. Stupid. Stupid. All for nothing.

He had grown up motherless.

His child – and he believed more than ever that it was his child – would grow up fatherless.

Helen for a mother; that would be enough, wouldn't it? She was good and strong. She, at least, understood the new world for what it was. She knew how to enjoy it at the same time as not falling for its vanities.

It was sad. Just when life was starting, he felt, it was ending.

He tried to reach the surface a second time, but his arms were wearier already.

Extraordinary.

A flash of memories.

Standing with his father on a hot day at Limehouse, looking down at a bucket of writhing eels.

Bunking off school to play with John Carmichael in the bomb sites around Paddington.

Never being able to march in step in the cadet parades at Peel House.

Once, when his father was losing his memory, he had said, 'There is a woman coming into this house without my permission.'

'That is your nurse.'

Lovely bouncy, bubbly, corkscrew-haired Sarah.

'She says she's my nurse. But she's not.'

'Yes, she is. She comes in every day.'

The odd twist of his father's hands as he spoke.

'She does? I wish she wouldn't. She smells awful.'

'No, she does not,' said Breen.

And Breen would make him another cup of tea and put it next to him.

Helen had been right. Breen was not good at trusting people. He was a policeman. Policemen learn never to trust anyone.

He had made exceptions, at a cost. There had been Sarah, hired to look after his father. For a while he was in love with her. But he had been wrong, his trust misplaced.

It had been 1966. Sarah was pretty, with blonde, curly hair. She didn't smoke; said if it wasn't Sobranie she wouldn't touch it. 'And I only smoke them if I'm drinking Madeira,' she said. She wore a ring on her thumb, often dressed in polka dots, enjoyed gambling on the horses, and liked three sugars in her coffee.

Strange how memories rushed at you.

There had not been many women in his life. Between work and looking after his sick father, he had had little time for them.

'What have you been doing?' he asked one day when he came back from work to find Sarah and his father sitting at the small dining table in the kitchen.

'Whist,' she said. 'We play it every day.'

By now his father could barely remember his son's own name, let alone learn a new game of cards. 'That's impossible.'

'Watch,' she said. She shuffled and dealt. His father took longer to pick up his cards, but to Breen's amazement was soon sorting through them.

'What are trumps?' he said.

'Hearts,' she answered. 'You lead.'

His father stared at his cards for a while and pulled out a three of clubs and placed it on the table.

'See?' she said.

She played a five.

'You play cards at work, don't you?' she said.

'Yes,' his father answered. 'I play cards at work. When it rains. Your go.' She led, and again his father laid on top of hers, this time picking up the trick.

'Did you win?' she asked.

'Trumped you,' he said, even though he had laid a club, not a heart.

'He always wins,' she smiled, winking at Breen. 'He's very good.'

'He's very good,' said his father.

He was amazed by the ease of her duplicity. For once, his loss of memory seemed to work to his advantage. The next day he went to an off-licence in Baker Street before catching the bus home and bought a bottle of Madeira.

Sarah drank only sips. He found the drink too sweet. She talked far more than he did. He didn't mind. Tired after a day at work, he liked to listen to her. Her father had been a boatbuilder, she said. 'Only not a good one, it turns out. He was lost at sea, in one of his own boats.'

'What a terrible way to lose a father.'

'Like yours, really. He's lost at sea.'

'But at least I know where he is. What's left of him, at least.'

His father was fast asleep in his armchair by then, hands twitching gently.

'True,' she said. 'But we had to wait seven years till they declared him officially dead. And that's a bit like yours too.'

He was shocked by her bluntness, at first, but then realised what she was saying was true, too. At least she talked about his father's illness.

He was working up to asking her to stay the night, but in the end, with what happened between them, he never got the chance.

Everything was slowing now. The cold made it easy not to care that he was dying.

Sometimes Sarah took his coat when he came back, and when she did, sometimes her hand would brush against his. She learned to make coffee the way he liked it. He bought a second bottle of Madeira.

'Are you seeing a woman?' Sarah asked one evening.

'No. When would I have time? Why did you ask?'

She actually blushed. 'Only I thought I smelt perfume when I came in this morning.'

'Why would you want to know if I was seeing another woman?' he teased her.

'No reason at all.'

The next morning, needing money to get a new front door key cut, because he had lost his spare a couple of days before, he went to the drawer, unlocked it and opened the tin where he kept a pound note for emergencies. The money wasn't there.

Assuming Sarah must have needed it for something, he thought nothing of it. The next day Breen replaced the money. This time he checked the drawer when he came home. It was empty again.

Then he asked, 'Did you need the money for something?'

'I was going to take your father for a haircut. Only there wasn't any money there.'

'I left a pound note in the tin.'

'No, you didn't.'

They went to the drawer, he unlocked it, showed her. Empty. He scrutinised her face but could see no evidence that she was lying.

Another day, he said, 'I left two pounds in the drawer.'

'Are you accusing me of taking them?'

'No. But they've gone.'

'Maybe your father took them.'

'He'd never manage the key.' It was true. His father had lost the simple ability to connect a locked drawer with the key that lay on top of it.

356

'I don't know. Maybe you forgot to put anything in there.' She shrugged and turned her back.

The Madeira stopped. Their friendliness disappeared. One evening, when Sarah had left and Breen discovered the tin was empty yet again, he asked his father, 'Did you take the money from the drawer?'

His father frowned a while, then in a brief, lucid moment, said, 'No. She did.'

'Who? Sarah? Did Sarah take the money?'

His father frowned again, picked at the stubble on his chin and asked, 'Who's Sarah?'

'The woman who looks after you while I'm at work. Did she take the money?'

His father looked away. 'I don't know what you're talking about. I want to go home.'

'This is home,' said Breen. 'Remember?'

The money kept on disappearing. So eventually he decided he had to replace Sarah.

When he told her she shouted, 'I didn't take your bloody money.' From her handbag, she pulled out her purse and dug out coins and threw them at him. 'Here,' she said. 'I don't care about money.'

And she stormed off, furiously, in tears.

He would have loved to have been wrong about her. When he realised Sarah had not returned her set of front door keys, he changed the locks. The agency sent another nurse.

When he got home for the next few days, he checked the tin and the money was always there. He wished it hadn't been. He wished he had been wrong about her. But it seemed he wasn't.

★

Drowning, the facts still rushed back to him in a strange order. The day he sacked her. For no clear reason he remembered her accusing him of seeing a woman; the smell of perfume. His father, he remembered, had also complained of the woman who smelt.

There had been a middle-aged woman who lived upstairs for a while in the rooms Elfie now shared with her boyfriend. She had worn perfume. So much that you could almost see it in the air around her.

And Breen had lost his key.

The memories swam together. Just because the facts fitted didn't mean that they were true. There were other ways of seeing them. The woman upstairs must have found the key and been letting herself into his flat. She knew perfectly well how ill his father had been then. She had been coming in, taking the money, and all the time he blamed Sarah for it. The same facts that he had used to condemn Sarah suddenly pointed to a different person being the thief. He had not trusted her. So stupid not to trust.

He would have laughed, but there was not the air.

He wished he could beg her forgiveness. He wished he could have told Helen. She would have said, 'I told you so.'

But there was no time.

And then something hit him hard in the chest, and it paused his movement long enough for him to grab hold of it.

A rope, stretched taut. Encrusted with slime, it was hard to grip with his frozen fingers, but he held on. And then pulled himself upwards on it, desperately.

So slippery he could hardly grip, feeling the current forcing him downwards as he tried to climb, hand over hand.

And then his head was above the water, gasping. He may not be drowning any longer, but knew he had exposure. He had to get out of the water fast.

He had somehow managed to grab the mooring line of a boat anchored close to the estuary shore. He looked around and worked out he was not so far from land. The question was whether he could make it there before his strength gave out.

And then he saw it. Downstream, a small light on the shore. Dim, behind dark curtains, but a light all the same.

There was no time to think; his body was cooling too fast. If he stayed here holding onto the rope he would die. But if he let it go, could he reach the shore?

There was no choice. He let go of the rope and thrashed in the water. His left arm had no strength in it at all. He had used it so little since the shooting. He pushed himself through the water, gulping air whenever he could.

He had been closer to the shore than he imagined. His feet touched the bottom, but it was silt and there was nothing to push against. His foot sank into the oily mud. For a panicked second he became terrified that the mud would suck him down, into it. It would be doubly stupid to drown so close to the shore.

The current was taking him past the light he had seen. With what seemed to be the last of his strength, he took another stroke with his right arm. This time, with the mud a little shallower, he seemed to find purchase on rocks under the silt. It was tough, forcing himself through the sludge, water pushing against him, but little by little he made it.

The shore was stony and hard. He fell on it, heart thumping, shivering so badly from the cold he could barely focus. Sharp shells dug at his skin.

'Help,' he said, but he had no voice.

The wind on his wet clothes was freezing him worse than the

water had done. He lay, incapable of any further motion. He would die soon of exposure, he realised, but felt oddly calm about it.

Help.

He was tired now.

And then he slept.

THIRTY

He half woke, shivering, cold, but surrounded by warmth. He could not move.

I am dreaming, he thought. I am asleep. That is why I cannot move.

Someone was singing, softly, to him. A strange, almost Middle Eastern song. He was conscious that the wet clothes that had almost drowned him were not there any more. He was naked but dry.

Something was bothering him, though. Within the smell of woodsmoke, another familiar smell. One he couldn't place. He didn't want to think about it now and so he lapsed back into unconsciousness.

Hurting, though. He must be sleeping oddly. That happened sometimes, didn't it? The dead arm, with pins and needles. Only it wasn't like that. His arms were aching. He tried to move them again but they were stuck

And that smell. Not strong, but unpleasant.

He recognised it suddenly. The smell of the butcher's shop. The scent of uncooked meat. Of flesh. Of blood.

He tried to scream, but couldn't. The noise died in his throat. He passed out again.

He opened his eyes with a start.

She was there, opposite him, naked, bound to a chair, disfigured and mutilated. Her hanging breasts were crusted with blood and her belly had been criss-crossed by a blade, like pork before roasting. The cuts were so deep that beyond the skin he could see the pale fat.

Not Hibou, who he had been searching for, but Eloisa Fletchet.

With horror, he realised that he too was tied to a chair. And naked as well.

Her eyes were shut. Was she dead?

But her chest rose and fell very slightly, very slowly. She must be unconscious.

There was a tarpaulin on the floor beneath both of their chairs. Under Eloisa Fletchet it was thick with blood that had run down her chest, her belly, her groin and her legs onto the floor.

Breen vomited.

Awake again.

Someone was cleaning the sick off his legs, his belly. Off his penis.

He opened his eyes.

A man with long hair, brown, but with a little grey in it. His head was lower than Breen's and the man's face was entirely hidden by the curtain of long hair that dangled downwards, swishing gently from side to side as he dabbed the sponge backwards and forwards, pressing it into the folds of skin at Breen's groin.

The tramp; Nicholas Doyle. He had cleaned himself, shaved off his beard, but it was the same man.

Breen tried to talk to him, but as he did so realised again that he could not speak. His mouth was now gagged. Instead he found himself making odd, animalish noises.

He must have passed out and been found on the shore. He had been dragged here, stripped of his wet clothes and tied to the chair opposite Mrs Fletchet. It was too fantastical a scene to comprehend. Pure horror.

He had almost drowned in water that would have been only a few degrees above freezing. He had been saved. He would have died out there on the beach. Perhaps that would have been better.

He would be suffering from hypothermia, he realised dimly. He knew it slowed your body and brain. It made understanding hard.

The man in front of him paused in his work. He too appeared at first to be naked, though when he stood, Breen saw he wore a pair of dirty khaki shorts that had a little blood on them. And a knife, sheathed in his belt. The strange man was bronzed, even in winter, and wiry, the outline of his ribs showing on his chest. He unclipped the knife and held it in front of Breen.

Breen's eyes widened; his head flinched backwards. Knives always terrified him. More than guns or bombs.

The man nodded and said, 'Shh.' Then he reached the knife around the back of Breen's head and cut through the gag. It fell onto Breen's naked lap.

'Where is Hibou?' Breen said, but his voice was unintelligible. His jaw felt like iron, his lips like cardboard.

'You are Nicholas Doyle,' Breen tried again. A croak, devoid of consonants. His lungs were weak, he realised. He had been exhausted by his time in the water.

The man said nothing, just kept sponging the vomit from Breen's body. The water was warm and trickled between his legs, but the man continued cleaning him. He was doing it carefully, respectfully.

'So you're not dead, after all,' said Breen, as loudly as he could manage.

'Oh, I wouldn't say that, exactly,' said Doyle. He spoke in a soft, soothing cockney.

'What's happening?' said Breen.

'Tell me how you found me.'

363

Breen tried to remember.

'Tell me. I will hurt you if you don't tell me.'

'You tortured her,' said Breen. 'Why?'

'No questions,' said Doyle.

'What about Hibou?'

'Shh,' said Doyle. 'Everything will be OK soon. You are Helen's friend, aren't you?'

Breen nodded.

'I've watched you,' said Doyle.

He squeezed the sponge into a basin and stood back. 'You're clean now,' he said. 'Tell me how you found me?'

'What about her?' said Breen, nodding his head towards Eloisa Fletchet.

'She's close,' said Doyle.

'Close to what?'

Doyle didn't answer. He left the room with the basin of dirty water.

For the first time, Breen looked around.

They were in a shack of some kind. It was a decrepit affair, smelling of seaweed and woodsmoke. To one side, driftwood was stacked in a pile next to a small iron stove. The room was lit by a single paraffin lamp hanging from a hook in the wooden ceiling. There were a couple of fishing rods leaning against the wall. It was still dark outside, but this was early spring. The nights were long. How many hours had he been unconscious?

In front of the stove, Eloisa Fletchet's eyes fluttered. Breen noticed the cigarette burns on her skin. The same as Bill Milkwood; the same as Alexandra Tozer. Breen thought for a moment she was going to regain consciousness, but she didn't. Her skin was pale. She had lost a great deal of blood already. The same slow, methodical torture.

Doyle returned with his knife unsheathed. Sharpened blades; Breen's phobia.

Breen stared at it, wide-eyed. Before he realised what Doyle was doing, he raised his hand over Breen's mouth and pressed, held the knife against Breen's belly and sliced once, diagonally.

Breen sucked in air through his nose. A silent scream, though surprisingly the cut had hurt less than he expected.

Doyle said, 'How did you find me?'

When his chest stopped rising and falling so hard, Doyle released his hand.

'Don't,' whispered Breen. 'Please.'

'How?'

'Police are out there looking for you.' His voice was powerless. Doyle leaned his head closer to his mouth. 'They know I went this way. They'll be here any moment.'

Doyle shook his head. 'I found you crawling outside over an hour ago. If they were behind you they'd be here by now. You're lying.'

Breen's heart fell. Helen hadn't persuaded them to follow. He was on his own. Doyle replaced his hand on Breen's mouth and sliced again.

This time it hurt. He felt warmth fill his lap. This was his own blood, dribbling down, mingling with Eloisa Fletchet's on the floor.

'How?'

'I had a photograph of you. From Kenya. Hibou recognised it.'

'Yes. She did.'

Dimly, Breen wondered where Hibou was. She must have tried to come here. But he couldn't see her.

'You were in Kenya,' Breen blurted.

'Yes. That's right.'

Breen was thinking desperately. Keep him talking. The longer he could do that, the longer he could postpone Doyle tying on the gag again. 'You must have seen terrible things.'

No response.

'I spoke to a Kenyan man whose girlfriend had scars . . .'

Doyle paused for a second. Nodded. 'Terrible things,' he said.

'You tortured people.'

Doyle was untying the knot from the gag.

'Was that where you learned to torture people?'

'You know about it?' he said.

'A little,' Breen said.

Doyle lifted the knife and scratched his chin with it.

'Jim Fletchet is a devil.' He was surrounded by blood and the body of a dying woman, and this man was calling Fletchet a devil.

'It was never about hurting people,' said Doyle. 'Not for me. You should understand that.'

Breen saw a glimmer. 'No? But for the others?'

'Fletchet, definitely. He is a bastard. A corrupter of men.'

'I need to understand,' said Breen.

Doyle didn't answer. He turned, opened the door on a small blackened stove and threw a piece of driftwood inside.

Where was Hibou?

'I've watched you,' said Doyle. 'On the farm. I watched you looking at where I left Alexandra.'

'You were there, all the time?'

Doyle nodded.

'You knew Alexandra?'

Doyle shook his head. 'Not really. I knew Jimmy was in love with her. I saw them fucking in his car. Are you in love with Alexandra's sister?'

Breen said, 'Yes, I am.'

Doyle nodded.

Breen looked in the hope that there would be daylight in the sky outside but it was still dark. He could keep Doyle talking. They would find them. But the longer it took, the less chance Eloisa Fletchet would have.

'I met Penny,' said Breen. 'In London.'

'How is she?'

'Sad. She thinks you're dead.'

'She is right. I am dead,' said Doyle. He walked over to Eloisa and held his face close to hers, feeling her breathing. 'Is Alexandra's sister in love with you?'

'No,' said Breen.

They were in a dirty wooden shed of a building, with a tortured woman dying next to him, and they were talking about love.

'And you? Are you in love with Penny?' asked Breen.

'I am dead, remember?' said Doyle. 'I am not capable of love. I haven't been for many years. It's strange how attractive that can make you to women like Penny. And Hibou.' He picked up Eloisa's limp arm and felt her pulse. Was he checking to see if she was still alive?

Breen looked at him. He had a crude tattoo on his left arm. Under a Union Jack, it read 'Queen and Country'. He was around thirty-five years old, but scrawny and fit still. Under his long hair, his face was sharp and angular.

'Is she dying?' said Breen.

'Not yet.'

'You can save her still,' Breen said.

Doyle snorted. 'Not her. She's not worth saving. I was in love once,' he said, taking out his knife again.

'Tell me about it,' said Breen, desperately.

Doyle glared at Breen, then suddenly seemed to relax. 'People tell stories all the time in Africa. You want to hear mine?'

'I'm not going anywhere.'

'No,' said Doyle. 'You're not. One thing I have missed is company.'

The cuts were starting to sting now. 'You're going to kill me, aren't you?'

'I don't have a lot of choice.'

'They'll know it was you.'

'The police think I'm dead in Spain. They've nothing to connect me to you.' He turned towards the dying woman. 'The only person who will know it's me is . . . your husband, Eloisa. He's known all along.'

Breen said, 'What about Hibou? She knows where you are. Did you kill her too?'

Doyle seemed surprised by the question. 'No. I decided not to.'

'Where is she?'

'She said she saw a photograph. She heard you talking about me as the man who had killed Alexandra. So she came to find out for herself.'

'She's alive?'

Doyle sighed. 'Don't agitate yourself. It does not help.'

'Tell me.'

'Yes.'

Breen heard a muffled banging from somewhere. 'Hibou!' he called.

The banging got louder. Doyle looked at Breen. 'Please. It's better for her if she is not stirred up.'

She must be in another part of the shed, tied to a bed or a chair, banging a foot against the floor or the wall.

'Shh,' said Doyle, louder. 'If you don't calm down, I'll have to tie you tighter.'

The banging stopped.

'Will you let her go?' Breen asked.

'How can I? Thanks to you, she knows who I am.'

'So you are going to kill her anyway?'

'Death is not important. You don't know that yet. But you will. I've seen a lot of people die. What is important is how you do it. If you are prepared, it doesn't leave marks on your soul.' The muffled banging from next door continued. Doyle stood. 'Hush, girl,' he called. 'Relax. Clear your mind, like I taught you.'

Breen could not turn his head fully, but the sound seemed to be coming from the other side of a partition made of planks of wood.

'Tell me about Kenya,' said Breen. Keep him talking.

'The energy is different there. Have you ever lived in a hot country? No? You loved it, didn't you, Eloisa? We agreed on that, at least. You used to say you adored the heat. I did too. I was in the police, like Mr Breen here, remember? Fresh out of Hendon. Spent a couple of months in Nairobi, then I was stationed in Nyeri with Milkwood. The White Highlands, they called it. And that was where all the Mau Mau militants were. Mickey Mau Maus you used to call them. And then, early '53, a couple of us were seconded to where you were, a tiny little place called Ngala. Myself and Sergeant Milkwood. It's where I fell in love.'

'Eloisa says you went native.'

'No. I just stopped being a cunt. That's what you didn't like, Eloisa, wasn't it?'

Doyle opened a tin and pulled out a hand-rolled cigarette. Opening the stove door, he lit a twig and used it to light the small cigarette, then he lowered himself onto his haunches, squatting on the floor.

'After Nairobi, Ngala was great. I was twenty-one. And in the morning the sun would rise behind a beautiful mountain called Mount Kenya. Some parts of the White Highlands were like World War Two, but the troubles hadn't come to Ngala, not then. It was paradise. We were kings, us white men. It was a little village. Everybody said, "Hello, sir." There was a little shop in the village.

Sold powdered milk for the tea. Stuff like that. "Hello, sir! Your usual?" Packet of fags. Bottle of beer. Can you imagine anything better? Me. A lad from Bow.'

'No,' said Breen. 'I can't imagine that.'

'You and your husband put us up in a chalet on their farm,' said Doyle. 'I thought you were wonderful. You had us round for dinner. Drinks on the veranda. Oh yes. You gave me the thirst. Isn't that right, Mrs Fletchet?' He addressed her naked, unconscious form, then looked back at Breen. 'But back then, I couldn't believe my luck. Great people. Plenty of everything. Because we were white, Bill and me, we were OK. Back in England I would have been shit to you, but out in Kenya, it was like I was a king. I had respect. Everything. Even me, I had a servant. Well, a houseboy, anyway. He looked after Milkwood and me at our quarters. Me. A lad from a back-to-back. Drinking gin and bitters on your patio. What were those little things you used to serve with the gin, Mrs F?'

Eloisa Fletchet groaned, but she didn't seem to be fully conscious.

'Gherkins. Pickled gherkins on little sticks.' He mimed holding up a toothpick. 'It was lovely. Though I'm not sure you approved of me, did you, Mrs Fletchet? You didn't like your husband mingling with a couple of mere coppers. But he knew what he was doing. We were new in the country. We needed taking in hand. He explained the things we couldn't see. How families like his had come here in the Thirties. His uncle had settled the place. How there had been nothing here when they arrived. They had made this place. He knew about the Kikuyu, the local people. Spoke a bit of the language. Said he admired them. Wonderful people.

'We heard about the Mau Mau atrocities everywhere else. All the white farmers were getting ready for their turn. Out in Ngala they didn't touch us. So we didn't have much to do, except file reports. I met the local schoolteacher, Ruth Wairimu. She was twenty-five. Older than me. She taught in the local Kikuyu School. One day I met her in the village shop . . . a tiny little outpost it was . . . and said hello. She asked me if I would read Shakespeare to her schoolchildren. Me. Read Shakespeare. She said she wanted her children to hear an Englishman read the Bard.'

The rain had started now. It spattered onto the window behind the blankets that hung as curtains.

'So I did. I always liked English. It was my favourite subject at school. Her school, it was this concrete block with a tin roof. All these desks lined up. And Ruth there in front of them all. She handed a book to me and made me read out of it. She gave me *Hamlet*,' he said.

'Who would fardels bear,
To grunt and sweat under a weary life,
But that the dread of something after death,
The undiscover'd country from whose bourn
No traveller returns, puzzles the will
And makes us rather bear those ills we have
Than fly to others that we know not of?'

He spoke it quietly, with feeling, looking straight at Mrs Fletchet. 'Bloody love Shakespeare. I don't know if they understood a word I said. Ruth explained it all to them . . . They loved it. All that murder and plotting. Next day we went for drinks on your veranda. Remember that, Mrs Fletchet?' No reaction. ' "Oh, I hear you've been getting chummy with the local schoolmistress," said your husband. "Yeah. As it happens . . ." He sidles over to me and says, "Word to the wise, old chum. Steer clear of the dark meat. If you want it, go to Nairobi. Plenty there. Not round here. Word gets around." So what if word gets around?

'I said, "She's not after my body, only my mind." We all had a good laugh at that, but you could see it there. And obviously I knew what he was getting at. We had our place. They had their place. Mess that up and it all goes wrong.' Doyle looked at his watch, then said, 'But I didn't want to admit it. I'd fallen in love with her from the start. She was beautiful. Not like you were beautiful, Mrs F. God, you were gorgeous, and didn't you know it? But Ruth was clever. And she didn't treat me like some piece of dog shit.'

Mrs Fletchet was waxy white. She did not have long left.

'In the evenings I would go and sit with her outside the house she shared with the other schoolteacher. There was this amazing noise, in the evening. All the crickets and toads. It was beautiful. We would sit on a bench where everyone could see us, so she could show everyone we were not getting up to no good, you know? I used to love to hear her talk. It was always about her kids. The stupid things they'd done. Out there, one moment it's the afternoon, the next it's night-time. The night comes down like a curtain in a play. And sometimes we would only sit there and just listen to the noise of the bugs. She was really funny and smart. I had to write reports and she'd help me with them. It was nothing more than just holding hands. I wanted more, of course. I did try, but she wouldn't let me . . .

'And then the raids came to Ngala. It was always at night. You never saw them, not at first. There was one on a farm fifty miles away, first. A settler's boy was killed. White. About ten. That was really shocking. They'd already killed half a dozen blacks, but now it was that they'd killed one of us, you know? Then a week later they raided your farm, but your husband was ready. He had guns there and paid men to stay up all night. The Mau Mau weren't expecting so many bullets to be coming their way and they scarpered. Your headman was nicked by a bullet, I think, but that was the worst of it. In the morning we went out and found the body of one of the Mickeys, hit in the middle of the chest by a bullet. The wound was crawling with ants, I'll never forget. First real dead man I'd seen.'

He took a puff from his cigarette.

'I was shocked by the effect it had on me. We were thrilled. We'd seen them off. Only when I told Ruth about it, I burst out crying. I couldn't help it. The shock of seeing someone dead, I suppose. She held my head in her lap like I was a child and I sobbed and sobbed. That night she took me into her room and kissed me, properly.

'Anyway, that was the beginning of the end of it. The worst raid was in September. I was in the police station when I heard all the Home Guard jumping into a Land Rover. Your husband was with them, Mrs F. He had his hunting rifle. Huge great thing. A Magnum.'

Breen remembered Eloisa Fletchet talking about the guns she had used to shoot elephants with.

'They said they had heard that the Mau Mau were preparing to attack the next farm to us. There must have been ten of us. Took us an hour to get there, so it was almost dark by the time we arrived. I remember how we waited for the Mau Mau, guns at the ready. My heart was going crazy. Out there it's so dark, you know, like a wall of black. And I was thinking: They're out there. Soon they'll start firing at us. Only they didn't. False alarm.

'So we got into the Land Rover and made it back to Ngala as the sun was coming up, exhausted. And then we heard it, over the engine noise. This wailing sound. And as we rounded the bend into the village, everyone was outside, crying.

'The Mau Mau had come in the night while we were all away and attacked the headman's house. They killed all his family. Two men, five women and three kiddies. All hacked to death with knives and machetes, then the whole place had been set alight. When we got back there were still bits of them everywhere. That was what they did, the Mau Mau. They wanted to make everyone afraid. And they did. It was dreadful. I wasn't used to dead bodies still.'

'You are now,' said Breen.

Doyle ignored him. 'But I didn't cry this time. I was angry. That night I went to see Ruth. This time it was her who cried. It turned out she taught two of the children who had been murdered. I was so angry. She was grieving so hard, it shocked me. As if they had been her own children. I couldn't stay long because I had to get back on duty. That would be the last time we were properly together. That same night, going back home to my quarters, I went down past the Home Guard station and I heard someone screaming. Someone really in pain.

'So I went inside. "What the bloody hell's going on in here?" There was a man called Jeremiah. A sergeant in the Home Guard. Short-arse with a round face and a big smile. He said, "We are questioning a suspect." And I could hear behind the door this man whimpering. Saying something in Kikuyu I didn't understand. "Let me see," I said. So they opened the door. And there was this naked man. Tied to a chair with wire. It was real dark in the room. But I could see he was bleeding from between his legs.

'His head was down. I didn't recognise him at first. Then he must have realised that someone else was in the room and he looked up. It was one of the guys who ran a shop in the village where I used to go to buy beer. I said, "This guy's not a Mickey. I know him. You all know him."

'"No, no, no. He's one of them," said Jeremiah. "He takes money for the Mau Mau. We raided his shop and we found the money." I was shocked. First that they had been torturing this guy I knew, then that they were saying he was a Mau Mau. I'd always thought he was OK.

'The guy looked up. I didn't know his name, but he recognised me. "Please, sir," he said. "Help me."

'I was horrified. I said to Jeremiah, "He's a local. You can't treat him like that."

'Jeremiah just smiled. And then I heard a voice behind me. "Of course he can. This is an emergency." It was your husband. And he was standing there, cool as anything.

'I said, "What's happening? There must be a mistake."

'But your husband said no, the Mau Mau must have had spies in the village, you see. The Mau Mau were all holed up in the Aberdare Mountains, miles away. The moment we had gone, somebody would have snuck out and told the Mickeys the village was un-defended. That's how they caught us with our pants down.'

Breen looked toward the window. The first daylight was breaking beyond the curtain. Doyle reached in the pocket of his shorts and pulled out his pack of tobacco again.

'You see, the shopkeeper had confessed. Milkwood told me how it worked. Behind our backs, the Mau Mau extorted locals to sup-port them. They might not even want to, but they had to. Otherwise they'd be attacked. That's why they'd killed the village headman and his family. Because he wouldn't pay. That's how the Mickeys sur-vived. And it turned out this shopkeeper was their book-keeper. They even found this ledger with the names of people in the village in it and sums of money next to it. The shopkeeper claimed it was just the money they owed him on account, but Jeremiah wasn't having any of it. Far as I was concerned, if he was the one that took the money, that made him just as bad as the men who chopped up those women and children.'

Doyle licked the new cigarette he was making. 'I was shocked, I admit. I had trusted this guy. I had bought goods from him. Given him ciggies. And here was your husband telling me he was a terrorist. Of course I believed him. I thought of Ruth's girls, chopped to pieces in front of their own mother and father. Fair enough. Hurt him all you want, I thought. He deserves it.

'I never found out what happened to the shopkeeper. I guess he died. If you'd asked me then, I'd have said, "Serves him right." I'd seen the dead bodies. I'd seen what the Mau Mau did, with my own eyes.'

He stopped talking and lit the new cigarette. He sucked in smoke, then leaned down to pick up the gag. Then he walked behind Breen and tied it around his mouth, so tightly that Breen's cheeks were drawn back against his teeth.

Breen tried to call out, but all he could manage was a squeak through the cloth.

'Only then, a couple of days later, I walked into the village for supplies and I saw the shop was still open, so I went in, apprehensive like. And there, standing behind the counter, large as life, was Jeremiah, with this big smile on his face. "Welcome to my shop," he said. "For you, sir, a special discount."

'I remember your husband saying, "So what? The loyal ones deserve their reward. If we don't support them, we'll be as bad as the bloody Colonial Office."'

Doyle sucked the cigarette once more until it was hot, then held it against the skin on Breen's right arm, just below his shoulder. Breen squealed with pain. He was going to torture him to death, just as he was killing Eloisa Fletchet.

'That was only the beginning. The Mickeys had more guns now. It seemed as if the Mickeys raided all the time at the end of the year. Always at night. It wasn't like you ever saw them. Sometimes we fought them off OK. Once they killed a couple of the Home Guard. Another time they caught two girls and raped and killed them. It turned out they were Jeremiah's cousins. Another time we found a body in the rice fields. This Mickey had been hit and had tried to crawl off, but he hadn't got far. I felt fine, looking at him, that time. Happy, even. It tears your sanity away, in the end.'

Doyle removed the cigarette, pulled on it a few more times, then pressed it against Breen's skin a little lower down. Again, Breen's scream was muffled by the gag.

'Fletchet was screening everybody in the villages for miles around now. That's what they called it: screening. Did you ever bother asking him what he actually did, Mrs F? The Home Guard were doing it, supposedly, but mostly it was your husband and Milkwood. They would go off in the Land Rover and come back with three or four people in the back. Then the screening would begin. Thing is, someone like me couldn't tell if they were Mau Mau or not. They all denied it. You would, wouldn't you? If you admitted it, you'd be sent for hanging. Or you'd have to become an informer, in which case the Mickeys would probably kill you anyway.

'At the beginning, I remember asking your husband, "How can you tell which is real and which isn't?" "That's the trick," he said. And he pulled out this lanky guy and we took him into the screening room. Because that's what we all called it now. The screening room. First off, Fletchet asked him for his ID. Guy said he had lost it. I remember Fletchet smiled at me. See? But that didn't prove anything, did it? I thought: Loads of them don't have proper ID.

'Then Fletchet said, "You're one of the ones who raided the Home Guard last week, aren't you?" The guy just shrugged. No. Not me. And he glared at Fletchet. This real dead man's glare. So Fletchet picked up this gun and swung it round at the man's head so hard he knocked the guy right off his feet. Crack. The guy got up and still said he had nothing to do with it. He was scared now, though. You could tell.

'So was he a Mickey or not? Fletchet said to me, "You think I'm being too hard, don't you? Well, I already have a list of five people who have already told me this guy is a Y1." We used to classify people as Z, Y or X. Y1 was a Mau Mau of lower rank. Fletchet used to write it all down in a ledger. Name, address, classification. He had all these little code letters too to show what we'd done to them; how far we'd had to go before they confessed. All neat it was, like it made what we were doing official.

'So this guy was down on his knees now. Pleading with us. I had thought he looked so genuine. The pleading looked real enough too. Your husband said, "See? You can't tell, can you?" But, look, we already knew he was one of them. I believed Fletchet. This man had taken the oath. And if they broke the Mau Mau oath, they'd be killed. So he had to deny it. No choice. Fletchet said the only way you're going to get it out of them is to make them more scared of you than they are of the Mau Mau. And he handed me the gun. "Go on," he said.'

Doyle moved around to the other side and started there. Fresh skin. Fresh pain. Breen threw his head backwards and forwards, trying to loosen the gag, but he couldn't.

'I thought of that girl who had been in Ruth's class. I had seen her body. One of her little hands had been cut off where she'd tried to stop the killer. And this guy in front of me was one of them. So when Fletchet handed me the gun, I had a go too.

'It wasn't as hard as you'd think, once you'd hit them the first time. I whacked him in the guts with the butt and it didn't take long until he started spilling names of people. I didn't enjoy it, but it was a result. It had to be done. And when I hit him, he gave the names of other people in the village. Fletchet wrote it all down in his book, but then he said, "We could send him to the magistrates' court. But they're so backed up with cases they probably won't even try him till next year. And if they do, one of those coloured lawyers from Nairobi will end up defending him. Maybe even getting him off. That would be ridiculous."'

Doyle shook his head, as if in answer to something Breen had said. 'I couldn't do it. Not that time, anyway. Fletchet did it.' Doyle made his fingers into a gun and held it to Eloisa's unconscious head. 'Bang.'

He stubbed the cigarette out on Breen's left arm. The pain was excruciating.

'Like I said, you get used to it,' said Doyle. He sat down in a chair. Blinked, relaxed. 'I didn't tell her what we were doing. But Ruth knew. It was only a small place. I remember going to visit her. She'd be sitting on that bench outside her house. After that first man I interrogated, that was it. When she saw me coming she stood up, she went inside and bolted the door. I knocked, but she wouldn't answer. She wouldn't have nothing to do with me after that. I was hurt at first. I said, "He was a Mau Mau. He's the reason why your pupils are dead."

'Your husband said it again: "You never know which side people are on, around here." I refused to believe that. I thought maybe it was just too dangerous for her to be seen with me now. So I spent more time with your husband and Milkwood. And anyway, things got worse. We spent each day screening people. The attacks carried on. I was spending all day in the station now. More and more and more of them.'

He left the room for a small bedroom to the right. Breen craned his head, but couldn't see where he was going.

'You quickly learned there was a point when everyone was going to start naming people. But I noticed something else. As people became more frightened, of us and the Mau Mau, that point became further and further away. Each day, what we had to do to get them to confess got worse. Your husband had started using pliers on their hands, by then. He would cut off fingers. Then we were putting electricity on their balls. They would jump up and down in the chair. I didn't do it. They did. I watched, though. You just got used to it. We really believed that unless we did it, the tide would engulf us.'

When Doyle returned he was holding a hunting knife.

'The Home Guard station had become a prison camp now. We'd made them build these huts and it had wire all around the place. By Christmas we were holding two, three hundred people, waiting to screen them. It was exhausting. I have never been so tired in my life. Every day we would be interrogating. All day, every day. We lost our minds. Every day this thing ran deeper. More people. More confessions. Then in the evenings we'd clean up, go to your house for a lovely gin and tonic, like everything was all perfectly normal. "Any news from home?", "What about the cricket?"

'Inflicting fear and pain becomes a kind of science. Your humanity disappears. But it worked, in a way. By the next spring, attacks were dying out. We had rounded up so many Kikuyu that we had ripped the heart out of the Mau Mau.'

Doyle stood in front of Breen; he held one hand on Breen's thigh, keeping him down. He sucked on the cigarette, then held it by Breen's nipple and pressed.

Breen bucked and wriggled, felt his eyes rolling back into his head. This was tender skin; Doyle had known that the pain would be far worse than before.

Doyle stood back and sucked the cigarette into life. 'Ruth never came near me all that time. Then one day, in the middle of the night, I heard a knocking on the door of our house. I was a little bit pissed. We'd been drinking at your place. I was drunk every day then, after work. It was the only way I could sleep. You had to be careful opening the door at night. I remember poking my gun out the door and looking round. And there was Ruth, scared to be out late, scared in case anyone saw her coming to see the white policeman.

'I was so happy to see her. I thought she'd come to see me. I realised how much I'd missed our conversations. I must have been babbling on to her, but she put her finger to her lips and said I was being too loud. She said we had arrested this boy. A former pupil of hers. She asked us to be merciful with him. She swore he was nothing to do with the Mau Mau. That he was a good, Christian boy. "How do you know?" I said. She wrote his name down on a piece of paper for me. I said I would do what I could but she'd have to kiss me first. If he was not a Mau Mau, he'd be fine. I was drunk still from all your gin, Mrs F. All I wanted was a single kiss. But she pushed me away.

'I was angry with her. It was hard, what we were doing. She should have understood that. Understood that I loved her. Next day I looked out for this fellow, all the same. I would have done anything for Ruth. Couldn't find him anywhere. I searched all the quarters. Asked all the Home Guard men. They all shook their heads.

'That night at Fletchet's place, I asked, casual like, about him. "He was a Mickey," Fletchet said. It turned out Milkwood had already interrogated him. He had confessed. One of the Home Guard had executed him that morning. "And why are you so interested in him, Nicky?" said Fletchet. "Would it have anything to do with that visit last night you had from the schoolteacher, Miss Wairimu?"

'I should have realised. Milky had heard Ruth coming to our quarters the night before. He'd heard her asking about the boy. "Did she offer to fuck you, for information?" said Fletchet.

'I was drunk again. Your gin, Mrs F. I told them they were talking rubbish. Ruth? She would never do that. Everything was getting out of hand. Fletchet called me naive. He laughed at me. Milkwood knew she was sneaking into my room at night, he said. She was a spy. How fucking dare he say that? I remember standing up and smacking him one in the face. That was the last thing I remember. Milkwood clocked me on the head. A gin bottle, I think it was, Mrs Fletchet. I went down like a sack of shit.'

Breen had discovered that if he sat still, the pain seemed to lessen. Some blood still trickled out of the wounds, down onto his naked thighs, but not much. He tried to listen.

'I woke up locked in our quarters. I screamed and hammered on the door but nobody came. They put food through the front door. Milkwood arrived, eventually, the next morning. He said they were sending me home to England. Compassionate grounds. I said, "Where's Ruth?"

'He said, "Forget about her." I ran to the screening station. They had taken Ruth that previous night after they'd knocked me out. I think they were both drunk. They raped her and tortured her, then left her for dead. She had confessed too, they said. She was a Y, they said. I saw her body too. They had left it in the ditch behind the screening camp. They had tortured her for the whole night and day. They had tortured her with cigarettes. They had cut her breasts. They had cut her stomach. Cut fingers off both hands. They had pushed a boiled egg into her vagina.'

'Like Alexandra Tozer,' Breen tried to say, but the cloth stopped the words.

'Everything I had believed in was a lie. Who had been Mau Mau

382

and who hadn't. It was all just madness. They didn't know. Nobody knew. That was the point. All they were doing was making everyone afraid of them. There was no logic. Only fear. When they let me out I refused to go back to England. I was sacked on grounds of ill health, they said. I went to Nairobi. I spent months there, writing letters to the head of the police force. To the Governor. To anyone I could think of, telling them what had happened.

'They didn't want to believe me. Nobody did. I tried to see the Central Province Commissioner and the Member for African Affairs. All of them refused to see me. They said I was unwell. I wrote home to the papers. But it was over now. Everybody wanted to forget it had ever happened. Even the bloody liberals and leftists. It was all in the past already, as far as they were concerned. I became known as a troublemaker.'

He leaned forward and removed Breen's gag. Breen sucked in air.

'Alexandra Tozer never did anything,' said Breen.

'Neither did Ruth. Neither did most of the people we tortured in Ngala. I killed people there. I could have gone mad after seeing what I'd seen and what I'd done,' said Doyle. 'Instead I became sane. I saw through the illusion. I travelled. I spoke to monks who taught me the meaning of death. Who helped me see that life was the illusion. But when I came back to England, what happened? I found out that you and Jimmy had become Lord and Lady. All the things you did. And you just sailed through it all.'

'Alexandra Tozer. She never did anything,' Breen said again.

'You're so hung up on death. You don't realise. That's part of the dream. That's why it hurts you so much to die. Once you know that, nothing can hurt you any more. When I got back here, I followed Jimmy around to see whether he had changed, like I had. But he hadn't. One day I saw them fucking. I was close by. She was beautiful. He had killed the woman I loved. So I could take her away from him, just as she had taken Ruth from me. Ruth had never done anything either.'

'Let her go,' said Breen, nodding towards Eloisa. 'She'll die. You can get help.'

'I don't need help. I don't want it.'

'You're going to kill me?'

Doyle didn't answer.

'You're blaming Fletchet, but it was you who did the torturing. You've admitted it. You're as guilty as he was.'

'And I'm going to be the one who punishes him. He knows that. Each time I do this he can see me coming. He knows I'm coming. He's afraid. Each time, he becomes more and more afraid. And his life will be hell for as long as I choose. He taught me well, didn't he?'

Doyle held the gag in his hands. He was going to kill him in the same way as he had killed Alexandra Tozer and Bill Milkwood.

Doyle looked at his watch.

There was a pattern. Each one the same. A long message to Fletchet. *I am still out there. I am coming for you.*

'Why did Milkwood pay you off?'

'He was a coward. He was scared. Wouldn't you be? But I persuaded him I could help him in return. I knew all about drugs. I started to give him information.'

'Real or fake?'

'Real, mostly. Not that the rest of the Drug Squad cared either way. As long as they got arrests.'

'But you killed him all the same?'

'I was coming down here. Back in January I saw police cars at the farm. You were visiting, but I thought the investigation was starting again. I realised I was running out of time. So yes, it was time for him to die.'

'But not before you'd given him information that you could use to fake your death. About drug gangs in Spain.'

'You knew about that?' Doyle tied the gag even tighter this time.

Breen was overtaken with a huge tiredness. The torture would be slow and long. And utterly pointless. And then he would die.

THIRTY-ONE

Outside, curlews called on the mud. A mournful note. The tide must be low now. It would be morning soon.

He was half awake. Then someone tugged on his left hand. He didn't know how long he had slept. Doyle lifted the palm and spread his fingers. Then raised up a pair of garden secateurs.

The blades were slightly rusty.

Breen shook his head violently from side to side. Screamed behind the gag. It wasn't rust.

With the limited movement he had under the wires binding him, he slipped his hand from Doyle's grasp, knocking the secateurs to the ground. It was not easy to remove a finger, even from a bound man. Doyle didn't seem particularly concerned by his struggle. It was as if he had seen it many times before. He knelt to pick up the cutters. They had fallen under the chair.

Behind him, Breen saw Eloisa now. She seemed to be still. He looked for any sign of rising in her chest, but there was none. A huge sense of sadness enveloped him for a second. He would be like her soon.

No.

Breen kicked at Doyle, who was on his knees, feeling for the cutters. Don't give up. Don't break. Doyle squealed.

When he stood, Breen saw Doyle was bleeding from just under the eye. Hobbled though he was, he had caught him with a toenail.

But Doyle didn't seem to be angered by this. He rubbed the skin and walked to the wall, to check it in a mirror.

Wriggling, still trying to loosen the bonds, Breen's left foot felt something under it. The secateurs.

His feet were closely tied, so kicking too far was hard. His first attempt barely moved them. He curled the toes of his left foot onto the floorboards and pressed hard down so that he was forcing his toes back, then in a single movement, uncurled his toes and flicked his foot as far as it could go. The secateurs spun across the floor and under a tool cupboard by the bedroom door.

Doyle saw the movement from the side of his eyes. He shook his head, then moved to the cupboard and squatted down, feeling for the tool. When he stood he was empty-handed. He could not find them.

Ha ha ha.

So Doyle opened the tool cupboard and pulled out a tenon saw instead. 'Your fault,' Doyle said. 'This will hurt more.'

Breen struggled in the chair. The wire cut his wrists and his ankles. Others hadn't escaped. Doyle had done this many times before in Africa. But to admit that would be to give up. The pain roused him, made him angry.

'Shh,' Doyle said. 'Don't worry. It'll be done soon.'

Fuck you, he said silently, under his gag. But however much he struggled with his left hand, Doyle was stronger. Doyle splayed the fingers over the edge of the chair and selected one, bunching the rest up under his fist and pushing down so hard to trap them there that the pain made Breen's eyes water. His ring finger alone stood out.

'I met a monk in Tibet,' said Doyle. 'He could drive a nail through his hand and not feel the pain.'

Doyle lowered the saw and started to carve. It cut straight away, tearing the pink skin just above the knuckle bone. The agony was fierce. But then, in an instant, Doyle was cutting into bone, which was worse. The vibrations made by the teeth travelled up his arm as the saw worked its way back and forth. His stomach wound had only bled a little; this was worse. Cutting deep, blood pumped onto the floor.

At the end, the bone gave way and his lifeless finger flapped from side to side, suspended only by a small piece of skin. Doyle removed the saw. Even half blind with pain, Breen could see his finger dangling down now, swinging gently. Doyle released his grip on the hand and put down the saw. He pulled out his knife and sliced through the remaining piece of skin and the finger dropped beyond Breen's sight.

And the blood kept pumping out of him onto the tarpaulin.

A shadow passed over the room. It all happened so fast Breen did not understand what was going on. Doyle looked up suddenly with a look of puzzlement on his face. And then there was the loudest noise the world had ever heard. Simultaneously, the curtains suddenly appeared to be horizontal.

And fire and glass.

And when the curtains fell slowly back into place, they were shredded.

And Doyle was nowhere to be seen.

The world rang. A high-pitched, all-enveloping note.

To his surprise, Helen was standing in front of him.

She looked great, he thought, but when he tried to tell her, nothing came from his mouth.

She was trying to say something to him too, but when her lips moved he could hear nothing either. Just the ringing.

And she had a twelve-bore shotgun in her hand.

★

He looked down at his feet. There was glass scattered all around, lying in his blood. She must have fired the gun through the window at close range before coming in through the door. Where was Doyle?

He craned his neck to the right.

He was there, propped up against the cupboard. There was blood all over his bare chest. Doyle held his hands across the wound. The shot had flayed his torso. You could see exposed ribcage where the skin had been torn away.

Doyle was saying something to Helen, but Breen could not hear that either. The blast must have deafened him.

Untie me, Helen, please.

She stood for a second with the gun raised and you could see the thought going through her head.

No, Helen. Please.

He could see her looking down the barrel at Doyle, finger tightening on the trigger.

No, Helen. Don't, he said. *Please don't.*

You're being stupid.

Think of the baby.

There is no need. He may die anyway. If not, we can lock him away.

Eyes closed, Doyle's lips moved, preparing for death.

She stared at Doyle for a second longer, then lowered the gun, propped it against the wall and turned and knelt in front of Breen. She picked up Doyle's bloodied knife and pulled out her shirt. Digging the knife into the cloth, she tore off a rough square and wrapped it round Breen's hand.

She said something to him but he still couldn't hear a word.

The gunshot deafened me, he tried to say, behind the gag.

This time she took the knife and knelt lower, trying to cut the wire that bound his wrists to the chair.

A train passed. He felt the vibration through the floorboards. The shack must be close to the track. There would be commuters on the way to work; post and parcels in the guard's van.

As Helen worked, agonisingly slowly, on the wires that bound him, he felt another more desperate knocking passing through the flimsy wood of the shed. He realised it must be Hibou, she too struggling against her bonds.

Hibou, he tried to call.

She would be frightened. She could not see what was happening.

And he was thinking of how lucky he had been when he saw Doyle start to move. Slowly at first. At first he felt gratitude. He was not dead. He would live. They could bring him to trial and punish him for what he had done.

But then, behind Helen, Doyle put his hands down on the floor and started to raise himself, slowly.

He stamped his feet to try and warn Helen, but she didn't seem to notice or hear. The shot must have deafened her too.

Slowly Doyle stood. His chest had been flayed by lead shot, and there were pockmarks dripping bloodily on his face, but his arms and legs seemed OK.

Helen! Breen screamed through the gag. *Helen! Helen!*

The bloody man looked around, saw what he wanted and leaned to pick it up.

The small-handled axe he used to chop wood for the fire.

Finally Helen looked up at Breen, worried now. What was he making all the fuss about?

But then she leaned down again, as if frustrated with how long this was taking.

In the very last second, she looked up at him again, puzzled. She must have seen something in his eyes, because she turned, twisting away as the axe swung into empty air, arcing down and missing Breen's bare knees by the smallest fraction of an inch.

A second time Doyle raised the axe, but she had her eyes on him now. Her back was to the wall she'd propped the gun against and Breen saw her desperately feeling for its barrel behind her. It was too far away to the left.

Doyle charged at her, axe raised again. She ducked and tried to barge past him.

But the floor was slick with blood, his and Eloisa's. Helen slipped, legs jerking backwards, body hurtling, face forward, onto the floor instead.

Doyle turned, stamped on her back as she flailed, holding her down with the right foot, raising the axe again.

No. No. No.

It was Hibou, appearing from behind the partition, screaming, that made Doyle pause just for that fraction of a second.

Unlike Breen and Eloisa Fletchet, she had not been tied up naked. She was still in her farm clothes, but her right wrist was bloody from where she'd been tearing the skin against the wire that had bound her.

Doyle's pause was long enough for Helen to get some purchase on the slimy floor and roll sideways, unsteadying Doyle.

And now Hibou came running at Doyle so hard he smashed back into the wooden wall.

She held him down, pinning him in a sitting position on the bloody floor, back against the wall. Farming had made her strong.

'Do it,' she was shouting.

Helen walked to the shotgun and picked it up. This time she didn't hesitate. Doyle lifted a hand as if to protect himself from the shot, but seemed too tired to hold it there for long. It fell to the ground.

'Hel. Do it.'

This time the bang was muted. A dull, faraway thud.

In that second, Doyle's head was entirely transformed. The skin left it, baring teeth and skull. His eyeballs disappeared, turned to jelly by the pellets. The shot destroyed the soft tissue of his throat completely. Blood pumped suddenly into the space that it had left, spraying up and covering the wall against which he lay, covering Hibou as she held him. She jerked backwards. For a second his head moved from side to side, as if what was left of him was convulsed by pain. Then he stopped and the skull fell forward onto the mess of his chest. Redness crept across the floorboards towards Breen's own blood.

And Helen, covered in blood, put the gun down and turned to Breen, expressionless.

She said nothing as she finally cut his hands free.

'Christ.' Hibou had her hand over her mouth, moon-eyed. 'Look at Paddy.'

Breen was weak now.

'Is that his finger down there? Oh.'

He had lost blood. Helen found a dishcloth and tied him a sling so that his hand was raised above his heart. That way the clotting blood seemed to seep less. Next, she knelt to cut the bonds at his ankles, and when she stood, the knees of her jeans were dark with his blood.

'Are you being sick?' said Helen.

Hibou nodded.

'Well don't. Find me a coat or a blanket or something. He's half frozen to death.'

'God. I fucked up everything,' said Hibou.

'Shut up,' said Helen.

Breen tried to move his feet, but he didn't seem to have the strength. When Helen finally untied his gag, his throat was so dry he could only whisper.

'Cold,' he said.

When Helen had found a grey blanket to put around his shoulders, she turned to Eloisa.

She put her hand on her head, then felt for a pulse. Eloisa's skin was a greyish yellow. She must have been dead a while now. There was an old mac on the back of the door, thin and dirty. Helen took it down, placed it over Eloisa, covering her nakedness. The empty sleeves hung down on either side. A grotesque, handless hunchback.

'Your sister,' he said. 'Alexandra.'

'It's finished now.'

'We need to go,' Hibou said.

'How did you know we were here?'

'I've been out since three in the morning, looking. Doyle's tent was empty.'

'Doyle's tent?'

'He'd been living in the marshes. I found it an hour ago.'

They found Breen's clothes but they were still too wet to wear, so Hibou took off her jumper and gave it to him. It was still covered in Doyle's blood, but at least it was warm.

Breen leaned against the outside of the hut. The estuary where he had almost drowned last night looked benign today, the water flat and ripple-less. 'I went to find you,' said Breen.

'I saw the photograph on your bed,' Hibou said.

Breen nodded. 'Thank you,' he said. 'You saved my life.'

'Really?' she said.

They had to cross the railway line to make it to the fields, tramping round the edge. Breen, an absurd figure in a woman's jumper, a grey blanket and huge waders that flapped at his bare legs, chafing them. Each step an exhausting challenge, even with Hibou on one side and Helen on the other.

When he could walk no more, they paused by a gate.

'Would I have liked your sister?' said Hibou. Breen could feel her trembling from the shock of what she had seen.

'Course,' said Helen. 'Everyone loved her. She'd have hated you, though. Farm girl. She wanted to move to the city. Get away from this dump.'

'It's not a dump. I love it.'

''Xactly.'

Now from the corners of the fields, white specks.

'Finally,' said Helen Tozer.

Policemen in shirt sleeves, running towards them across the sodden fields. They would make a ghoulish sight, the three of them, skin and clothes so bloody.

When he saw them coming, Breen lay down on the damp soil. He could go no further.

Hibou sat next to him and took his injured hand. 'Can we call my mum and dad when we get back?' she said. 'I need to say sorry. I thought I was never going to see them again.'

He asked, 'Why did you run away?'

The policemen seemed to be taking an age to reach them. Hibou looked at Breen and said, 'It was stupid. I stole money.'

'How much?'

'One hundred and seventy pounds.'

'Is that all?'

'Don't laugh. I knew they'd be angry if they found out. They're good people. They didn't deserve me.'

'Nothing more than that?'

'It was meant for the British Legion. There had been a fete. Mum had all the money.'

'You took it?'

'I just wanted some proper clothes. I wanted to be fab, like all the girls on TV. They were just giving it to old people, anyway. But then I bought them and I couldn't wear them because they'd know. It doesn't feel like so much now. I always make stupid mistakes. One mistake after another.'

He held up his bloody hand. It didn't throb so much that way. 'Think about it. If you hadn't been here we would never have got him,' he said.

'I lied to you.'

'It doesn't matter.'

They lay on their backs on the cold ground, exhausted.

A V of geese flying overhead, all perfectly spaced.

THIRTY-TWO

He has cooked breast of lamb slowly in the oven, then coated it in egg and breadcrumbs.

The rich smell fills the flat.

The table is laid for six. Breen doesn't have enough chairs, but Elfie has brought down one of hers from upstairs. Her boyfriend has called to say he'll be working late at the advertising agency and they are to start without him.

'Typical,' says Elfie. 'He's working on this ad campaign today with Twiggy. It's for the new Mini.'

'I met her once,' says Amy. 'She came to the cinema.'

Carmichael hadn't turned up yet, either. He must be working late too.

Breen has painted the entire flat. All the old wallpaper is covered. The front room is white and modern-looking now. He has bought a new Swedish armchair and thrown out the big old dark one of his father's. He has put a framed poster from a Rembrandt exhibition over the fireplace. And he's bought one of those big Japanese paper lampshades, though it hangs too low from the basement ceiling and sometimes he knocks it as he passes. He should have bought something smaller. Maybe he needs to find a bigger flat instead, now there will be three of them.

His bedroom is white, too. The spare room, however, has yellow walls and red skirting boards. The colour hurts Breen's eyes, but

Helen likes it. It's her room now. You'd never know his father had lived there in his dying days.

There is still work to be done. In Elfie's flat they've painted the floorboards. It makes the whole place look light and European, somehow. Breen thinks he should do the same.

He is back at Marylebone CID. A familiar grind, but he is happy there. It is a novelty coming home to a flat with a woman in it. Helen has stopped saying she'll move out when she's had the baby, though she insists it's only temporary, staying here. When he bought a cot for the baby from Swan & Edgar, Helen was angry at first. She said she was planning on getting one second-hand from Brick Lane. But they've put it up in her room, at the end of the bed, anyway. She's in there now, doing her make-up while he chops the vegetables.

His hand is still bandaged. He's been learning to type one-handed. He was never that good with two anyway.

Helen emerges from the bedroom finally in a black-and-white maternity dress. She's cut her hair as short as it's ever been. 'I look like crap,' she says, staring down at her belly.

'You look beautiful,' he says.

'Pervert,' she says.

She's not as pregnant as Elfie, though. Elfie is huge, a fecund half-sphere poking from under her cotton top. Unlike Helen, who looks uncomfortable being pregnant, Elfie luxuriates in it. She has brought knitting with her and sits at the table, clicking needles.

'Where's John?' Helen asks Amy.

'Bloody pub, I expect. Friday night. He said he'd be here at seven.'

Elfie says, 'You're lucky, Helen. I'd love to have grown up on a farm.'

They have been talking about Hibou. Her parents had come from Buckinghamshire to visit her at the farm this week to see where she had made her new life.

Amy has brought a bottle of Mateus Rosé and they've opened it already. Elfie says she can't drink any more, it makes her feel ill.

'I'll have yours then,' says Helen.

'Know what I read in the papers today? James Fletchet is going into politics,' says Elfie. 'They say he's been offered a job as a shadow minister, for whenever they get Wilson out.'

Amy says, 'I don't believe in politics.'

Helen lights a cigarette and says, 'God. Shut up about James bloody Fletchet, won't you? You go on about him all the time. It's like you fancy him or something.'

Elfie says, 'I do, actually. I think he's quite cool for his age. Racy. Know what I mean?'

Amy and Elfie laugh; Helen doesn't.

In April Breen and Helen had to travel to Exeter to go to the coroner's court for the inquest into the murder of Eloisa Fletchet. Fletchet stayed away. Breen was glad of that. If she'd seen him, he wouldn't have been surprised if Helen had tried to kill him.

'Think about it. You two are heroes. You saved the life of a peer of the bloody realm,' Elfie says. She reads every little detail of the case in the papers and quizzes Breen or Helen about them whenever she has the chance.

Over the last few weeks there have been several sympathetic articles written about Fletchet. About the tragic loss of his wife. About the embittered and disgraced policeman turned drug dealer and murderer who was jealous of his success and wanted to kill him. They finally printed extracts from the furious letters Doyle had written in Nairobi. But there is no mention of Fletchet being a torturer in those articles. They sound like the ravings of a madman. Instead, Fletchet is described in the papers as a heroic former settler who was a key figure in combating the brutality of the Mau Mau.

Fletchet would be relieved that Helen had killed Doyle; it would have been inconvenient if he'd been arrested. What happened in Kenya was best forgotten.

'I like living above people who lead such exciting lives,' says Elfie. 'I've told all my friends.'

Helen rolls her eyes. According to the society pages, Fletchet's been a regular gambler, staking large sums at the Clermont Club. There is no tutting, only sympathy. A man trying to run from his sorrows.

'I know what you said about him, but do you actually believe James Fletchet really tortured those people?' says Elfie. 'I don't. They would have said that in the papers, if it had happened. There's been nothing about it. I mean . . . Doyle was mad, wasn't he? They said he'd taken LSD. I wouldn't be surprised if he had made it all up. It does your head in, you know?'

Helen refuses to look at any of the papers. She says it makes her feel sick, thinking about him. He got away with what he did. His sort always do.

'Can we change the subject? All that's done with now.'

Though Breen knows it isn't. It's still there in their heads. The pictures of Alexandra. The vision of Eloisa's body. The gun firing at Doyle's face.

He's been sleeping better, though, finally. There's still a scab on the stub of his finger, but the doctor says it's healing well.

The lamb is looking dry. It should have been served half an hour ago at least, but Carmichael is still not here. He looks at his watch. It's unlike him not to have rung.

'It was all so . . . wild, that's all,' Elfie says.

Amy takes the knitting away from Elfie, holds her hand and says, 'I think they don't want to talk about it any more, OK?'

'OK. I'll shut up. But I just want to say, what they did was so fab.'

'What are you going to call the baby?' asks Amy, to change the subject.

'Jimi,' Elfie says, without hesitation. 'After Jimi Hendrix.'

'What if it's a girl?'

'Jeanne, after Jeanne Moreau,' she says.

Amy turned to Helen. 'What about you? Have you decided on a name yet?'

Helen looks down at her growing belly.

'Alex,' says Breen.

Helen looks at him and smiles.

'What if it's a girl?' asks Amy.

'Alex,' says Helen.

They wait a little longer, but Carmichael still doesn't come, so Breen serves the food and opens another bottle of wine. He pours a glass for Helen, another for himself and Amy, and they eat and talk, about pop records and Ted Heath and Concorde and the theatre, and it feels good to be here, eating food in his flat with friends. It's like, after years, he has finally rejoined the world.

The baby will be born soon. He will help look after it, even if Helen won't let him marry her. What is that going to be like? He has so little experience of real families. He doesn't want to say, but though he's excited, he's a little bit scared too.

He's disappointed in the lamb. It was slightly overdone, but the women all say it's delicious. Especially for a man. He's almost finished his when he looks up from his plate, thinking he hears Carmichael coming down the stairs. Amy looks up too, expectantly, but it's only Elfie's boyfriend, who is somewhat drunk and isn't hungry but still has another glass of wine anyway.

Breen recognises the look in Amy's eye, though. Part

disappointment, part exasperation. And a little bit of apprehension too. Has something happened to him?

He picks up his wine and takes too large a gulp. And before they know it the second bottle is empty and Elfie and her boyfriend say goodbye and go back upstairs, but Carmichael is still not here.

AUTHOR'S NOTE

This book is a work of fiction, though the details of the torture are real. They are taken from Caroline Elkins's *Britain's Gulag: The Brutal End of Empire in Kenya* (Jonathan Cape, 2005), compiled from the testimony of Kikuyu witnesses. I also relied on David Anderson's excellent *Histories of the Hanged: Britain's Dirty War in Kenya and the End of Empire* (Orion, 2005).

Thanks, yet again, to Jon Riley and Rose Tomaszewska for all the clever things they said, and to Nick de Somogyi for not losing his mind unravelling my timelines over the course of three books. Also to the five kind people mentioned in my dedication, and to Jeff Humm, Karolina Sutton and Jane McMorrow.

BOOK CLUB QUESTIONS

'The 1960s were really just the 1950s for most people.' Based on the way life is depicted in the book, how much do you agree with this statement?

Were you surprised by the methods of policing depicted in the book? How do the processes – the lack of communication, the attitude of witnesses, the corruption and incompetence of police – structure the investigations and the plots? How do you compare this approach to other crime novels?

Breen often considers the generation gap. Helen Tozer, he thinks 'understood the new world for what it was. She knew how to enjoy it at the same time as not falling for its vanities'. How are the differences in society bridged between the two characters, and do each of them change as a result of becoming closer?

In what ways does Shaw use humour to characterize Helen Tozer – and other characters – as a subversive force? What is revealed and what is disguised by their wit?

'It is an inconvenient memory.' Colonial history plays an important role in the series. What do the characters of Fletchet, Doyle and Sam the Kenyan professor lend to Shaw's portrayal of its impact on British society? Are the problems discussed in Kenya relevant today?

The murder of Alexandra Tozer haunts the series, but she's one of several teenaged girls that become victims. How does she compare to Morwenna (Ijeoma's murdered girlfriend) and to Hibou? How does Helen Tozer react to these girls, and how does she set herself apart?

'I'm not marrying nobody just because I'm pregnant.' Is the way that sexual liberation is explored – its uses and its hypocrisies – typical of the way we understand the sixties? Is it instrumental to Breen and Helen's relationship in a way it couldn't have been in any other decade?

At the climax of the book, the detective, Breen, is rescued by the pregnant Helen. How does Shaw challenge traditional tropes of detective fiction throughout the book and how does this compare to other crime novels you've read?

As a policeman, Breen remains politically neutral. Confronted with the Kenyan Emergency and Fletchet's protected establishment, how do you imagine he is affected? Do you think the author has a political agenda, or simply a historical one?

'An elegy for an entire alienated generation.' Do you agree with this review? The sixties heralded a sea-change from a closer, community-minded society to independence and toleration of difference. Who is liberated in this book and who is left behind?

Read on for a sneak peek at William Shaw's new novel

THE BIRDWATCHER

Published May 2016

ONE

There were two reasons why William South did not want to be on the murder team.

The first was that it was October. The migrating birds had begun arriving on the coast.

The second was that, though nobody knew, he was a murderer himself.

These were not the reasons he gave to the shift sergeant. Instead, standing in front of his desk, he said, 'God's sake. I've got a pile of witness statements this deep to get through before Thursday, not to mention the Neighbourhood Panel meeting coming up. I haven't the time.'

'Tell me about it,' said the shift sergeant quietly.

'I don't understand why it has to be me anyway. The constable can do it.'

The shift sergeant was a soft-faced man who blinked as he spoke. He said, 'Ask DI McAdam on the Serious Crime Directorate. He's the one who said it should be you. Sorry, mate.'

When South didn't move, he looked to the left and right, to see if anyone was listening, and lowered his voice. 'Look, mate. The new DS is not from round here. She needs her hand holding. You're the Local District lead, ergo, McAdam says you're on the team to support her and manage local impact. Not my fault.'

It was still early morning. It took South a second. 'Local impact? It's in my area?'

'Why else would you be on the team? She's outside now in the CID car, waiting.'

'I don't understand. What's the incident?'

'They didn't say, yet. It's just come in. Fuck off now, Bill. Be a pal and get on with your job and let me get on with mine.'

It was an ordinary office in an ordinary provincial police station; white paint a little scuffed on the walls, grey carpet worn in front of the sergeant's tidy desk from where others had come to haggle about the duties they'd been allocated. The poster behind his desk: *Listen. Learn. Improve. Kent Police.*

'Could you delegate it to someone else?'

'It was you he asked for.'

'So if I show her round today, will you get someone else on it for the rest of the week?'

'Give me a break, Bill,' said the shift sergeant, blinking again between words as he turned to his computer screen.

Over twenty years a policeman; a reputation as a diligent copper: but South had always avoided murder.

Maybe it would only be for a day or two. Once the new DS had found her feet, he'd go back to normal duties, back to the reassuring bureaucracy of modern police work, and back to getting things done in his patch. He was a good copper. What could go wrong?

William South paused before walking through the glass door at the front of the station. Outside, the blue Ford Focus was parked in the street, engine running. Behind the wheel sat the new woman, and right away the sight of her made him nervous.

Late thirties, he guessed, straight brownish hair, recently cut; a woman starting a new job. Her fingers tapped on the steering wheel impatiently. She would be running outside inquiries for the murder investigation; a new arrival, first case on a new force, keen to get on, to make a go of it. Lots to prove.

A good copper? There was a part of him already hoping she wouldn't be.

He sighed, pushed open the door. 'Alexandra Cupidi?' he called.

'And what should I call you? Bill? Will?' she answered.

'William,' he said.

'William?' Was she smirking at him? 'Well, then, William . . .' She stretched his name to three syllables and nodded to the empty seat beside her. 'I'm Alexandra, then.'

He opened the passenger door and looked in. She wore a beige linen suit that was probably new too, like her haircut, but it was already crumpled and shapeless. And the car? It was only Tuesday, so she could only have had it for a day so far, and already it was a tip. There were empty crisp and cigarette packets in the footwell and wrappers and crumbs all over the passenger seat.

'Sorry,' she said. 'Bit of a late one last night.'

He sat down in the mess, buckling the seat belt around his stab vest. She'd been with the Met, he'd heard, which was enough to put anyone on their guard.

DS Cupidi reached out, took a gulp from the coffee cup in the cup holder, then said, 'So. You're Neighbourhood Officer for Kilo 3, yes?'

South nodded warily. 'That's right.'

'Good.' She switched on the engine.

'And there's been a murder there? Shouldn't I have been informed?'

'You're being informed now. What's the quickest way?'

'To where exactly? It's a large area.'

'Sorry.' She dug into the pocket of her linen jacket for a note-book, opened the clip and flicked through until she had found the most recently scribbled page. 'Lighthouse Road, Dungeness,' she said.

He turned to her; examined her face. 'You sure?'

She repeated it.

Right now, he thought, he should just get out of the car and walk back inside the police station. Say he wasn't feeling well. 'This is the address of where it's supposed to have happened?'

'What's wrong?' she asked.

'They're not pulling your leg or anything? First week on the job?'

'What are you on about?'

'That's my road. That's where I live.'

She shrugged. 'I suppose that's why the DI said it was so important you should be on my team.'

South thought for a second. 'Who is it?'

She indicated and pulled out into the traffic, glancing quickly down at the open notebook and trying to read her own notes. 'No name. Address is . . . I can't make it out. Arm Cottage?'

'Arum Cottage.'

'That's it.'

'Robert Rayner,' said South.

She raised her eyebrows. 'That must be it. The woman who reported the crime is a Gill Rayner.'

'Bob Rayner is dead?' William blinked. They pulled up at a zebra crossing where a woman in a burqa pushed an old-fashioned black pram very slowly across the road.

She turned and looked. 'I'm sorry. You knew him?'

'A neighbour. A friend.' South looked out of the side window. 'Arum Cottage is about a hundred yards away from where I live.'

'Good,' she said. 'I mean. Not good, obviously, sorry.'

South said, 'So I shouldn't be part of the investigation. Because I know the deceased.'

Cupidi pursed her lips. 'Shit,' she said. The woman with the pram finally made it across to the other side of the road. DS Cupidi drove over the crossing, then pulled the car up on the zigzag lines on the other side, hazards flashing.

'Give me a minute,' she said, pulling out her mobile phone. She dialled and then held the device to her ear. 'DI McAdam? Something's come up.' He heard the DI's voice.

Amongst the noise of the traffic, he couldn't make out what the DI was saying. Cupidi paused, turned to South. 'He wants to know, were you a close friend?' she said.

'Close? I suppose,' said South. 'I saw quite a lot of him.'

'Hear that, sir? . . .' She looked at her watch. 'Do I have to go and drop him back at the station?' She listened some more, said, 'I understand,' a couple of times, then hung up.

When she'd replaced the phone, she reached out, put the blue light on and swung back into the traffic, the cars ahead scattering in panic, mounting pavements and braking, not knowing which way to move.

'Well?' said South.

'He said you can stick with me, strictly on an advice basis. For today at least, while we find our bearings. Just don't do anything unless I say, OK?'

Unfamiliar with the local roads, she was cautious at junctions and the town's many roundabouts. Only on the outskirts was she able to build speed, heading out towards the coast road.

'What happened?' he asked when the road opened out in front of them.

'I don't know, yet. Call came in from a distressed woman about an hour ago. Scene of Crime are there doing their thing.'

He remembered. Bob had said his sister was coming to visit. She arrived there once a fortnight; it was an arrangement the two of them had.

'God. I'm sorry. Are you going to be OK to do this? I mean, if he was a friend . . . ?'

'I shouldn't be involved,' he said.

'But you are, though, aren't you?'

The flats on their right-hand side gave way to council houses, then to semis and bungalows and caravan parks, the flashing blue light reflecting off their windows. The further they travelled, the more open the land became.

On the left, occasional gaps in the breakwater gave glimpses of shingle running down to the sea. The traffic thinned and Cupidi gunned the engine. Overtaking, she flashed her lights at an oncoming car.

'You actually like it here?' she asked.

'I've lived here almost all my life,' he said.

'Not that there's anything wrong with that.'

'But what?'

She was concentrating on the road ahead. 'But nothing. I just can't imagine it, really. It's very . . . flat, isn't it?'

They were passing through the marshland, its grass burnt brown by the wind. 'So why did you move here?'

'Oh, you know. Just fancied a change,' she said, but a little too lightly, he thought.

'Slow down,' he said. 'The turning's any minute.' He shifted in the seat. Something was poking into his behind. 'Left,' he said.

The thinner road was pitted. At the shoreline, loose stones crackled under the tyres. Flat land to the north; flat sea to the south. Weather-beaten houses with rotting windows and satellite dishes dribbling rust-marks down the paintwork. An oversize purple and yellow UKIP flag flapping in the wind.

'Must be bitter in winter,' she said.

'Bitter all year round.' It was a wide low headland extending south from the marshes, exposed to winds from every quarter.

As they drove towards the point, South noticed some people sitting round a fire on the shingle.

'Go slowly,' he said to DS Cupidi.

'Why?'

South looked out of the passenger window. The low light was behind them and they were too far away to see their faces clearly; he didn't think he recognised any of them, anyway. Fires on the shingle were always a risk. The flints exploded sometimes in the heat, shooting hot stone splinters out at the drunks.

'Rough sleepers?' she said.

'They come down here, break into the old fishing huts and burn the wood. They haven't been around for a while though,' he said. The vagrants were huddled close to the fire, trying to warm themselves in its dying heat.

'Can't stop now,' said Cupidi. South pulled his notebook from his vest and wrote, '*3 men, 2 women?*', then replaced the elastic band around it and put it back in his pocket.

They were nearing the end of the promontory. The road veered suddenly to the right, away from the sea.

'Now left,' he said, and she turned again.

'God, it's bleak.'

'It's how we like it.'

A track led away from the main road. DS Cupidi looked ahead, at the massive buildings in front of her. 'Jesus. What the hell is that?'

'Nuclear power station,' said South.

'Wow. I mean . . . I didn't realise it was here.'

Behind the black tower of the old lighthouse, the metal and concrete blocks that surrounded the two reactors rose, unnaturally massive in the flat land. These colossal shapes were surrounded by rows of tall razor-wire fences. As Cupidi and South approached, the buildings seemed to grow still larger. Their presence made this landscape even more Martian. To their north, lines of pylons marched inland across the wide shingle beds.

'Aren't you worried it'll blow up?'

This was where he had lived since he was thirteen. A freakish, three-mile promontory of loose stones built by the English Channel's counter-currents.

The single track road led to Bob Rayner's house and, beyond, to the Coastguard Cottages. Under the looming geometry of the power station, small shacks were dotted around untidily, as if they'd dropped accidentally from the back of a lorry. In recent years, the millionaires had arrived. Some cottages had been rebuilt as luxury houses, with big glass doors and shiny flues. Others still looked like they were made from scraps pilfered from a tip.

'People live in those?' said DS Cupidi.

'Why not?'

South pointed to the row of houses, an oddly conventional-looking terrace a little further away from the reactors. 'My house is over there,' he said.

The car slowed. A dog was lying in the road. Alex honked the horn at it. The dog got up slowly and sauntered off into the clumps of mint-green vegetation.

William South felt something vibrate as they bumped over the potholed road. His phone? But when he pulled it out of his pocket, the screen was blank; no one had called or texted. He was just putting it back when DS Cupidi said, 'That must be the place, then.'

He looked and saw Bob Rayner's bungalow. A small wooden construction, with two small gables, like a letter M, facing the track. A couple of chimneys stuck out of a tiled roof. The wood had been painted recently in red preservative, but it was already starting to flake. It sat on its own on the shingle, sea-kale and thin grass strug-gling to take hold around it. Like most of the shacks here, it would have been built originally almost a century ago as a poor man's getaway, long before the nuclear power station had arrived.

Today, there were police cars and vans parked outside the small building. Half a dozen, crammed on every available piece of the narrow track.

'Shit,' he said, quietly.

Bob; his friend.

'Are you going to be all right?' said Cupidi, peering at him as she pulled up the handbrake. Not sure if he was, he looked away towards the sea, avoiding her gaze.

A memory. Police cars outside the house . . .

❋

He was thirteen years old, late for his tea and running hard up the hill. He should have been home half an hour ago. Usually his mum wouldn't have been bothered, but after everything that had hap-pened, she'd have been going mental.

It was all Miss McCrocodile's fault. She had spotted him lurking in the Spar and been all over him. 'Ye poor wee snipe, Billy McGowan. The people who did this terrible thing will not escape the wrath of the Lord. For God shall bring every secret thing into judgement, whether it be good, or whether it be evil.'

She bought him a packet of Smith's Crisps, at least.

Now he ran, past the hum of the electricity substation, past the playground where the climbing frame there had been recently painted in red, white and blue (and not by the council either), past the bored squaddies on the checkpoint, rifles pointed towards the tarmac, and finally on to the estate: NO POPE HERE, touched up only a few days earlier. The black ring on the grass of the field where the bonfire had been.

The McGowans' house was at the top, where the town ends and the fields begin.

When he reached the start of the cul-de-sac, he stopped dead, panting.

There were two police cars outside his house. One of those big new Ford Granada Mk IIs with the orange stripe down the side, and an old Cortina that had seen better days. They were back again. He ducked behind the Creedys' chip van.

He was getting his breath back now. But he stayed there, peeking out from behind the chipper, waiting for the police cars to drive off.

He started shivering, even though it was summer. He closed his eyes tightly, wishing he had never even existed.

He should just kill himself now. They must know. He is in such trouble.

JOIN US

Want to know more about policing in Sixties
London? Government corruption? Celebrity
scandal? Or just love the books?

Follow William Shaw for

Music playlists from the Breen & Tozer series
Interactive maps of Sixties London
Articles and histories
Prizes and freebies
Tour dates and signings
News and updates
& more!

Get the newsletter williamshaw.com/subscribe

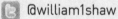 @william1shaw

www.quercusbooks.co.uk